I0823824

MOVING Serafina

Moving Serafina

a novel

by **Bob Cherry**

TCU Press • Fort Worth, Texas

Library of Congress Cataloging-in-Publication Data

Cherry, Bob.
Moving Serafina : a novel / by Bob Cherry.
p. cm.
ISBN 978-0-87565-356-3 (alk. paper)
I. Title.

PS3553.H3563M68 2007
813'.54--dc22
2007001929

TCU Press
P.O. Box 298300
Fort Worth, TX 76129
817.257.7822

http://www.prs.tcu.edu

To order books: 800.826.8911

Jacket & Book Design / Margie Adkins Graphic Design
Jacket photograph / © 2007 Arthur Meyerson

DEDICATION

for Carol

BIRDWINGS

Your grief for what you've lost lifts a mirror
Up to where you're bravely working.

Expecting the worst, you look, and instead
Here's the joyful face you've been wanting to see.

Your hand opens and closes and opens and closes.
If it were always a fist or always stretched open,
you would be paralyzed.

Your deepest presence is in every small contracting
and expanding,
The two as beautifully balanced and coordinated
as birdwings.

—Rumi 1207-1273 A.D.

CHAPTER 1

Clayton Elliott stopped his old pickup truck and sat for a moment, allowing the wake of dust to boil up and over the cab. Through the haze, he saw the small picket fence he had built around the gravesite of his baby daughter, Serafina, twenty-five years ago. The fence leaned loose at one corner, no surprise to Clay, who had driven the sixteen miles of two-track dirt road snaking southwest from the little town of Solitario to his now-abandoned ranch house. For months he had made this trip each week to feed his old bay horse, Palo, and his few remaining *corriente* steers and to mend Serafina's fragile little fence. And to talk with Serafina.

He shut off the engine and stepped out onto the soil, hard and leached. Except for the occasional high desert plant, the terrain ran almost barren all the way to the Rio Grande. He looked to the south, but he could not see the river. He knew it snaked between Texas and Mexico, just five miles from his gutted ranch house. The water ran mirror flat at that point until it reached the abrupt anomaly of Santa Elena Canyon. There it swept through gray rock walls in muddy turmoil for only a short distance. When it exited the canyon, it widened again and once more its mood became senile and serene, all the way to the Gulf of Mexico.

He thought again about that shallow section of river just to the south of where he stood. For decades, that stretch had served as an easy crossing for hundreds of illegal Mexican nationals. Six years of severe drought across the West had diminished the flow of water even further. The United States Border Patrol now focused major attention on this easier part of the river. But the *coyotes*, these new traffickers in human beings, had simply become more crafty with their methods as they shuffled groups of anxious people across into Texas and to points north, preying on their dreams of unlimited opportunity. Clay and his ranching friends considered this type of coyote far more diabolical than any predator they had ever encountered.

Clay shook his head when he thought about how it had all changed. The old adobe house seemed far more wasted than these past few months of neglect might warrant. But the heat had not changed. Even on this spring day, it quavered up from the rangeland, the temperature already inching above one hundred degrees. "Hot," Clay said to no one, just a statement of fact. He lifted his hat and ran the back of his hand across his forehead and replaced the hat, just so, a reflex from some long past and impetuous youth.

He turned back to his task and thought about his plan for this special day, this first of May. He glanced inside the cab at the extra cushion on the seat. He knew he would need this pad on the ground next to the grave to protect his wasted knee joints as he knelt. He would also need the baling wire in the bed of the truck to mend Serafina's little fence as he lingered in the failing light with the white paint and the narrow brush, taking all the time he wanted because he had a special thing to say to Serafina.

Clay stood beside his pickup and listened to the ticking of the engine as it tried to cool. Again, he regarded the old adobe house with its covered patio wrapped around three sides, vacant for months and now vandalized by illegal immigrants or locals on four wheelers or both. All its glass lay in shards on the hard earth and one corner of its porch roof sagged as if it had also given up, just like the little fence guarding Serafina. Farther back stood the small tack shed, also adobe but compact and windowless and double padlocked, though it held nothing of value except to Clay: rusted barbed wire, his worn saddle and a cracked leather wagon harness.

Though it tormented him to do so, Clay thought about the one-horse ranch wagon he could not see behind the tack shed. The obsolete relic rested there with the front axle still propped on a rock, its one loose wheel against the wall where he had leaned it all those years back. The old wagon, passed from his grandfather to his father and in turn, to Clay, who had used it occasionally until it fell into disrepair. But now Clay refused to look at it, or to burn it as he had threatened after Serafina's death. Even out of sight, it still haunted his memory of that night when Serafina died, and so Clay tried to ignore the fact that the wagon had ever existed, tried to erase it from his memory. ***Push it back, push it down, leave it!***

Clay shifted his attention to his old gelding, Palo, standing stiff, leaning against a protesting corral rail, testing his own boundaries as though he too felt abandoned. The only thing that seemed alive was the stubborn windmill, gap-toothed but cycling above Palo in a small thermal from the afternoon cooling, sending as if by providence intermittent spurts of water into the trough within easy reach of the old horse. Clay and his wife, Adelita, had built the fieldstone trough with their own hands after they erected the windmill but before they had made the house. Before they had made their only child, Serafina.

Adelita had insisted on the trough. "We can pack our own water inside," she declared. "After our house is built. But our animals can't wait."

Clay knew this. But he had said nothing. He loved his wife's definitive voice, this strong voice with its Spanish accent inherited through Adelita's own strong grandmother. Clay smiled as he remembered the story Adelita loved to tell. The grandmother was a *soldadera* from the Mexican revolution, a woman soldier who had endured not only the hardships of that struggle but all the trauma of being a woman amongst hardened *Zapatistas*, revolutionaries who would have banished her—or worse—had they discovered she was pregnant and would soon be unable to tend a cook fire, much less ride a horse or wield a rifle. The grandmother finally sought the only refuge near her, just across the *Rio del Norte*, the Rio Grande, thus making her only child, Adelita's mother, a citizen of the United States when she was born. And as Adelita's mother had become a citizen, so too had Adelita upon her own birth north of the Rio Grande.

But Adelita was not only a second-generation citizen of the United States; she was a Texan. And at the right moment to the right people and to Clay's continuing delight, she would quietly proclaim herself as such, and if these people happened to be the occasional band of cow-hardened gringo Texans dropping by, there would for a moment fall a silence over Adelita's kitchen as thick as the adobe walls, with only the sputtering of rolled tobacco followed by an approving round of nods and murmurings and mugs of Adelita's strong coffee lifted to her in unison.

But breast cancer knows neither nationality nor border, selects no particular generation. Adelita's voice, at age sixty-two, weakened and finally fell silent this past March second, despite all the efforts Clay had made. March second, the date in 1836 when Texas had declared its independence from Mexico, the irony of which had not escaped Clayton Elliott.

The cost of moving Adelita to El Paso this past January for radiation and chemo treatment soared to impossible amounts. Shortly after they were told by the specialist that Adelita's condition was terminal, Clay set about finalizing a contract to sell this same rank ranchland to water developers in order to pay the hospital. These El Paso entrepreneurs had hounded him for years about tapping deep into the West Texas aquifer, far below his parched ground, in order to pipe the water two hundred miles northwest to an expanding and thirsty El Paso and beyond.

It was an impossible and insane scheme and ordinarily Clay laughed, dismissed it, and went on his way. But to pay the bills and move Adelita back to Solitario and make her as comfortable as possible, he needed the money. So he had contracted with these wildcatters, who called their company Agua Hondo, Deep Water, for a handsome down payment. The remainder of the money would follow as soon as the deed transferred. Clay thought about that deadline set in their agreement. It loomed only two weeks away, on midnight of May fifteenth.

Now, just as their daughter had rested silent all these years, Serafina's mother lay mute below the earth back in the county cemetery at Solitario where Clay was forced to bury Adelita because as soon as the deed transferred, he would no longer own even an inch of this ground on which he now stood. To help assuage his guilt about having to bury Adelita that sixteen-mile distance from Serafina, Clay had splurged with some of the down payment and purchased the expensive crushed white rocks which he spread atop the mound of soil covering Adelita. And though Adelita rested in the town of Solitario, far closer to Serafina than had been Adelita's medical ordeal in El Paso, they were still miles apart. And this is what Clayton Elliott wanted to speak to Serafina about on this first day of May, on the birthday of this daughter, their only child.

He stretched over into the bed of the pickup and retrieved the can of paint and the brush in one hand and the pliers and wire in the other. When he reached the corner of the old house, he paused for a moment and glanced at an eyeless window. He turned to look inside at the little bedroom that Serafina had used, where at three years of age she had lain, waiting with the fever. Waiting in vain with Adelita for Clay to return.

He stopped and thought about the old wagon again. "No sense in doing this to myself either," he scolded. "No sense at all."

When he turned to move away from the house, he thought he heard a sob or some quick and painful intake of breath, or at least a sigh from inside the bedroom. But he did not turn back. Memory can play tricks on an aging man, he thought. He shook his head and blinked memory away and moved on. "No sense at all," he repeated.

He crossed the fifty feet of rough ground to the gravesite next to the windmill and set down the materials. Then he walked over to the corral where Palo raised his head and scissored his ears, but that was the only movement the old horse made. Clay saw that the hay he had left days ago was scattered but not totally eaten.

"I'll put some fresh out in the morning anyway," he said, but the horse did not move. "Yeah, I know." The horse remained immobile. "You're lonesome out here, right?" Palo lifted his head a little and Clay reached and cupped his palm over his velvet muzzle and then glanced at Serafina's grave. "So's she."

He swirled a hand inside the water trough and looked into the clear liquid and absently reached for the water dipper, the one he had fabricated years ago from a tomato can and a broken mop handle. He scooped up a can full of the sweet water, drank slowly and then hung it with its lanyard of wire back onto the bottom rung of the ladder that ascended the side of the windmill. Then he walked past the house again without a glance, and, this time, he brought back the cushion from the pickup seat and stood next to the grave.

"A man has only so many times he can kneel," he mused. "And I've abused these knees far too often, Sera." With the toe of his boot, he smoothed aside the rocks next to the leaning pickets and dropped the cushion. "I don't think they're good for much more."

He bent forward with his hands on his thighs and relaxed his knees as far as he could and finally dropped his thin body the last inches onto the cushion. His face tightened from the pain in the arthritic joints but he allowed himself no sound, nothing that would disturb his daughter on this her special day.

With care, he reached over and righted the little fence and twisted tight a strand of wire at the top corner. He threaded a second piece halfway down the corner pickets and made secure a spiral of wire-against-wire with the pliers, almost to the breaking point.

"There," he said, and thought about what he planned to tell Serafina. "That'll hold." He dropped his hands and let the pliers fall to the ground. "For now, anyway."

Clay relaxed a little from his upright kneeling, rested his butt against his boot heels in the familiar position for talking at a campfire or scanning the horizon for stingy cloudbanks or stray *corriente* steers. Or for telling good news or bad news or both. He reached for the paint can, shook it, levered it open with the jaws of the pliers and picked up the brush. Then he dipped it into the paint and stroked the white across the thirsty wood.

"I'm gonna move you, Sera," he said. He tried to speak these words without any tightening of voice or mumbling or justification for these weeks of procrastination that Clay knew even an adult might not understand. Just flat, not even joy, another statement of fact. "Into Solitario. There with your mama." He dipped the brush into the paint.

That was all. He did not say her mother had died. This had been impossible to explain to Serafina, or even to articulate aloud to himself, but the unspoken had invaded everything else he had spoken, infected his every action, stalled him all these months to the point of almost total denial. And it seemed better not to speak the other words even now; say only that he would move Serafina so she could be with her mother.

Each of the past three nights he had awakened in the rented apartment on the second floor at the Hotel Solitario where, months earlier, Adelita had weakened and died. He had paced across the creaking oak floor as he practiced how he might finally say all this with great elaboration, telling his baby daughter how he would do it and when. And with whom because Clay knew he could never do it by himself anyway, never release Serafina from twenty-five years of case-hardened soil, not with his bone-on-bone knees and knotted hands. And this too had stalled him. But he would arrange it with whatever help he had to enlist. And now Serafina knew the most important part. He did not need to explain more.

He placed the paintbrush across the lip of the can and studied the backs of his outstretched hands. Wrinkles eroded flesh at each joint and all the way from the knuckles to the wrists, hard lines earned from more than fifty years of tending cattle and horses and barbed wire. He slowly curled his fingers forward into his palms, tried to erase the knots at the joints, tightening the flesh into something smooth. But the wrinkles would not disappear until he squeezed his hands into fists, hard, white at the knuckles. He knew his face was the same, the premature furrows there accentuated in the coming shadows now inching across the rangeland, making silhouettes of the *ocotillo*, the *agave*, and the *sotol* brush. As if in apology for the heat of the day, the dusk also brought with it a cooling zephyr that whispered in his ear.

"Well . . ." he said. "Sometimes kneeling is necessary. But sometimes it takes a fist."

He flexed the hands open and closed and thought about how they seemed larger than before, as if they had continued to grow as separate beings at the ends of his arms, even as the remainder of his body seemed to wither over the sixty-four hard years he had abused it, especially these past few in combat with the drought. And now Adelita's battle.

"But maybe sometimes it doesn't take a fist either," he mused. "Maybe just a smile, even though it puts more wrinkles in this face." He stopped moving his hands and smiled down at the mound of earth, suddenly remembering the game he had played with the little girl all those years past.

"Make the wings, Papa," she says. "With your hands. Show me."

Clay brings his hands close to her face, splays his fingers and then locks the thumbs together as a hinge. And then he articulates the hands at the pivot of the thumbs, making bird wings of his hands. He purses his lips and releases small staccato whistling sounds as he flies the bird around her face and then over her kept hair, iridescent as a raven's wing, and makes the bird disappear behind her head, thus encircling the child inside his arms. He puffs a few whistles into her face, causing Serafina to flutter and then close her eyes. Then he stops whistling, smiles and lifts his eyebrows to widen and distort his own eyes. When the child opens hers, he exposes each hand in turn from behind her head to say, as if by magic, he has made the bird disappear.

Serafina squeals in laughter and attempts to duplicate the action. And Clay laughs also, as does Adelita from across the kitchen.

"Again," Serafina insists. "Again!"

And Clay makes the wings again. And again.

Clay looked around, a little embarrassed even in such an isolated spot, and then he attempted to lock together his stiff thumbs but it was no good. They were beyond use as hinges for bird wings. "I'm sorry, Sera."

But these hands could still hold the paintbrush, which he lifted again with a sense of urgency from the coming darkness or perhaps spurred by the little breeze that once more seemed to carry the sound of some soulful voice. Or perhaps it was simply the wind sharing some secret absolution for the human flaws of a Clayton Elliott, whispered inside his ear by Serafina or Adelita, neither of whom he had been able to save.

He finished painting the little fence and with a rock tapped the lid back onto the can of paint and pushed himself up from his knees. First he arched his back, sliding his hands into his rear pockets. To relax some of the stiffness, he pressed the heels of his palms into his lower back and took in a breath of cool air, held it, released it. Then he bent to place all his materials onto the cushion, folded it and lifted the whole array against his chest.

Clay inspected his fencework and then studied the little mound of earth, capped with a jigsaw puzzle of flagstones, the weeds invading the cracks. He looked at the white headstone he had chiseled himself, the single shadowed word, SERAFINA, legible in the tangerine light from this sun, cut flat now by the horizon.

"I'll get flowers," he whispered. "Your purple wildflowers. Tomorrow. And I'll pull these weeds."

He walked past the old house with its darkened and hollow window sockets. He moved on to his pickup, tossed the armload into the bed and opened the door. But then he paused and frowned as if considering what he might have left behind. He shook his head and scolded himself again for fading memory.

"I'm not *that* damned old," he said, but he thought about how some of his friends had observed that Clay seemed to have aged even more on the inside than on the outside. But he did check off in his mind anyway the list of items brought that day. As far as he knew, the only important things remaining right now were the few good memories and old Palo and Serafina herself, but he needed help to take her away, regardless of his age, inside or out. And in so doing, perhaps he could leave behind the bad memories. But he would have to do it soon. He ducked into the cab of the old truck and cranked it and sat a moment listening to the idling engine. Then he pulled on the headlights, shrugged and meshed the gears and drove away, leaving far more than he realized cowering at that moment in the shadows filling one hidden corner of Serafina's bedroom.

CHAPTER 2

On the second floor of the Hotel Solitario, Miss Jovita Seals stepped out of her early morning bath. She stood at the gauze-curtained window of her apartment, looked through it and down on the empty main street as she toweled herself dry. The curtain was unnecessary. Even if someone had looked up from the center of the street with binoculars, Jovita doubted that anyone would be interested in a never married, sixty-one-year old female body, even nude.

She chuckled, pushed back the curtain in a moment of brash feminism and held it open, exposing herself to the world. Or at least to Solitario, Texas. Not one of its 1,328 citizens shouted *Bravo!* No one jeered or called out obscenities. And even if some chance passerby did report this momentary public display of her assets, she doubted that anyone at the front desk would ask her to leave the hotel. After all, the hotel itself was one of her assets.

She turned and faced her antique beveled mirror, reflecting a body that still pleased her, despite its age. Then she brushed back the still damp salt-and-pepper hair until it lay sleek against the nape of her neck. There she held the hair in her left fist and moved into her closet where she opened a drawer filled with fresh silk scarves, each one red. "What color . . ." she teased. "What color today?" She lifted one of the scarves. "Maybe this?"

She smiled as she shook the scarf and bound her hair against the back of her neck with this same Ganado red trademark she had worn as long as she could remember. Though everyone in Solitario wondered about it, neither the scarf nor its color signified a thing. It was just a simple way of keeping distractions out of her eyes and away from her concentration as she supervised whatever needed supervision each day at her hotel. And it was easy to shop for, even if she asked someone to do it for her in El Paso. But she also liked the mystery of it, the same color, the same hairdo year after year, and she liked the questioning eyes as other women in the little town glanced up at it and then with envy, surveyed the entirety of Jovita's still firm body. Surveyed everything except her eyes. Not many dared look directly into Jovita's eyes, unblinking and confident, set like turquoise stones perfectly matched with the color of the jewels she usually wore.

Jovita continued to dress, slipped a cool white blouse with an open V-neck over her head and pulled on a pair of pressed slacks and stepped into comfortable leather loafers. She fingered through the large tray of Native American jewelry at her dresser and finally selected from its velvet bag a hand-wrought necklace of tiny silver squash blossoms, one her father had acquired years ago in some horse trade behind his Hotel Solitario. He brought it into the hotel in a paper bag because the string of the necklace was broken. Its former owner warned her father before the trade that it might not be complete. "But if it *is* . . ." the man smiled and whispered the secret into her father's face, "If it *is* . . . I got no damned idea what it might be worth."

"Same goes for the mare," her father whispered back into the man's grinning face, an expression that slacked a little as the man glanced at the mare but then he frowned as he peered once more into her opened mouth. He inspected her teeth, then finally turned back to shake hands.

Her father had dumped the pieces onto the long mahogany table in this same apartment on the top floor of his Hotel Solitario and declared to his teenage daughter that he was not certain if he got the better of the deal, but if Jovita could assemble it, she could have it.

"It's the chase," he said as he always did after one of his dubious deals, and then he bellowed with laughter. "Not the conquest. Remember that, Jo."

"Sure, Papa." She tried to sound elated with her new treasure and then echoed his favorite creed because she knew he wanted her to say it. *"Never look a gift horse in the mouth, right?"*

So Jovita had spent days bent over the puzzle of the necklace, placing each increasingly larger hollow silver bead next to its matching squash blossom in what she thought were their proper positions, until she was certain that it would all fit and was complete with its turquoise-embedded silver amulet in the front center. Then she strung it back together with strong dental floss and placed it in a purple velvet bag with a faux gold drawstring, one of the many that had once contained a carved glass bottle of her father's favorite bourbon, long since drained at one of his famous all night poker games in his bar downstairs. She wore the necklace over the years, long after her father's death, but now only on special occasions because some hotel guest—a trading post owner who had stopped overnight off the passenger train—cautioned her about the risk of wearing it in public, as he appraised it for the finest he had ever seen, worth a great deal of money.

"Why wear it today?" Jovita said. She touched the turquoise amulet hanging centered as if to draw attention not to itself or to her matching eyes, but to the open neck of her blouse. "What's so special about an ordinary Sunday?" she mused. "In Solitario, Texas?"

She shrugged and walked back to the open window and looked again down onto the short main street of Solitario with pickup trucks and a few cars now pulled against the curb, probably carrying men delinquent from church, arriving early at the hotel for coffee or to meet their wives later for the Sunday brunch, but not until they had sneaked a wistful glance at Miss Jovita Seals when she strolled into the restaurant. "Too late boys," she whispered through the window. "Enjoy the necklace when I come down. You'll only have to guess at what else you missed."

She brushed past the mirror without inspecting herself and closed her apartment door behind without locking it. She paused at the opposite door across the hallway and tapped three times to rouse Clayton Elliott, just as she had done each morning these past months since he had returned from El Paso with an ailing Adelita and they had settled–at Jovita's insistence–into the apartment across the hall. She said nothing at the door but moved on to the stairwell where she paused again and listened because she had not yet heard his usual groaning awake. Absently, she tilted her head to one side and blinked as she adjusted the knot in the scarf, waiting. When she heard nothing, she descended the worn but elegant carved oak stairway into the cool lobby, took note of its freshly mopped and polished Mexican floor tiles and smiled approval at Rafín, the clerk behind the desk.

"Buenos días, Miss Seals," he said, but she only nodded, said nothing. After her breakfast, she would talk about the day with Rafín.

She went on back into the kitchen where Beatrice Hernandez reigned over her huge cast iron cookstove. Even though it had been retrofitted many years ago for natural gas instead of wood, Jovita often begged Bea to let her replace the relic with some stainless steel marvel, but Bea had refused.

"Buenos días, Bea," Jovita said. "How's it working?"

Bea smiled but said nothing. She simply nodded and turned back to the grill where thick peppered bacon hissed, one piece already done just as Jovita liked, set aside on a paper napkin. Jovita picked it up and bit into it, closed her eyes in ecstasy. She chewed slowly and swallowed. Then she tucked the remainder into her mouth.

It was only then that Bea stopped what she was doing. *"Buenos días* to you also."

Jovita opened her eyes, winked once and smiled back to her and, without words, touched Bea on the arm. It was a silent ritual. One piece of bacon, taken in seclusion, not acknowledged to the world by either of the women, who each understood that this item with its unknown quantity of deadly chemicals and artery-clogging fat simply did not exist and that the healthy bowl of cereal with fat free milk, alongside fresh-squeezed orange juice, would arrive on time at Jovita's usual table out front in the small restaurant of her hotel. Jovita poured herself a cup of coffee and walked out into the dining room.

She was surprised to see Clay already sitting in his place at the table next to hers. He looked up at her over the top of his coffee mug.

"Morning, Jo," he said and sipped, dropped his glance. He was obviously a man with a mission for the day.

"You're up early," Jovita said. She surveyed the room and smiled and nodded at the smattering of customers, all men.

"Mmmm . . ." Clay held the mug, blew across the lip of it, sipped again.

"You got back late too," she said with feigned detachment. She knew exactly where Clay had been yesterday, the first day of May, and why. "If it's any of my business, I mean." Jovita sat at her table, her back to him.

"Well . . ."

"How was it?" She sipped her coffee and pretended to study her morning newspaper placed on the table in front of her chair each day by the desk clerk.

"About the same," Clay said. "Busted fence, weeds. Old worthless horse to match a worthless house. All the windows broke out now, about the same, except . . ."

"Yes."

"She wasn't—"

"Yes," Jovita interrupted again. Clay did not need to remind her that for those long weeks before her death, Adelita had refused to ride out there with him.

"I fixed the fence though, painted it. I'll take flowers out this morning, pull the weeds. Put out more hay for Palo." Jovita nodded this time, but with their chairs back-to-back, Clay could not see this. "Maybe you could tell Yebbie and Dobb I'll be back soon," he said. "If they come in today."

"Was there an earthquake?" Jovita said and smiled.

Clay turned around and stared at the back of Jovita's head. "A what?"

"An earthquake." She frowned, pretended to study the newspaper, ran her finger down the columns on the front page. "I don't see a thing here. It's not likely either of those two would miss Bea's Sunday morning brunch unless there'd been something serious."

"Come on, Jo," Clay said. He turned back to his coffee. "Just tell them I'll be back before noon for sure. Maybe they could have coffee or breakfast or something till I get back."

"I think you can count on that."

"Just say I got something to talk over with them."

"Okay."

"No big deal, just something . . . well, I'd appreciate it, Jo." He shoved back from his table, drained his mug and picked up his hat that he had stowed on an empty chair, crown down, with his leather gloves inside. He stood facing her, holding the hat by the brim in one hand, the gloves bunched in the other.

"Sure." She folded the newspaper and looked up at him. "Cow talk?"

"Nope. Tell them I already ate."

"But you didn't." She nodded at the lone coffee mug.

"Bea's making a couple of burritos for me to take," he said, and Jovita thought he might say more.

"You already have the flowers?" she said. "You could take some from the lobby you know."

"That's okay. She likes those wild ones."

He smiled at Jo and she nodded. "Right."

"Those purple kind," he said.

"Yeah."

"If I can find any out there," he sighed. "Damn dry, that's for sure. And hot, hot for this time of year. Weeds don't seem to care though."

"Should be some out there," Jo said. "Somewhere."

"Maybe under the windmill . . ." Clay said but he had turned and spoken this to no one as he paused and stared absently out the window.

Jovita nodded. Bea came out of the kitchen with Jovita's breakfast on a tray. She placed each item in front of Jovita, poured her a fresh cup of coffee and then handed the foil-wrapped burritos over to Clay. "They're still warm," Bea said. She went back into the kitchen.

"Thanks, Bea," Clay called and then walked away. He stopped under the thick arched doorway to the restaurant and turned back. "You'll tell them?"

Jovita did not look up. "I said I would." She poured the milk into her cereal and then turned around in her chair and looked at him. "Clay . . ."

"Yeah?"

She hesitated and stared at him a long while and then said, "Ever wonder why it is we always sit back-to-back in here?" It was not scolding and more an observation than a question. "Adelita's been gone quite a while now, Clay."

"Yeah," he agreed. "Several months now . . ."

"Yes," Jovita said and hesitated but finally added quietly, "Or maybe longer than that, Clayton. Far longer."

Clay shrugged and studied the gloves in his hand. "Well . . ."

"You be careful out there," she said and turned again to her newspaper. "It's become a real war zone down that close to the river. It's all over the front page here, and that's the truth."

He said nothing and walked out of the restaurant past the front desk and pushed through the wooden front doors of the hotel, their age and mass as dark and heavy as the unspoken words left suspended in the air between himself and Jovita. Outside he paused and looked up the street one way and then the other.

"Well," he repeated.

Like everyone else, she would learn soon enough about his plan to move Serafina. And whatever he had felt for Jovita in their untamed youth had been buried far longer than Adelita. He blinked into the early morning sun and pulled on his hat and set it right, then moved toward his pickup, parked in front of the hotel.

"No sense doing that to myself either," he muttered, and it seemed to Clayton Elliott that more than usual these past few days, he had been scolding himself about putting to rest the things he loved. And perhaps still loved. "No sense at all." ❧

CHAPTER 3

Clay drove south from Solitario for two miles and then turned off the blacktop onto the two-track dirt road, twisting the sixteen miles southwest to his old ranch house. He settled into thought as he listened to the rocks ping against the inside of the fenders.

Jovita had been kind about the spare apartment just opposite hers on the second floor of the hotel. It had remained idle for years because, like himself, he knew Jovita guarded her privacy and would not allow just any drifter to occupy it. Yet, she had insisted that Clay and Adelita move their Spartan furnishings into it and to use it toward the end of Adelita's ordeal. And so they did. And it had been Jovita who comforted Adelita as only another woman could after that final session in Doctor Boone Maddox's office across the street from the hotel on his weekly visit to Solitario.

"It's going to be fine," Jovita said to Clay as the two sat alone in the hotel restaurant after the meeting. She had helped Adelita upstairs where she lay in the dim apartment, waiting, refusing to come down even to eat. "There's always hope, Clay."

"Boone said they'd done about all they could in El Paso with the chemo." Clay studied his hands on the table, slowly rubbing the palms together. "Said he wouldn't put her through any more of that pain, even if it was his own wife." Clay paused and scowled down at his wrinkled hands as if–like himself–they had become totally useless. "They took both breasts . . ." He began and then looked up into Jovita's eyes. "Over there in El Paso."

"I know. But they're doing a lot more things now, Clay. Maybe they don't know everything. Boone doesn't know everything," Jovita said but she looked at Clay for reassurance. "Different things. I've read about them."

"Well, I dunno. Maybe something, Jo," he said but there was no conviction in his voice either, and in less than a month, Adelita weakened and was gone without once more having ridden in Clay's old pickup truck out to visit Serafina's gravesite, even though Clay had begged her to try.

On that final day, Clay sat on the bedside, exchanging whispered words with Adelita, her painkillers from Boone Maddox adding a dreamlike haze to their dialogue, flowing unpunctuated for hours, each tiptoeing around the inevitable until late in the afternoon the subject changed from the mundane reminiscences about their years of marriage to the grim matter at hand. Clay continued whispering in the same uninterrupted monotone as he said . . . *and you'll be with her . . . I mean after* . . . and then as if Adelita had anticipated that this would come up, she interrupted Clay . . . *like we talked about, Clay, please* . . . and for the only time that day, and then only for a brief moment, Clay paused and then he said . . . *Yes* . . . and she said . . . *here, Clayton, in the cemetery, under that cottonwood, please* . . . and he said . . . *okay* . . . and she said . . . *with Sera, Clayton . . . you promise? Please*

. . . and then he promised again though he had already told her this . . . *Don't you worry none about that* . . . and she said . . . *with my baby, okay* . . . and then Adelita stopped breathing before she could hear Clay again say . . . *oka*y . . . and before either had gathered the courage–or perhaps the terrible anger–to insert even as a kind of benign and final catharsis into their dialogue a single word about the blackest subject that had infused and stained their relationship for all those years: the circumstances of Serafina's death itself.

So Clay put her in the cemetery at Solitario under that lone cottonwood tree. Jovita and Bea Hernandez came, of course, as did Locket Wagner, the deputy sheriff stationed in Solitario, and Doc Boone Maddox. All three of the county commissioners came: Dobb Campbell in from his ranch and Yebbie Riggs in from his, and old Henry Bennett, the chairman of the county commissioners who lived alone just above the meeting hall in Solitario. Clay's best friend, Augústin "Gus" Muñoz and his younger brother, Alvaro, drove over from Los Arbolitos, their ranch just north of the village of Redford. A few other ranchers from the area showed up, longtime friends with Clay. They all left store-bought bouquets of real flowers shipped over from Alpine, and they walked past the closed casket with the brims of their hats clutched low in both hands. Later they all ate in silence with only the scraping of Hotel Solitario silverware across Jo's earthenware dishes, all this in the large private back room of the hotel where Bea Hernandez and a few wives had brought in enough food to feed twice the number who came alone, most of whom were either widowers like Dobb or simply had never married, like Yebbie and Henry and Gus and Locket and Jovita and even Bea. Or divorced like Alvaro, twice now. And now, Clayton himself, among the widowers.

Clay spat out the open window of his pickup into the morning air. If not there already, he guessed it was approaching one hundred degrees. For a few minutes he slowed, searching through the window into the borrow ditch and inside the seared gullies for the purple flowers. But he saw no color at all except the beige of the parched earth, and soon the heat forced him to roll the glass back up. He punched on the air conditioner, which rattled and whirred and struggled but soon began to cool off the cab.

He tried to remember how many of these same people had come when they buried Serafina. Perhaps their daughter's death had not been widely known or maybe people just did not know how to mourn the death of a three-year-old. Twenty-five years was a long time to practice forgetting, especially those circumstances surrounding Serafina's death, his own guilt as oppressive as this Southwest Texas heat. Only Jovita and Doc Maddox knew what had happened that night, and both were at Serafina's burial. And of course, Adelita knew, but she stood beside the grave in too much shock to shed tears. Dobb and Yebbie and Gus Muñoz were there, he remembered, all of these friends much younger then, of course, but he could not remember if any of the others who showed up at Adelita's funeral in town had also driven the primitive road out for Serafina's. It did not matter. No one then, or since, could lift any of the anguish from Clay's shoulders or from Adelita's now-stilled heart. If he could, Clay would finally have to take care of his problem for himself.

Yebbie and Dobb and Gus had helped hew out the small grave from the hardpan and lower Serafina into it. Yebbie had brazed together the tiny casket from a small oval horse trough, using heavy brass hinges removed from an old wooden icebox and attaching these to the lid, which he had also fabricated from matching galvanized metal.

But even though Yebbie had polished the makeshift metal casket with its hinges for hours using fine steel wool and it looked very presentable to Clay, glinting in the bright sunlight, Adelita could not bear to see them fill the grave. She rushed back into the house and Clay remembered hearing her wails even through the thick adobe walls. It would be months before she would venture out the back door of the house toward the windmill with its adjacent gravesite, and only then because Clay assured her he had mounded the earth and capped it with fieldstones and then chiseled a flat white rock with Serafina's name and even built the pure white fence as protection from whatever black evil had taken her in the first place.

Clay stopped the pickup on a small rise. He got out and looked to the southwest where the little house sat forlorn and forgotten, parts of its dried mud adobe already crumbling back into the earth from which it had come, but in truth, Clay knew this had been happening during all those years since Serafina's death. He thought about how much he too had aged, perhaps as the others had observed, far more on the inside than the outside. And then he glanced at the old windmill and wondered how long it would continue to pump into the rock livestock trough, and he wondered exactly where the new owners would punch their big hole, far deeper than his old well, down through the hardpan where they would extract the billions of gallons of water they swore lay below in the aquifer. And where the hell they would run that big-inch pipeline all the way from here to El Paso. Or wherever.

"Well right now, I'd just be happy with a dipper full," he said and chuckled. "It's a cinch they ain't drilling nothing till I get you moved, Sera. I seen to that."

But then he remembered the negotiations with the representative of these new owners this past January in El Paso and how two alternate deadlines had been agreed upon. He had asked his hired lawyer about the process of moving Serafina from her grave because with Adelita's turn for the worse at the time, he had been thinking it over. His attorney in turn suggested to the other attorney, a man named Dalton Simik from Agua Hondo, the company buying his land, that perhaps language speaking to the removal of Serafina's remains could be written into the agreement.

Simik balked, but Clay said he was not signing a damn thing unless it said something about his right to move Serafina *before* they ever set one foot on his place. When Clay got up to leave Simik's office, Simik stopped him at the door and said maybe they *could* write something into the contract for deed, just a line that spoke to Clay's right to move this Serafina. Some kind of compromise.

"I mean *before* you can even come out," Clay insisted. "I don't want nothing happening out there till I get that done. Nothing. Understand?"

"How's that sound?" Clay's attorney said.

"Well, how soon's that going to happen?" Simik said and he tried to sound sympathetic. "I mean, we can't just wait forever and—"

"Soon," Clay said and he thought about Adelita withering at that moment in a stark white hospital room just down the street from where they now sat. And he had no idea how long she might last. "Soon as I can get it done, I mean."

"How about if we do it for you, Mister Elliott? We could bring out a backhoe and—"

"No way," Clay interrupted. He moved toward Simik and stabbed his index finger at him as he spoke. "I put her in the ground. I'll get her out and I'll move her. I don't want no machines tearing up her grave and her little coffin." He sat back down.

"Well, at least let's put a cap on the time frame," Simik said. "Say, next month? We go in as soon as you remove the remains . . . or after midnight on February fifteenth, whichever happens first, of course."

"My wife's sick," Clay said, and Simik nodded. "Don't you understand? That's what this is all about. I told you that from the get-go."

Clay studied Simik for a long while and finally lowered his voice and said, "Truth is, she's not just sick. She's dying." Simik nodded again and Clay thought about the doctors who had given Adelita a month at best. He went on, "And even after that, I'll have all kinds of paperwork to take care of, and then there's all her medical bills to think about, talk over some kind of plan to pay these people up the street."

Simik looked first at Clay and then at his attorney. "I understand all that," Simik said. "How about no later than midnight, *March* fifteenth then?"

"It ain't something I can just schedule, goddammit," Clay said and frowned at his hired attorney, who did not seem to be earning his pay.

"Well?" Simik said.

"Well what?" Clay continued to study his attorney's face, but the man simply shrugged and tilted his head as if to say it would have to be Clay's call.

Clay paused for a long while, shifting his eyes from one attorney to the other, the muscles working in his jaws. "Fine," he finally said. "Write it in."

"Midnight, March fifteenth?" Simik repeated, somewhat surprised.

"No," Clay said and then added, "May. I'm talking May, Mister Simik, not March. I ain't never rushed anything in my life and I sure as hell ain't gonna rush Adelita, not now, not ever. Or Sera either."

"May fifteenth?" Simik said, losing his composure. "And who's this . . . Sera, Mister Elliott?"

Clay rose again and this time pulled on his hat. "Serafina," he said. "I already told you that." He scowled at Simik, who saw he would get nowhere with the contract for deed to the property unless he agreed to some compromise.

"Well, Agua Hondo can't deal in *maybes*," Simik said. "We're running a business here."

"How about the deed transfers midnight, May fifteenth, or as soon as Mister Elliott has the remains moved, *whichever comes first*," Clay's attorney suggested and smiled at each party, pleased with what he thought was some great new compromise. "And in all likelihood, Mister Elliott will have her moved long before that, Mister Simik, and you can go right onto the place at that time. I mean, considering all the circumstances my client has already been through–and will soon have to go through–you should allow him to do it in his own way and in his own time. Within reason, of course, considering all the other things he'll have to take care of and also with the proper respect he needs to give Serafina."

"Well what if this . . . this *Serafina* hasn't been moved by that deadline?" Simik said. "What if, as you say–considering all the circumstances–she's still in the ground at midnight on May fifteenth and—"

"Don't forget, Mister Simik," Clay interrupted—and his voice came wearily now—"Number one, I got major bills hanging over me. Major. Honest to God, I'm wanting all this settled as much as you do. Number two, I'm not only needing that down payment you're offering right now just to get a little slack for myself, I'm needing every penny of the money you're offering when the deal's done to settle it all up and get all of them off my back for good. I'm wore down. I want this thing closed out as much as you guys want to get in there and drill your big well, trust me on this. I know you may not have more important things to think about at the moment, but I sure as hell do. And that'll take me a little while. Or I should say, that'll take my *wife* a while. But to speak the untainted truth, Mister Simik, Adelita might be the first to say she'd just as soon it *didn't* take a while."

No one spoke for a long while after Clay said this.

He sat studying the patterns in the maroon carpet on Simik's office floor. Finally, Simik sighed and looked at his watch.

"Okay, write it in," he said to Clay's attorney. "I'll get two copies of it typed up out front and we'll do a final review of it right now. Agua Hondo moves in immediately upon removal of the remains or after midnight, May fifteenth . . ." Simik paused, shook his head but then continued, " . . . whichever comes first between now and then."

"With $25,000 down immediately?" Clay's attorney said.

"Yes," Simik said. "Earnest money, just to lock us in right now, today, contingent on our review."

"You mean to lock *me* in, don't you?" Clay grumbled.

Clay's attorney glowered in his direction and Clay softened when he saw this was as good as it would get. "Well, that'll help," Clay said. "That'll help a helluva lot. But no amount of money will do everything right down this street that I wish it could. Don't seem like nothing can do that now though."

"Call it a show of our good faith and trust," Simik said and now he feigned a smiled. "Agua Hondo's trust that you'll carry through with your end of the deal . . ." He reached to shake Clay's hand. " . . . *as soon* as possible."

"Like I said, Mister Simik, I want Sera moved a helluva lot more than you do," Clay reminded him but he did not take Simik's proffered hand. "I'll have to do that in my own way, understand?"

"Maybe *you* shoulda been a lawyer," Simik said.

He put his hands in his pockets and laughed, but Clay was not certain if it was a joke or a jab at Clay's hired attorney. And so they signed the contract and notarized it that afternoon; it was done. Clay left Simik's office with the largest check he had ever seen.

"Who the hell's this Serafina anyway?" Simik grumbled as he gathered his copy of the papers.

"His baby daughter," Clay's attorney said. "She's the one being moved."

....

On the road now just above his old house with Serafina's grave out behind, Clay took off his hat and wiped his forehead with his shirtsleeve, then got back into his pickup to drive the final distance. He thought about the long weeks since that meeting with Simik and all the reasons why he had not yet moved Serafina. At first Clay answered each of Simik's certified letters of inquiry about Adelita, but then he began to ignore them. Simik knew the deal was signed and there was nothing legal he could do.

Adelita's final agony had drawn out and then there were the arrangements for her burial in the cemetery at Solitario. And then with the drought worsening, the temperatures rose to the hottest on record this spring and Clay refused to ask any of his friends, even Gus Muñoz, to help him in that heat. And then it was spring calving and branding and the busiest time of the year for Gus, so he did not bother him then either. Even though their bodies were as worn as his, Clay kept promising himself he would get together with Dobb and Yebbie and maybe even old Henry Bennett and tell them everything about the sale and the deadline and ask if they might be able to help him during April. But the truth was that Clayton Elliott had rarely depended on anyone for help, so like many things in his past, he simply put it off with what he considered good reasons.

It had also taken a great deal of time to go over the necessary paperwork with his hired attorney concerning Adelita's death and getting a clear title to the property, and when that was finalized, he paid the lawyer off first. Then he had taken two more extended trips back to El Paso on the passenger train out of Alpine, using up more of the earnest money on lodging and meals and payments to Adelita's medical staff. But even that did not pay the full balance, and now the earnest money was gone. The medical center also sent certified statements each month in the mail for the remainder of the money but Clay had stopped opening them a month ago.

"Deadline ain't up yet," he said and once again surveyed the remnants of his past that lay just ahead, now desolate and crumbling and empty except for Palo and Serafina. "Hell, who knows, maybe before it's all said and done, I'll be trespassing out here on my own damn place. Some things just take time. . . ."

He drove down past the old house and parked next to Serafina. He got out and inspected his fence repair and his paint job in the harsh light of the morning sun. Satisfied, he walked over to the base of the windmill and looked around at the sometimes damp area for the little flowers and to get a cool drink from the rock trough with the makeshift dipper. But he saw no purple anywhere.

"Hey, Palo," he said to the old horse who appeared to be standing in the same tracks where he stood yesterday afternoon. "How's the hay holding up?"

The horse did not budge. He had still not eaten much of the bale Clay had scattered the week before, and he wondered if Palo had given up.

"Putting things off too, ain't you? Eating ain't something you can put off for long though, hear me?"

Clay thought about the old wagon again, hidden behind the tack shed. Its front wheel remained unrepaired and useless, and still there it was against the wall of the shed where he had leaned it all those years ago, his body younger and stronger but even then, too stubborn to ask for the assistance he knew he would need to restore it and lift it back onto the heavy axle of the wagon. He stood next to the trough with his hand on the horse's neck and he stared down into the cool water and saw his reflection alongside Palo's, and he wondered if he, too, should just give up.

"Damn thing's worthless anyway," he said, but he was not speaking about the aged horse. "Who needs some damned rattling junk with a loose wheel to remind you of what's long past. I ought to just burn it and that rotten harness inside the shed to boot. I never used them anyway. Never needed them . . . except that once. . . ."

He stopped and regarded his image in the water as he said this and saw the guilt fracture his face. He raked his fingers across the top of the water, warping that image further and Palo's image also inside the ripples. But this only distorted his guilt; it did not remove it.

"Well," he said and he reached to fill the dipper. It was then he noticed traces of water still in the bottom of the can.

Had it not been one hundred degrees the day before and already that warm today—far too hot to allow any lingering moisture from yesterday—Clay would not have thought much about it. Had all the windows in his old homestead been intact and had Jovita's words of caution not still teased his mind, he would simply have dipped the can into the water and drank and then looked around in the coulees for the flowers. But even in the heat, a small shiver walked across Clay's shoulders, especially when he remembered the sounds he had heard last evening, sighs or sobs that he imagined at the time as simply the soughing of the evening breeze in his ears.

Do I turn and look around slowly . . . do I walk casually back to my truck, retrieve the pistol from under my seat . . . do I just get in and drive away and get Deputy Wagner back out here. . . .

Like he had done all his adult life, Clay decided on the studied and calm course, though others might call it wasting valuable time. He dipped the can, lifted it and put it to his mouth. As he sucked in the water, he made a casual turn, glanced up over the lip of the can and from under the shadow of his hat brim. He took in everything for almost a complete circle. Nothing. He lowered the dipper and in an uncharacteristic move, especially for Solitario County, splashed what was left of the precious water onto the dirt and released a loud satisfied groan, accentuating his pleasure with the cool water for anyone in earshot. Then he turned and bent over the gravesite and coaxed two tenacious clumps of grama grass from the edge of the mound, tossing them aside.

Minutes passed, but it seemed an hour before Clay felt this charade was sufficient to warrant his returning to the truck. He opened the door, bent forward and felt under his seat for the loaded revolver. With his back to the house, he stuffed the barrel of the pistol inside the waist of his pants but then reconsidered, realizing how silly he would appear when he turned around, so he lifted out the revolver and held it alongside his thigh, muzzle straight down. Then he turned and approached the house.

Clay had never considered himself a man of exceptional courage. Perhaps it was the thought of some stranger invading his sovereignty, even as useless and empty as the old house now stood. Perhaps it had to do with some imagined threat to his physical safety or to Serafina herself. He did not know what careless impulse urged him to the side of the house, out of view from someone—or some *thing*—inside. Nor did he think twice about his own safety when he recognized for certain these were sobs coming from Serafina's bedroom. He simply moved in front of the empty window, his revolver still at his side and useless in that position. He looked inside and straightened, startled at the sight of the young woman crouched in the shadows, her face in her hands.

"What are *you* doing in there?" he said as if he might be speaking to Serafina or Adelita. It was not a demand but a simple request for some explanation. *"Quien estas?"* he said when he saw she was obviously Latina and probably from across the border and then, *"Habla Ingles?"*

The young woman removed her hands from her face and stopped the sounds, but she did not look up. She tensed, and Clay thought she might rise and bolt from the room, but then he saw she wore no shoes, her feet blood-caked, probably from walking across the broken window glass outside to get to the water at the windmill.

"Esta bien," he whispered. "It's okay. I won't hurt you."

She looked at him, and Clay saw terror in her eyes.

"Esta bien," he repeated, and her eyes softened a little when she saw he was not the source of her terror but perhaps someone who might even help. She looked at her swollen and bloody feet and then back at Clay.

"They took my shoes," she began, as if stating that fact in English might explain everything. "And they took my–"

"I see that," Clay interrupted and smiled at her. He had other questions, but he was certain Deputy Sheriff Locket Wagner would have many more. "Can I come around inside there?"

A flash of terror returned to her face for a moment, but then she nodded. Clay went around to the back doorway and came through the darkened kitchen, his boot steps hollow inside the gutted rooms. When he walked into the bedroom, the woman saw the gun, and cried out burying her head again in her hands.

"It's okay," he whispered. "It's not for you. See. . . ." He shoved the pistol into the waist of his pants. "Look." He held out his hands, palms exposed. She glanced up through her splayed fingers and saw this. She sucked in several staccato breaths, relaxed, exhaled slowly. "Let's get you out of here, okay?" Clay said.

The woman nodded this time but dropped back to her knees when she tried to stand on her cut feet. Clay moved over and bent to help her. "Here," he said. "Take my arm."

She reached up and grasped his forearm and with

his help, pulled herself onto her feet. "Careful," he said. "Take it easy." They worked their way to the front door and out onto the porch next to the weathered railing. "Wait here. Just lean against the rail there, but lean easy."

Clay steadied her and then went to his pickup. He stashed the pistol under the seat and took the extra cushion and tossed it onto the floor of the passenger side. Then he cranked the engine and in a moment, he was parked with the door on the passenger side next to the old porch. He punched the dash control to the rattling air conditioner into full mode and got out to help the young woman.

"Put your feet on that cushion when you get in," he instructed. He saw her look down at her bloody feet and then back at him. She shook her head. "On the cushion. It's okay," he said and smiled at her. "Go ahead. It ain't gonna hurt that old thing."

She got into the seat and brought in one leg and then the other. She lowered each foot in turn onto the soft cushion. Some relief came to her face.

"Better?"

"*Sí,*" she sighed. "Thank you."

"I'll get some water." He moved to the windmill again and brought back a dipperful which she finished right away. "More?"

"Please."

He went back and refilled the dipper and brought it. She dribbled part of this over the tops of her feet and then drank the remainder and gave the empty dipper back to Clay. He tossed it into the bed of the pickup and got in on the driver's side. "That's burritos." He nodded at the foil-wrapped food on the seat between them. "Bea made them."

She did not ask who Bea was. Nor did she wait for encouragement. She unwrapped one and bit into it and shut her eyes as she leaned her head forward into the cold air vent. She sucked in another deep breath as she chewed.

"You got a name?" Clay said. He shifted the gears and accelerated onto the dirt road back toward Solitario and thought how stupid the question was. "Course you do. "

She did not offer it. She took another bite.

"Well?"

The young woman swallowed and then said "Perfidia" and bit again.

"I see. Where you from?" he said. She did not answer. "*De donde va?*" he repeated in Spanish because he knew that if her name was not obvious, where she had come from was, and he realized this too was a stupid question. "I understand."

He glanced at this young woman, this Perfidia, as they moved along the two-track dirt road. She finished both burritos by the time they reached the junction at the blacktop. There, she grew increasingly nervous as they turned toward Solitario, visible just up the pavement. For a moment as he slowed at the intersection, he thought the young woman might open her door and dash back into the desert, but he saw her glance down at her bare and useless feet and he saw a look of resignation come to her face.

"Hey, it's gonna be okay," he said. "But I already said that, right?" He looked at her and smiled but she saw no humor in this, so he said in a very resolute voice, "I promise you . . . Perfidia? You said, Perfidia, right?" She nodded. "Well Perfidia, nobody here's gonna bother you."

He looked up the blacktop with fingers of heat already rising from it, blurring the little town of Solitario and he thought about some of its citizens, some of his lifelong friends even, and he considered the fragile truth of his statement so he repeated it, as if to convince himself this time, "Nobody'll bother you here in Solitario."

Clay concentrated on the road now and did not notice this young woman, this Perfidia, as she turned her shoulders away from him. She pretended to study the passing fence posts. He did not see her press her palms to the outside of her damp blouse and against her breasts, trying to relieve the pain. ☙

CHAPTER 4

Locket Wagner studied the map on the wall of his branch office, two doors down from the Hotel Solitario. He traced his finger along the perimeter of the vast area that he was assigned to cover as deputy sheriff of Solitario County, an expanse of land that bordered the Rio Grande River.

"What am I doing in here on a Sunday?" he said. "It's like combat duty now. Impossible to prevent a damned thing even working seven days a week."

He thought about the call on another Sunday just three weeks ago, a dispatch to a remote sidetrack of the railroad ten miles west. No one had dared open the lone boxcar, left there months prior by the rail line due to a faulty brake. When Locket approached on foot he knew immediately why someone had vacated the area and placed the anonymous phone call to the sheriff's office over in Presidio. Even without a breeze in the heat of the day, the odor came wafting toward him, halting him in his tracks. Instinctively, he held his pistol ready as he lifted the heavy bar on the locking lever of the sliding door and pushed open a two-foot crack. But there was no need for the pistol.

The stench was unbearable. Locket backed off a few feet and gagged, trying to maintain a semblance of a defensive stance. Then he holstered his weapon and buried his nose in the crook of his shirtsleeve and moved forward to look inside. Even in the shadows he could count five, six, maybe seven bodies strewn about, one a child, no more that a couple of years old.

"*Bastards*," he hissed. He was not cursing these destitute Mexican victims inside, but rather the *coyotes* who, in some panic or a simple act of viciousness, had locked these people inside this inescapable oven, perhaps abandoned them at night in haste to avoid detection themselves.

"*Scum* . . ." he said.

Locket had the bodies removed to the Presidio station of the Border Patrol for difficult if not impossible task of identification, along with the help of Mexican authorities from across the border in Ojinaga. With the U.S. Immigration Service, Locket was still on the case because it was a homicide in his jurisdiction. Thus far, as usual, no one knew a thing.

Locket leaned one palm against the map now, trying in vain to cover his assigned area with one hand. Then he tried using both palms. Even with two hands sprung from his six-foot-four, two hundred and forty pounds of mostly muscle, Deputy Locket Wagner still could not hide his duty area on the map. "Why in hell do I keep doing this?" he grumbled. "You gotta be nuts, Wagner."

He turned away from the map and took his hat from the rack and walked toward the door. "At least they still let me eat," he said. "When I have the stomach for it." He thought about Bea Hernandez and her special Sunday brunch only two doors down and smiled.

"Maybe she's made *carne adovada* today."

Outside, he turned the key in his office door and moved toward the Hotel Solitario. He thought about the time not so many years past when no one on the little main street of Solitario ever locked their doors during the day, except maybe Doc Maddox, who was only there one day a week. He paused at the hotel door when he heard Clay Elliott's ancient pickup bump to a stop against the curb behind him.

Locket glanced over his shoulder and saw the young woman in the seat beside Clay. It did not take a trained lawman to notice through the dust of the window the abrasions on her face and the disheveled hair. That she might be a Mexican national–and probably not here legally–made no difference whatsoever to Locket because he had no jurisdiction on illegal immigrants anyway, unless they had broken some local law. Or gotten themselves slaughtered in the heat of a boxcar. He simply recognized that this was another human being who might need some help and where she was from was irrelevant. When he saw Clay exit and come around to her door to let her out, Locket walked back and stood on the sidewalk in front of the truck.

"Need a hand, Clay?" he said.

"Yeah," Clay said without looking up. "I don't think she's gonna be able to walk on these feet, Locket."

Locket nodded and moved to the truck. Perfidia had swung her feet out and Locket saw her grimace when they touched the hot doorplate of the pickup. He said nothing. When she glanced at his white straw hat and his matching white shirt with the brass badge, and then his sidearm, she brought her feet back in and tried to close the door, but Clay held it. She crossed her arms as if protecting her chest and sat sullen, staring out the windshield.

"It's okay," Clay said. "He's not Border Patrol, not *La Migra.*"

That did not seem to matter to Perfidia. She sat immobile.

"You can't stay out here in this heat," Locket offered. He bent down to look inside the truck but he did not approach. "I ain't gonna arrest you for having cut feet, lady."

She seemed to relax a little and Clay held the door wider and said, "We need to get you inside, take care of those feet."

Locket nodded and waited. Perfidia turned her head toward the two men and blinked into the sun. With one hand she tried to smooth her hair back but it sprang up again in tangles.

"Don't worry about your hair," Locket said and turned to Clay. "I could carry her inside, I guess."

Clay lifted his shoulders and gestured at the young woman. "It's her call. And yours. Probably be a good idea though."

Even in this heat, Clay had no doubts about Locket Wagner lifting and carrying into the hotel what could not be more than one hundred and ten pounds, unless she happened to be kicking and screaming and clawing.

"Well?" Locket said. He was talking to Perfidia now. "Whatta you think?"

She finally nodded, once, and pushed herself around again, this time holding her feet suspended. Locket leaned in and slid one arm around her back and the other under the crook of her knees. When he lifted her, she seemed far lighter than he had anticipated.

"Hang on," Locket said expecting that she might at least bring a hand up and grasp his shoulder to assist, but she did not move either arm. He wondered if they might be broken.

Clay held the hotel door and they moved into the lobby. Rafin glanced up from whatever he was doing behind the counter and then back down, but then with wider eyes, looked up again at this parade standing under the ceiling fan. He walked quickly into the back office and was soon in the lobby with Jovita.

"*What the—*" Jovita began and then, "Who's this?"

"It's a long story," Clay said. "Where can we take her?"

"Well, back where she came from might be best," Jovita offered and then she saw the young woman's feet. "Bring her back here, Locket."

By now, Dobb Campbell and Yebbie Riggs and several other people from the restaurant had heard the commotion and wandered into the lobby, their post-Sunday brunch iced tea still in their hands. Clay looked over at his two friends and shrugged. "Hey, thanks for waiting," he said. They stood silent, blinking at him.

Clay went with Jovita and Rafin back into the hallway where they all followed Locket carrying the young woman into the first empty guest room. Dobb and Yebbie looked at each other, baffled.

"Well, I ain't gonna wait forever," Yebbie called but Clay had disappeared behind the guest room door. Dobb went back into the restaurant and straight for the dessert table and soon Yebbie was there beside him.

Inside the guest room, Locket set the woman on the bed. Jovita elbowed the men aside and stood inspecting the woman's feet, then her hair and her bruised face. And then she looked at her torn blouse, obviously damp in front, even though she sat with arms crossed over her breasts.

"You men get out of here," Jovita said.

"I gotta ask her some questions," Locket said.

"Send Bea back here, Clay," Jovita said, ignoring Locket. "And Doc Maddox if he's still in the restaurant." She turned to the men, who all stood immobile, as if she had not spoken a word. *"Go!"* she said and they hurried from the room.

She moved to the door and locked it and then went into the bathroom and wet a wash cloth. She came back and sat on the bed beside the young woman and gave her the damp cloth. The woman dropped her crossed arms and took the wet rag. For a long while, Jovita watched as the woman washed the dried blood from her face and dabbed at the torn lip and tried to smooth back her hair. Both seemed to avoid the question of the cut feet until finally Jovita said in a quiet voice, "I can wet some towels for those too."

The woman nodded. Jovita moved a wooden chair next to the bed and lifted the woman's legs onto it. She went back into the bathroom and returned with two towels soaked in cool water. Then she carefully wrapped the towels around the woman's feet and lowered them to the seat of the chair.

"There," she said and then, "We'll clean these and get something else on them too. You just cool them off right now, okay?" She looked up into the woman's face.

"What's your name?"

The young woman sighed. Twice today she had been asked. "Perfidia."

"Do you want to lie back on the bed?"

"No."

Jovita nodded. "You're from across the river."

Perfidia hesitated for a moment but then said, "Yes."

"Where?" Jovita said but it was not difficult to figure this out.

"Ojinaga."

"Where is your baby?" Jovita said.

The woman's eyes widened at this. "My baby . . ." she whispered.

"I have eyes," Jovita said and nodded to the front of Perfidia's blouse.

Perfidia tried again to conceal the fresh dampness, at first as if to make it go away but then she dropped her arms and began to sob. "They have her," she whimpered.

Jovita sat on the bed again next to Perfidia and this time, she put an arm around her.

"Who?"

"The *coyotes* who brought us over."

"Where? Why?"

Perfidia seemed confused now with all of Jovita's questions. She looked up at the door and next the window and then into the corners of the room, as if disoriented, or perhaps seeking an avenue of escape.

Finally, Perfidia looked at her useless feet propped on the chair and stumbled through her words, "I . . . I could not pay enough. When we got here, they wanted more to take us all the way to El Paso. I only had a little left. They took that. And then they took my baby daughter." She stared at her hands, nervous and busy in her lap with the hem of her blouse. "Then they beat me and took my shoes so I would die in the desert."

Jovita took her by the shoulders and gently turned the woman toward her but Perfidia still held her eyes lowered. "Look at me," Jovita said. "Please . . ."

Perfidia finally turned her eyes up. Jovita searched to see if these eyes might be lying. But when Jovita glanced down again at the front of Perfidia's blouse, she knew she was not lying about having a nursing infant, a baby who was not with her now.

"But why?" Jovita repeated. "Why take your baby?"

Perfidia sat mute.

"Why?" Jovita pressed. "Why would they take a nursing infant? Just because you didn't have enough money for them? That's insane."

Perfidia lowered her head and shook it hard, as if to purge all this from her mind. When she stopped, her long hair fell forward, concealing her face. Jovita said nothing, waited. There was a long silence before Perfidia sighed and then slowly gathered the hair from her eyes in both hands and raked it back over her ears with curved fingers. She looked up and across the room at nothing. Jovita saw a mist come to the corner of her eyes.

"They said if they kept her alive and healthy," Perfidia continued in an even voice, as if by a simple and unemotional explanation, she might distance herself from it. "Then they could get a good price for her."

"Sell her?" Jovita said.

"Yes."

"Sell your baby?"

Perfidia nodded, once.

"My God," Jovita said. She took the young woman in her arms and held her tight but Perfidia seemed stiff and lifeless as the two rocked gently back and forth on the edge of the bed. "My God . . ." Jovita repeated and for the first time in many years, her own eyes began to fill. ☙

CHAPTER 5

Bea was clearing the last of the brunch from the buffet table when Clay and Locket walked into the restaurant, gesturing and talking low with their heads inclined toward each other. "If you two are thinking about eating, forget it," she scolded. "It's all cold anyway."

They stopped and looked up at Bea who skittered away. Then Locket went over and sat with Dobb and Yebbie, who were finishing slabs of pie and mugs of coffee. Clay saw that Doc Maddox had already gone, along with everyone else except these two. Clay moved closer to Bea and walked back toward the kitchen with her.

"Jo wants you," he said.

"Wants me to what?" Bea stopped and turned, her arms full of platters.

"Wants you to come over to that first guest room down the hall," he said. "When you get a chance, of course."

"Why?" Bea said, pretending she knew nothing about what had happened in the lobby, even though the buzz had swept through the little dining room. Clay knew there was no way Bea was unaware but he said, "Where we took that woman, Bea."

"That's none of my business," Bea said. "I just run the kitchen, I don't smuggle Mexicans or anything else over the river."

"I know, Bea," Clay said. He followed her back into the kitchen. "I think Jo just wants some help. I mean, another woman, you know. She run us off."

Bea set the platters into the big sink and turned back frowning at Clay. "I don't know anything about those things," she said. "I don't *want* to know anything."

"Come on, Bea. Nobody thinks you're involved in anything," Clay pleaded. "That's silly."

"Well, silly or not, I know how some people think," she said. "It's not like I don't care, Clay. But it doesn't matter that I was born and raised there in Solitario County and that three generations of my family have lived here. Or that I've lived around here all my sixty-nine years. We're Texans, just like you. But if you're also Hispanic in this area, well . . ." She turned back to the sink and opened the hot water onto the dishes. "You know about that." She looked at Clay. "Adelita knew. . . ."

And Clay knew. For a moment, he thought about all of these conflicts concerning citizenship and racial bias and talk of illegalities and amnesty, all of which had seemed to reach a crisis point in recent years. But because Clay and Adelita had chosen to live in such isolation, most of the issues themselves seemed alien. Now he often wondered if it had been only his choice to live such a solitary existence. Adelita had never been asked for documentation because she had never needed to work outside their ranch. In addition, she was second generation and a native Texan and that would have made her a citizen, even if she had not been married to

Clay. There was plenty of work on the ranch, and they got by without outside income. Sometimes just barely, though Adelita might have said *always* just barely.

"Well, whatever. But you'll have to tell Jo yourself," Clay said. He walked back toward the kitchen exit into the restaurant. "I'm just passing on what she said, Bea. Sorry. Never meant to upset you."

Clay drew a lukewarm mug of coffee from the big urn inside the restaurant and went over and sat at the table with the other men. Locket looked at him but Yebbie and Dobb just picked at the last of their pie. No one said anything. Bea finally came out of the kitchen with a plate piled with *carne adovada* and beans and a tortilla in one hand and a piece of pecan pie in the other. She set the *adovada* in front of Locket and the pie in front of Clay.

"You already had burritos," she said curtly to Clay and then to Locket, "The rest of all this is cold anyway," she repeated but no one raised a single objection. Then she turned away and moved out into the lobby and toward the hallway.

"Bea's getting soft in her older days," Locket said.

"If you only knew," Clay sighed. He looked with envy at the food in front of Locket, cold or not. "I gave my burritos to that young woman. There ain't no way in hell I'd bring that up with Bea, though. Can you reach that hardware over there, Dobb?"

Dobb nodded and retrieved two cloth napkins rolled with silverware from the next table. He gave one to Locket and the other to Clay and then he looked at Yebbie, sitting impatient, sipping. Both watched the two eat.

"Well?" Yebbie finally broke the silence.

"Well what?" Locket said.

"Wasn't talking to you, Mister Deputy," Yebbie said. "We been sitting here waiting three hours, Clayton. What is it you wanted to talk about?"

"Take it easy, Yebbie," Dobb said and then wryly, "You'll have the deputy here whipping out his handcuffs. And the food in his jail ain't like this."

Locket looked up and poked an empty fork at the two. "You guys never give up, do you? It's only when somebody breaks into your barns or shoots one of your damned old fleabag horses that you talk nice to me. Or when you need votes to get you back on the county commissioners." He stuffed another piece of meat into his mouth and shook his head and lifted his eyes to the ceiling. "Why do I do this job?" he said through a mouthful.

"Well, you gonna arrest her?" Yebbie said, unable to let it go.

"Arrest who?" Locket frowned at him.

"That woman you carried through the lobby, that's who."

"Why?"

"Cause she's a *wetback*, that's why," Yebbie said.

"How do you know?" Clay injected. "Mind your own damned business, Yebbie."

"Well then, where'd *you* get her?" Yebbie turned on Clay. "How come *you* showed up here in Solitario with her in the first place?"

"Well, it's like this," Clay began and then lowered his voice to a false whisper. "See, her and me and Lock here are in cahoots with a Mexican dope lord. We smuggle dope over all the time. People too. Didn't you see my brand new pickup out front?"

Yebbie snorted, folded his arms and sulked. "Well I don't care what you say, if she ain't over here legal, then she oughta get sent right back. Hell's bells, we got millions of 'em here already."

"Okay, you two," Dobb said. "Joke's over."

Clay stopped eating and set his fork beside his unfinished pie. "You didn't see her feet I guess. Neither of you."

"Wasn't me making no joke," Yebbie said to Dobb and then to Clay, "What about her feet?"

"They're cut all to hell," Locket said. "But that ain't illegal, far as I know. But I can check it out for you, Yeb."

"Cut?" Dobb said. "How?"

"On all that broken glass around my old homestead," Clay said. "I guess they—" He stopped and looked at Locket. "I guess whoever brought her over stole her shoes and then left her out there."

"Why'd they do that?" Yebbie said, his voice mellowing a bit. "That's just stupid, sneak her over and then leave her afoot without shoes. Where's she from, anyway?" Yebbie paused and then said, "But I expect we can guess that though."

"We didn't get her biography," Clay said dryly.

"Don't matter," Dobb said. "If she's hurt, I mean. She's still a human being. I'm glad it was you found her, Clay, and not somebody else who might have just left her there," he scowled at Yebbie. "I think she's lucky to be alive with the way things are going on around here."

Locket nodded grimly, remembering the stench

from the boxcar. "Yeah, some ain't so lucky." He too stopped eating and put down his fork, pushed the plate back. No one spoke for a long while, not even Yebbie, all considering what Locket had said.

Finally, Clay cleared his throat. "Well, anyway, this sorta trumped what I was wanting to talk to you two about today. Actually, I been intending to speak to you ever since . . ." Clay paused.

"I'd better check back there," Locket inserted and rose to go. "Ask a few questions."

"They'll let you know if they need you, Lock," Clay said. "I think maybe they had some woman talk to do first. Bea's back there too."

"Yeah . . ." Locket said and sat back down. "I guess I'm due a little down time once in a while anyway. It ain't like she might be a serial killer or something. Truth is, I got no jurisdiction at all. That's Border Patrol and that's Immigration and *that's* Feds." He looked at each one in turn and said, "And now that all three of you know that, you can just give it a rest."

Dobb nodded and shifted the conversation, "What's up, Clay? What was it you wanted to talk about?"

"Well, truth is, it's about Serafina and Adelita," Clay began.

"I see," Dobb said.

"Yeah." Clay looked at each face and then said, "I'm gonna move her."

"Move Adelita out there with her?" Yebbie squinted and pulled on an ear. "Well, it'd be a helluva a lot of work fixing up your old place, but if that's what you're thinking about doing, I could sure understand that. City living can get to you." He paused and looked at Dobb.

"Solitario ain't exactly a city, Yeb," Dobb corrected and then turned to Clay. "But I can see your point, Clay. Frankly, I always wondered why you put Adelita in here in the first place and not out there. And then you stayed around town here yourself. You know, big *city* living as Yeb here says. It's not like you, Clay, but I never said nothing. None of my business, you know. It's been tough for you," Dobb said and lowered his eyes as if remembering the loss of his own wife a few years back. "Probably still is. . . ."

"Yeah," Yebbie said and shook his head. "Tough call the way your place had been broke into and run down so quick. Damn meskins coming over in droves now, getting into everything." Yebbie's face grew taut and angry and he continued. "Hell, just this last week some of them broke into my—"

"Yeah, you told us, Yeb," Dobb interrupted and then looked at Clay and waited for more, but Clay said nothing so Dobb went on, "But if you been waiting all this time to ask us to help you on this, Clay, you shouldn't have done that. If you're needing some help fixing it up out there, hell just say the word."

"Yeah, you shouldn't have done that," Yebbie said. "Just you say the—

"It ain't that," Clay said. "You guys ain't understanding. It ain't Adelita I'm moving. And I ain't moving back out there either. I'm moving Serafina. Here, into Solitario, right next to her mother. I ain't fixing nothing up out there. That's all."

"You mean just keep living upstairs here?" Locket

said. "In town the rest of your life? Like Dobb says, that sure as hell ain't like you, Clay."

"You guys shut up," Dobb injected. He tilted his head and inspected Clay. "I don't think Clay's finished. Are you?"

Clay sighed and went on. "It's been working on me ever since Adelita died and I put her in the ground here in town. I just think it's time that her and Sera were together. Adelita wanted to be together with her too. She said that the day she died. . . ."

"I see." Dobb nodded.

Yebbie said nothing, remembering the little casket he had constructed for Serafina all those years back.

"Oh," Locket said but that was all.

"I see," Dobb repeated. "Well, you shouldn't have waited so long, Clay. You shoulda just done it."

"Truth is, Dobb," Clay said. "It ain't all been just excuses or pride. I can't do it by myself, and that's the problem. Knees and my back and these hands and all . . ." He lifted the gnarled hands he had held resting on his thighs, not to show to the others, but to inspect them himself as if perhaps some miracle had healed them and he could just walk away. He studied them for a moment and then replaced them again out of sight under the table. "Anyway, if you two will remember, she ain't very deep," he continued. "But it's gonna take pickaxes and shovels and spud bars just to loosen up twenty-five years of hardpan. And then, there's the getting her in here to Solitario and . . ."

"And you need some help, right?" Locket said. "From us? Hell, just *say* it, Clay."

"That's right. I sure as hell ain't gonna ask just

anybody. No way," Clay said and now that these words were out, others that had been dammed up for months burst forth. "You Dobb and you Yebbie and maybe even old Henry Bennett too but I don't know if he's up to it because I think Henry's more wore out than any of us and you too Locket if you'd a mind to and had the time and I'm sure Gus Muñoz would—"

"Okay, okay," Locket interrupted. He paused and considered his pending cases and his recent seven-day work weeks and now, this assaulted woman. Even an illegal immigrant had a right not to be assaulted. "Maybe. We'd just have to see about my helping right now, Clay. I may have to get involved pretty strong with the situation in that room back there. You understand? I'd do what I could, though."

"When did you want to do it, Clay?" Dobb said.

"Yeah, when?" Yebbie said.

"Well, that's sort'a the catch too. It ain't like I got much selection now," Clay said. He lowered his eyes and searched for the right explanation, speaking slowly and deliberately. "See, when I sold out, I signed this contract for the deed to my place. In it, they gave me a certain amount of time to move her." Clay paused again and in the silence, looked around at the blank faces.

"Sold out?" Yebbie finally said. "They?"

"Yeah, you know," Clay continued. "The new owners."

"You never said you sold out, Clay?" Dobb said.

"No I didn't," Clay confessed. "And in fact, it ain't a done deal yet. I mean it's a *done deal* but no deed's been transferred over there in the county office. I just never thought much about it, I guess, until lately with the deadline coming up. You know, all them big bills and me broke and everything else happening . . . well, I got some earnest money from them and I went back and forth over there on the train to El Paso and used it up on a lawyer and getting the medical people off my back at least till the rest of the money comes in after the deed does transfer."

"I remember them trips, Clay. Tough time for sure, Adelita gone and. . . . anyway, I guess we never really had a chance to talk about much of anything since then," Dobb went on. "I can sure understand that too. Like I said, though, nothing I wanted to poke my nose into . . . friends don't do that. They ought'a just be here for you and I was."

"Me too," Yebbie said and paused. Then he narrowed his eyes. "Who's this new owner gonna be anyway?"

"Outfit called Agua Hondo," Clay said.

"Cattle company?" Dobb said and smiled.

"Well, not exactly," Clay said and paused. "They're kind of a water company, I guess."

Everyone at the table nodded but did not speak. Second only to cattle or now perhaps illegal immigrants, nothing aroused more interest in far West Texas than water.

"Never heard of them," Locket said.

"Me neither," Yebbie said.

"They've been around West Texas a while, I guess," Clay continued. "Hit me up a few years back at the stock show in El Paso but I wasn't selling then, of course. Didn't need to back then." All nodded, understanding, but said nothing more about Adelita's ordeal.

Clay went on, "Anyway, they've got this dumb-ass idea they'll pump water out of there and sell it."

"Sell water?" Dobb said, very curious and then he brightened again. "That might be good. Haul it around and sell it to people here in the county with dried up wells or something. Might relieve this six-year drought a little." He smiled at Clay who did not smile back. "I mean, if the price was right, of course. What *is* their plan, Clay?"

"Bring in a rig, drill a well," Clay explained. "Just like that, I guess. Right there at our old windmill. Tear that down, doze in the buildings, flatten everything, knock over the corrals so's they can park all that machinery and stuff. Then drill it right there, right next to where Sera's been all these years."

"I see," Dobb said. "So you gotta get her out of there, no question about that."

"Well, it's not like that's the *only* reason," Clay said. "Mainly, I just want to put her here in town at the graveyard, right next to her mama under that big cottonwood tree, so's they can be together. It's what Adelita wanted. And I want it too. Y'all understand." Everyone nodded again but no one said anything.

"Why don't they just go a little deeper and put in a bigger windmill?" Yebbie said. "I done that south of my house a year ago when three of my windmills and that one spring all went bone dry about the same time. You seen that new big sucker I put up, Clay? Works good, lot's more water, even in a little breeze. Hell, I only had to go down another thirty feet or so and then—"

"I seen it, Yebbie," Clay interrupted.

"Hell, I'll loan them my old cable drilling rig,"

Yebbie said and he straightened his back and grinned. "Wouldn't tear up so much stuff that way. She's old but she still works good. Kinda like myself, I guess."

"Don't think that'd do it," Clay said.

"Why not?" Dobb said. He frowned at Clay.

"Because . . ." Clay began but then stopped. "Anyway, I only got till midnight of May fifteenth to move her but I want to get it done sooner than that. And I'm just asking for your help, that's all. Contract says as soon as I get her moved, they can go in there, but not before. I didn't want them moving machinery all over where she is. I saw to that in the contract."

"You say they couldn't just use Yeb's old rig?" Dobb pressed. "Why not?"

Clay sighed and stood. The three at the table swung their heads in unison as he went to the coffee urn where he tipped it and filled his mug with tepid coffee. He spoke with his back to his audience. "Because they're going all the way down into the aquifer, that's why." He turned back and stood rigid and from across the room said, "Deep. Real deep, maybe a thousand feet. Tap the aquifer with a pump. A *big* pump."

"What the hell for?" Yebbie said. "Why that deep?"

"Yeah?" Locket was now caught up in this. "What's happening to the water?"

"They're planning to *pipe* it outta here," Clay said. "Not haul it. They say there's billions of gallons down there."

"Billions?" Dobb said and repeated, *"Billions?"*

"That's what they say, Dobb."

This too was out now. Clay moved back and sat

at the table. "Anyway, I just need your help with Sera so they can pay me the rest of what they owe me and the deed will be theirs. They can do whatever they want to with it then."

"Why?" Yebbie said, more baffled than ever. "We all could use a little in our stock ponds and such, but billions? Whatta you gonna do with billions of gallons of water?"

Dobb was even more dubious. "Yeah, and what happens to all our windmills and springs that are already drying up? And to those little trickles of water still struggling down the creeks? What happens to all that if they do pump billions of gallons out of our aquifer too, Clay?"

"It's for El Paso," Clay said, answering Yebbie and then to Dobb, "Nothing. Nothing at all happens to surface water, Dobb. That's the same question I asked them and that's what they said, but . . ."

"But what?" Dobb said. "And whatta you mean, *El Paso?*"

"Truth is, I don't know for sure what will happen to surface water," Clay admitted. "And I'm not certain they do either. How the hell was I to know all that? I just needed money for Adelita's bills, the money I needed to try and keep her alive, dammit." Everyone at the table nodded but said nothing. Clay went on. "Anyway, their plan is to push all that water through a big pipeline all the way over to El Paso."

"For some damned city?" Yebbie was incredulous. "So's they can build more houses and golf courses and lawns?"

Clay sat silent. So did Dobb and Locket. Yebbie

went on, "Damnedest idea I ever heard of."

"Well, y'all in?" Clay said and looked at each man in the eyes. "I mean, on helping me with Sera?"

Locket spoke first, "Like I said, Clay. I'm pretty busy. We'll just have to see."

Clay understood this.

"So they can't move in out there till you move Serafina?" Dobb said.

Clay nodded again. "Or that deadline in the contract. Whichever comes first."

"And that's when?" Dobb said.

"Like I said," Clay looked at Dobb. "And it ain't changed since I just told you five minutes ago, Dobb. Midnight, May fifteenth, this month. It's in the contract." He turned to Yebbie who had detected Dobb's reluctance. "Whatta you think, Yebbie? Can you squeeze in a few hours between now and then?" Clay said.

Yebbie hesitated for a moment and then said with strained determination, "You know I'll do it in a heartbeat. You know that, Clay."

"Dobb?" Clay said and he waited in silence for the true verdict. He knew Yebbie would do whatever Dobb decided.

"It's like Locket says, I'll have to think about it too, Clay." Dobb said.

"Think about it? Then you're saying no, Dobb?"

"Course not, Clay." Dobb said. He looked at his friend and sighed. "It ain't moving your Serafina I'm balking at. You know that. But if I'm hearing you right, they can't do a thing out there till she's moved or that deadline's passed, right?"

"Whichever comes first," Clay said wearily

and frowned at him. "Where are you going with this, Dobb?"

"And nothing happens in the meantime? I mean till midnight, May fifteenth?" Dobb said.

"Yeah," Clay said. "I already gone over all this, Dobb."

"You don't really have to be in any hurry then, right?" Dobb said. "I mean, you've waited all this time to move her, so you wouldn't really have to rush now."

"Well, it's no crisis, Dobb, if that's what you mean," Clay admitted. "And no, I don't always get things done exactly like they oughta get done maybe. But I just want to get them together now, that's all. Like I promised Adelita and I promised myself." Clay paused and studied Dobb. "And truth is, I promised Sera too. Yesterday, as a matter of fact. On her birthday, kneeling right out there next to her grave. And if that sounds nuts or silly to you guys, so be it."

"It ain't silly, Clay," Dobb said. "It's just that we might need to study on it a bit. That's all I'm saying. Maybe we need to get Henry Bennett to call a special meeting of the county commissioners and talk about all this. After all, it is *water* we're talking about too. Lots of it."

"Water?" Clay said with anger but only a hint because he knew this was a very important part of everything he had been tiptoeing around himself. "I'm talking about Serafina, Dobb, not water. It's simple as far as I'm concerned. We don't need some damn meeting of the commissioners. We bring her up, we move her, as soon as possible. That's it. That is if you guys ain't turning me down. I don't see how it's any of the county's

business anyway except that you three commissioners control the graveyard. I hope you ain't saying I can't put her there close to her mama? Well?"

"Course not," Dobb said. "If that's what you want, that's a given as far as I'm concerned. We never said putting her in the cemetery would be any problem, Clay. And we never said we wouldn't help you."

"We never said that," Yebbie inserted. "No. That ain't what Dobb's saying at all, Clay."

"Well, what are you saying, Dobb?"

"Hell, I'm just saying maybe we need to study all this water drilling business and tapping deep down there into our aquifer. It ain't like it's affecting only you. It's under all of us, right? We don't know what the hell it's all about, Clay. Hell, this is sudden, you know. You ain't really had time or any inclination to think it over either, Clay. We all understand that. But maybe we ought to find out if we should fight this somehow? I mean as a county. Try to stop it before it's too late?"

"Stop it?" Clay said. "You're talking like I done something wrong, Dobb. And I realize it ain't just me. But hell, my little parcel out there is just small peanuts. I got no idea what else they may be up to. Lots bigger stuff than mine probably." He paused and looked down into his cold coffee. "Anyway, big or small, mine's a done deal."

"How do you know that, Clay?" Dobb said. "How do you know it's a *done deal?* Maybe they don't have all the regulations in place or something. Maybe they just want to use your land for their first test well and then see what else they can do? Suck what's under you dry and all of us who border your place dry too and then what?

Who knows?"

"Like I said, I *don't* know." Clay sighed and shook his head and his voice became weary. "But what I do know, Dobb, is that I've already signed the contract and spent their $25,000 earnest money paying off some of Adelita's medical bills. And I owe another $150,000 to that medical center and they're coming after me." He looked at Locket and Yebbie and then back at Dobb. "Hard."

The amount seemed to shock the three men but no one said anything. "And I know they can come in there at midnight on the fifteenth with backhoes and diggers and run roughshod right over my baby daughter if I don't do it before then," Clay said and once more looked around the table at the three, all avoiding his eyes now, men he had known most of his life. "And anyway, Sera don't wanna stay out there any longer either. That's the bottom line. Don't you guys see that?" He got up to leave but stood still when Jovita came into the restaurant and moved over to the table.

"Sit down, Clay," she said. "You need to hear something."

Clay thought he had heard about enough for one day, but he sat again.

"How's she doing," Locket said. "Can I talk to her now?"

"No," Jovita said. "She hasn't broken any laws, Locket. Not any of yours, anyway. You know that. Bea's with her. She's sleeping."

"Bea stayed in there?" Clay said, remembering Bea's reluctance to have anything to do with it. He was not surprised, but he felt moved by this sudden change.

"You couldn't get Bea out of there now with a team of horses. And I wouldn't go rattling the door unless you want Bea right on your asses."

"What's up, Jovita?" Dobb said. "I need to get outta here too."

"Simple," Jovita said. She tilted her head and toyed with the knot in her red scarf. Everyone at the table knew that when Jovita Seals rearranged her scarf, nothing to follow would be simple, but she spoke calmly, with an almost matter-of-fact voice. "The bastards beat the hell out of her, took her shoes so she'd die in the desert. They left her there and took her baby with them."

"Baby?" Locket leaned forward in his chair. "You sure?"

"Keep still, Lock," Jovita said. "Yes, I'm sure."

Locket sat and waited. The others fell mute.

"You're going to need all the help you can get, Lock," Jovita said. "It's big country out there."

"I'll call the Border Patrol," he said. "This afternoon. We need to get on this."

"Just hold on," Jovita said. "As soon as they find out, they'll want to send her right back over the border."

"They might," Locket admitted. "Depends, I guess."

"Well, I don't think we can count on that *not* happening. Not with Immigration Service, not the Feds. It's usually cut and dried with them," Jovita said. "The letter of the law, you know."

"What do you have in mind, Jo," Locket said, skeptical. "I can't do something illegal."

"Is it illegal for you to see if you can find a lost child?" she said. "Even if it's not a citizen of the United States?"

"Course not," Locket said. "But you're saying *lost child.* If folks know it's an *abduction* and a *baby,* that'll mean something different."

"Right," Jovita said. "But folks don't need to know anything immediately. Don't you guys keep stuff secret for special reasons sometimes? So you won't tip some criminal off, put the baby in even more danger?"

"Sometimes," Locket confirmed. "But I can't keep this a secret for long, you understand. At the very least, I'd have to report it to the office in Presidio. I don't know what Sheriff Gil's gonna want to do."

"I understand," Jovita said. "And is there any reason someone else couldn't help you find this *lost child?*"

"Depends on what you mean by help me," Locket said. "I can always snoop around for information on the QT. We solve a lotta stuff that way."

"I mean us," Jovita said. She swept her hand toward the men. "Why couldn't we all help you? You know, ask around, snoop around like you say?"

"That might not be smart," Locket said. "Or safe. And if you mean be my posse, absolutely not. This ain't the Old West and I ain't Wyatt Earp. Neither is Sheriff Gil and he's the boss. And it's a cinch I never know where his mind might be on this kind of thing."

"What about a citizen arrest," Clay suggested, relieved that the topic had shifted now. "I mean if one of us found these bastards. Is that just a myth or what?"

"Yeah, sure," Yebbie said. "You're gonna citizen arrest some *coyote* with a hostage baby, some guy with an automatic gun who's probably involved with dope smuggling too? I gotta real big picture of that, Clay.

Hell, how do you know she ain't lying just so she won't be sent back? And if she ain't lying, how do know the kid ain't dead by now anyway?"

"She's *lactating*, you dumb shit," Jovita fired back. "That's how I know she's not lying."

"Lac . . . *what?*" Yebbie said. "What's that mean?"

"It means she's been nursing a baby," Dobb said. "Keep quiet, Yebbie."

"She said they told her they'd sell the baby on the black market," Jovita continued. "For the money she couldn't pay them. So they'd be keeping the baby alive. At least for now. But if there's a lot of media and law pressing on them . . ." Jovita looked down and lowered her voice. "Well, use your imagination."

"Geezus, I'm out of it," Dobb said and rose to go. "All this is making me dizzy. I got enough trouble just keeping a lid on my ranch and worrying about county roads." He brushed past Jovita.

"Me too," said Yebbie. "It ain't easy being a rancher in a drought, much less a county commissioner to boot."

"Dobb?" Clay stopped him. "What about the other thing?"

Dobb turned back. "I said we'd study it."

"Yebbie?" Clay said but Yebbie had also risen to go. He stood and looked Clay in the eyes this time but refused to comment about moving Serafina.

"We neither one said we *wouldn't* do it, Clay," Dobb reminded him. "Remember that."

"Well, I guess that sounds okay," Clay said. He took in a deep breath, released a long sigh. "Looks like I might not get to it soon anyway."

Jovita turned to Clay, "What other thing you talking about?"

"Moving Serafina," Clay said. "Into Solitario."

"Moving Serafina?" Jovita said.

"Yeah," Clay said. "I thought I might be able to put her in here with her mama pretty soon. But that's okay. Maybe something more important's come up," he said and he looked up at Yebbie and then Dobb. "And it ain't water." He lifted his hands to the tabletop again and studied them, made fists so the wrinkles would disappear and spoke softly to no one in the room. "I can always do it later," he muttered. "And maybe this new thing won't take too long. . . ."

Dobb studied Clay for a long while but Clay never looked up. Dobb turned to leave and Yebbie followed him.

"Dobb? Yebbie?" Locket stopped them. "Maybe you two ought not say anything about this woman and her baby, hear?" They nodded and left without words.

Clay glanced up as they exited into the lobby. He thought about Serafina and the little purple flowers and he remembered he had not placed any on her grave yesterday and had not had time to search for them today. But he thought about how he had found something else—or rather someone had found him—this young woman, Perfidia, right in Serafina's own bedroom, and he could still see the terror in her eyes as she sat there in those shadows.

"I'm in, Jo," Clay said. "Maybe it's all meant to be this way or something. What is it you want me to do?"

"I wish I knew, Clay," Jovita confessed. She looked

at Locket for guidance.

Locket shook his head. “Hey, I’m not sure either,” he said. “But whatever we do, it’s gotta be done soon.”

CHAPTER 6

Running a hotel was one thing; finding a kidnapped infant was another. After everyone left, Jovita sat in the vacant restaurant, looked out into the afternoon sunlight and tried to think of some plan. Nothing seemed possible. Even Locket himself seemed at a loss for action, unusual for him, talking around the subject as if he were still not certain anything was workable. Or legal. But one thing was certain. A young woman, beaten and bruised, lay in one of Jovita's back rooms, swearing that her infant was out there at this moment, probably in some heat-stifling place, with who knew what kind of care.

"Locket was right," Jovita mused. "We have to do something. And it needs to be soon."

She rose and went back through the lobby and tapped lightly on the first guest room where Bea was with the young woman. Bea came to the door with her finger across her lips. Jovita nodded and gestured for her to come into the hallway. She could see Perfidia stretched out across the bed, still asleep. Bea came out and closed the door.

"How is she?" Jovita said.

Bea shrugged. "She's talking in her sleep," she said. "And crying."

"Listen, we're going to find her baby," Jovita said with conviction. "And we're going to find it soon. But I need you to take care of her, Bea."

"Where?" Bea said. "She can't stay in this room."

"Will you keep her with you?"

Bea hesitated and then said, "You mean in my apartment?"

Jovita nodded.

"You're asking a lot," Bea said. "If Immigration found out . . ."

"I know," Jovita said. "But don't forget, I'm in on it too."

Bea stood rigid, said nothing.

"And Clay," Jovita went on and then, "And so's Locket."

"Locket?"

"Yes."

Bea sighed. "Well, who am I to say no then." She looked at Jovita and softened. "And I want to anyway. If you're going to do something, I want to be a part of it."

"Thanks, Bea," Jovita said. "I knew I could count on you."

"When should I move her?"

"Well, let's wait until later in the evening," Jovita said. "A couple of guests are still here but they're checking out in the morning."

Bea nodded. The restaurant always closed on Sunday evening. "I'll go back and get a bed ready for her."

"Fine."

"Can you get some clothes? She's small."

"Well, mine sure won't fit," Jovita smiled. "Maybe

I'll have to do some shopping."

"In Solitario?" Bea raised her eyebrows. "Good luck."

"I'll drive down to Presidio," Jovita said. "First thing in the morning. You go ahead, Bea. I'll sneak back in and sit with her."

Bea went off down the hallway toward her apartment, secluded at the back of the hotel behind the restaurant. Jovita watched her go.

"Well, it's not much of a plan," Jovita confessed to herself. She opened the door and went into the room and sat in a chair next to the bed, staring at the young woman. "But it's a start," she whispered and Perfidia stirred just a moment but then seemed to relax, as if she had heard and understood the determination in Jovita's voice.

Two doors down from the hotel, Locket and Clay poked fingers at Locket's map, like two generals before an invasion.

"They could have gone east, but not likely west," Locket said. "Nothing's next to your old place out that way but desert. They'd need water and somewhere to get their own asses outta the heat. And they'd need it soon."

"Yeah," Clay said. "Probably over east to Presidio. Maybe even that same night they dumped her?"

"That's what I'm thinking," Locket said. "Or maybe even farther east, on over to Redford. There's been lots of action crossing the river here where it's really shallow with a sandy bottom." He poked his finger at the map where the river widened below Santa Helena Canyon and bent, slowing down the water and depositing silt and sand.

"And Redford ain't that much farther east of Presidio anyway," Locket went on. "They'll probably try to dissolve into the Hispanic community some way, somewhere. Maybe we oughta check with the Muñoz brothers over there, Clay. Their place spreads out all over above that area. If anybody knows what's happening there, it's those two. Maybe they saw something, heard something."

"Well, I don't think they'd be connected to anybody that'd help those bastards. But like you say, they might have seen something or might be able to find out something. I could go over and see them. I ain't seen Gus much since Adelita's funeral anyway. But there's way more people and houses in Presidio, Lock," Clay observed. "A lot of abandoned houses there now with people moving out of the area. Wouldn't that make more sense? I mean, a baby'd stand out more over around Redford, you know. More places to hide in Presidio with it."

Locket agreed. "I have to go down there to the main office tomorrow morning anyway, Clay." He turned from the map and paused, looked at Clay for a long while. "You know I'll have to report this to Sheriff Gil."

"I know. . . ."

"But I'll poke around over there too, of course." Locket turned back and using his thumb as a pivot, drew a span with his hand on the map. "Presidio's about . . . twelve, thirteen miles east from your old place. And on foot with a baby? That's a helluva hike, Clay. You think they got into some vehicle?"

"She said two of them led them across the river. Said there were some others in her group and that they were all afoot."

"Yeah. Well, the *coyotes* are used to hiking across this stuff," Locket sighed. "Scum like that ain't hardly human, more like animals. But the others aren't. Anybody they brought across that couldn't make it on foot after that, they'd just leave out there too because they got their money anyway. Surprises me a little bit that they didn't have all of this woman's money up front." Locket turned and looked at Clay.

"Yeah, I don't know how it works, Locket. Maybe she knew one of them or something," Clay said and shrugged. "She didn't say."

"Well anyway, they could have made it across here to Presidio in one night." Locket turned back and traced the distance again with his finger on the map. "One long night. A baby'd slow them down some though."

"They probably zigzagged to confuse their trail, then swung up and filled their own guts with water when they seen my windmill," Clay said. "Maybe even carried some in something. But what about the baby?" They looked at each other but neither said anything. Clay finally spoke. "Maybe she had time to feed it before they beat her up and dumped her."

"Maybe," Locket said but he turned away. He moved from the map and sat at his desk. "Did she say anything about the baby being able to take a bottle? I know she was nursing it, but . . ."

"Dunno," Clay said. "I could find that out too, I guess."

"Well, it don't really matter." He stood again and

moved back to the map, crossed his arms and studied it. "It's crazy. But I never am able to figure out what they're thinking anyway. What I'm thinking is that we're gonna find that little baby daughter and we're gonna find her soon."

"Yeah, soon," Clay said. He stood silent behind Locket as both focused on the map again for a long while, as if the concentration might reveal some veiled secret, and finally he said, "Lock?"

"Yeah?"

"Maybe *soon* don't mean tomorrow. Maybe it means right now," Clay said. "This afternoon . . . tonight . . ." He remembered just a few hours ago in the restaurant once more promising Serafina that he would move her . . . *soon.* And he remembered saying that same word as he promised to return all those years past when he saw Serafina alive for the last time.

Locket turned back to him and nodded, but he said nothing. Clay moved to the door and opened it to go.

"Clay?"

"Yeah."

"If you're still carrying that old pistol under your seat, I don't even want to know about it. Hell, you never could hit a damned thing with that rusty hogleg anyway," Locket said and he paused. "You be careful over there at Redford, hear?"

Clay looked back at Locket who had returned to his desk, propped his feet up and stared again at his map, shaking his head. Clay moved out the door and onto the sidewalk toward his pickup.

Back in the hotel room, Perfidia stirred again and

opened her eyes, alert now, as if she had been right there in the office, listening to Clay and Locket. She sat up in the bed and looked around the room, frantic. *"Where is she? My baby?"* She blinked and then realized where she was.

Jovita stood from her chair and sat down beside Perfidia on the bed. "It's okay," she cooed. "She's alright. We're going to find your baby. I promise."

"Who is?" Perfidia said. "How?"

"All of us. Clay and Locket and Bea and . . . lots of people," Jovita said. "But you have to move out of here."

"Why?"

"With Bea. Into her apartment. It's just down the hall, Perfidia. You'll be fine. But you can't come out, not for a while."

"Why?" she repeated.

"I think you know why," Jovita said. "If Immigration finds you here, they might send you back."

"Without my baby?" Perfidia whispered and Jovita saw she was completely disoriented.

"I said they *might.*"

Perfidia began to weep again.

"Listen, you'll be fine. Bea is a kind woman and she'll take very good care of you," Jovita said. "So will I. Tomorrow we'll get Doc Maddox over to look at your feet and see if you're okay."

Perfidia nodded but she continued to whimper. Jovita stood and went to the door. "You wait here. I'm going to get some antiseptic and some socks for your feet and check on Bea. We'll move you in with Bea. You go ahead and rest." She flicked off the light and opened the door to leave and then looked back. "I promise."

After Jovita left, Perfidia lay back onto the bed. In the fading light from the window she closed her eyes and thought about her baby.

Behind her eyes Perfidia sees herself clinging to her daughter as she wades into the water and there are voices all around her, some frail and frightened and some harsh and angry and cruel and she tries to move as rapidly as she can in the darkness but it is not fast enough. The others outpace her but she struggles out on the opposite side, exhausted, and then the cruel voices become angrier and even more abusive and they grab her and twist her and pull until she collapses onto the rocks atop the embankment but she realizes now her baby is gone and she feels the warm blood on her face and she struggles again to rise but she has no strength. And then all is blackness and silence except for the movement of the water below the embankment and the fading scurry of footsteps running into the darkness of the desert.

Perfidia jerked awake and sat upright and searched the dark room but there was no one there. Then she felt the warmth of the socks on her feet and so she moved her legs over the edge of the bed and stood on her still useless feet. Even though the pain was piercing, she slowly worked her way to the door from under which a thin sliver of light invaded the blackness of the room. She hesitated with her hand on the doorknob, then went back across the room to the window but she knew it was two floors up and there would be no escape this way.

She returned and sat on the edge of the bed and stared at her silhouette outlined in Jovita's beveled dressing mirror across the room. Her face lay dark and empty in the shadows and she could feel the tears on her face but she could not see them in the mirror. She wondered if they were truly there. ❧

CHAPTER 7

Augústin "Gus" Muñoz tugged the last bale of hay from the back of his pickup and tossed it onto the ground. Immediately, the *corriente* steers began to bully him aside for the hay. He raised his arms and shouted and they moved back a little.

"At least wait till I've cut the wire, dammit." He bent with the cutters and snipped the baling wire and kicked the bale open. Then he moved back and leaned against the bed of his truck, watching the range-wild *corrientes* go at the hay.

Though he cursed them and wondered why on earth he tolerated such crazy cattle, Gus did admire their single-minded instinct to rush at whatever they sought without flinching. Like the open gate at the far end of a rodeo roping arena. But in this case, it was the hay they went for. He had scattered it across the hardpan that these Muñoz Brothers steers had stripped of every blade of grass, without conscience. When it came to this grassland that was his heritage, Gus hoped he had maintained conscience enough for all of them, including his younger brother Alvaro. The drought would not last forever, and some little rains would bring the grass back to life. Gus knew this, though a West Texas sun devoid of any conscience at all had parched one year into another and now, had tempered even his faith with it.

"Well, that's why they like you in the roping arena," Gus sighed, changing the subject in his head back from the heat to the steers. He smiled. "They wouldn't pay me what they do if you just stood there and waited for somebody to put a rope around your horns."

Gus tossed the strand of wire on top of the others bunched in the bed of his pickup, a tally of how severe this spring had already been here north of Redford. But it was the same all the way up to the Pecos River and Fort Stockton and back west to El Paso, this entire section of Texas where he and Alvaro supplied these steers to the rodeos for the bulldog and team roping events.

Muñoz Brothers Rodeo Stock. Gus thought about the business. It had always sounded too formal for him, but he went along with his younger brother about the name. After they had built the herd of *corrientes* to over three hundred and now owned three cattle trucks moving back and forth to events all across West Texas, Alvaro insisted they needed to put their names on the doors of the eighteen wheelers. And get business cards printed.

"Esta bien," Gus had said. "That's fine. But I'm not carrying any of your damned fancy business cards. You'll have to spread them around yourself, *Alvarito."*

Gus preferred this end of the business anyway, this isolation under a quiet sky, even if the sun had hardened the land even more each year. He hated being cooped up inside the cab of one of their trucks, schmoozing rodeo promoters. But Alvaro considered thundering down the interstate inside one of their newly branded eighteen wheelers more a vacation than a vocation. Gus wondered how his younger brother did it, how he could drive days at a time without rest. He was concerned that Alvaro might be pushing the limit of legal drive time for truckers. But Gus was more concerned about Alvaro pushing himself beyond the limit of his own safety. And the safety of others.

"I stop and fuel up a lot," Alvaro explained once from inside an idling truck, loaded with *corrientes* and parked in front of their huge barn at Los Arbolitos. "And sometimes I even put something into the fuel tank of the truck too." He smiled and roared out of their ranch compound, working through the gears of the eighteen wheeler far more aggressively than Gus thought necessary.

Gus had never pushed that issue further. Perhaps his devotion to his younger brother carried with it a dangerous shade of denial for Gus, who had raised Alvaro from a child after their mother died and then their father only two years later. If Alvaro was not perfect, Gus felt it sprung more from a lack of their parents than anything Gus had done . . . or not done. Gus never found time for marriage himself, though Alvaro had now been through two wives.

"I guess you'll have to carry on the name, little brother," Gus teased Alvaro at his first wedding reception. "Get busy."

But when that relationship soured and failed and Alvaro went into—and shortly out of—his second marriage, Gus wondered if the Muñoz name might just die. He had not mentioned it to Alvaro since, and his brother did not seem to have much concern for anything beyond right here, right now.

Well, maybe he'll meet some nice woman over in Fort Stockton today, Gus mused and got into his truck. He tapped the horn several times but the steers did not move until his grill guard nudged one on the rear and they made a little room for him. In the quickening dusk, he pulled on his headlights and swung his pickup back along the ridge and dropped down into a dry wash and then over the next rise above Los Arbolitos (The Little Trees,) the Spanish name his great grandfather had given to the compound he had built here by Arbolito Creek in 1800s on the Texas side of the river.

When he drove into the yard, his headlights swept Clay's pickup, parked in front of the ancient adobe hacienda. In his lights, he saw Clay sitting with his head cocked back against the seat, his straw hat over his face. Gus killed his lights and his engine and got out and walked toward Clay's truck. He slapped the hood with his bunched gloves as he walked by.

"This damn thing still run?" He put one boot onto the running board and bent forward and with his gloves slapped the dust from this boot and then did the same with the other. "Whoever you are, you're trespassing," he said to the dark ground and then he straightened and leaned inside the open window.

Clay did not answer except for "Hmmm . . ." But then he sucked in a deep breath of the cooling evening. "Arrest me," he said from under his hat.

"No," Gus said. "We don't do that here. We shoot gringos first, especially old wore out gringos, ask questions later."

Clay sat up, adjusted his hat onto his head. "Do I get any last words?"

"Few," Gus said. "Damned few."

"How about *you got anything to eat?*"

"Beans," Gus said. "Tortillas. And more beans. With jalapeños, though. You know how we meskins are."

"Yeah, I know," Clay said and he thought about Bea's fine pecan pie. As good as it was, it remained the only thing he had eaten today while he watched Locket scarf up her fine platter of *carne adovada.* With beans.

"Come on in," Gus said and turned toward the house. "We got real lights inside now," he teased. "Electric. And a real refrigerator and propane hooked up to the old wood cookstove. Hell, they even let us buy cold beer over in Presidio now. With an ID, of course."

"Works for me," Clay said. "Looks like you guys are moving right up the social ladder."

"Sí," Gus mocked. He opened the door and snapped on the front patio lights. "It only took a hundred years or so. Watch out for the cactus, gringo."

Clay moved across the yard and onto the covered flagstone patio with its huge wooden *vigas* overhead. He turned to look along the front side of the massive adobe house then back toward the other end, the patio lined with latticed leather chairs and a variety of cacti inside giant pottery vessels, their outside glazes glowing under the soft light with the patina of age. "Nice place," he said, as if he were seeing it for the first time. "How long you say your people have been here?"

"All my life," Gus said and held the door open. "So far anyway. That'd be fifty-three years, all hard."

Clay moved into the tiled entry and on back through the familiar hallway and entered the high ceilinged great room, the unplanned décor of which would turn some southwest interior designer green. "If you're looking for pity, forget it," Clay said, admiring the room as he always did. "And I seen your pickup too. You didn't buy that with food stamps."

"So you're selling something door-to-door, Mister Gringo?" Gus quizzed. "Come on back." He went through the great room and into the kitchen, equally impressive with its huge old cast iron cookstove and ancient copper utensils hanging above the ceramic tiled work counter. "Beer?"

"Naw, I ain't selling beer," Clay shot back. "But if you got it, I'd have one. If it's cold and if it's free."

Gus smiled. He moved to the refrigerator and rattled two longnecks onto the counter, twisted the lids off and put one in front of Clay. They tapped the bottoms together and leaned back and swallowed deep. "Sit down," Gus said. "I'll heat something up."

Clay groaned as he sat at the little round kitchen table, feeling the long day in every bone. "Got any aspirin," he said and sipped his beer.

"That's extra, old man," Gus said. He swung open a cabinet door, retrieved a bottle of aspirin and brought it over to Clay. "Fifty bucks each."

"Where's Alvaro?" Clay said. He opened the bottle, spilled out three tablets, tossed them down with a long draft of beer.

"On the road," Gus said. "As always." He moved back to the refrigerator and brought out a large bowl and some tortillas wrapped in plastic. "Over toward Fort Stockton."

"I thought they only roped goats down there?"

"They do that too," Gus said and grinned back at Clay. "But when they want a real challenge, they call Muñoz Brothers."

"You're proud of that, ain't you, Gus? You gotta right to be. How many head of *corrientes* you guys got now anyway?"

It would have been a question on the edge of propriety between any other two ranchers. Gus just shrugged. He dumped the beans into a sauce pan and put it onto the stove. Then he struck a match and cranked open the propane burner under the pan. The gas popped and then whispered into blue flames when he touched it with the match.

"This won't take long," he said. He whipped the match flame dead.

Clay sipped the beer. "You in the market for any more?"

"Depends," Gus said. He turned around to see if Clay was joking. "Why?"

"I still got those twenty-five head of *corrientes* I need to get rid of," Clay said. "Everything else is sold."

"Sold?" Gus said and frowned.

"I guess I ain't had a chance to tell you either," Clay confessed. He sucked in a long breath, exhaled. "It's been a while since we talked. I'm getting out of it, Gus."

"Cattle?"

"Everything," Clay said and then, "Deal ain't complete yet but it's moving along okay, far as I know. I got some earnest money anyway but that's already gone."

"You're selling it all?"

"Yeah," Clay said. "I really didn't have no selection the way Adelita went and . . . well, you know all that part. Expensive, but I'd never done it any other way. I just wish . . ."

"Right," Gus said and lowered his eyes.

"Except Palo, of course. And they don't want those steers. They don't even make good hamburger. And to tell the truth, Gus, there's not much else left out there of any value anyway." Clay thought about the old wagon and how he would simply burn it now, his last act of retribution before he left the place for the final time, after he moved Serafina.

"We'll take them, Clay," Gus said. "You know that. What's your timeline on it?"

"Well, anytime on the steers, but . . ." Clay began. "The rest of what's happening right now is a longer story. It's got a little complicated, Gus. You sure you wanna hear all of it?"

Gus came over and sat across from him. "Sure," he said. "I didn't figure you'd come all the way over here on a Sunday night just for beans and free beer. What's up?" He looked into the worried face of his old friend. "I got all night and it ain't like there's a houseful of people here. Just you and me and all the ghosts of a fading family. Lots of empty beds. You can take your pick," Gus said and Clay heard the remorse in his voice. "And don't forget, there's a case of longnecks." He pointed the mouth of his bottle toward the refrigerator and then tipped it up, swallowed deeply. "Cold. And it's all free tonight." ❧

CHAPTER 8

The next morning, Clay awoke and came out of the back bedroom and down the long hallway and into the kitchen where Gus already sat with a mug of coffee. Gus rose and went to the old camp style coffeepot on the stove, poured a mug for Clay. "Sit down," he said. "How's your head?"

"It's been better," Clay groaned. He moved his palms across his forehead and over the top of his hair and then rubbed his eyes with the tips of his fingers. "What time'd we quit?" He reached for the bottle of aspirin, still on the table.

"Oh, maybe five longnecks after midnight," Gus said. "Want another?"

Clay snorted into the hot mug, shook his head. *"No gracias."* He opened the aspirin and this time spilled four out onto the table.

"Hungry?"

"Not that either." Clay blew across the lip of the mug, sipped, set it down. Then with the edge of his hand, he scraped the aspirin across the tabletop into his other palm and tossed them into his mouth.

"How is it?"

"You'd make somebody a great wife," Clay said around the tablets in his mouth. He sipped again, swallowed the whole mixture, washed it all down with more coffee. "You ever think about that, Gus?"

"No woman would put up with me," Gus said. "Anyway, I'm too damned old."

"Hell, you ain't either. Seriously."

"No woman could make *huevos rancheros* like I do," Gus said. "You oughta try them."

"I have," Clay said. "But I gotta pass this morning. I need to get back on the road."

"You come through Presidio?"

"No. Over the back road. Rocky and rutted more than ever. Like maybe somebody's been driving eighteen wheelers over it," Clay said. "Hard. Loaded with cattle, maybe."

Gus smiled. "That ain't illegal, you know. And it's a helluva lot shorter across there if you're coming down Highway 67 to here."

"Yeah."

"Maybe you'll bump into Alvaro out there."

"Hope not. For your sake. My old truck's not insured but I know all yours are." Clay grinned. "I'd get rich."

Both worked on the coffee but neither said anything for a long while. Finally Clay glanced up at the antique shelf clock and said, "Okay, how much of all that other shit did I tell you last night?"

"I was hoping to hell there wasn't more." Gus sighed.

"Yeah."

"It's a helluva story, Clay," Gus said. More silence and then, "So you've sold out and you're moving Serafina into Solitario?"

"Yes. There with her mama, you know."

Gus nodded. "And you got a little time to finish all that up?"

"Yeah. May fifteenth, midnight . . ."

"That ain't much time," Gus said. "We could move her tomorrow if you want to, Clay. When I come over for your steers. Won't take long to gather up and load them *corrientes.* Just say the word if you want to do that too. You know I'm there, even if those others are dragging their feet like you said." Gus ran a finger around the top of his mug. "Shit, we could do it *today,* Clay."

"I told you them reasons I can't move Sera right now, Gus," he said but he was uncertain if he had told him everything last night through all the beer. "And I told you the *main* reason I'm holding off right now, didn't I?"

Gus looked at him for a long while and then said, "Yeah, you told me, Clay."

"Well?"

"Well, what?" Gus said.

"Well, can you help us with that *other* thing? Maybe it shouldn't be, but I guess that's been bumped up to my first priority right now, Gus. Don't matter whatever else might be involved, this is one thing that's got inside my gut now and I ain't the only one."

"I slept on that one," Gus confessed. Clay waited. "And I understand what you're saying. But I just don't know how I can help on that kind of thing, Clay. Honest to God, as sad as it all sounds, I just don't know what I can do about it."

"Gus, there's a baby girl out there somewhere." Clay leaned across the little table. "And her mama's laying up in Jo's hotel, crying her eyes out. She's hurtin,' Gus. And I got a pretty damn good sense what that feels like. . . ."

"I understand. . . . I told you that last night."

"And there's a damned good chance Immigration might just send her right back across the border *without* her baby if . . ."

"You said all this last night, Clay." Gus rose and went to the stove, brought the coffeepot over and refilled the mugs. He sat down and studied the dark liquid inside his mug again. "You also said Locket's on it."

"Well he is. . . ." Clay said. "But then he ain't. Not the way I'm talking about. I mean, he's gonna have to tell Sheriff Gil about it at the very least and that's gonna tie his hands some probably, but he says the rest of us might have some slack time till all hell breaks loose, I mean, Border Patrol looking for sure, maybe FBI and, well, if the rest of us could just find out something before all that—" Clay sat back in his chair. He looked at his friend for a long while.

"The *rest* of us?" Gus finally said. "Why me? Hell, why *you?*"

"I dunno, Gus," Clay confessed. "I ain't had time to study it. I guess it just seems right. I mean she just sorta shows up out there outta nowhere, right there in Sera's old bedroom and it was all kinda creepy, Gus. That's all. And you know how it can be with this kind of scum that brought her over. If they get under a lot of pressure, you know what they're likely to do. You read the papers."

Gus sipped, looked up at him and sighed. "Alright. Alvaro's due back sometime today."

"Alvaro?"

"Yeah," Gus said but he avoided Clay's eyes again. "You know, he's in the bars around here sometimes and, well, could be he'd know *somebody* who might know *somebody* who . . ." Gus cleared his throat. " . . . knows something about all this."

Clay nodded but he kept quiet.

Gus went on, "I'll see what we can come up with. But I make no promises, *comprende?*"

"I understand," Clay said. "Thanks, Gus. Like I said, I feel like it's just something I need to do. You understand? I owe you big time."

"You owe me nothing," Gus said and smiled. "Except maybe a case of longnecks."

"Yeah, I owe you lots of painkiller," Clay said and he replaced its top and dropped the bottle of aspirin into his shirt pocket. He drained his mug and got up and went into the front hallway and retrieved his hat and set it on his head, just right. He went back and took his friend's hand and then turned to go.

"Clay?" Gus said.

Clay looked back over his shoulder.

"Good seeing you," Gus said. "Let's get an early start in the morning on them steers, okay?"

"I'll just meet you out there at the old place if that'll work?"

"That'll work," Gus said. "I'll bring a horse and one of our rigs to haul them in." ❧

CHAPTER 9

Earlier that same Monday, Jovita walked out of her apartment in the hotel and as before, paused at Clay's door across the hall but this time she did not knock. Late on Sunday evening, she had gently slipped the socks on Perfidia's feet while she slept in the guest room and then helped settle her in with Bea. Afterward, Jovita waited in her apartment, listening for Clay to come in across the hall but finally gave up and went to bed.

This morning, Jovita moved straight to the staircase and went down into the lobby and back into the kitchen. Bea busied herself at the stove, but Jovita could see she was nervous.

"Buenos dias," Jovita said and then her usual, "How's it going?"

And as usual, Bea said nothing until Jovita had a mouthful of the peppered bacon. "Not so well," Bea said. Jovita knew she was not talking about the old stove this morning.

"Porque?" Jovita said, chewing. "What happened?"

"She sat up most of the night," Bea explained. "Crying and crying."

"Oh . . ."

"She finally slept, about four."

"You?"

"I'm okay," Bea said. "I just don't know how long she'll make it this way."

"I'm going right over to see Doc Maddox," Jovita said. "Maybe he can give her something."

"Yes," Bea said, she cracked eggs onto the grill. "But I don't know about her—"

"Her feet?" Jovita said. "Yes, I'll ask him for something to put on those too. She may need some antibiotic."

"Her breasts," Bea whispered. "I know they're bothering her and maybe some of it's just in her head but still . . ."

"I'll ask Boone about that too," Jovita said. "Or he can talk to her if she'll do it."

"Maybe I should be in there too," Bea said. "In case she'd rather talk to him through me."

"Sounds to me like her English is pretty good," Jovita reminded her.

"Yes," Bea said. "When she wants it to be."

"I see," Jovita said. "That's fine. Thanks, Bea. I think that's a good idea. I'll try to explain all this and get Boone to come over here. We can trust him. But I'll drive on down to Presidio and get some clothes and things for her. Maybe I'll ask around the stores there too. Won't hurt."

Bea nodded. "Sit down out there. I'll bring your breakfast before I feed those two guests."

"No time for that today, Bea. Just get those two fed so they can check out and then close down in here. You need to be ready when Boone comes over, okay?"

"Well, at least have one more piece of bacon." Bea reached to the back of the grill and placed two more pieces onto a paper napkin and gave them to Jovita.

Jovita smiled. "I thought you said *one* more?" Bea turned back to the eggs. Jovita folded the bacon strips into the napkin and walked out into the lobby and through the front doors.

Outside, she looked up the main street of Solitario and then down the other way. No one stirred this early, even on a Monday morning, but she did expect to see Locket's patrol car in front of his office. It was not there. Doctor Boone Maddox always parked his car out of sight behind his clinic across the street, and she wondered if he would be there today either. He was.

"You sick, Jo?" he said when he unlocked the door and opened it for her.

"Some of us work for a living," she said. "We get up, we get going early. Especially on Monday. Bacon?" She held out the napkin with one piece still on it.

"That stuff'll kill you," he said and then, "This isn't your workplace over here, you know. Unless I lost my lease or something." He picked up the last piece of Bea's bacon and stuffed it into his mouth and wiped his hand on his shirtsleeve.

"I need your help, Boone," she said. "And I'll just cut to the chase."

"So how's that any different?" he said through the mouthful and gestured at a chair in the small waiting area. "Sit down, Jo. What's up?"

"I don't have time to sit," she said. "Can you go over to the hotel?"

"Somebody sick over there?"

"Well, maybe not sick, but she needs your help. She can't walk far."

"Sure," he said. "But maybe you could give me just a wee bit more info so's I know what the hell to take over there?"

"Her feet are cut pretty bad," Jovita began. "And she's been dehydrated and . . . well . . . she's lactating and I know that's been painful for her too and—"

"Hold it, hold it," Boone said. He held up a palm and then ran it over his bald head. "Let's back this wagon up. Who's this *she?* And you mean her baby won't nurse or what?"

"Not exactly."

"Alright, Jo," he scolded. "You said you'd cut to the chase but this is ridiculous."

"Okay, it's like this, Boone," Jovita said, slower this time. She leaned forward. "But you can't say a word to anyone, okay?"

"Call it patient-doctor confidentiality if you want to, Jo. And I know you wouldn't put me in some awkward legal position now, would you, Jo?" Boone looked into Jovita's fixed eyes for a long moment and then said, "Course you would. . . ."

"Now don't freak out, Boone. It's not all that bad," Jovita said. "She's from across the river, okay. But she was left out there in the desert without her shoes. Left to die. Clay found her hiding out there at his old place yesterday morning and brought her in."

"I see . . ." Boone said, waiting for the remainder of the story.

"Well, I guess she couldn't pay the extra money that the *coyotes* demanded after they got her over here . . ." Jovita stopped, not for dramatic effect but because her voice had left her.

"Okay. . . . Go on."

"They took her baby, Boone," Jovita whispered.

Boone's mouth parted a little, his cool medical composure shaken. "Took her baby?"

"Yes," Jovita said. "She says they intend to sell it on the black market since she couldn't pay enough."

"*Sell* it?" Boone shook his head in disbelief. He sighed and turned away from the eye lock Jovita held on him. "I see," he repeated but any cold professionalism had disappeared from his voice. "And she was nursing her baby."

"Right," Jovita said. "She's staying back there with Bea. She didn't sleep much last night Bea said."

"Course she didn't. I wouldn't have either," Boone said. "Damn. Sure, I'll come over, Jo. I'm not busy till this afternoon anyway. Just let me tape a note up on the door."

"Thanks, Boone," Jovita said. "I'm going down to Presidio and get some other things for her. Her clothes are all torn and she's got no shoes. She can't use them now but she'll need them sooner or later. Her feet look pretty bad to me."

"You know cut feet won't be the big problem, Jo," Boone said. He went to the locked wall cabinet and retrieved some items, put them in a small valise. "I can give her some antibiotics for her feet and something to help her sleep." He walked back over to Jovita and stood looking again at her. "But she'll need to stop taking the sleep medication if . . ." Boone paused and corrected himself. "I mean, *when* she starts nursing again. But she's gonna have a bigger decision to make right now than taking these meds."

"I know," Jovita said. "And if it's what I think it is, I don't envy you telling her that."

"Well, I'll take over a manual breast pump for her to use. That'll keep the milk flowing," he said.

"How long?" Jovita said and then embarrassed, "I'm not exactly up on all this Boone. Never needed to know . . ."

"As long as she wants to keep doing it," he said. "But her baby might not want to take her again right away if it's not nursed her for a while. Depends on what's happening to it right now." Boone scratched some words on a notepad and attached a piece of white adhesive tape to it. He went to the door and stuck the sign on the inside of the windowpane and then held the door open for Jovita. "I mean, if whoever's got it is giving it a bottle and it gets used to that . . . and let's hope to hell they are. Of course if it looks like it might take a while to find her baby, or if, God forbid, they decide they might *not* give it back at all . . ." Boone stopped abruptly and looked down and then cleared his throat. "Well, what I mean is, she might just decide to let herself dry up. . . ."

Jovita moved toward the open door but then stopped and stared at Boone again but he did not look up this time. "You gonna say *that* to her, Boone?"

"No way in hell I'd say that to her, Jo," Boone said. They went out the door and Boone locked it behind him. They stood on the sidewalk. "That's not an option I'll even mention. I don't care who she is or where she's from."

"Thanks, Boone," Jovita said. She moved across the street toward her car parked in front the hotel. "Talk with you when I get back." ❧

CHAPTER 10

Locket walked through the outer office at the sheriff's office in Presidio and straight through the rear hallway where he tapped on the frosted door pane marked Sheriff Gilberto Romero.

"It ain't locked unless it's Locket," growled a voice from inside.

It was the same rhetorical response to anyone knocking on the sheriff's door, especially on a Monday morning, and Locket had heard it often. Locket knew it was more bark than bite. He walked on in and closed the door. Sheriff Gil did not look up from the stack of paperwork strewn across his desk. "Sit down, Locket," he said and then, "What's up?"

"Not much, just thought I'd stop by."

"Yeah right," Sheriff Gil said. "Then why'd you shut the door?" He looked up at Locket, pencil poised as if to take down his deputy's name.

"Well, I was just wondering what the outcome was, with those seven in the boxcar."

"The boxcar seven?" Sheriff Gil said. "That's what we've been calling that situation."

"I see," Locket said. He noted the casual title the sheriff had given the grim case. Locket also knew it was not black humor, not from his boss. "It does help sometimes to get distance from situations like that."

Sheriff Gil nodded. "Immigration finally got around to delivering the bodies back across inside that reefer truck we had to store them in. I don't know what's happened since then."

Locket sat silent.

"So what else you got?" Sheriff Gil said. He tilted his head. "Coffee's out front, Lock. If you can stand it. Don't let the doorknob hit you in the ass on your way out." He returned to the paperwork on his desk.

Locket leaned forward as if to go, but then he sat back, rubbed his unshaven chin. Sheriff Gil looked up again, sighed and then rose from his chair and came in front of his desk. He crossed his arms and stood with his butt resting against the desktop but said nothing. He studied his boots. The air conditioner filled the silence with a sudden humming rattle, cycling in response to the rising heat outside. Finally he said, "You know I been at this almost thirty years, don't you, Lock?"

Locket nodded.

"Some day you'll be sitting in this hot seat. If you keep your nose clean and tip your hat to the right voters."

"Yeah, maybe," Locket said but he did not look up at his boss.

"And I guess I'd have to say I know you pretty damned well," Sheriff Gil said. "Most of your life. Almost like the son we never had."

"Don't get mushy on me, Gil," Locket said. "How is the family anyway?"

"Everybody's fine. But that ain't what you drove down here to check on. You needing a hot meal or what?"

"You know I'd jump at the chance to sit at your wife's table anytime, Gil, but . . ."

"Okay then, why the hell'd you drive down here so early on a Monday morning? Phones out? Ain't you got nothing to do up there?"

Locket snorted, "Yeah right. Nothing."

"Then like I said before, what's up?"

Locket had expected this. And he wanted it to be in the open, get Sheriff Gil involved, someone he could trust with good advice. But actually telling the sheriff face-to-face was different. "Well, it's a . . . situation."

Sheriff Gil looked at him and sighed again, "What isn't?"

"This one's way different, Gil," Locket shifted in the uncomfortable chair.

"Figgered that," Sheriff Gil said. "Right after you come in and then shut my door behind you. And I seen you ain't shaved yet and look like you're hungover to boot."

"I need a shave, yes. Hungover? Nope," Locket said. "Just tired. What we may have is a kidnapping, Gil. I'm pretty sure anyway."

"Oh yeah?" Sheriff Gill's expression did not break its professional deadpan.

"Yeah. It's a long story but Clayton Elliott over at Solitario brought in a young woman he found out there at his old place yesterday. No shoes, feet cut, dehydrated. Jovita and Bea Hernandez are taking care of her over there in the hotel."

"Illegal?"

"You got it. And battered pretty bad too."

"Go on."

"Well, cut feet ain't exactly against any law that I'm supposed to enforce, so I just let it slide for a few hours getting her taken care of. I found out later in the afternoon some of the details. I guess she couldn't pay her *coyotes* enough so they took her baby as payment. Said they'd sell it for the money she owed them."

"Shit," Sheriff Gil said and now his stone face contorted. He shook his head as he moved back behind his desk and sat. "I thought I'd seen the worst of these things. Seven bodies in a boxcar is bad enough, but still . . ." he said and then, *"Sell* it? That's a new one."

"Anyway, Jovita and Clay and some of them over there say they want to, well, help her out a little more than just fix up her feet and feed her."

"Help her out?"

"Well, you know how it is sometimes, Gil, folks get all worked up, especially if there's a baby involved. They thought maybe they could just find the baby before we got all fired up. They knew if we got involved, then the Border Patrol would get involved and maybe wouldn't believe the woman about having a baby at all and they'd just send her right back over without it and—"

"Hold it, hold it," Sheriff Gil interrupted. "Whatta you mean, *if* we get involved? Sounds to me like somebody's been watching too damn much TV."

"Maybe. Anyway, they thought those scumbags might panic and kill the baby or something bad like that if they knew all this law enforcement was involved and closing in on them and so—"

"And so you just let it slide overnight, right?" Sheriff Gil interrupted again.

"Well, sorta . . ." Locket looked up at his boss again.

Sheriff Gil stood and turned toward the window. He punched the air conditioner on high fan, but it did little good. "Damn thing's wore out," he said. "Looks like they could break loose a few bucks for a new air conditioner for the sheriff of the hottest seat in the hottest county in the nation. Maybe not for my deputy's office, but at least for mine." He slapped the top with the heel of his palm. "Maybe they figger this sheriff's wore out too, just like this goddamn thing."

"I just thought since it was an immigration thing too and we had no real jurisdiction that maybe . . . ," Locket went on. He stopped and looked at his boss but Sheriff Gil stood with his back to him. Locket saw no reaction so he fell silent, waited.

"You know that's horseshit, Lock. Sure, they might have to send the woman back over. They might not have any choice. But in this country, a kidnapping's a kidnapping," he said and sat back down behind his desk. Locket saw his face now, frozen with the familiar determination he had often seen. "Don't matter where you're from. And just helping an illegal immigrant with cut feet is one thing, but *transporting* one *away* from the border looks a helluva lot different to most any lawman because there's a law against that. And you're saying Clayton Elliott did exactly that? That's a federal offense. You know that, Locket."

Locket knew. "Well hell, what was Clay supposed to do, Gil?" he said. "Let her die out there in that heat?" Sheriff Gil said nothing. Locket went on, "That kind of law makes no sense to me, but okay, it was a bad call on Clay's part and mine too. So now what do we do? You gonna put both of us back there in the same cell?"

"Simple. We find that baby," Sheriff Gil said. "But that's *our* job, Locket. Not a citizen's job. And we'll get all the help we need. Legal, professional, whatever."

"You mean—"

"I mean get some people out there on the exit highways and I mean pretty damn quick," Sheriff Gil said. "Hell, you know the statistics on a kidnapping, Lock. These guys play for keeps, you know that."

Locket knew.

"Chances of finding the victim alive start to drop off real quick even after a few hours," Sheriff Gil said. "And that's based on *adult* victim stats, not on a hungry screaming baby with dirty diapers."

"Yeah," Locket said. "Hey, I'm sorry."

"Well, it'll take me a while to get this cranked up," Sheriff Gil said. "You get on out there and see what you can find out. Ask around here before you go back over to Solitario."

"Okay."

"And get one of them electric razors out front from the secretary and shave first, hear? At least be presentable in public."

"You got it, sheriff."

"But just you remember, this ain't like television, Locket. You know, the program where the chief gives the renegade deputy and his beautiful blond girlfriend just forty-eight hours to find the killer and blah, blah, blah. . . ."

"I know." Locket squirmed in the chair but tried for some levity. "But I ain't got a girlfriend, sheriff."

"Well, what you got is some time," Sheriff Gil said, not amused. "But it ain't gonna be forty-eight hours with nothing else going on, I guarantee you. You say the mother's over there in the hotel?"

"That's where she was last night anyway," Locket said.

"They'll want to talk to her sooner or later," Sheriff Gil said. "Probably sooner. The Border Patrol."

Locket nodded. "And they'll want to send her back over, right?"

"Hellfire, Lock, how do I know what they'll do?" Sheriff Gil said. "I'm just gonna do my job. I can't do theirs, but I gotta tell them about her." He picked up the phone and punched in some numbers. "Maybe they'll cut her some slack. Now go." ❧

CHAPTER 11

After Clay left Gus, he drove onto the same dirt back road he had used coming over to Los Arbolitos. It was a shorter route than the blacktop that looped the long way south and then west, around through Redford and Presidio and then north back into Solitario. Even though the dirt road was much rougher, Clay preferred the isolation because he could think better. The road ran through the ghost town of Casa Piedra but then due west toward Solitario. At Casa Piedra, he stopped and got out of his pickup and urinated in the road, the moisture immediately soaking into the dust.

For a moment, Clay felt as if he might throw up, but he had eaten nothing Gus offered so there was nothing to come up. He gagged a little and then went back to the truck and poked around under the seat for something to drink, anything liquid to help with the nausea and the headache that had come on like a hammer in the mid-morning heat. A lone can of beer rolled out and fell onto the hardpan. He looked down at it, hesitated.

"Well, it's something wet anyway," he said and then, "And it won't get any cooler laying there. Damn you Gus."

He reached down and retrieved the can and pulled

the tab. Foam erupted from the lid and ran over the edge of the can. Clay lipped it quickly and then tipped his head back and sucked in half the tepid liquid, glancing over the top of the can to the north where the massive domelike structure of once molten rock called The Solitario marred an otherwise uninterrupted horizon. He lowered the can and walked over and sat in the shade of a wall, the only remnant of a rock house once standing among half a dozen others in Casa Piedra.

"You two are just alike, ain't you?" he mused, squinting at The Solitario and then down at the can of beer in his hand. "One lonesome spewed-out beer, one lone spewed-out blister of rock. Except that one's famous," he said and held up the warm beer. "You ain't."

He drank again and thought about the geologist from the college over in Alpine talking about it once at a community meeting in Solitario, explaining how the town's name had come from this million-year-old landmark of rock. He had emphasized that the formation was not an extinct volcano but simply a rare bubble of lava, long since collapsed into itself and back into the void of the earth from which it had flowed, leaving only the huge circular rim of cooled rock. The man explained that the word in Spanish meant hermit or that which stands alone.

"Fits pretty good," Clay muttered. He tipped back the beer. "Pretty damned good."

He thought about his friends: Dobb, a widower, and Yebbie, the cantankerous old bachelor cowhand who seemed never to have needed many male friends, much less female. And old Henry Bennett and Locket and the reclusive Gus and his lone-wolf brother Alvaro.

And then there was Bea and Jovita, each living alone, two floors apart though they shared the roof of the Hotel Solitario. And this young woman who had entered all their lives, now alone without her baby. And, of course, Clay himself, now that Serafina and Adelita were both gone. All Solitario in their own ways.

"Except for each other, I guess." He thought even if they did have each other, he would not go so far as to think of the group as connected, not like family anyway. Not kinship. Except for Gus and Alvaro, none of the others were blood kin like Clay and Adelita and Serafina. But then he considered Perfidia's connection to her baby, not unlike his to Serafina. "Except her too, I guess. . . ."

Clay rubbed his temple with the tips of his fingers and then remembered the aspirin in his shirt pocket. He fingered the bottle out and opened it and tossed a few tablets into his mouth, washed them down with the remainder of the beer and belched loudly. Then he lay back in the shade. He closed his eyes and thought about Adelita and Serafina and how it was Clay himself who had chosen the isolation of their home and their lives. It was he who urged Adelita to let him build their house in the desert—with adobe *from* the desert—sixteen miles of dirt road segregating their world from everything else. She did not protest. She too wanted no part of living close to neighbors. She loved the animals and saw the sparse grass of the high desert, greening in the spring despite stingy cloudbanks, as a sign of returning hope for themselves. She considered Clay and herself to be like the grass, hardy and firm-rooted and able to resurrect themselves from even the worst of conditions. But there were negatives attached to the isolation that neither had considered until Serafina came into their lives.

Behind his closed eyes, Clay sees Adelita sitting next to the wash basin in the kitchen, Serafina draped across her lap. The child is limp and listless and Adelita mops her forehead with cool water, squeezes the rag dry, dips it again into the last of the water Clay has brought from the windmill. "She is so hot," Adelita says and she smiles, unconvincingly. "But she played so hard in the sun today."

Clay nods. Serafina moans and he sees she is not responding to the cool rag. Adelita looks at him and at the empty basin. He stands and reaches for the pan and holds it for a moment, looking into the eyes of his wife.

"I'll get more," he says and he leaves and walks back to the windmill where the cold water comes in small but steady spurts from the spout in the late afternoon breeze. He places the basin on the flat fieldstone under the stream of water, waiting for it to fill and looks into the face of his old mare, just over the rail of the corral where she is kept with the milk cow. The mare is heavy with her new foal and he knows she is uncomfortable even with the cooling senility of a late afternoon sun, but she has plenty of oats and hay and also the cool sweet water from deep in the earth now in the rock trough right at her chest.

"Don't worry old girl," he says to her. "I won't be working you for a while. Not till the foal comes. But I wish I could get you out of the sun too." He reaches over the rail and palms the velvet muzzle and the mare rumbles deep in her throat and lifts her nose into his hand but there is nothing sweet there. "But I'll keep you in under the loafing shed when you foal. I promise."

She lifts her nose again and again. "No time for sugar right now old gal," he says and notices the wash basin running over.

"Maybe later."

He lifts the basin of water and moves across the hardpan and back into the house. Adelita meets him just inside and now instead of a frowning concern, Clay sees panic in her eyes.

"She threw up," Adelita says. "All over me."

"What did she eat?"

"Beans and some meat," Adelita says. "And some cactus preserves on a biscuit."

"What else?"

"Milk. She had some milk."

"Was it sour?"

"I don't think so . . . it's from yesterday."

Clay goes to the big porcelain crock sitting in a pan of water to keep it cool. He lifts the lid and places his face into the opening. He sniffs and then lowers a dipper into the milk, holds it to his nose and then tastes it. Immediately, he wrinkles his nose.

"Well, it's not the freshest, but I've tasted worse," he says.

"But it's not good?"

"No," Clay admits. "It just got too hot I guess, even setting in the pan of water. I'll dump it."

Adelita frowns and turns and takes the basin of cool water from Clay and moves back into Serafina's bedroom where the child lies across her bed, groaning now. Adelita continues to mop her head with the water, but Clay can see that Serafina is not responding. He goes to the door of the bedroom and leans against the jamb, watching.

"Maybe she just needs to sleep," he says but there is no conviction in his voice.

Adelita senses this. She sighs and glances back at Clay, who looks at her for a moment and then down at the floor as if considering some other course of action.

"I'll get the pickup ready," he says and turns away. "Don't

worry. I'll take her into town. That new Doctor Maddox comes there today. I think."

Clay moves rapidly to the kitchen, retrieves his gloves and hat and exits from the front door and into the yard where the old pickup sits. He opens the passenger door and tosses oily rags and fencing pliers and hammers and an assortment of other items from the passenger side back into the bed. He reaches in and tries to brush the dust from the tattered seat.

"That'll have to do," he mutters and moves around and enters on the driver's side where he reaches down and twists the key in the ignition. The starter cranks. And cranks. But there is no response. There is not even a single firing from the old engine. Clay pumps the accelerator and tries again. Still nothing.

"Shit!" he says and even though he knows the gasoline gauge has not functioned in years, he glances at it. "Can't be out of gas. I just filled it yesterday in town."

He gets out and goes to the back and twists off the filler cap. He reaches over into the bed of the pickup and straightens out a length of barbed wire and inserts it into the filler neck and retrieves it. Nothing shows on the end of the wire.

"Christ!" he says and reinserts the wire. Again nothing. Clay drops to his knees and leans under the bed of the pickup and immediately smells the gasoline which has dribbled from the fresh rock puncture in the gas tank and soaked into the ground overnight.

Clay sits back up. He sighs and lifts his hat and swipes the forearm of his shirt across his head and looks up at the sky, nothing but cobalt blue from horizon to horizon.

"Maybe she'll sleep," he says but when he gets back inside the house, Serafina is flushed scarlet and now there is a light foam at her lips. Adelita looks at him, her eyes pleading with him for some words she cannot find from herself. But all he can whisper is,

"It won't start."

Clay bolted awake from the sudden noise of the empty eighteen wheeler, rumbling on the dirt road toward the ruins of Casa Piedra. He sat and blinked at the sound coming from the west where only a thin coral sliver on the horizon remained of the sun. For a quick moment, he wondered how long he had been asleep but then it occurred to him that he did not have the luxury of contemplation. His pickup was sitting in the late dusk, right in the middle of the road where he had left it earlier in the day.

"Sweet Geezus!" he said.

He scrambled to his feet and rushed to his truck, his knees crying out. He flung open the door on the driver's side but he did not take time to shut it or even to pull on its headlights as a warning to the oncoming vehicle because the lights of the eighteen wheeler bore down on him without slowing.

"Damn!" He twisted the ignition key, hard. And for an instant in his head he was back twenty-five years, sitting in front of his old adobe house in a different old pickup at that terrible time . . . and again now, sitting in another worn-out pickup with yet another senile engine that would not fire. He looked up into the headlights of the truck and for another brief moment, wondered if this was what death looked like.

And then it was all in black-and-white and slow motion and he knew for certain that he was dying . . . or maybe already dead. The headlights of his imminent death seemed to inch to his left and the noise of the diesel engine seemed to hush as the entire mass of steel moved off the road to his left. He closed his eyes and waited for what seemed to be hours. And then he felt a sudden jarring, maybe his last shuddering breath. When he opened his eyes, Alvaro Muñoz was standing at the open window of his pickup, just as his brother Gus had done the day before, but Alvaro was shaking him by the shoulder.

"What the fuck you doin' parked on the road?" he demanded and then relaxed his grip, leaned further into the window. "That you, Clayton?"

Clay nodded but he was not sure Alvaro could see this, so he tried his voice. "Yeah," he wheezed.

"You goddamned near killed us both," Alvaro said. "What the hell you doin' parked out here in the dark?"

Clay decided he had best not say he had been sleeping or that he had a hell of a hangover caused by Alvaro's own brother or that he had simply been dozing on the hard ground out there, contemplating his own mortality. "I'm stalled," he said. He pulled out his headlight switch but the left light did not come on.

"You ought'a be dead," Alvaro said.

Clay thought he should agree with Alvaro, but instead, he opened his door and got out and stood silent for a long moment. The eighteen wheeler leaned into the barrow ditch, but otherwise seemed intact. "Hey, I'm sorry," he said. "You okay?"

"Yeah," Alvaro said and he released a long breath. "Wore out though."

"Where you been?" Clay wanted it to sound casual. "You loaded?"

"If you mean is my truck loaded, no," Alvaro said wryly. "If you mean myself, well . . ."

Clay said nothing to this. He moved to the front of his pickup to inspect the left headlight. The front of the fender lay peeled back, the entire headlight and grill gone from that side. "Looks like that tire ain't scratched a bit," Clay said. "Lucky I guess."

"Yeah, lucky."

"What about your truck, Alvaro?"

"Well I ain't exactly had time to look it over." Alvaro turned and walked the length of the cattle hauler, stopped at the cab and retrieved a flashlight, then came back. He inspected the underside of the trailer with the light. Clay followed him as he circled the end of the rig and then worked his way around the opposite side and finally they both stood in front of the headlights, Alvaro's engine still idling.

"Seems okay," Alvaro said. "Except for this scrape on my bumper." He rubbed the chrome with his hand. "Like you say, Clayton, you're lucky."

"Will she climb outta the ditch?'

"Oh yeah. This won't slow me down much."

"Good."

Alvaro climbed up into the cab and set the gears low and hammered with his foot on the accelerator as he released the clutch. The rig jerked forward, spun its wheels in the loose rock and finally caught. It easily rolled up out of the ditch and back onto the dirt road, the aluminum slats of the empty cattle hauler rattling. Alvaro got out and came back. The two stood in the glow of the amber running lights on the side of the trailer.

"Where the hell you going, Clayton?"

"Solitario."

"What are you doing out here then?"

"You already asked me that, Alvaro."

"Well?"

"I been visiting your brother."

"The hell you say? Hope he's got cold beer and hot beans ready," Alvaro said. "I got to get loaded up and get back out on the highway."

"You can count on the beans," Clay said and smiled. "Don't know if there's any beer left. You come down 67?"

"Yeah," Alvaro said. "Lots of traffic too. All going north. Fast."

"Traffic?" Clay said. "This time of day?"

"You mean night, don't you?"

Clay looked again at the horizon to the west, nothing but a layered hint of pink showing now. "Yeah, guess it is."

"Well, some of the traffic looked like John Law to me."

"Law?"

"Lots of it. Sheriff cars and a couple black-and-whites too, stopping traffic going north."

"Maybe an accident?"

"Didn't see anything coming down. Could'a been something behind me though."

"Maybe a drug bust or something . . ." Clay offered, stopping short of saying what he was pretty certain the sudden excitement was all about. "It's getting real bad."

"Well, you're not exactly in the best place if there's a drug shoot-out," Alvaro said. "I mean, it seems to me this old back road might be just right for a deal."

"I wouldn't know," Clay said and released a long sigh. "I'll see if I can get this damn thing started." He went to his pickup and got inside and cranked the engine over and over until the battery almost gave out.

"Give it a rest," Alvaro called. "At least a full minute."

Clay sat. He counted in his head what seemed to be a full minute and tried again. Nothing.

"You sure you're not out of gas?" Alvaro pressed. "You goddamned gringos never got any gas in your pickups. I said wait a *full* minute."

"I got gas," Clay shot back, raw memories invading his voice and then he whispered, "I got gas. . . ." He counted again and then certain it had been more than a minute, turned the ignition key and held the accelerator to the floorboard and soon the engine coughed and stuttered alive in a cloud of white exhaust.

"See." Alvaro was standing at his window again. "Better try her out, see if that fender's dragging your tire."

Clay put the truck into gear and moved a few feet. "Seems fine, except for only one headlight," Clay said.

"Hope all that law don't see you with only one light," Alvaro said. "You'll get stopped for sure."

"Maybe. I'll only be on the pavement a while though. Say hi to Gus. Tell him I'll see him tomorrow morning at my old place."

"Your place?" Alvaro said. "What's up?"

"I sold out, you know. He said he'd take my *corrientes.*"

"Damn you say? Sold out?"

"Yeah."

"Well, I'm sure brother Gus meant to say the Muñoz *Brothers* would take your steers, right?" Alvaro corrected. "Not just him."

"Yeah," Clay said but that was all. He was thinking about more pressing things. He meshed the gears of his injured pickup and drove off like a man ablaze, leaving Alvaro standing silhouetted in the amber running lights of the Muñoz Brothers rig. ❧

CHAPTER 12

Jovita studied the road in front of her car. Though the headlights opened up the moonless dark, she hated driving late at night. She never knew what to expect on this lonely stretch of pavement between Presidio and Solitario, even though it was only twenty miles and a quiet Monday night. She wished Locket had decided to drive back to Solitario behind her, but with the information they had discovered that day, she knew he would be very busy in Presidio. She thought about their conversation when they bumped into each other that afternoon in the general store.

"Whatta you doing here?" Locket teased. "Shopping for new scarves?"

"Yeah," she said. "I'm out of red." She moved closer to Locket and spoke low. "What did the sheriff say?"

"Said all hell was about to break loose."

"Can he stop it?"

"If he wants to," Locket said. "Thing is, I don't think he could, even if he wanted to."

"What's that mean?"

"It means my ass is sort of in a bind," Locket said. "Means he's got a job to do and thinks maybe I shoulda got on it sooner myself."

"Oh. . . ."

"Yeah. And he thinks all you people ought'a go back to watching TV shows," Locket said. He looked at Jovita, who said nothing. Her face hardened and she blinked at him. "He wants to talk with the mother," Locket went on. "But, hey, I guess the bottom line is we got some time."

"We?"

"Yeah, a little anyway," Locket said and paused. "But don't sell him short, Jo. You know Gil couldn't very well say, *'Just round up your friends and do whatever the hell y'all decide is best.'* He understands what a lot of pressure from the law might do to the chances of getting that baby back—"

"Alive?"

Locket paused again and then said, "I keep having to say that. I don't like having to say that. . . ."

"I know, Lock. None of us does. But you just have to do what you have to do. And so does Sheriff Gil."

"Yeah. How is she?"

"I sent Boone over this morning to check on her. Bea's hovering like a mother herself. I think the young woman is as well as could be expected."

"Well, I'm going to ask around a little over here today."

"They won't talk to you, Lock. Not anyone who knows anything."

"I got sources. . . ."

"You mean like me?"

Locket looked at Jovita, puzzled. "My turn for the question now," he said and then, "What's *that* supposed to mean?"

"It means you might want to make me a deputy after all." Jovita smiled. She cocked her head, repositioned the knot in her red scarf.

Locket knew this gesture well. "Okay, I'll bite. Why?"

"I found out they have some clothes her size here, see?" She held up several items of female clothing. "Not much, but some."

"And?" He crossed his arms, moved out of the narrow aisle for a customer with a shopping cart and waited.

"And I found out they've been real busy in here this weekend," she teased. "Especially with certain items."

"Come on, Jovita, get to it."

"Things like throwaway diapers and infant formula and bottles and, well, *things.*"

"Who told you all this?"

"Well, it's not exactly CIA stuff, Lock. Just ask for all those same things yourself and the clerk gets to talking and then it's easy. One comment leads to another, that's all. Lots of mothers come in for that stuff, but she said one buyer was, well . . . *different.*"

"Different?"

"Yes."

"How? She say who? When?"

"I figure that's your job, deputy." Jovita said. "After all, I'm not getting paid."

"Yeah, I do get paid." Locket sighed and looked around the little store. "But it's a cinch I ain't getting rich." He turned back to her. "And you can take *that* to the bank. Which one is it you talked to?"

"The short one. Young. She's also a mother. . . ."

Jovita looked across the store at the dry goods section. "She's over there."

"Okay."

"She said something else, Lock." Locket waited again. "She said it was kind of sad that a parent of a baby on formula and still in diapers would also be buying that many cartons of cigarettes."

"How many?"

"I don't know . . . she said several."

"A woman bought cigarettes and all that baby stuff too?"

"She didn't say it was a woman at first. She only said *parent.* But when we talked more, she said it was a man and she thought he was a Mexican national but then, lots of her customers are and lots of them take American cigarettes back across the border. Said maybe he was stocking up on them or something. Many of them like these American brands. But she said it was real unusual for someone to take that many at one time, though."

"Yeah, maybe."

"But that wasn't what she said was the strangest thing, though."

"Go on."

"She said he also bought enough diapers and formula to last for several weeks," Jovita said. "And she said hardly anyone ever does that who's right across the border. They got all that baby stuff over there, too, and lots cheaper. Same brand. No import tax if they buy them over there, you know."

"Yeah." Locket picked up a package of gum and looked toward the checkout girl. "Well, you better go out first, Jo. I'll follow this up in here." He turned to move away from her.

"Just like spies on TV, huh?" she said and he turned back to her. When he glowered and said nothing she regretted saying it.

"Sorry, Lock," she said. "I know it's serious. Anyway, I've got a dozen other chores to do down here. I've put them off too long. If I don't pay our utility bills they'll turn off our gas and then Bea won't be cooking your *carne adovada* or anything else next week."

Locket glanced at her to see if she was teasing again. She was not. "I'll be late going back up," she sighed and smiled at him. "And you can take that to the bank too. What's your plan today, anyway?"

"I don't know. Depends. I need to get on this before things get, well . . . *noisy.* I'll probably be late too. "

"Hey Lock?"

"Yeah?"

"Be sure you pay for that gum. Or I can loan you a dollar till payday if you need it." She smiled again at him and Locket grinned back this time. She walked to the counter, checked out the things for Perfidia and left.

Jovita had worried all day as she tried to rush through her mundane list of items to take care of. She finished paying bills and picked up some fresh produce for Bea and then ate a quick dinner at the little restaurant in the back of Julio's Bar. But by then, it was already late into the evening. She watched for Locket's patrol car but had not seen it all day long.

Now on a sharp turn in the blacktop fifteen miles north of Presidio, her headlights illuminated Locket, standing on the shoulder of the opposite side of the road next to his vehicle, his headlights on. She slowed and then pulled across the two lane and stopped nose-to-nose with his patrol car. She rolled down her window and then killed the engine but left her headlights on. Locket came over but not to her open driver side window. Instead, he got into her car on the passenger side and removed his hat and sat silent for a long while, staring out the side window into the night. She could hear his patrol car idling.

"What?" she finally said, speaking to the back of Locket's head.

"I been waiting for you," he said but he did not turn back. "I guess Bea called dispatch."

"Bea?"

"About an hour ago. They relayed the message to me. Where were you all this time anyway, Jo?" He turned to her now.

"I had dinner at Julio's. And a couple drinks," Jovita said. "I needed them."

"All evening?"

"What is this, Lock? A DWI? You gonna put the cuffs on me or what? Why'd Bea call?"

"She said we got a new problem."

"New?"

"She's gone." Locket sighed. "Disappeared."

Jovita did not have to ask who had disappeared. "When?" She turned away from Locket and she too now stared into the darkness, considered all the grim possibilities. "What else?"

"Just this evening, I guess. But I dunno what else. I didn't talk to Bea," Locket said. "The sheriff got on the horn after that and put out an alert on the woman, but nothing's showed up yet."

"Who's looking?" She turned back to Locket.

"He'd already sent two units out earlier on both highways leaving the area, one north on 67, the other to the east on 170. Those were for the baby though, but now with the mother gone too. . . ." Locket looked at her in the headlights glaring through the windshield from his patrol car. "Looks like all hell's broke loose now, Jo, Texas State Highway Patrol, Border Patrol, you know, the whole catastrophe. They're checking everything leaving, all the way north of Solitario up to Alpine and east from Presidio over to Redford and beyond."

"Well, maybe that's good at this point." Jovita released the breath she had been holding and sat silent for a long while. "Where do you think she went, Lock?"

"I got no clue," Locket said. "Hell, maybe they came back for her or something."

"You mean just walked into my hotel and dragged her out? With Bea hovering right over her?" Jovita snorted at this. "I don't think so. . . ."

"Well . . ." Locket cleared his throat, realizing the folly of this. He knew he would not want any part of Bea Hernandez on a defensive rampage. "Probably not."

"You think she just panicked, Lock, and went out looking for her baby on her own?"

"More likely," he said. "Something like that."

Jovita leaned her head back on her headrest. "Like I say, maybe that's best. Maybe Sheriff Gil was right. Maybe it was stupid to think we'd just walk into some abandoned house and find her baby unharmed, like on TV."

"That's what I'd hoped too," Locket said. "And

that's exactly what I did."

Jovita sat up. Locket was not forthcoming and she realized maybe she was the one being toyed with now. "Okay, Lock, I'll bite. What'd you do?"

"Well, I didn't find the child," he admitted. "But I think I did find where they'd kept it and my hunch was right. I just asked around a little more and one thing led to another and I found something in one of those abandoned houses."

"Where?"

"Over in that old neighborhood by the river," he said. "Lots of indication that a baby had been there, dirty diapers, empty formula cans."

"What else?"

"Cigarette butts." He sighed and leaned forward. "Lots of them. But no baby and no perps just waiting for me to arrest them."

"Perps?"

"Perpetrators," Locket said and then, "It's law talk, Jo. Sorry."

"Oh . . . Well, where do you think they took the baby?"

"Dunno that either. Maybe they just panicked and went back across the river, but that'd be damned hard to do right there so close to town." He lifted the handle and pushed the door open. He sat in the glare of his headlights and now the yellow of the dome light. "Or maybe something worse."

"Don't even go there, Lock," she pleaded.

"Well, you gotta know it would be a helluva lot easier crossing over the bridge without a baby, Jovita. Or even wading back over the river on down the way."

Locket paused for a long while and then replaced his hat and said, "Either way, they wouldn't risk taking a kidnapped baby back over. They're stupid scum, but they ain't that stupid."

Jovita looked at him but could not see his eyes shadowed now under his hat brim that he had tipped forward into the lights. "I know that makes sense, Lock. But you know something that doesn't?"

"What?"

"If Perfidia's disappeared into the night," Jovita said, and she reached into a bag in the back seat, "how would she do it without these?" She held up a new pair of women's shoes. "Without any help and with cut feet?"

Locket studied the shoes for a long moment. "Nice work, deputy," he said. "Just like on TV."

Jovita smiled but said nothing. Locket got out and shut the door but stood in the middle of the two lane blacktop for a moment, looked to the north and then back to the south as if expecting something to come out of the darkness. Nothing did. He walked back to his vehicle.

Jovita pulled onto the road and stopped in the oncoming lane adjacent the patrol car, her open window next to his. "See you for breakfast in the morning, Lock?"

"Dunno," he said. "I'll probably run up and down those back roads the rest of tonight just like I did last night, see if I can find anything. Doubt if I'll get back for breakfast in Solitario. You can count me in for lunch and dinner both, though, if nothing else happens out here."

"Is it my turn again?" she said but did not wait for

permission to speak. "What's all *that* mean?"

"Well, it means that if nobody finds the woman and nobody finds the baby and nobody finds any evidence that either ever existed . . . well then, the whole thing might be considered just a hoax or a prank and all this would cool off, that's for sure. After I got my butt chewed out, of course."

"And all that heavy pressure we've been worrying so much about would suddenly disappear?" Jovita said and smiled. "Just like Perfidia? Disappear right into the night? Is that what you're saying, Lock?"

Locket did not reply but even in the darkness, Jovita thought she had seen a slight smile come to this face. She rolled up her own window and drove back into the night, north toward Solitario. ☙

CHAPTER 13

"Well in Texas, it's called the Rule of Capture." Henry Bennett was speaking from behind his battered oak desktop in the county commission's office, just across the street from the Hotel Solitario and downstairs from his living quarters. He yawned, sipped on what was once a white porcelain mug, now stained brown inside and out and cracked. He looked out the front window where long morning shadows were withdrawing back across the empty street into the sunrise. "Is that all you two got me outta bed for?"

"What's that mean?" Dobb Campbell said. "Doesn't sound very legal to me."

"Me neither," Yebbie echoed.

"Oh it's legal," Henry said. "And it's been on the Texas statutes since the Republic was founded and that makes it older'n dirt."

"Just like you, Henry. But come to think of it, I've seen dirt look better than you do this morning," Dobb said. "You okay? Maybe you need a wife."

"Just get on with it, Dobb," Henry said. "You two seem to be doing just fine without wives and family and so am I. Hell, I'm eighty-eight years old and ain't no woman's gonna put up with me now. I like living upstairs right here, by myself. It's worked for me and the county for all these years and besides, I got all these county and state documents to keep me company. And they don't nag me like a wife." He gestured to long rows of gray bound documents lining the shelves in the office. "Friends," he said. "Ever damn one of them."

"Okay, okay, Henry," Dobb said and held up both palms toward Henry. "You don't need to read the whole shelf. Just tell us how the hell that law works."

"Like I said, that Rule of Capture is legal. You wanna see the statute?" He rose to reach for one huge binder of documents behind him but he wavered in mid-stance.

"Sit down, Henry, before you fall. We don't need that, dammit. Just tell us how it works, okay?" Dobb said. "I think as county commissioners, Yeb and I both need to know about it."

"Fine," Henry said. He sat back down. "But why the hell you need to know all about it at six A.M. on a Tuesday morning in May beats the hell outta me."

"Because we just might want to put it on the agenda at the next meeting," Dobb confessed. "For discussion."

"Discussion?" Henry said. "Why?"

"Goddammit, Henry," Yebbie said. "Just walk us through it. And then you can get on back to bed. We don't wanna look like idiots in front of the whole damn county if it comes up or something."

"Why would it come up?" Henry said. He coughed and sipped the stale coffee. "And the whole damn county ain't in my lifetime ever been at a single one of our meetings anyway. We're lucky to have two rangy cowhands show up and they usually just wander in after somebody's kicked them out of a bar somewhere." He coughed again, a rheumy rattle from his chest.

Dobb looked at Yebbie and then back at Henry. "You sure you're all right, Henry?"

"Yeah, I'm okay," Henry wheezed but the other two looked at each other again, unconvinced.

"Okay, it's like this," Dobb continued. "Clay's sold his place, right?"

"Yeah," Henry said. "That's what I been hearing. But they ain't been no deed transferred yet in this office. And I'd know about that. I also know it's been tough on him, his wife and all. I don't blame him a bit if he's got something in the works."

"Well, the new owners-to-be made a big earnest money payment and Clay's already spent it on some of Adelita's medical bills. The rest of the money comes to him after the deed transfers."

"And that don't happen till midnight of the fifteenth of this month," Yebbie said. "And now Clay wants to bring his daughter into Solitario and bury her with her mama but if he moves her before—"

"To cut it short, Henry," Dobb interrupted, "they plan to drill deep down into the aquifer out there soon as Clay moves Serafina but they signed an agreement that they can't get the deed until she's been moved or after midnight of the fifteenth, whichever comes first."

"The aquifer?" Henry said. "Why?"

"Well, that's the big problem as we see it," Dobb went on. "Some screwball idea about piping billions of gallons of our water out of here and over to El Paso. Figure they'll make millions because of this drought, I guess."

"And probably want it handy for a zillion more houses and golf courses too," Yebbie said. "And not just pipe it over there to El Paso neither. Hell fire, there'd be no end of it."

"I see," Henry said and sighed. "And you think we ought'a stop it?"

"Well, I don't even know if we can," Dobb said. "But I think we ought to look into it. Hell, we don't know what'll happen if they pump all that water out of the ground. Neither do they. So anyway, how does this Rule of Capture work, Henry?"

"Simple," Henry said and held both hands out, palms up. "Here's one piece of land, owned by one guy . . ." He raised one hand. " . . . and here's another, owned by somebody else." He raised the other hand. "Way down there deep underneath both of them is this big ole pool of water and it's underneath everyone else around them too, as far as you can see. One big pool. Or it could be just a little piss-pot full, don't matter."

"So?" Dobb said.

"Yeah, so what?" Yebbie echoed.

"Simple," Henry said. "Whoever's got the *biggest* pump in his palm wins."

"Hmmmm . . . you mean they could just suck out all the water they wanted, even if it run everybody else around there dry?" Dobb said. "And they'd own that water the minute they got it out of the ground? Is that what you're saying?"

"Yep. Soon as it's outta the ground, it belongs to whoever brings it up."

"And nobody around him could do a damn thing?" Yebbie said. "Windmills and springs might dry up?"

"Might," Henry said. "Ain't ever been done way out here, so I guess nobody knows for sure."

"Don't seem right to me," Dobb said.

"Me neither," Yebbie said.

"Well you know, it don't make a shit what you two hardheads think is right, or me either, or even the *three* of us as county commissioners for that matter. That's just the way the law reads in Texas."

"Then if they come onto Clay's place and drill that deep hole and put a big-ass pump on it, they could eventually suck us all dry?" Dobb rose to leave. "Just don't seem right to me."

"Me neither," Yebbie said again and he too rose and moved toward the door.

"Well just for the record, it don't seem right to me either," Henry began. "And they could do it legally without a hitch . . . *unless* . . ."

Both men stopped, turned back. "Unless what?" Dobb said and he looked at Henry askance.

"Unless you've got a county water board in place."

"Water board?" Dobb said. He moved back over and sat again.

Yebbie stood at the door, his hand on the doorknob. "What's that mean?" he said.

"Well, it ain't that we've ever really needed one here in this county since there's never been that much water around here to worry about, at least not close to the surface. Basically, we're watering livestock and putting enough in our town water tower for drinking. It ain't like we're irrigating cactus or something."

"What does this water board do?" Dobb said.

"You might say it controls all county water in a sense," Henry said. "Above and underground water rights and stuff like that. And no single owner can do something without it going through this county water board."

"You mean, sorta like us three on the county commissioners?" Yebbie injected.

"Go on, Henry," Dobb said.

"Well, that's about it," Henry continued. "If someone was to plan to suck water out of our aquifer, our county water board could put a halt to it if it wasn't in the interest of the people in the county. If we had one of these boards in place, that is. It's in the Texas statutes."

"Why can't *we* just do that?" Dobb said. "Us three as commissioners?"

"Well, you can do it two ways," Henry continued. "The town could elect a separate board, just like the commissioners. Or we could appoint ourselves as a temporary board till that happened. For a while, we could be both. That's also in the law."

"And if we did that, we could set those regulations?" Dobb said. "And if they're in place, this new outfit would have to come to us before they could drill?"

"Yep," Henry said. "They'd be in place after we had a hearing, of course. Can't do any kind of regulations without a hearing. You guys know that. First you gotta notify Austin and get that paperwork done, then there's the legal notice that has to run in the newspaper, then we could—"

"Okay, okay, Henry, I understand," Dobb interrupted again. "But you're saying it *could* be done?"

"Oh hell yeah," Henry said. "Sure it could."

"One more question, Henry," Dobb said.

"Shoot," Henry said.

"What if some landowner, somebody holding a deed to some ground in the county, knew this water board was in the works and decided to get cracking and drill on that land *before* we had a chance have a hearing and all?"

"Well, they'd be grandfathered in, I guess, if they held the deed to the property at the time the regs passed. And they wouldn't have to abide by any new regulations. The county would be shit outta luck on that particular piece of ground."

"They'd still be under that stupid Rule of Capture?" Yebbie said. "What if they ain't hit any water yet?"

"Don't matter," Henry said. "All they need to do is apply for it under the Rule of Capture and get a hole going. They'd be doing it without any local county regulations in place when they began, see. That's the way I read it. Ain't no way any regulations could be retroactive. That'd be unconstitutional."

"Retro . . . *what?*" Yebbie said.

"Shut up, Yeb," Dobb said. "And they could suck all they wanted out of the aquifer without anyone stopping them, Henry? Do anything they wanted to with it? Even after our regulations went into place?"

"Yep. If they hit any water, of course. Haul it or pump it anywhere they wanted to. Like I said, Rule of Capture equals the biggest pump wins."

"So any regulations after that might just stop *us* from doing the same, even if we wanted it for ourselves?"

Yebbie said. "The county, I mean. But it wouldn't stop *them* at all?"

"Yep," Henry said. "Depends on how tough we worded it I guess. It'd be sort of a double-edged sword. In any case, they'd be free of the regulations."

Dobb clenched his jaw and sucked in a long breath. He stared at Henry for a while and then turned to Yebbie who had moved over and stood at his shoulder. "Looks like we need to be the ones to get cracking on this water board thing, Henry. Before any deeds get transferred and any holes get started."

"Sounds like that might get real complicated," Henry observed. "What with Clay hot to move his daughter and all. If he does that before we can do anything, well it's 'Katy bar the door.' When's he wanting to do it anyway?"

"Well, you know how Clay is," Dobb said. "Everything's usually *tomorro*w, but he's put me and Yeb under the gun to help him right away since he's also under the gun. Come midnight on the fifteenth, they'll go in whether he's got her outta there or not. He don't figger he can do it by himself and I don't think he can either."

"But he could get somebody else to help," Henry said. "Right?"

"Says he wants only his friends. His good friends," Yebbie said.

"Clayton may be a little quirky that way, but he's not stupid. He knows this water thing is bigger than just what he wants to do right now," Dobb said. "He won't admit it. But I don't think he's gonna do it real quick though in any case."

"Why's that?" Henry said.

"It's a long story," Dobb said and looked up at Yebbie. "Something else came up, though."

"Yeah," Yebbie said and then very seriously, "what Dobb means is *someone* else who—"

"Shut up, Yeb," Dobb interrupted. He cleared his throat. "That don't need discussing here." He stood and reached out and shook Henry's hand. "Thanks, Henry."

Yebbie shifted and looked down, then frowned at Dobb. "Well, we got time at least to eat breakfast before all this gets cranked up?"

"Yeah," Dobb said. "We got time for breakfast, Yebbie."

"Well, you wanna get this on the agenda for the next commissioner meeting?" Henry said.

"You mean the regular meeting?" Dobb said. "Thursday night?"

"That's right," Henry said. "Thursday."

"Can we get it on the agenda that fast, Henry?"

"Only the chairman of the commissioners could do that, Dobb," Henry reminded him and beamed. "And last time I checked, that's me, right? I think the other two commissioners can count on it."

"And that'd be us, right?" Yebbie said and he too brightened.

"Sounds like a plan to me," Dobb said. "Now you get back in bed, Henry, hear?" Henry nodded, sipped the coffee again but made no effort to stand. Dobb turned and left with Yebbie. Outside, they crossed the still empty street and entered the front doors of the hotel.

Back in Bea's kitchen, Jovita stood looking at her

early morning strip of pepper bacon on the napkin at the back of the old stove. As usual, Bea had not responded to Jovita's *"buenos dias"* until the bacon had been tasted. But this morning, Jovita did not pick up the meat. In one arm, she held the clothing she had purchased in Presidio and a shoebox in the other.

"Tell me again," she said to Bea, though they had been over and over everything late last night when Jovita returned to the hotel. "She was just gone when you went back to your apartment?"

"Sí," Bea said. "After I cleaned up out here." Bea poked with a fork at more bacon strips sputtering on the grill. "It was late. . . ."

"And you saw no one go back there?"

"No."

"You think she just left?"

"I don't know," Bea said, but she would not look at Jovita. "Maybe . . ."

"Just ran off into the night?"

"Yes."

"I see," Jovita said. She set the clothing on a work table and moved back over and picked up the bacon. She bit into it, chewed, swallowed, pushed the remainder of the bacon into her mouth and wiped her fingers on the napkin. Then she went back to the clothes and lifted the lid from the box with the new shoes. "Without these?"

Bea turned and looked at the shoes. Her face drained. She said nothing. Jovita returned the lid to the shoebox and came back in front of Bea. "Maybe you could see to it that she gets this stuff, okay?" She smiled at Bea. Then she filled a mug of coffee and turned to walk out into the restaurant.

"And *buenas días*, to you," Bea said. She held a small smile on her face.

Out front, Jovita moved to sit at her usual table but then stopped. Across the room, she saw Clay sitting with Dobb and Yebbie. Locket was not in the restaurant. The men seemed very intense. She went over and stood next to their table. "Looks serious," she said to them. "Actually, I'm feeling a little serious myself this morning. Mind if I join you?"

"Sit down, Jo," Clay offered. "We're just yakking."

"Yeah," Yebbie said. "Just yakking."

"Well, if it's cow talk, I'm not interested," Jovita said. "I can read about cattle prices in my newspaper."

"It's not that," Dobb said. "Sit."

She sat. "What's the crisis today?"

"Water," said Yebbie, unable to hold it.

"Water?" she said.

"Actually, it's the aquifer," Dobb corrected. "But it's all real boring, Jovita."

"Hey, boring sounds just fine to me," Jovita said. "Especially after last night." The men looked at her in silence. When there was no effort to explain anything about their water discussion or even to quiz her about her comment, Jovita said evenly, "Okay, where is she?"

She studied the face of each man in turn, first Dobb, then Yebbie and last, Clay who appeared drawn and exhausted. But no one gave any indication that he understood what she meant.

"She?" Dobb finally said and Yebbie echoed the word. Clay said nothing.

"Perfidia," Jovita said. "As if you knotheads didn't

know." They all frowned and appeared baffled. Jovita went on, "She's gone."

"Gone?" Clay said. "Whatta you mean, Jo?"

"I mean she just up and disappeared."

"When?" Dobb said.

"Last night sometime," Jovita said. "That's what Bea says."

"Hell, I didn't even know she was with Bea," Dobb said.

"Me neither," said Yebbie.

"Well she was," Jovita said. "And don't all of you play dumb. I've got a feeling one of you knows something about it and maybe all of you do."

"Why the hell would we have anything to do with it, Jo?" Clay said and he seemed crushed. "That's just stupid. That's just more trouble for somebody and we all got enough of that already."

"Yeah, maybe she just walked back into the desert or something," Dobb said.

"Not without shoes," Jovita said. "And even *with* shoes, not likely with the shape her feet were in." They all nodded. "Anyway, Lock says they may just call off the whole search, maybe just consider it a hoax or something and let it drop."

"Well, whatever," said Clay. "Maybe that's best. Just let Locket and the law take over."

"Yeah," Dobb said. "Maybe it's best this way."

"Yeah, best thing," Yebbie said. "We can get on with other things maybe more important."

"Yeah, like moving Serafina," Clay said and turned to his old friends. "Right? And the new owners can take over my place and I can collect my money and pay off my bills and that's all done and . . ."

"Let's not get too hasty, Clay," Dobb inserted.

Yebbie picked up on this. "Yeah, not too hasty."

"Why's that?" Clay said, tiptoeing around the issue.

"Yeah, why?" Jovita said.

"Okay," Dobb began. "It's another matter we been thinking about, Clay, and you know all this. He turned to Jovita. "It has to do with what we were just talking about before you come in, Jovita. Drilling the aquifer."

"I just told you again, that's a done deal, Dobb," Clay said. "Ain't no going back on it now."

"I know. We all know now. But there's a little time-frame situation we didn't talk about," Dobb said.

"Time frame?" Clay said.

"Yeah," Dobb went on. "I didn't think we'd need to get into it today, but it goes like this. . . ."

Dobb explained the Rule of Capture law and how getting a county water board in place before the deed to Clay's land transferred would be critical to installing some regulations before the new owners attempted to drill into the aquifer.

"So you see, moving Serafina before we can do that is gonna affect us all, Clayton. It's not just your problem now," Dobb said. His voice held more plea than anger. "Sooner or later, it's gonna affect the whole county."

Clay sat silent. Jovita seemed dazed with all this, but she said nothing either.

"I just thought with your new focus on this woman and her missing baby slowing down your moving Serafina, we didn't need to get in such a big rush right now, Clay. But now if *she's* disappeared and that pressure's off, well, I know you're gonna want to get on with bringing Serafina in, right?"

Clay narrowed his eyes at Dobb. "Why would I, Dobb?" he said. "You know damn well I wouldn't just stop looking for that woman's baby now. You know me better than that. In fact, I'm even more concerned now. If that baby's not been found, then there's no way in hell I'd give up now, no matter where her mama's at." Clay paused and looked at the other faces and then back to Dobb. "But maybe that's why *you* took the woman, Dobb? Thinking that if nobody found the baby and now the mother too, they'd just keep searching. Keep us all busy. And you knew damn well I'd keep searching too and forget all about Serafina, admit it. Leave Sera right there, stall any drilling. Is that what you were thinking?"

"I didn't say *forget* about Serafina, Clay," Dobb snapped.

Clay went on. "But you never figured that it all might just get dropped suddenly by Locket and the law, like Jovita's saying, and you never figured that I'd drop it too, feel free to go ahead with moving Serafina, right? You never calculated that, did you?" He glowered at Dobb and then turned on Yebbie. "And you're in on it too, aren't you, Yebbie?" He looked back at Dobb who sat mute. "Like Jo says, Dobb. Where *is* she?"

"Okay," Dobb said and sighed. "I'm sorry, Clay. I just got ahead of myself and I apologize. Of course we didn't take that woman. Come on, that's about as far-fetched as you could get, Clayton. And of course we'll do whatever it takes to help find her. And her baby too, right, Yeb?" Yebbie nodded, totally baffled with all this intrigue. "And that'll be *our* priority too if you think that's what's best. But that doesn't mean we can't—or *shouldn't*—move ahead on this water board thing. And we'll just get that in place *before* your deadline on moving Serafina. Ain't no reason it all can't get worked out if we cooperate. Hell, I think we can agree on that." He held out his hand. "As friends?"

Clay looked at Dobb's proffered hand, hesitated so long that Dobb started to lower it, but then Clay shook it and turned and held his hand out to Yebbie. "Sorry. I apologize too. To both of you. And like you say, as long as Serafina's still in the ground, can't any drilling be done, Dobb. Don't matter whatever's keeping her there now. Y'all know that. We *all* know that. And whether or not anyone believes it, I'm also concerned about the welfare of this county."

"Hey, I care about this county as much as anyone at this table," Jovita said and turned directly to Clay and put her hand on his arm. "And you know I care about getting your Serafina back with Adelita, Clay. But I'm also invested in that young woman and her baby out there now, emotionally anyway. I'm interested in knowing how she is and seeing her baby back with her too." She pushed back her chair and rose. "And believe it or not, I'm interested in seeing you hardheads stay friends, so let's just all cool off and see what Locket has to say when he gets back."

She moved away and went over to her own table where Bea had laid out her breakfast. When she saw her morning newspaper was not on the table, Jovita walked back into the kitchen.

"I think we're all interested in doing what Jo says,"

Dobb added after she was gone.

"Then that settles it for now," Clay said and he too stood. "I'm glad we're finally on the same track. You two and Henry just go ahead with your plan on that water board, if you think that'll help. I understand all that but you guys need to understand there's not a damn thing I can do about my contract to sell. I'm boxed in too. If I don't get Sera moved by midnight on the fifteenth of this month . . . well, I think we've hammered all that stuff enough. You know what they'll do out there at that point."

He looked at Dobb and then at Yebbie and both lowered their eyes and nodded their heads and muttered they did not want that to happen. Clay went on, "And you know I'd tell you two in a second about when I'm gonna move Serafina. Like I've said from the get-go, I wouldn't wanna do it without you two helping anyway. *Couldn't* do it, actually. Not in the shape I'm in. But right now I'm late for an important meeting of my own."

Neither asked Clay what meeting was so important. They were just happy to see some of the anger subside and a semblance of agreement in place.

"Thanks, Clay," Dobb said. "I really think all this can work, though. If we keep our heads on straight and get it all timed right, get the board in place first and then we can get Serafina in here next to Adelita. I think it'll be a tight squeeze but I believe it can work. Henry's got it on the agenda for the regular county commissioners meeting Thursday night. It's our next legal meeting and the quickest we can get a hearing set. I hope you can come to the meeting, Clay."

"I'll be there," Clay said. "I just hope nobody from

Agua Hondo shows up. Soon as they find out about all this, you can bet they'll start pressing the hell outta me to move Sera."

"Yeah," Dobb said. "I expect they'd do that for sure."

"Well, I'll cross that bridge when it happens," Clay said. "*If* it happens. But she'll get moved before they tear up all hell out there where she's buried. Y'all can count on that. Right in here with her mama. One way or another." He stared at the two for a long moment and then turned and left the dining room.

When Clay got into his pickup in front of the hotel, the clothes for Perfidia lay on the seat, concealed under Jovita's morning newspaper. "Thanks, Bea," he whispered. He smiled and cranked the engine. It started immediately. ☙

CHAPTER 14

"Morning," Gus said when Clay pulled up in front of the corral behind his abandoned ranch house. Gus sat on the top rail stroking Palo's neck, his cattle hauling rig parked nearby. "How's your head?"

"Still a little rough," Clay said. He got out of his pickup. As he walked over, he glanced at his old house and then at the little gravesite.

"Looks like you been busy." Gus indicated the *corrientes* already inside the corral. "Riding night herd, just like the Old West? Hope you had a good flashlight. Won't be needing the horse I got loaded up front, I guess. You must'a rode this old horse hard."

"Ain't nothing like the Old West anymore, Gus. That's long dead. But Palo never complains and he's always ready to go. He got that from his mother. . . ." Clay's voice trailed off. He thought about the mare and the night Serafina died. And he thought about the derelict one-horse ranch wagon, still hidden behind the tack shed. "He's not like some things I know. And some people I know. Always complaining about one thing or another." He reached through the rails beside Gus and palmed the old gelding's muzzle. "You been here long?"

"Not long. And you know I ain't the one complaining, don't you?"

"Thanks for coming, Gus," Clay said and sighed. "Sorry. I didn't mean you."

"I said I would." Gus frowned and then said, "Did you think I wouldn't?"

"Sorry."

"You already said that . . . what's up? You sure you're okay?"

"Nothing." Clay turned away. "Still hungover a little, I guess. Ain't like the old days, right? Drunk one night and ready to go the next. Takes me at least three now. And then add to that my Serafina's still waiting under that hardpan over there."

"Yeah," Gus looked at the grave and then back at Clay. He smiled and said, "Hey, we're gonna take care of her. Whenever you say so. And by the way, we haven't talked about your money for these steers either."

"I ain't worried, Gus," Clay said. "Let's just get them loaded. Won't take long."

"What about Palo here?" Gus said. He stepped down from the rail and stood next to Clay. Both stroked the old horse's neck. "You didn't sell him too I hope?"

"Nope," Clay said.

"You want me to load him up front with mine?"

Clay thought about this for a long moment and finally said, "No, I don't think so. I'm not sure what I'm gonna do with him. I don't want him to be a bother to you over there."

"He wouldn't be any trouble to me, Clay. What are you talking about?"

"Well, maybe I'll bring him over there when I pull the rest of that stuff out of the tack shed here."

"What's left in there?"

"Junk," Clay said. "My old saddle, some wore out harnesses. And my granddad's rotten old wagon out behind there. You know, just junk."

"I could store all that for you," Gus said. "No problem."

"Maybe. It's a cinch Jo ain't gonna let me keep it in her hotel," Clay said and he looked at the tack shed and then across the dry earth, distorted by the heat already rising. "I been threatening to burn that old wagon for years, Gus. Maybe burn all of it, saddle, harness, the whole pile of junk."

"Why?" Gus said. "I thought that old wagon was a family antique?"

"Yeah, burn it," Clay said. "And I sure as hell wouldn't call any of that stuff antique. It's all worthless, useless. One of the wagon wheels has been busted ever since before Sera . . ." He paused and looked at Gus. "Why the hell would someone hang on to a dead past, Gus? I mean, I can understand why you'd keep all that nice old stuff over there at Los Arbolitos. That's all historical and it's like family to you, right?"

"Well . . ." Gus looked down, toed aside a rock with his boot. He did not need to remind Clay that there were more important things from the past to hang on to besides furniture and houses. Things dead or not.

"Only family thing left out here is Palo," Clay said. "And Serafina, of course, but . . ."

"Yeah."

"Truth is, Gus, I'm not likely to need all that shit in the tack shed ever again anyway." He moved away and entered the corral, closing the gate behind him. "Let's just get these steers loaded, okay?"

Gus nodded but said nothing. He went to his rig and backed the cattle trailer up to the loading chute and set the brake. When he came back, he climbed over the rail and into the corral where Clay had begun hazing the steers toward the loading chute. The *corrientes* were having no part of this. They easily skirted around him and stood bunched against the opposite rail, eyeing the two men as they approached.

"You gotta whistle," Gus scolded. "And yell. Hell I wouldn't give ten cents for a cowhand who couldn't whistle and yell." He edged to the far end of the corral opposite Clay's position.

"My head don't feel like yelling," Clay said. "Or whistling. Like I said, this ain't the Old West." He walked as fast as he could toward the steers from his side but he was quickly winded. They bolted toward Gus who held his ground, waving his arms, yelling and whistling. The steers turned and Gus ran at them, hazing them toward the loading chute. At the last moment, all but one circled back but Gus closed in. Clay slowed but held his side of the haze. When the remainder of the cattle saw the lone steer stumble up the ramp, they followed, crowding and slipping but soon the whole group rattled into the metal-sided trailer. Gus moved quickly up the ramp behind them, closed the tailgate and latched it.

"See," Gus said. "Just like the Old West." He stood at the top of the ramp and looked down at Clay, bent over catching his breath. "You okay?"

"Yeah," Clay said.

"I love these rangy bastards," Gus said. "Don't you?"

"Hell no," Clay stood erect, still gasping for air.

"In fact, how much do I owe *you* for taking them off my hands."

"We'll settle up. Don't worry," Gus teased and moved back down the ramp. "It'll be big bucks, though, I promise you that."

The two walked out the corral gate and stood under the windmill. Clay looked for the dipper, but then he remembered he had tossed it into his pickup bed on Sunday.

"Join me?" Clay said. He leaned over and brought up water from the trough in his cupped hands. Gus did the same, twice. When Gus turned around facing the old house, he saw Perfidia like some apparition in one gutted window, watching the two.

"Holy shit," Gus said. "Clay?"

"What?" Clay turned around.

"Who the hell's . . ."

Clay said nothing for a long moment, staring back at Perfidia. "Meet Perfidia, Gus," he said evenly and gestured toward the house.

Gus turned but Clay said nothing more. Instead, Clay walked away from Gus and went to his pickup, retrieved the clothing Bea had concealed on the seat and went into the house. In a few minutes, he rejoined Gus who had hunkered down, scratching at the ground with a stick. When Gus looked up at him, he saw Clay held a pair of worn boots.

"These didn't fit her," Clay said. "They're mine and way too big but we made do with them last night. She's got new shoes now. And a change of clothes. You won't have to worry about all that, Gus."

Gus rose and stood looking at Clay in bewilderment

but neither spoke. Finally Gus widened his eyes as if suddenly understanding, stepped away from Clay and said, "Hey, don't even think about it."

"I got no selection, Gus," Clay said. "I had to bring her out here last night with blankets and stuff when I came to gather these steers. She slept on the floor in there." He looked back toward the old house and thought about all the broken glass and insects. "Wasn't very comfortable I guess but things were closing in on her at the hotel. I figured that out as soon as I hit the road north of Solitario, buzzing with law vehicles. Just like Alvaro told me when I bumped into him on the back road."

Gus nodded. "Yeah, he told me about that too when he got in last night. Sounded like it was him, though, that did the bumping into. . . ."

"Yeah . . . well anyway, I figgered it was just a matter of time till they took her in and sent her back across the river." He paused and turned again to Gus. "And without her baby, Gus."

"I understand all that, Clay. But what in the hell can I do about it?"

"I just need some place for her to be," Clay said. "Until something else works out."

"Something else? Like what?"

"Well . . . something. We're gonna find that baby, Gus."

"Or maybe something like me getting led away in cuffs? Something like that?" Gus protested. "And it ain't *across* the river that they'll send me."

Gus sighed and walked away from Clay and went back to the water trough but he did not drink. He swished one hand around and around in the cool water and stared at his face warped in the ripples. He thought Clay had moved behind him, but when he turned, it was Perfidia who stood there. She had managed to pull on the canvas shoes and the new socks Jovita had brought for her and she held her old clothing bundled in her arms across her chest.

"Clayton said you would find my baby," she whispered. "You're Augústin?"

Gus looked at her, his face somber and determined. "I said I would *ask* around, that's all."

Clay moved to join them. "No Gus, you said Alvaro would."

Gus pulled Clay aside and held their backs to the woman. He whispered in a harsh voice, "Alvaro's leaving, goddammit. Back on the road. He may already be gone."

"You said not till after Cinco de Mayo," Clay reminded him. "Remember?"

"Yeah," Gus said. "And that's tomorrow but then he's gone again and—"

"I need your help, Gus . . . *she* needs your help."

"I'm sorry. . . ."

"Hey, if anybody's gonna get led away in cuffs, it's me."

"I said *no.*"

"Her baby needs your help, Gus. And she needs Alvaro's help too."

"How do you know she even has a kid? How do you know she's not just pulling something on all of you?"

"Look at her, Gus," Clay turned him around to face Perfidia. "Do them bruises on her face look like she'd be lying? And besides that—" he began but he stopped, too embarrassed to speak of the little pump he knew from Bea that Boone Maddox had given her. She held it hidden inside the bundle of torn clothing. "Well, you just gotta take my word for it. She's got an infant . . . somewhere. Trust me."

Clay watched Gus who did not ask for further explanation. Clay saw his face soften and soon Gus lowered his eyes and sighed. "Okay. But only because it's you, understand? What is it you got in mind?"

"Just take her with you, Gus. Keep her out there at Los Arbolitos until we can sort things out. They may just call off the search for the baby anyway since Perfidia's disappeared now too. Pressure would be off of us. They're thinking just like you did, Gus."

"Me?"

"Yeah," Clay said and he smiled at him. "That it's all a hoax."

"Well . . ." Gus said. "But I ain't keeping her long, understand? And I don't know what Alvaro will do."

"Did you talk?"

"Yes. But only about him asking around. And he even balked at that, just like I thought he would." Gus glanced over his shoulder at the woman and looked at her for a long while and finally said, "There hasn't been a woman at our place for a long time, Clay. It might get awkward."

"For you or for her?" Clay said.

"For Alvaro," Gus said. "And probably for her too."

"Maybe if he meets her, he'll change his mind," Clay said and then, "Like you just did."

"Don't count on it," Gus said. He walked away. "Get her inside the truck."

Clay crossed to Perfidia and said, "He's a good man. You can trust him."

"Where will you be?" she said.

"I'm not sure."

"Will I see you?"

"Yes. I'll come over soon as I can and let you know what's happening. But you have to stay out of sight. They won't find you over there."

"My baby?"

"We'll try hard. I'll get everybody I can into Presidio tomorrow to ask around during Cinco de Mayo. People get a few beers partying and sometimes get to talking. You keep up your hope. Gus is going to help."

"He said Alvaro?"

"Him too. The brother I told you about," Clay said but there was little confidence is his voice about this. "Now you need to get in the cab there. It'll be cool inside."

Perfidia nodded. Her limp was not as bad in the softer shoes but Clay helped her over to the truck anyway. Gus fired up the diesel engine when Clay opened the door for her. She looked up at Gus sitting sullen behind the wheel without looking back. Perfidia stiffened and turned to Clay.

"Go on," Clay said. "It's okay."

She stood for a moment and then said to Clay, *"Gracias."* She stepped up into the cab. "Thank you . . . again."

Clay nodded and without thinking said, "You got . . . *everything?"* She held up the bundle of torn clothing, the only things she owned. Clay regretted asking but he knew what she held concealed inside the clothing. "Stay low when you get out there on the blacktop," he said to her. "It's only for a few miles north and then you'll be on another back road." He shut the door.

Gus accelerated the rig and moved out onto the dirt road, the *corrientes* bawling and shuffling against the sides of the trailer. Clay watched the rig disappear inside a wall of dust and soon the diesel grew more muffled and then there was silence. The dust held, suspended in the morning air for a long while. Clay turned and walked back to the corral to Palo who stood under the windmill next to the cool water.

"I'll bring out more hay next time," he promised. "Maybe you can rest up now without them steers jostling you around in there."

He turned and walked over to Serafina's grave and stood for a moment. Then he remembered the purple flowers and he walked around the area but again, he saw none. He returned and with great pain, knelt on the rocky ground, today without the cushion for his knees.

"Can't stay long anyway, Sera," he said. He reached inside the little white fence and pulled a thistle sprung up through the cracks in the fieldstones. From the corral, Palo grumbled deep in his throat. Clay looked over at him. He ignored the stinging in his hand from the thistle and sat back on his heels to relieve some of the pain in his knees. He stared back at the grave and let his eyes go out of focus.

Inside his head, Clay sees the pregnant mare standing in that same spot where her foal, Palo, stands now as Serafina lay with the fever inside the house and his old pickup truck dead, the gasoline drained through the fresh hole in the bottom of the tank. He walks briskly to the old wagon behind the tack shed, pulls the broken wheel up out of the weeds and inspects it but he sees that the steel rim on the hub is still broken and not somehow miraculously repaired and he curses the wagon, "Goddammit!" But he knows he is also cursing himself for not mending it. And Clay recognizes he cannot depend on the old wagon to carry Serafina into town. And then he sees himself in the house and Adelita, frantic, clutching the child to herself on the bed, the rag in and out of the cool water but as useless as the truck and the wagon.

"It won't start," he says as if this statement will solve everything, as if this will bring Serafina out of the twilight and all will be well. But he knows this will not happen. "I'll have to go in and bring back Doc Maddox," he says and he tries for confidence in his voice. He knows it is sixteen miles by the dirt road and only a little shorter if he cuts through, riding the mare down the dry wash the back way, but then it is sixteen full miles back out in Doc Maddox's pickup. Adelita remains hysterical but she nods. Clay touches his wife on the cheek and then puts his palm on Serafina's head and feels her heat. He turns away briskly and leaves the house. Outside, he retrieves his old bridle and saddle from the tack shed and cinches the saddle onto the pregnant mare as tight as he feels he can, apologizing all the while. She protests for a moment, shifts away from him but then accepts the saddle and the bridle. "I'm sorry old gal, but we need you," he whispers. He mounts her and rides onto the road in a fast trot but he knows he cannot lope the mare nor can he keep up a fast trot for sixteen miles.

Then the late afternoon sun turns into thin rays of blood-orange behind him, like stilettos spiking out of the horizon and Clay turns in the saddle to look into it. And he curses the oncoming darkness because he knows the mare's pace has slowed and slowed from the fast trot to a walk and he cannot be but halfway there. In a short while, the mare begins to stumble on the rocky road and then begins to founder next to the culvert under the road that crosses the dry wash. He urges her on but finally, her knees collapse onto the ground. Clay gets off and stands with the reins in his hand. "Get up old girl," he begs. "It's not far now." But he knows that is a lie. She rolls to her side and breathes harder and Clay realizes that she is in labor. And he realizes he must choose to leave her and walk down the dry wash and on into Solitario or take the time to get the foal on the ground and then ride the mare the remainder of the distance. But he knows that even at a walk with a new foal beside her and Clay on her bareback, she can make it into Solitario faster than he can walking in his boots, so he leans to her ear and speaks to the mare in a whisper, "Okay, gal. Let's do this first. It won't take long."

He loosens the saddle and removes the bridle and tosses both to the side of the road. Then he goes back to her rear and feels around in the darkness and immediately, he knows she is dilated and the foal will come very quickly and that will be good. But it does not come quickly. It is a long and tortuous labor and an hour later, Clay finally reaches up inside the mare and feels the legs of the foal and knows it is breech. His heart sinks. He sits on the dirt road and swallows hard and fights back tears of anger because he knows he must act very quickly now. He retrieves the bridle and takes it back to the rear end of the mare. He loops each rein into a slipknot and then reaches back inside the birth canal where he finally is able to secure the slipknots over the legs of the foal. Then he kneels and puts the bridle over his head and around his chest and exhales. And he pulls. But nothing moves. Then he pulls again, leaning his weight into the bridle and this time, he feels some movement. He continues to pull a little at a time and slowly the foal begins to emerge. He feels a sudden release and he knows the foal is almost free. He turns around and takes each leg in a hand and pulls one final time. The foal comes out onto the dirt road and there is a little movement and then there is more movement. Clay stands and takes out his pocketknife and cuts the cord and in a short while, the foal is also standing.

Clay is breathing hard. But the mare lies still. He calls toward her head but there is no response. He moves over and feels behind her and then realizes that a great mass of her insides have also come out and she is dead and this cold knowledge hammers him back to his knees. This time, he allows the sobs to surge in a heaving staccato into the darkness.

At the graveside, Clay straightened and remembered that there had been none of this shooting pain in his knees inside that blackness all those years ago. Not inside his younger knees. All the pain at that moment had stabbed directly through his chest and needled his exhausted lungs. His heart lay on the hard ground next to his mare which the foal now tried uselessly to nurse. The rest was just motion, also useless. And numbness. He left the foal standing next to the dead mare and walked down the dry wash on into Solitario and hours later he and an also much younger Jovita Seals shook a groggy Doc Maddox awake in the hotel and he and Doc made a skidding and tossing trip back to his house in Doc's pickup. It was too late.

"I'm sorry, Sera," Clay said as he knelt beside her now. "I'm so sorry, baby. I did all I could," he said but even decades later he wondered if he truly had. He straightened one side of the little white picket fence he had painted just last Saturday on her birthday. But the fence needed no straightening.

Adelita had never truly accepted Serafina's death because to do this would be to acknowledge Clayton's guilt as well. Even though she stayed in the adobe house and went through the motions, she was never the same. And so Clay himself grew ambivalent but not toward their house or even the harsh rangeland that had insulated them from the remainder of the world. He simply fell into a perpetual lovers' quarrel with isolation, the self-imposed solitude that had always fed some unarticulated need. But he knew it had taken Serafina from him. And in his heart, Clay knew it had also taken Adelita, long before the cancer did.

"I'm gonna move you, baby," he whispered and now the words sounded hollow and impotent but he spoke the remainder of the litany anyway. "I'm gonna move you in there with your mama. And I'll find those flowers. I promise. . . ." He struggled to his feet and looked around his old place, the splintering corral and the frail old gelding and the tack shed with the mute ranch wagon in back, all constant reminders of Clay's culpability. And the weeds, more tenacious than ever, and now the crumbling house to match everything else, all collapsing around him in the inertia of complete neglect. "But I just felt like I had to move someone else first. . . ." ❧

CHAPTER 15

"They never did celebrate much on this one," Gus said to Alvaro. "Maybe you were too young to remember." Gus sat at the little round table in the kitchen speaking of their parents to his brother who stood at the stove. "Cinco de Mayo isn't what a lot of people think it is anyway. Not across the border here in Texas, not even some Mexican citizens who haven't been here long. But our folks knew it was not Mexico's Independence Day. They always celebrated the *real* one on September first, not May fifth."

"What's today all about then?" Alvaro asked because he knew his older brother wanted him to.

"Today's about a whole different thing. But it's important too. Cinco de Mayo is when Mexico kicked the shit out of the French down there and ran them out of the country. You should know that, Alvaro." Gus thought about the days he had sent false messages concerning Alvaro missing school as a teenager. Gus held no illusion that his brother even knew Texas history, much less anything about their parents' Mexican heritage.

"If you want to know the truth, I don't give a shit what either one is," Alvaro said. He poured himself a cup of coffee. "I just like to go in and eat the *carne asado* and drink beer at Julio's Bar. That's where everyone else who doesn't give a shit will be, out of the sun, in where it's cool. And did I mention, drinking cold beer?"

"Then you *will* go?"

"To Presidio? Oh yeah," Alvaro said. "Hell, this is the only vacation I ever get, right? One day, and it don't make a shit to me what holiday it might be across the border or over here either."

"You can take as many days as you want, Alvaro," Gus said. "You know that, even if you don't know what holiday it is. And you'll ask around?"

"Hey, that's some deal between you and Clayton Elliott," Alvaro said. He joined Gus at the table, his back to the hallway. "It's none of my business."

"You better eat something."

Alvaro picked up an orange from a bowl on the table, inspected it, put it back. "Not hungry."

"I could fix him something," a voice came back. Perfidia had padded in silence down the hallway, her bare and healing feet cooled on the maroon Mexican tile. She had stood at the doorway, listening behind them. "Or for both of you?"

Alvaro held his coffee mug suspended. Even though it was a strange voice, he did not seem startled. He looked over the mug at his older brother and frowned, but Alvaro did not turn around to the voice. "Well, I haven't had that kind of offer in years," he said. "Not in this house anyway."

Perfidia moved into the kitchen and stood near the table, waiting. She had showered and dressed in the new clothes and brushed her long hair until it shone like a raven's wing. Gus looked first at Alvaro and then both stared at Perfidia, her quiet beauty escaping neither, even with a cut lip and bruised cheek and bare feet. But she appeared as though she had not slept well and there was no vitality in her face. No one spoke for a long moment.

"That'd be fine . . ." Gus finally said and then said her name. " . . . Perfidia."

"Perfidia?" Alvaro studied her. "You'd be—"

"The one I told you about," Gus interrupted.

"You never said she was back there, brother," Alvaro said.

"You weren't around when I came in yesterday," Gus reminded him.

Alvaro moved his hand across his morning beard. "You said you brought Clay's steers over. You never said you brought something else." He looked at Gus. "She's pretty quiet . . . for a woman."

Perfidia lowered her eyes. "I can make something to eat," she repeated, her voice almost inaudible.

"What?" Alvaro said. "I couldn't hear you." He continued to study his brother.

"I said I could make something," she raised her chin and spoke louder. "If that will be okay?"

"Sure," Alvaro said. "Whatever. Hey, I'm just the little brother, right? But I don't know what you'll find in that refrigerator except mold."

"There's eggs," Gus offered. He rose and crossed to the refrigerator and opened the door, inspected the contents. "And bacon." He turned around and held the door and smiled. "See? And hey, beans."

Alvaro snorted, shook his head. Perfidia allowed herself a taut smile and moved over beside Gus. "You sit," she said.

"Hey, she's taking right over," Alvaro said. "First thing you know we'll be having to shave and then who knows, maybe even shower."

"Wouldn't hurt a bit," Gus grumbled. He poured another mug of coffee, set it on the counter for Perfidia who was already cracking eggs into a skillet. She lit the stove and laid strips of bacon on the grill. Gus refilled his mug and brought the coffeepot over and refilled Alvaro's. "Especially you."

He took the pot back to the stove. "You sure I can't help?" he said. Perfidia shook her head, set the skillet with the eggs on a burner and poked a spatula at the bacon which began to hiss. He returned and sat across from Alavaro, his back to her now. He watched his brother's face, a picture of skepticism, Alvaro's lips mouthing the silent words, "You stupid shit!"

Gus sighed, shrugged, avoided his brother's glare.

Perfidia soon brought over plates of scrambled eggs and bacon and warm tortillas. She dumped the stale coffee grounds, filled it again and set a fresh pot on the stove to perk. Alvaro immediately tucked into the hot food but Gus kept his palms on his knees. He looked around at Perfidia. "You're eating too," he invited. Alvaro looked up over a forkful of eggs but he did not slow down.

"I'm not hungry," she muttered and moved toward the hallway.

Gus rose and stood in front of her. "Yes you are," he said. "You didn't have a thing yesterday . . . all day. You sit over there." He gestured at the third chair and then went to the cupboard and pulled out another plate, filled it from the stove and brought it over. He placed the food on the table. "Now sit."

Alvaro smiled at all this. "Better do as he says. Like I told you, he's the big brother."

They ate in silence. Alvaro finished first, mopping his plate with the last of a tortilla. He rose and started to leave but Gus said, "Your plate. You always forget that."

Alvaro paused, looked up at the ceiling and turned around. "Okay, mama," he said. He took the plate and mug to the sink, reached into the cupboard for a toothpick and once again moved to leave.

"Sit down, Alvaro." Gus said this with the authority Alvaro had not heard since he was a teenager. When Alvaro turned, he wore the same sullen attitude Gus had seen most of his life. Gus stopped chewing and stared at his brother. Perfidia tensed but she did not look up.

"I'll just stand," Alvaro said, a declaration that he might listen, but at his age now, he would not be obeying his brother. He crossed his arms and leaned against the doorjamb and chewed the toothpick. And he waited.

Gus swallowed, sipped his coffee and then leaned back in his chair. "We might as well get all this out," he said. He looked at Perfidia who stared at her half-eaten food. "Look at us, Perfidia."

"What can I say?" she whispered and looked up into the surly face of Alvaro. "They have my baby. Isn't that enough?" She began to cry.

"If we're going to help," Gus said softly. "We need more than that. Don't you see?"

She looked at Gus and shrugged and said, "What more?" Then she turned to Alvaro, repeated it and he heard her voice crack. He dropped his arms to his sides and removed the toothpick. His face softened a little.

"Well, who are we looking for?" Gus said. "How many? What do they look like? That'd be a start."

"Two," she said but she seemed uncertain. She shook her head and said, "I don't know, just two guys. Mexicans from Ojinaga."

"Two Mexicans?" Alvaro entered the conversation. "Hey, that's a big help. I just need to go into Presidio, drink a few beers during the celebration and look around town and in the bar for a couple of Mexicans, right? Maybe walking around with a baby?"

"I thought you weren't going to help?" Gus said to him.

"I'm not," Alvaro said and then, "I mean I *might* not."

"One had a hard time walking," Perfidia continued, encouraged now by what she was hearing. "I think he may have been hurt or something."

"Maybe he had bad shoes," Alvaro said. "Mexican made shoes will do that."

"They weren't shoes," Perfidia said and she seemed to be remembering details now. "Boots. Both of them wore boots."

"Mexican boots?" Alvaro said. "That'd be even worse. How do you know this?"

She looked at him and her eyes hardened and then she spoke haltingly, as if remembering something she had tried to forget. "Because they kicked me with them . . . and kicked me some more when I came out of the river. . . ." She buried her face in her hands.

"And then they took her baby," Gus finished for her. He glowered at his brother. Alvaro looked away, said nothing. "What kind?" Gus continued. "What color?"

Perfidia stopped sobbing but she spoke with her cupped palms over her face. "I don't know. Maybe gray . . . with a . . . a white tip."

"Okay," Gus said but he knew she was not certain of this. "Anything else he should watch for?"

"He?" Alvaro injected. "I never said I'd do it yet. Not for sure."

"My baby," Perfidia said evenly and she looked up now at Alvaro with enough cold intensity that even he could not hold his eyes on hers. "He should watch for my baby, that's all. My baby daughter." She stood for a moment and then picked up Gus's plate as well as her own and took them to the sink. She began running hot water over the dishes.

"You don't have to do that," Gus said. "We need to talk anyway. Just me and Alvaro."

Perfidia looked back at him and understood. When she moved past Alvaro in the doorway she said, "I'll wash them later."

When she was gone, Gus sat silent. Alvaro worked on the toothpick until it was frayed and then moved back to his chair at the table.

"What were you thinking, anyway?" Alvaro said. "Something about all this don't sound right to me, brother. How'd she wind up over here anyway?"

"I brought her over yesterday," Gus began. "I told you that. Clay had to move her out of the hotel in Solitario where Bea Hernandez was hiding her. I guess things were heating up and they worried she might get sent back."

"Yeah," Alvaro said. "Like I told you when I came

in, I saw all that heat myself, on the highway Monday night. So what?"

"Sent back across the river without her baby," Gus said. "That's what."

"So?" Alvaro sat sullen. He toyed with the toothpick in his hand, rolled it between his thumb and forefinger. "You know, I just don't get it, brother. Why is this any of our concern? Hell, there's thousands of Mexicans wading the river every day and it's just going to keep on. And probably a lot of them have babies that get snatched too."

"And a lot of them die," Gus said. "Locked in some boxcar in hundred-degree heat . . . without water."

"Okay, so it's not right," Alvaro conceded. "But why should we get involved with this one? Why not just turn it over to the law? Hell, they're not going to just send her back without her kid."

"Maybe not," Gus said. "But you don't know that. And neither does anyone else who knows about her. Even Locket Wagner knows."

"Wagner? And *he's* looking the other way?" Alvaro shook his head. *"Damn!"*

"Not exactly. But he's not being aggressive either," Gus said. "At least, that's what Clay tells me. And besides, Locket says they might just call it a hoax because she's disappeared now and let it go at that."

"Well?"

"Well, if that happens, it gives us more time to see if we can find her baby."

"We?" Alvaro scoffed. He shoved his chair away and stood. "Just because all of you guys have bought into this doesn't mean I have. What's everyone else doing? Is

it just on my back?"

"I never said that. Clay says they'll be looking around today too," Gus said. "In Presidio and all over. Just more eyes, but . . ."

"Great, we'll all just have one big party at Julio's," Alvaro said. "You know, me and Clay and Locket and Bea and Jovita Seals and, oh yeah, them two *coyotes* from across the border and hey, don't forget, with that baby they got too. Just one big happy family at Julio's. And what about you?"

Gus looked at him but he did not reply.

"What are you going to do?" Alvaro pressed.

"I'm not good at that," Gus finally said. "I mean crowds and all."

"Oh," Alvaro said. "I see. You don't drive cattle rigs, you don't deal with rodeo promoters, you don't cook and you don't do crowds." He leaned on the table and into his brother's face. "What the hell *do* you do around here?"

Gus fell silent again. He looked hard at Alvaro as if he might cuff him, like he had done many times in the past in helpless frustration when a teenaged Alvaro seemed to be completely out of control, drinking and missing school and wrecking one pickup after another.

"I failed you, brother. After they were both gone," Gus said quietly. "I know that. I won't make excuses. But it was hard for me, too, losing both of them so close together. I had no idea what to do with a wild young kid. And I think I lived each day in a kind of panic over it until it became just part of our lives. Must have been hard for you, living in fear. Maybe it hardened you too much."

"Maybe," Alvaro said. "But we're doing okay now."

"No we're not," Gus said. "Sure, the business is fine and we've done okay there, but . . ."

"But what?"

Gus studied Alvaro's face for a long while and finally said, "Why the drugs, *Alvarito?* If it's all okay, why the drugs?"

"What drugs?" Alvaro narrowed his eyes and tried for indignation but it did not work on his brother.

"You know what drugs," Gus said. "The same ones that broke up both of your marriages, the same ones you talk about as 'extra fuel' on the trips." He paused again and then said, "Maybe cocaine, for a start?"

"Bullshit!" Alvaro rose abruptly and turned his back. "That's total bullshit."

"Maybe," Gus said. "But I don't think so. I'm not stupid."

"There's no *maybe* about it," Alvaro scoffed. "Okay, I use something once in a while, just to keep me on the road twenty hours straight, goddammit. Just to stay out there pushing Muñoz Brothers's stock. But never cocaine. And I *never* pushed anything but our livestock, either."

"Look at me, Alvaro," Gus said but Alvaro held his back to him. *"Look* at me!"

Alvaro turned around and said, "What are you going to do, brother? Hit me?"

"I'm past that," Gus said. "Long ago. What I wanted to say was . . . you're my brother, *Alvarito.* Family. And dammit, I love you."

Alvaro seemed stunned. He could not remember

his brother ever saying that, or if he had, the words were long lost in the fog of his hard living.

"And if this isn't something you want to do," Gus went on. "Then don't do it. *Any* of it."

Alvaro stood silent for a long moment and then his face yielded a little and he said, "It's no problem. Hell, I'd be in Julio's either way today. After all, it is Cinco de Mayo, right? I'll ask around."

"I don't mean just that," Gus said. "Not just that woman's problem back there. I mean everything. I mean the business, everything. I don't want to pick up your cold body beside some interstate, crushed inside one of our rigs, or bleeding in a ditch behind some bar."

"That won't happen."

"How do you know?"

"I'm more careful than that."

"I don't think so, Alvaro," Gus said. He moved over and tried to put his hand on his brother's shoulder but Alvaro stepped away. "Think about it, though. What are you doing different than you did fifteen years ago? When you were totally out of control, drinking and wrecking pickups?"

"I'm different," Alvaro assured him. "And how about yourself, brother? How much beer did you guzzle lately?"

"More than I should," Gus confessed. "I know that. And maybe it's a poor excuse and maybe I should give it up too, but . . ."

"But what?"

"Well, I'm not out there on the interstate all fuzzed out," Gus said. "And that worries me too, Alvaro. If something happened out there, it might not be you dead in the ditch. It might be some van full of school kids. Could you live with that?"

"I'm telling you it's not like that," Alvaro said but there was no certainty in his voice. "I'm just more alert doing it this way. That's all."

"Then why not just coffee?"

Alvaro had no response.

"Okay," Gus said. "I'm just asking you to think about it. And if selling out the business is what we need to do then selling out is what we'll do." He moved away from Alvaro and walked into the hallway. "That's all I'm asking," he repeated.

"Hey, don't worry about it, brother. I'll be real serious today. For that woman back there." He watched Gus disappear into the hallway. "And her baby." After a long while he spoke again but Gus could not hear this, "If she's even got one, which I doubt. But I'll do it for you, too, brother." ❧

CHAPTER 16

Locket walked into Julio's in Presidio at midday on Cinco de Mayo and, to his surprise, found a single barstool still vacant. When he saw Locket, Julio moved from the far end, drew a frosted mug half full of tonic water, twisted a lime in it and set it in front of him.

"You want the rest of that filled with gin, right?" Julio said. He pretended to reach for a gin bottle.

"Yeah . . . right," Locket said. "I always do that on holidays." He sipped the tonic water. "Especially when it's hot and I'm on duty and everyone in the county is watching me right now. Go ahead."

"Well, I'm afraid you'd arrest me for not checking your ID," Julio said. He toweled the bar in front of Locket with one hand and swept over a bowl of chips and then salsa with the other. "Have some lunch, anyway."

"Is this a bribe?" Locket dug into the chips, dipped one into the salsa and buried it inside his mouth. He spoke around the food. "If so, that's even worse."

"No." Julio said. "If I wanted to bribe you, I'd do it with cocaine."

"Is that happening today?" The word was an instant red flag to Locket. He paused, narrowed his eyes at Julio but then helped himself to more chips. After he had left Jovita on the blacktop to Solitario, he spent much of Monday night driving the back roads for any sign of Perfidia or anything else unusual, but he found nothing so he went on into Solitario for the remainder of the night. Tuesday, he did the same in the daylight with the same negative results.

"You figure it out," Julio said and shrugged. "It's Cinco de Mayo, isn't it?"

"Something you wanna tell me, Julio?"

"Well, I don't rat on my customers," Julio said. "You know that. Besides, I wouldn't know if it did happen. These guys in here are just beer drinkers and a little tequila, that's all."

"Well let me put it this way, Julio. If someone *was* to be doing it, who'd you most suspect?"

"What is this, a drug bust?"

"Just doing the job you elected me to do," Locket said. "Something like what we're dancing around could lead to all sorts of things."

"I didn't vote for you," Julio confessed. "But my wife did."

"Who'd you vote for?"

"I don't vote," Julio said. "A bartender has to be neutral, you know." He saw Locket push aside the chip bowl with only crumbs left in it. "You still hungry?"

Locket looked at him. "I'm on duty."

"Yeah, I know," Julio said and then repeated, "You still hungry?"

Locket looked at him but said nothing.

"You're still hungry," Julio said. "It's only *carne adovada* today though. You're probably not interested."

Locket looked beyond Julio and spoke to his own

image staring back from the mirror behind the bar. "Arrest this man for bribery."

Julio smiled and disappeared into the kitchen. Locket sipped his tonic water and looked again into the mirror, this time surveying the noisy crowd behind him. He knew Julio was right. This group of locals might drink a few too many beers on a holiday, but they were mostly good citizens who held political offices and paid their taxes and sent their kids to school and worked hard. All were well aware of their proximity to the Mexican border and all the problems that presented. But these were second- or third-generation citizens from Mexican immigrants themselves, and some were first generation, but all regarded highly their status in their new country. These citizens were often more harsh than the authorities were on illegal Mexican nationals, and especially the human smugglers, who cast a bad reflection on the entire Hispanic community on both sides of the border. There would not be a person in his view at the moment that would be dealing drugs or harboring *coyotes,* especially with a baby for sale.

And that is why Locket became more than curious when Julio set the steaming platter of *carne adovada* and beans and tortillas in front of him, leaned closer and whispered, "Alvaro Muñoz was in. Him and another guy."

Locket looked wistfully at the food but held back. "When?"

"Earlier this morning," Julio said.

"Drinking?"

"Oh yeah," Julio said. He set more hot sauce in front of Locket. "But that's all."

"All?"

"As far as I know. Just beer. At least in here."

"Who was he?" Locket could hold off no longer. He tucked into the food.

"Don't know," Julio said. "Never saw him before."

"Yeah?" Locket said. He chewed, nodded, swallowed. "What'd he look like?"

"Alvaro? Well, he seemed a little high," Julio said. "But he usually does. Long as I've known him anyway. He'd started celebrating early, I guess. That other guy looked a little too nervous for just being over here enjoying a holiday."

"Well, we get a lot of people back and forth on Cinco de Mayo," Locket said. "But you know that. Nobody thinks too much about it, especially today."

"I know," Julio said. "I serve a lot of them. Nothing illegal about that. No more than you having a beer over there. And that's why I notice things."

"Things?"

"Yeah," Julio said. "They weren't just having a friendly drink. I think Alvaro was getting pissed off about something and started raising his voice and then the other guy got pissed off too and they finally just left out the back door without finishing their beers."

"You hear anything at all?"

"You kidding? Listen inside here right now. . . ."

"Yeah," Locket said. He forked more meat into his mouth and nodded. "I'm barely hearing you this close. Anything else?"

"He was dressed pretty slick, for an Ojinagan. If that's what he was."

"How so?"

"Fancy shirt, snaps on the pockets and boots with those silver tips on the toes."

"Boots?"

"Yeah. Real sharp toes. Looked like some of that fancy skin, alligator or lizard or something like that. I could see them in that neon sign on the wall by their table when I took over their beers. "

"Yeah?"

"Looked dark gray in that light, but hey, I dunno. Coulda been black. Kinda goofy looking if you ask me," Julio said and stepped back. "You seen these?" With pride, he lifted one foot into the bar light.

"Nice," Locket said but he could not see the boot well in the pink neon beer sign. "They look a little pink to me. But nice, Julio. Very nice."

Julio lowered the boot and moved close again. "Compliments will get you nowhere. You just want a refill on the tonic, that's what you're after."

"Nope," Locket said and drained the mug. "But hey, I wouldn't look down on another plate of *adovada.*"

Julio nodded, considered Locket's left-handed compliment, and then took the platter and said, "You got it."

He returned with another pile of meat on the platter and he refilled Locket's mug. "That's the end of it," he said. "Don't Bea ever feed you over there at the hotel?"

"Not today," Locket said and started on the meat again. "And incidentally, I'm a paying customer, *there* and *here.*"

"Yeah, right," Julio said. He looked around the

barroom. "Where's all your friends? They usually come in on Cinco de Mayo."

"My friends *are* here," Locket said. "If they're old enough to drink, they're old enough to vote. But if you mean Jovita, she said she was coming, but decided against it I guess. Too hot maybe. Bea's over here somewhere. Probably at the bingo hall where it's cool."

"Yeah," Julio said. "Well, neither one of them two exactly keep my bottom line in the black. And it's a cinch Bea wouldn't be eating my *carne adovada* here."

Locket nodded but declined to compare Julio's *adovada* with Bea's. "Clay musta had something else going on this morning too. I guess he's coming over later and the rest don't really celebrate this holiday."

Locket finished the food and sighed heavily. He turned away from Julio and looked into the crowd which was getting noisier. "I guess I'd better get back to work."

"Work?" Julio scoffed.

"Yeah," Locket said. He spun back around on the stool. "Some people do have to work, even on holidays. How much I owe you?"

"It's on your tab," Julio said. "Just don't forget where you got it and be sure to swing back by here later this evening. I'll still be *working.* You'll probably be able to earn your dinner in here by then. I might even have a customer for you."

"Well . . ." Locket sucked his teeth and retrieved a toothpick from a nearby holder and rose. "Sure nice and cool in here," he said, trying for sympathy from Julio. He got none. "It'll be hotter'n hell inside my patrol car by now," he said to no one and then back to Julio, "You say they went out the rear door?"

"Alvaro?"

"Yeah."

"That's right. The other guy was close behind him. Real close."

"Pushing him?"

Julio frowned and looked aside. "You know, it's hard to tell in here, Lock. I didn't hear them, but come to think of it, he did have a hand on Alvaro's shoulder when they opened the door."

"I thought you said they'd been riled up?"

"Hey, he could'a been shoving him, how do I know? Hell, I was busy, Lock."

Locket nodded. "Stay cool," he said and walked through the crowd toward the front door, then changed his mind and came back. His stool at the bar was already filled before Locket exited the rear door. ❧

CHAPTER 17

Clayton Elliott had never dwelled on the mortality of others in Solitario. As devastating as it was, the irony about Serafina's death was that it had become a birth for Clay's other obsession. Her tragic ending had established a beginning from which a painful focus on his own mortality—and Adelita's mortality—would spring. Of course, Serafina's dying never left him or Adelita. It simply layered itself like some dark collage across each day for all those intervening years and then with even greater agony during the long days of Adelita's dying. And since he had buried his wife, everything else paled in comparison to the single certainty of his mortality, leaving only the pain itself as the very core of Clayton Elliott. With the *corrientes* gone and the selling of his place also a certainty and the imminent reuniting of Serafina with her mother, the only other thing driving him now was his parallel compulsion to do the same for Perfidia with her own daughter.

Clay did not question the added irony of this new situation either. It was simply something he had to do. If it mirrored his own private hell—to reconnect things from his past to his present—he simply had not had time to ponder that either. Too much had to be done. And so placing Perfidia in the hands of his oldest and closest friend, Gus Muñoz, was just one more step toward moving Serafina.

And his decision to avoid all the celebration on this Cinco de Mayo also sprung from that core, to reconcile at least for a few hours his deep need for isolation against his primary mission which involved the help of others in moving his baby daughter. Today, he needed to avoid crowds and noise and speak quietly to Adelita about all this.

He left the hotel well before the breakfast hour because he knew Bea would not be serving on this holiday anyway. He had promised Perfidia that he would get everyone into Presidio to look around today, but yesterday when he had asked Jovita to do this, she smiled at him and said, "Look around for who? Perfidia? Come on, Clay, you know she's not in danger now."

He was surprised a little by Jovita's statement until he realized how transparent his sneaking Perfidia out of Bea's apartment on Monday night had been. And Bea was not the best at hiding things either. Jovita was not stupid.

"Okay, I don't need to play games with you, Jo," he had said. "Of course I know where she is and you're right. She's safe."

"That's fine," Jo said. "Somebody needed to do that with all the pressure coming. I don't even want to know where. I just need to know if the baby is still missing and I'll keep doing whatever I can on that, okay?"

"It's still missing," he said. "I don't know what Alvaro will—" He stopped, another secret exposed, and looked at Jovita who averted her eyes and pretended not to hear. "Well, just say that *someone* else besides Locket is involved now and maybe he can help."

"Listen, Clay," Jo said. "It's fine and I hope it all works out for her. I'll get with Lock at least and see if he'll let me ride over with him tomorrow. He's found out a few things but I don't expect anything big to happen on Cinco de Mayo. Why in hell would *coyotes* come out to celebrate? Are they just going to walk into Julio's with a baby in their arms and order a beer?"

"Probably not," Clay confessed. "It'd just be good if we kept looking, I guess."

"You're not coming over tomorrow?" she said.

"Not right away," he said. "I gotta do something else first."

"Oh," she said but did not question him.

"I just want to go by and see Adelita and let her know what's happening and . . . it's always been a special day for her too."

"Right."

"I'll come on over later, okay?"

"Sure, Clay," she said. "I understand."

Jovita had been right yesterday, he thought as he walked through Solitario now toward the graveyard. Clay wondered if they were all being impractical about finding an abducted infant. Perhaps he should not have moved Perfidia. Perhaps he should have just let Locket and the law take over and place the young woman in their hands.

It was certain that Dobb and Yebbie wanted no part of it. Clay was not stupid either. These two old friends, who would otherwise have been right in the thick of it, had no reason to see Clay stop this search.

They viewed it simply as a delay in his moving Serafina, and that served their purposes quite nicely now. They knew Clayton Elliott and they understood perhaps better than Clay himself why he would not be moving Serafina until this other baby was found and back in the arms of its mother. It did not take a psychologist to figure that out. What Clay did understand, and now accept, was that this delay for whatever reason allowed the county commissioners time to get a water board established before he moved Serafina. And this delay, of course, prevented Agua Hondo from drilling. Or at least it would slow them down until some regulations could be put in place. But that remained a larger problem for the county commissioners, not for Clayton Elliot.

But if drilling the aquifer were inevitable, so too was the eventuality that Serafina would lie next to her mother in the graveyard, both under that great cottonwood tree. Clay was determined to see that. So on this Cinco de Mayo morning it was with an increasing feeling of apprehension and then dark despair that Clay moved toward the fresh mound of earth directly adjacent Adelita's grave in the shadow of that gigantic and solitary cottonwood, the only tree in the cemetery.

He stood over the newly opened gravesite and spoke into it in a businesslike voice, as if by doing so he could prevent something. "Whoever you are," he heard himself say. "You're going to be in the wrong place." He looked around for someone, anyone with valid authority, who might hear him.

"You'll be in the wrong place," he repeated louder. He went to the other side of Adelita's grave where another headstone had long marked the resting place of

Jackson Kelley, a long deceased citizen. He stood there for a moment and then went back to the fresh grave on the other side of Adelita and spoke again, "She'll be blocked in, don't you see?" Then he moved to stand at the foot of his wife's grave as advocate to argue his case further. "Whoever you are, you'll be over here, see . . ." he pointed at the hole and then back to the other man's grave. " . . . and old man Kelley's been over there for years and Adelita would be trapped between you two. But see, Serafina needs to be right where you've dug, right here next to her mama and . . ."

Clay stopped. He looked up through the leaves on the cottonwood tree. Thin shafts of morning light lay across his face making shadows like iron bars. His eyes filled but he held the wail inside his lungs until he could not bear it and then it came out as a long and mournful whine, just like the night he had lost Serafina, and again when he had lost Adelita. But no one heard him this time either.

He moved and sat heavily onto the ground, his back against the cottonwood tree, and he stared into the empty grave. "Who are you?" he whispered, over and over. He could not remember anyone mentioning a death in Solitario. But that was not unusual. Many of the old timers from the surrounding area passed away quietly and were buried without fanfare because that's the way they wanted it. They lived in isolation and died in isolation and preferred to be buried that way, many on their own ranches in the hard ground they had battled their entire lives. And had Clay been able to sustain his own isolation, that's exactly where Adelita would be: beside Serafina out there at their homestead where he too could be someday. But all hope for the three being together out there was gone now.

He rubbed his palms across his face and pressed his eyes with the tips of his fingers as if to wipe away this self-indulgent and momentary lapse of determination.

"I shoulda locked in Sera's gravesite, Adelita." He stood and thought about this, trying to lay in place the steps he had taken for all this, the steps he had not. "Don't matter how many people I've told about moving her, I just never got the paperwork done on it. Even in Solitario, you gotta follow some rules." He thought about rules and how few he had ever followed in his lifetime and how he had needed no rules whatsoever to bury Serafina. "I guess that's it," he admonished himself to Adelita. "I'm sorry."

He looked at her grave again and waited a long time, thinking about how often he had said those two words to Adelita. He tried to see her face inside the dark earth or to hear her voice, some absolution, but nothing came back.

Finally he said to her, "I'll just have to see if I can stop this other burial, Adelita. Somehow." He pushed himself up and stood again and stared at Adelita's expensive granite headstone. And he thought about the white crushed rocks he had purchased for the mound of earth covering her, all of which had taken not one second of his grief away. "And dammit, I gotta stop wallowing in my own torment, Adelita. Get off my ass and stop feeling sorry for myself."

He looked again into the empty grave and shook his head. "But who the hell *are* you?" he whispered and glanced down the main street of Solitario and wondered if Henry Bennett would be awake this early. "He'd know," he said. "It shouldn't be any trouble to dig a different grave for this person somewhere else, especially with a county backhoe. And if anybody can change a county gravesite, it'd be Henry." ❧

CHAPTER 18

When Clay walked out of the cemetery and onto the main street of Solitario, he saw Jovita entering her car in front of her hotel. She backed into the street, but when she saw Clay, she pulled again to the curb and waited for him, her engine idling. She rolled down the window on the passenger side when he approached.

"Get in," she said.

Clay opened the door and sat. He removed his hat and turned his face into the air conditioner which had begun to cool down the inside of Jovita's car. He did not look at her. He said nothing.

"I thought you might be in Presidio," Jovita finally said. "I never heard you come in last night. Locket's already gone."

"What the hell could I do in there?" Clay said. He would not look at her. "Ain't I done enough?"

"You've done plenty, Clay." She leaned forward to look at him, but he turned his face and stared up the street.

"Well . . ." he said.

"More than any of us," she said.

"Maybe it's time to just let Lock take over," Clay said and turned to her. "I'm tired, Jo."

"What's happened, Clay?" she said. "Where is she?"

"If you mean my baby girl," he said. "She's still out there in the ground under that hot sun."

"I know." Jovita looked away now.

"If you mean Adelita," he continued. "She's up there in the cemetery. By herself. Under the cool shade of that old cottonwood."

"I know that too, Clay," she said. She turned and touched his arm. "But that's not who I meant either. You know that."

He wiped the inside of his hatband with a palm, set it back on his head. Neither said anything. They sat and listened to the whirring of the air conditioner and the idling of the engine. Finally, Clay leaned back against the seat and brought his hat over his eyes.

"Go on, Clay," Jovita said. Her reaction was not one of surprise. "Sounds like you need to just talk it all out. Nobody can hear you but me right now."

"I'm just weary, Jo," Clay said from under the hat and then, "Perfidia's with Gus, if that's who you mean. I moved her out to my old place Monday night with some blankets and stuff. She slept out there. It was getting a little heated up and I just didn't know what else to do with her. Bea knew."

"I know that. I knew it when I saw Bea's eyes yesterday morning. And then the clothes I bought her were suddenly gone and I knew she hadn't just run off. And if Bea knew, I figured she was fine. That's why I didn't panic." Jovita smiled. "You two would make terrible criminals."

"I didn't want Locket to know," Clay said. "And I didn't want you to feel like you had to lie to him. It'd just be an added burden for him and you both. He's got enough on his mind."

"Yes."

"Gus came over for my *corrientes* and he took her on over to Los Arbolitos yesterday. She'll be safe there for now. I stayed out there till dark looking for those little purple flowers Sera loved. You know the kind, Jo? No bigger than your thumbnail?"

"I know. I don't see them much anymore either."

"Damned drought," Clay said. "I looked all around the place and even over into Alamito Creek but nothing."

"Yes."

"She's fine," Clay went on. "Gus says Alvaro promised to ask around over there in Presidio today." He sat up and moved his hat back in place. "And that's the best I can do right now, goddammit."

"Hey, nobody's saying you need to do a thing," Jovita scolded. "You've taken this thing with Perfidia on yourself, Clay. And I think it's wonderful and if pressed, so does everyone else. Dobb and Yebbie and all of them. But it's not all yours to—"

"She's a mother. She needs to have her baby with her," Clay interrupted. "That's all. And maybe that makes it my concern more than anybody else's."

"I understand . . ."

"Maybe you don't," he said. "Maybe nobody does."

"But I know what happened, Clayton," Jovita said. "With Serafina all those years ago. And I also know why. You can't carry that around with you the rest of your life, Clay."

He sat silent.

"And I know how it was at the end with Adelita," she went on. "All that's been hard for you. But you have to remember that you weren't alone in any of this, Clay. And you're not now. You have friends. You always have."

"I know, I know. . . ."

"Well, give some of that load to *us*," she said. "You know that Locket and Gus and even Alvaro will do what they can about this woman and her baby. And Dobb and Yebbie didn't say they wouldn't help move Serafina, they just want to know more about this water thing and—"

"I understand all that, Jo. But how do you think I feel about it? Knowing I probably set that water problem in action too and the one thing—the *only* thing I wanted—was just to get Adelita settled in some peaceful place and then move our baby next to her. But that's all been shot to hell now. Maybe if I'd been able to get it done sooner, that woman and her baby wouldn't have been a problem for any of us. Maybe if I'd paid more attention to things—"

"Stop it, Clayton," Jovita said and shook his arm. "Just stop feeling sorry for yourself. Nobody's saying you caused Serafina's death. Or Adelita's either. And it's ridiculous to feel like you alone are responsible for finding this baby. Just because Perfidia showed up at your old place doesn't mean you're jinxed or something."

"She didn't just show up out there," Clay said. "Don't you see, Jo? She was right there in Sera's bedroom. That's where I found her."

"Okay, but so what? You're acting like she's some

kind of spirit or something and she's here to haunt you."

"So maybe I'm just not supposed to move Serafina or something," he said.

"Oh bullshit," Jovita said and shook her head. She leaned back against the seat and crossed her arms. "I give up. . . ."

Clay sighed and thought about all this. "Maybe you're right," he finally admitted. "I'm not superstitious or even a religious man, Jo, but it does seem like—well, maybe a sign or something."

"I can understand that too, Clay," Jovita said. "But maybe it's a sign for all of us, not just you? Maybe it's meant to bring all of us closer or something. Like family. Maybe people around here just shouldn't be so damned stubborn and independent."

"I dunno, Jo. Like I say, I'm just weary, that's all."

"And maybe hungry too?" Jovita touched his arm again, gently this time. "Look at me, Clay." He turned to her and saw the familiar turquoise eyes. "You eat anything this morning?" she said.

"Not yet." He turned back and stared out the front window.

"Coffee?"

"Not yet."

"Me either," she said. "Come on inside."

"Bea's gone today," he reminded her.

"You think I don't know that? And I hope she's winning a bundle over there at the bingo hall in Presidio. But what makes you think I can't fix us something to eat?"

"I didn't mean it that way."

"Then get your ass out of the car and come on

in." Jovita killed the engine and opened her door. Clay did not move.

"Jo?" he said and he tried to maintain as much composure as possible, say this other thing unemotionally, as one would say it looks like it might rain. "I don't mean to whine, you understand, but there is one more thing to add into all this."

She bent back inside her opened door and looked across at him, waited.

"Who died?" he said. "Who's going into that new grave in the cemetery?"

"It's already been dug?" Jovita said with genuine surprise.

"You knew about it?" he said but he would not look at her. "Who is it for, Jo?"

"I guess nobody's had a chance to tell you yet," she said.

"Tell me what?" Clay bent toward her and a sudden flash of joy came to his face when he realized Jovita might be talking about some secret effort by all his friends to move Serafina into this new grave. "Who is it for?" he repeated and smiled at her.

"It's for Henry Bennett," Jo said quietly. "I guess he had a bad stroke last night. He's gone, Clay." ❧

CHAPTER 19

Clay sat silent across from Jovita at her special table in her restaurant. He could not remember having ever sat there before. He picked at the food she had prepared for him, but he ate very little of it. Jovita ate slowly, watching Clay absorb what she had told him outside about the suddenness of Henry's death. She had not seen him in this much despair since Adelita's burial. She knew it was not because of some close attachment to Henry Bennett.

"What?" she said. "It's sad, but it's not like Henry hadn't been sick, Clay. He's been going downhill for months. So eat something."

Clay looked at her. "They've dug his grave right there, Jo. Right next to Adelita's."

"They *did?*" Jovita stopped with her fork in midair. "But that's where you—"

"Yeah," Clay said. "That's what I'm talking about. Why there, Jo? And why the big rush? I don't understand."

"It wasn't any bigger rush than anyone else's grave would have been, Clay," she offered. "I guess they just have to get these things dug early before the heat sets in."

"They?"

"Well, I'm just guessing Dobb and Yebbie probably had it done," Jovita said, as stunned as Clay by all this. "They're the ones found him early this morning and they're the only members left on the county commission. Henry had no living relatives, you know."

"Figures," Clay said. He stared at the plate of food. "And I guess that kills any of my thoughts that this might all be fate somehow. You know, that maybe I shouldn't try to move her at all."

"What figures, Clay?"

"Well hell, those two had good reason to hurry it up. And it ain't the heat."

"Okay." Jovita set down her fork and sipped her coffee. "I see where you're going with this."

"Well? Think about it, Jo. Hell, the best way to stall this water drilling is to make sure I don't move Sera in here beside her mama," he said. "It's that simple." He looked up at Jovita. "Or *can't* move her. And if looking for Perfidia's baby might not work any longer, this sure as hell would."

Jovita said nothing. Clay continued, "Makes sense, don't it? Hell, they could've dug a grave for him anywhere else in the cemetery, right? Think about it."

"I don't know, Clay," she said. "Honest to god. But just remember, though, they are your friends."

"My friends? Who says? They sure as hell ain't been acting like it."

"Why don't you just drive out and talk to them, Clay? At least give them a chance to explain it to you. Maybe you owe them that?"

"Maybe it's them owes me something. Something like a little warning at least," he said. "They coulda looked me right in the eyes and told me what's happening. Give me a chance to do something about Sera first."

"Well it's not like they *caused* Henry to die," Jovita scolded. "And you haven't exactly been walking around the main street here, bumping into them or anything. My god, Clay, you're talking like it's some kind of conspiracy."

"Well, it sure as hell ain't nothing spiritual, that's for sure," Clay said. "It ain't like God stepped in and took Henry right now, or something like that, right?"

Jovita said nothing. Clay sighed and turned in his chair and stared out the window into the empty street. After a while, he retrieved his hat from the adjacent seat and placed it on his head. "But maybe you're right, Jo. Maybe I should just go out there and plead my case or something. Maybe it's high time I show a little backbone here and quit feeling so damned sorry for myself."

Jovita sat silent.

"Maybe they'll put Henry somewhere else, let me put Sera in that one," he continued. "Hell, it don't hurt none to ask about it." He rose and started to go, then turned back. "Listen, thanks for the food. I'm sorry I didn't do it justice, Jo."

"It's okay, Clayton"

"And thanks for listening to me." He looked at her for a long while and she stared back at him and then he frowned. "How come you put up with me, Jo? All these years? You don't need all this bullshit."

"Get outta here," she said and smiled. "I don't have time to explain every damn thing I do."

He offered a small smile back at her and then walked away. "Let me know when you get in," she said.

She heard the big front doors of the hotel thud closed and soon heard Clay's old pickup rattle off to the north toward Dobb's place. She stood and moved to the window to watch him drive off. "Good luck," she whispered and she thought about how she and Clay had been very close, long before he met Adelita.

Their relationship had been youthful and wild, far more passion than common sense, and Jovita's father saw no future in it for her and fought it with all the passion—and the power—that he could muster. But all these intervening years now and the continuous drama that invaded Clay's life had tempered even the memory of that for both of them, far more than her father had been able to do.

She thought about the other men, a few, but never anything serious. She stood and reached to adjust the knot in her scarf, hesitated and instead, began to stack the plates, a chore just like making the meal which she had not forgotten how to do. As she did this, Jovita thought about how many years it had been since she had made love with a man. She smiled because she was certain this too was something she had not forgotten how to do. ❧

CHAPTER 20

On the pavement north from Solitario, Clay practiced what he might say to Dobb and Yebbie about Henry Bennett's open grave. Dobb's much larger ranch sat to the east of Yebbie's hundred and sixty acres, both just a few miles off the blacktop. He would bypass Yebbie and go straight to Dobb first because he knew Dobb was the key player in all this. If Dobb would go along with moving Henry's gravesite, he knew Yebbie would also agree.

The plan he devised as he turned off the pavement onto the two-track road running past Yebbie's place was simple: he would ask Dobb if he and Yebbie would help him move Serafina, not days nor weeks from now, but *today.* He would insist. After all, the gravesite was already dug, he would argue. It would be a simple matter of going out to his old place when it cooled off, carefully opening Serafina's grave and moving her into town.

He would be firm but they would protest. They knew the moment she was out of the ground, it would then be legal for Agua Hondo to start drilling. But how could they refuse a lifelong friend this?

And even if neither Dobb nor Yebbie would help him right away with moving Serafina, that would be fine. That was not his real intention anyway. Not today.

He would just put them on the spot today and that would be enough to get Henry's gravesite changed. At least he would be able to lock in that gravesite right next to Adelita now that Henry would be buried elsewhere. Clay could then get all the neglected paperwork in place for that spot to be Sera's, pay whatever fees he needed to, and even offer to pay for moving Henry's gravesite after the remainder of his money came in. How could they possibly refuse?

"No way in *hell,"* Dobb said after Clay had parked in front of his house and found him in the cooler shadows of his barn. Dobb stood bent over with a currycomb as he worked on the side of his favorite gelding. "Ain't happening." He did not look up.

"But why?" Clay said, baffled. He moved around and leaned over to look into Dobb's face. "It just makes sense."

"*Two* reasons," Dobb said. He stopped and looked at Clay. "Number one, Henry's had that next gravesite locked up for years. Site's been paid for. Paperwork's been in place for years." Dobb pursed his lips and squinted his eyes at the rafters, remembering. "It's even in the county commission's minutes somewhere, a resolution in honor of all his years of service. Says something like, *County Judge Henry Bennett is hereby entitled to the very next one in the event of his death.* "

Clay backed away. "But it doesn't say *that* one, the one right there? Does it?"

"Yep," Dobb said. "Damn sure does. That one right there. It's the only one left under that same old cottonwood that Henry planted himself, probably fifty years ago."

Clay said nothing. He thought about all the times he had promised himself he would do the paperwork on Serafina's plot. Dobb continued, "We had no selection, Clay. Don't you see?"

Clay leaned his butt against a hay crib. "You could put him on the other side of the tree." Clay said, grasping. "Why couldn't you just put him over there? He wouldn't know now anyway."

"That ain't the point. That ain't where he wanted to be," Dobb said. He went back to combing the horse. "Same reason you wanted your wife and daughter there on the east side maybe. Henry always said he'd rather see the sun rise than see the sun set."

Clay thought that no one in the graveyard would ever see the sun rise nor set again anyway, but he did not say it. "Why didn't you just tell me about this, Dobb? Earlier? Where'd you think I was planning to put Sera anyway?"

"Truth is, Clay, I just never thought about it. Figured a grave just nearby I guess. Maybe on that other side of the tree, just like you're saying for Henry. Hell, nobody knew Henry'd up and die anyway."

Clay thought about this. In his grief during Adelita's dying, it was another step in the process he had neglected. Had he gone ahead with the paperwork on Sera's gravesite at the same time he did for Adelita's burial, this thing abut Henry's gravesite would have come up and it could have been worked out then. Maybe.

"You said *two* reasons?" Clay said.

Dobb stopped for a moment, looked at the dirt floor, then went back to working on the horse. "You know the other one," he muttered. "And by the way, we've postponed the commission meeting until Friday night. In respect to Henry. We'll bury him tomorrow morning early, before it's too hot. Hope you can be at both events, Clay. At the meeting, we're going to get cracking on appointing a replacement for Henry. And then move right on with that . . . *other* business."

Clay stood rigid, watching Dobb's back for a long while. Finally Clay said, "Well, say it." Dobb kept working with the currycomb but he said nothing. "Ain't you gonna say it? That *other* reason for not wanting Sera moved today is that *other* business you're talking about, right? Even if we moved Henry's gravesite and I said I wouldn't move Sera till all that *other* business was taken care of, you still wouldn't go along with it, right? You just don't want to risk me doing it anyway. Right?" Clay pressed but when he saw Dobb was done, he turned and walked out of the barn, got in his pickup and drove off.

At first, Clay had given up the idea of stopping at Yebbie's place to plead his case with him, but just as he reached Yebbie's turnoff, he changed his mind and angrily swung his pickup into the lane. The truck edged in the loose gravel and fishtailed, sending the left back wheel into the barrow ditch where it spun for a moment before Clay let off the accelerator. He left his engine idling and got out, leaving the door ajar. He looked at the wheel and saw he was not stuck, so he returned to get back inside and ease the truck out. When he drew his right leg up to enter, he noticed his old revolver that had skidded from under the seat and onto the rubber floor mat.

Clay paused for a moment, regarding the rusty weapon, then reached in and picked up the pistol. He reentered the truck and sat looking down the dirt road at Yebbie's old shack set at the edge of a dry wash. As he did this, he absently cocked the hammer on the gun and slowly released it as he thought about all that had happened in the past week.

Events had been swirling around him far too fast. Perhaps this small event—stalling in a dry ditch—was intended to give him a brief moment of respite just to think. Clay acknowledged that he had never been one to plan too far down the road. He always thought at least there had been forks in the road that gave him some options, even if they were not the best. Just as he knew he had enough traction right now to ease out of this ditch, he had never felt that he had been presented with an absolute dead end. Even with Serafina all those years ago and then with Adelita, there had been options, though both had ended in bitter and agonizing conclusions. At least he had been presented with choices, poor as they might have been at the time.

But now, there seemed to be no selection about his moving Serafina next to her mother. Even if he convinced Yebbie that Henry Bennett could be placed in some other gravesite and promise that he would respect their plan and not move Serafina yet, he knew Yebbie would have no power over Henry's documented last wishes. Yebbie too would have to go along with Dobb's thinking.

And he knew that Dobb and Yebbie needed time. Clay sighed and again acknowledged this to himself. Time to appoint another member of the county commission, time to set up a water control board, time to establish regulations before anyone could begin to drill into the aquifer. But Clay also recognized that his lost option now on moving Serafina to the gravesite next to Adelita had nothing to do with all this commissioner business, this water business. There was simply no place to put her next to her mother now. Period.

Clay seemed to see for the first time the rusty revolver in his hand and for a moment, he considered that this old weapon might be one of those less than desirable options. It was a fleeting thought and Clayton Elliott had never envisioned himself as some kind of desperate mass murderer, slaying all those who might have gotten in the way of his mission. But it did present a choice, crazy as it might be, not unlike some of the less desirable options with which he had been presented his entire adult life. He snorted and released a nervous chuckle.

"That'd be a helluva deal, wouldn't it?" he muttered. "On Yebbie Riggs and Dobb Campbell. Hell, maybe I'd just invite them to a shoot-out on the main street of Solitario, Texas." He cocked the pistol, lowered it to his hip, and raised it swiftly, practiced it a few more times and then said, "Fast draw, just like in the Old West. I wonder what the hell my two friends would say about that invitation. Two of my *best* friends. Nothing else seems to work. Wonder what the hell kind of traction that might get me on all this?"

He placed the revolver on the seat beside him and turned his attention to rocking the old pickup from reverse to low and soon he was out of the ditch with a finesse that surprised him. He was able to back out with ease and point his truck again toward Solitario. With just the traction he needed. ❧

CHAPTER 21

Attending Henry Bennett's burial was difficult for Clay. They had never been close but Clay always respected Henry, a loner much like himself but far more dedicated to the county and the little town of Solitario where he had lived all of his eighty-eight years. But to see Henry's casket waiting next to the fresh grave into which Serafina should be going sent Clay into a deep depression that everyone mistook as grief for Henry.

Since Henry had never married, there was no immediate family crowded around the gravesite early Thursday morning for the combined funeral service and burial. The county commissioners, consisting now of only Dobb and Yebbie, decided it was far too hot to conduct a separate service and a burial in one day because there was no air-conditioning in the church. And everyone agreed it would be best to just get Henry into the ground and move on. However, Dobb and Yebbie did postpone till Friday the regular Thursday night meeting in respect for the deceased judge and had hastily posted notices to that effect around the community.

Dobb and Yebbie arrived together for the burial and most of the adult community members were represented. A smattering of people from Presidio and the outlying areas of the county also came. Bea stood next to Locket, who appeared weary from the previous day of active duty on Cinco de Mayo. Jovita dressed appropriately in black slacks and black blouse and sunshades. She wore no jewelry but she refused to wear anything in her hair except her trademark red scarf. She stood next to Clay at the edge of the crowd and heard him whisper too low for anyone else to hear, *"It's Sera's grave. Can't y'all see that?"* Jovita hooked her arm through his when he muttered this and again, everyone misinterpreted Clay's grim visage and Jovita's sigh as grief for Henry. Halfway through the service, Gus arrived and walked up behind the crowd, his hat in hand. Clay saw that Alvaro was not with him.

"He didn't come home last night," Gus said to Clay after they had lowered Henry into the grave and the crowd began to disperse. "That's not unusual on Cinco de Mayo, but I'm a little concerned after we had our discussion about—" He stopped and looked at Jovita, who still held Clay by the arm.

"It's okay, Gus," Clay said. "She knows."

Jovita nodded but said nothing.

"Well, we had a little disagreement over all that," Gus went on. He looked around and continued when he saw no one was within earshot. "About what he might be able to find out and what he might be able to do that nobody else could."

"I wondered if he'd balk," Clay said.

"Well, I couldn't tell for sure. He's stubborn, always has been. But if he makes up his mind about something being right or wrong, he clamps down on stuff like a Gila monster and just won't let go. He'll do it his own way."

"I know," Clay said. "Takes after his big brother."

"Well," Gus said. "It gets us both into trouble sometime."

"You talk to Locket yet?" Jovita said. "He was over there all day yesterday but I don't know if he saw Alvaro."

"Locket knows *she's* over there?" Gus hissed, startled at this. "I mean, at *our* place?"

"No way," Clay said. "That'd been real awkward for him. But he does know Alvaro might be asking around about the baby."

"Locket will be over at the restaurant after this, Gus," Jovita said. "If you want to talk. He's on duty but he wouldn't miss Bea's food for anything short of a riot."

"You're coming over too aren't you?" Clay said. "Bea and the others will have it all laid out by now."

"Sure, for a while. Then I'd better get on back," Gus said and then awkwardly, "She's out there by herself."

They moved away from the gravesite but not before Clay glanced one final time into the hole which now held Henry's casket. He stopped and then looked back at Adelita's grave and drew in a deep breath but said nothing.

"How is she?" Jovita said to Gus.

"She's crying," Clay said before Gus could answer. Jovita saw Clay was staring at Adelita's grave. "I think she's probably crying."

"I meant Perfidia," Jovita said. She reached over and took Clay's arm. "Come on. . . ."

"She's okay," Gus said. "She's staying busy. She don't have to, but it's the best Los Arbolitos has looked since our mother died. I guess that helps her some, but still I hear her crying in the night down the hallway." Jovita nodded and then pulled Clay gently away from the gravesite and the three left the cemetery.

Everyone had already crowded inside the hotel restaurant when Jovita and Clay walked in with Gus. An array of covered dishes lined the long table and people moved down both sides, filling paper plates. Bea and some of the men had set up folding chairs around the walls but some still had to stand with their plates poised in mid-air.

After most had finished the meal and sat murmuring over coffee, Dobb stood and walked to the end of the room. He tapped on a glass with a spoon and when everyone stopped talking he said, "Henry Bennett was a friend to all of us." He looked at Clay, who glanced away. "And as a county commissioner, he always took pride in keeping the county looking good. Stuff like roads and fences and that little park on the hill. But especially, the cemetery. Henry always said it ought'a be a place of rest, peaceful and well kept. And he's right where he always wanted to be. In fact, Henry himself planted that big cottonwood he's under. Must'a been fifty years ago as a matter of fact. Ain't that about right, Yebbie?"

Yebbie nodded and said, "That's about right, Dobb. Leastways, that's pretty close if it ain't right on, far as I can remember."

Dobb stopped and let this sink into the crowd. "Of course, we did put it in the form of a resolution.

Not that Henry himself brought it up, but me and Yebbie thought it ought to be there, kind of official, you know." Nods and murmers of agreement went around the room. Dobb went on, "Henry would want us to continue to move forward with the business of the county. And in respect for Henry, we've postponed the regular meeting tonight till tomorrow evening at seven. It's all been posted legally. He'd not think this wrong to mention it at this time. Yebbie and I'll bring it to order and then immediately vote on a temporary replacement for Henry."

"We don't need an election?" someone voiced from the back of the room.

"Yep, we do need an election," Dobb said. "You're right on that. But not till November. Yebbie and I can legally appoint a replacement till then. We have a couple of names in mind, but if anyone else wants to be considered, you'd best let us know today."

Dobb waited for any other questions about this or names to put into consideration. When no one made a suggestion, he said, "Okay, maybe now it would be appropriate to hear comments from any of you about Henry. That is, if you want to say something."

Dobb sat down and one-by-one, people offered kind words or stories about Henry, about how cantankerous he could be but how in general, Henry Bennett was one of the most kind and selfless men who had ever lived in Solitario County. Clay stood leaning against the wall at the end of the group, listening to all this. When at last it came his turn to speak, he stood straight, clasping his hat brim in both hands against his belly.

"Well, Henry Bennett was a friend, that's for sure,"

Clay began. "A *true* friend." He glanced first at Dobb and then at Yebbie, held his gaze there for a moment and then continued looking at the other faces in the room in turn. "And I'll miss him. We'll all miss him. And it's . . . well . . . real nice that my Adelita is gonna be right next to old Henry under that big old cottonwood tree . . . for ever and ever." Clay's voice trailed off. When he did not continue, Dobb allowed the silence to linger for a while, then stood again, but before Dobb could speak, Clay said, "Well, since you asked, Dobb, I guess I did have one more thing. . . ." He looked at Jovita, who stared back. Afraid he was about to mention Serafina's now occupied gravesite, she shook her head just slightly as if to say, *Not now, Clay, not this, not now!*

He paused for a moment more but then continued, "I'd like to put a name in the hat for you two commissioners to consider tomorrow night, okay?"

"Well . . . sure, Clay," Dobb said.

"Yeah, go on, Clay," Yebbie encouraged. "Who?"

"Jovita Seals," Clay said evenly. "I think you ought to consider her for Henry's spot on the board."

The room grew silent again. Not since Jovita's own father had served on the commission had the name Seals been used in public service. And indeed, he had served for many years with distinction. No one in the room would ever question the name of Seals in a public office. It was just that there had never, in the entire history of Solitario County, been a woman in any public office. ❧

CHAPTER 22

On Friday morning, Jovita went through her regular routine: bath, underwear, shoes, slacks. And as usual, she even stood briefly at the window overlooking the main street. But with the exception that she wore no scarf in her hair, she stood fully clothed this morning behind the gauze curtains. Had she been there nude as she often did during her early morning affront to the sensibilities of the world, Dalton Simik would surely have noticed her as he stepped from his nondescript black sedan into the street and glanced up at her window. His was not a casual acknowledgement that Jovita Seals resided behind these curtains. The man did this as though he knew exactly where he was looking and it sent a small shiver across Jovita's shoulders.

"Welcome to Solitario, Mister Simik," she whispered and took one step back from the window but continued observing Simik though the curtains. "I expected you'd show up. Come on in."

But Dalton Simik hesitated, looked toward the front doors of the Hotel Solitario and then up the street toward the cemetery, as if deciding which way to go first. He removed his sunshades, inspected each dark eyepiece against the morning sun, adjusted them back on his face and then moved toward the cemetery.

"Don't get too excited, Mister Simik," Jovita said. "She's not been moved there . . . yet."

She turned away from the window and went into her closet to select a scarf for her hair. Simik obviously had a choice: check into the hotel or see if Serafina had been moved. But today, Jovita did not even go through her usual pretense of choosing the scarf from the dozens in the drawer. She removed one without looking and wove it into the back of her hair and only paused a moment in front of the mirror before she left her apartment. She went directly across the hall and tapped on Clay's door.

"Get up," she said. "We got a guest about to check in and I think he's probably here to talk to you."

She heard Clay stir behind the door. "Ummm . . . who?"

"Your friend Simik, I think," she said and walked away. At the top of the stairwell, she smiled as she heard quick steps across the old oak floor and the toppling of a chair inside Clay's apartment.

"I should mention that name more often," she said. "Gets him moving right fast."

Downstairs, she went through the routine with Bea in the kitchen, but this morning after she sampled the bacon and greeted Bea, she said, "How's Perfidia?"

Bea made no pretense of ignorance about this but she did not look at Jovita. "Don't know about today . . . ." she said. "But Augústin said at the funeral she was crying and crying. Except for that, she seemed okay."

Jovita nodded and went into the restaurant and sat. When Clay walked in, he went straight to her table.

"Join me," she said after he had already sat.

"Where is he?" Clay said. "Did he check it?"

"No."

"I thought you said he was here?"

"I said a *guest* was about to check in," she said. "I don't know for certain it's him. But whoever it is, he went up the street first. Coffee?" She turned and retrieved a mug from Clay's usual table behind her, filled it and then one for herself. "Black fancy sedan, thin as wire, dark glasses . . . nobody would mistake him for a resident of Solitario, that's for sure."

"Yeah, sounds like Simik alright," he said and then, "Not much question what he's doing up there. And he'll see a fresh grave today." He sipped and continued. "But it won't have the name on it he's looking for."

"How do *you* feel about that, Clay?" she said but instantly regretted it. "I mean, this morning, after you've slept on it and all?"

"I didn't sleep on it," he muttered. "And I don't really wanna talk about it if that's okay, Jo."

"Sure," she said. "Why don't you eat something, Clay? Bea could fix you some huevos rancheros . . . or something?"

He sat silent, staring into the coffee. "That's okay," he said. "Maybe in a while."

"Well, I shouldn't be so damn nice to you this morning," she said. "You disappeared pretty fast yesterday."

"Well . . ."

"If I'd caught you, you'd have even less hair today," she teased. *"I think you ought'a consider Miss Jovita Seals for Henry's place on the board, blah, blah, blah. . . ."*

"Well, you can always withdraw your name," he said. "Besides, they ain't voted on you yet."

"Why'd you put my name in anyway, Clay?"

"Seemed like the thing to do," he said. "Just seemed like the right thing."

"I hope you don't think that I can get Henry Bennett moved or something."

"Nope," he said. "I've given up on that idea. It's just that someone here in town ought'a be on the commission. Henry lived in Solitario. Don't need another rancher from outside the town, that's for sure."

"You know there's never been a woman on the board," she reminded him. "Never."

"That right?"

"Yeah."

"Well, maybe it's time one was on it," he said.

"Never thought about it that way. Maybe it's time. You know, shake up some of that stale thinking from Dobb and Yebbie, guys like them."

"Why not you, then?"

"Same reason," Clay said. "My thinking's pretty much like theirs."

"Except when it comes to drilling into the aquifer."

Clay looked at her for a long moment. "That's not true, Jo," he finally said. "I never said that was a *good* thing. In fact, I've always said it was a dumb ass idea from the get-go. I even told Simik that, right to his face. I always figured selling my place to Agua Hondo was a little like selling them my old pickup for big bucks and telling them it ran like new. You know, *buyer beware?*"

"I see. . . ."

"Anyway, it's a done deal and Henry's in that grave and that's a done deal too," he went on. "And come midnight May fifteenth, they'll probably be punching a hole out there and then we'll all find out what's down there."

Jovita sipped her coffee, held it to her lips and spoke into the mug as if to muffle her words. "So you intend to leave Serafina out there?"

"Well, I damn sure ain't moving her today," he said. "I just need to think about it one day at a time."

"Maybe we could figure something else out, Clay," she offered. She had noted the change in Clay's voice. But she could not decide if it was optimism or something much blacker he had in mind. "I mean, if you want me to help. Especially if I get on the commission."

"If you get on the commission, you'll have one major thing on your agenda, Jo," he said. "And it ain't moving Sera."

"Something about water regulations I've heard," she teased.

"You got it."

"Yeah, it's like a gun at Dobb and Yebbie's heads," she admitted. "I can tell that."

"And at yours too now, if they appoint you tonight."

"Yes."

"You'll have about a week to do all that," he said.

"I know," she said. "It's not like I haven't thought about all that. I didn't sleep much last night either."

"That is, one week *if* Sera stays right where she is till then," he said. He sipped as he glanced over the lip of the mug at her.

Jovita cocked her head and looked back at Clay from the corner of her eyes, but she said nothing about his last comment. Bea came out of the kitchen and stood next to the table and said, "Okay, what's for you two this morning?"

"Huevos rancheros," Jovita said. "And bacon and toast, *buttered* toast."

"But what about you?" she said back to Jo.

"That *is* for me," Jovita said and turned to Clay. "I don't have a clue what's going on inside this guy's head."

"I'll have the same, please," Clay said. "And maybe you could stir in some of those *habañero* peppers too, Bea. I'm feeling like pushing the edge this morning."

"You sure?" Bea said and frowned.

"I'm sure."

Bea shook her head and turned to go.

"Bea," Jovita said.

"Yes?"

"Me too," Jovita said.

"Everyone's gone crazy," Bea said as she flipped a hand into the air and disappeared into her kitchen.

Dalton Simik walked into the restaurant just as Bea set the steaming plates of food in front of Jovita and Clay. He paused under the arched entryway, removed his dark glasses and surveyed the room. It did not take him long to pick out Clayton Elliott from the smattering of breakfast customers in the restaurant. He moved abruptly across the room and stood behind Clay who had his back to the doorway and did not see Simik enter. Clay had started to eat but Jovita had not. She watched Simik move quickly toward them but she did not have time to alert Clay.

"We need to talk," Simik said. "Since you haven't

returned my calls or answered my letters. My *certified* letters."

Clay stopped eating, chewed the mouthful but did not turn around.

"Now," Simik said.

"I'm eating," Clay said through his mouthful of food. "And this is hot stuff." He lifted another forkful of the huevos, tucked this into his mouth and turned to look up at Simik. "Hungry?" he said.

Simik stood silent, glaring into Clay's eyes. Finally he said, "I'll just check in first. I got a couple phone calls to make back to El Paso."

"Don't count on doing it from your room," Clay said. "I ain't got one either, by the way. Hotel phone only rings down here and the desk clerk don't speak much English." He looked back at his food. "Sometimes I just don't get my messages. Strange, ain't it."

"There's a pay phone in the lobby," Jovita offered.

"That'll work," Simik said. "Just need to report on what's happened here." He turned toward the lobby, paused and said, "Or rather, what's *not* happened here. And I understand there's a big meeting tonight too?"

Without missing a beat on her breakfast, Jovita said, "Word sure gets around, doesn't it? But you're right, Mister Simik. County commissioners. The regular meeting was postponed till tonight." She looked at him. "Of course, if you've been up to the cemetery, you'll know why. But I suspect you didn't come all the way over here from El Paso on vacation or just to check the names in our cemetery, now did you?"

Simik looked at her but said nothing.

Jovita went on, "Oh, and don't worry, the special meeting's been posted."

Simik turned and walked away.

"It's all legal, Mister Simik," she said as he reached the entryway. "Just like a contract someone might sign." He did not look back.

"Thanks for the help," Clay said when Simik was out of the room. He smiled at Jovita, who still held her jaw set firmly. *"Commissioner."* ❧

CHAPTER 23

Gus Muñoz was himself enjoying huevos rancheros on this morning. Even with the mysterious absence of Alvaro the second morning in a row, this had become usual fare at Los Arbolitos this past week and Gus was savoring every bite. Perfidia had also filled a plate and now sat silent across from Gus as they ate.

Anticipating that he would have to take the *corrientes* himself to the rodeo in Pecos, Gus had loaded them into an eighteen wheeler in the early hours that morning. They jostled and bawled now inside the metal slats of the hauler attached to the truck, parked next to the barn. With the noise of the raucous cattle, Gus did not hear Alvaro's pickup as he pulled into the yard.

"Everybody invited to this party?" Alvaro said. He leaned against the doorjamb at the entry to the kitchen. He was unshaven and had on the same clothes he had worn the morning of Cinco de Mayo, two days ago. "I gotta long haul ahead of me."

"You ain't gonna make it over there in time if you stop to shower and eat both," Gus grumbled.

"Who said anything about a shower," Alvaro said. He moved into the kitchen, poured himself some coffee and slouched into the extra chair at the table. "You saying I stink or something, brother?"

Perfidia stopped eating. She sat stiff and would not look at Alvaro.

"And how're you doing?" Alvaro leaned forward and cocked his head so he could look into her eyes, but Perfidia diverted them to the floor. "Not so good, I guess," he said. "Maybe you had a couple of rough nights too?"

"Okay," Gus said. He slapped his napkin onto the table and stood. "So you had a party. So what else is new?"

"Lots," Alvaro said. "You gonna finish this?" He did not wait for Gus to answer. He reached across and scraped the remainder of his brother's eggs into a flour tortilla, rolled it up and stood. "Lots is new."

Alvaro moved toward the entryway and out the front door onto the patio. Gus followed but he turned at the door and looked back at Perfidia. She remained rigid and intense, as if she might suddenly flee from the room, thus avoiding any news Alvaro might have brought. Gus thought he might say something to try and calm her but he said nothing. More pressing matters awaited him in the yard.

Outside, he confronted Alvaro who sat on a bench against the adobe wall, eating the burrito he had made. "Well?" Gus said.

"Well, what?" Alvaro said.

"I don't need to know where you've been or who you've been with or what they sold you," Gus said. "Or what you might have bought for the road. I just want to know if you've found out anything for Perfidia?"

"Oh, it's *Perfidia,* now?" Alvaro said. He stuffed

one end of the burrito into his mouth, bit it, chewed. "Been cozy here, huh?"

"No," Gus flared. "That's her name, dammit. And as a matter of fact, it's been a little bit of hell."

"Hell for you or hell for . . . *Perfidia?*"

"Okay, that's enough," Gus shot back. "You gonna tell me anything or you gonna fuck around?"

"Ain't me been fucking around," Alvaro said. "Can't be sure about you though, brother."

Gus stalked over, poked a finger into Alvaro's chest and leaned into his face. "Then just get into the goddamn truck and get them steers up the road, hear?"

"Yes *sir,*" Alvaro said. "Whatever you say." He stood and stuffed the remainder of the food into his mouth and walked into the yard. At the wrought iron gate, he stopped and turned back. "Oh, in case you're wondering, my information is that your Perfidia didn't come across the river where she said.

"What do you mean?"

"Well, seems there were several others with her and also a family."

"So where did they cross?" Gus said and then, "But that don't really matter anyway."

"Might matter if it was Santa Elena Canyon," Alvaro said.

"No way," Gus said. "Nobody comes across there."

"Well, they did," Alvaro said, gloating. "Down into the canyon and across that swift water and back up the riverbank on this side. Tough and rocky trail too. And it ain't no fucking wade across there where it narrows. But then, you're a smart man. You'd know that."

Gus stood silent, weighing all this. Finally he said, "What do you mean a *family?*"

"A younger guy and his wife," Alvaro said. "They all came across there."

"And I guess your . . . *friend* . . . was with all of these people?"

"Leading the pack, so to speak," Alvaro said. "And oh, his partner, maybe the one with those fancy boots she told us about, the one she says kicked her? The one I was with had dark ones alright, but no white tip as far as I could tell. Anyway, seems the other one went back across days ago. Maybe his were gray. This one I was with just hung around to . . . well . . . let's just say to do some *business* with me. He's back over there by now too."

"Business?" Gus said.

"Yeah, just a little something to help me stay on the road," Alvaro said. He patted his shirt pocket. "That old winding road, you know? Good price too, but hey, the information was free."

"I hope to hell you don't get stopped," Gus said and he wondered if maybe this might not be a good idea after all. "You said family? Just a man and his wife?"

"Nope," Alvaro said. "They had a baby too." He turned and went through the gate.

"Well, did you ask him about *her* baby, Alvaro? Just tell me that much anyway."

"Yeah," Alvaro said. "Funny thing about that, though. The guy just clammed up, wouldn't say a damn thing about your friend inside there or her baby daughter. Just kept changing the subject back to that family and how they were still hiding out somewhere.

That's all I could find out. He never said where. He was getting suspicious, I guess, so I shut up."

"Nothing else?" Gus said. Alvaro shrugged and walked away toward the truck. "You think he might have left her baby somewhere or what?"

"I told you he didn't say," Alvaro said over his shoulder. "He wouldn't talk any more about that. Leastwise not in the two days I was with him. Course, we weren't always as clearheaded as we should have been, I guess. Maybe they already got rid of the kid." He turned at the truck and grinned back at his brother.

"Nothing else?" Gus pressed.

"Just that the family with the baby is still around there in Presidio or somewhere in the area. Hiding out, waiting to sneak out of here like all of them do. You know, packed like sardines into some van or truck heading north. That is, them that don't get caught first. But only those who've *paid* for that second part of the trip can go, of course," Alvaro said and waited for Gus to respond. When he did not, Alvaro continued, "Not those who *didn't* pay . . . or *couldn't.* Even then, they wait till all of this law heat's died down." Alvaro climbed up into the truck, leaving the door open.

"Wait a minute," Gus said. He moved closer and held Alvaro's door open. "You think it could be Perfidia's baby?"

"Don't think so, brother," Alvaro said. He shut the door and fired up the engine, then rolled down the window. "He said that baby was a *boy* . . . not a girl." Alvaro meshed the gears and roared out of the work yard, leaving Gus standing inside a wake of dust.

CHAPTER 24

Even though there had been several knocks on his apartment door during the day on Friday, Clay remained silent inside, refusing to answer any of them. He wondered if one might have been Jovita, but then, she would have said something. He knew it was Simik. Just before the meeting started at seven o'clock that evening, Clay peeked out into the hallway and seeing no one, went across to Jovita's door and tapped on it.

"I'm almost ready, Clay," she said from inside her apartment.

He put his face close to the door and said, "How'd you know it was me?"

She opened the door and stood looking at Clay. "Well first, I don't get many gentleman callers anymore," she said. "Not even on a Friday or Saturday night. And second, I didn't hear anyone come up the stairs."

"You're getting to be a real detective, Jo."

"Well, it's not that hard to figure out."

"Yeah, guess I'm a little nervous," he said. "You ready for all this?"

"No, but thanks to you, looks like I've got no choice."

"You have options," he said and thought about his

own choices and how they had slowly withered. "You can just walk away from it."

"Not likely," she said. "They have my name on the table, but it's anybody's guess how Dobb and Yebbie will vote."

"What if it's a tie?" Clay said.

"Relax, Clay. And think about it," she said. "Dobb'll vote first on whichever name he's inclined to support."

"Yeah, probably."

"And then it'll be Yebbie's turn to vote on the person he's favoring, right?"

"Right. . . ."

"Well, how the hell do you think Yebbie's vote will go?"

"Yeah," Clay said and he grinned at Jovita. "Like you say, it ain't that hard to figure out. Anyway, it just made sense to put your name in there. Maybe there won't be any others come up."

"Might make sense to you," Jovita said. "And maybe even to me too. In fact, I thought about this all day and the more I bumped into that Simik snake coming and going downstairs there, the madder I got. I might just enjoy putting a burr or two under his saddle." She shut her door and moved into the hallway. "But even if I do get on the board, Clay, I hope you're not expecting . . . something."

"What do you mean?"

She stopped and stood with her hands on her hips. "He's got a contract for deed, remember?"

"Of course. That part's a done deal. Midnight, May fifteenth, it's his, one way or the other. Why?"

"Well, it's just that a lot has to happen between now and then. Regulations have to be put in place before Simik gets that chance to take over. And let's face it, I'm not up to speed on all that legal stuff and neither is Dobb or Yebbie."

"Can't be all that hard to figure out, Jo," Clay said and smiled. "There's all those law books over there and you can always call Austin. You're a smart woman. Smarter than either of them *and* Simik."

"Damn, I'm sorry I ever mentioned it now," she said.

"Mentioned what?"

"Figuring things out." She moved toward the stairwell. "Let's go."

Clay followed her down the stairs, still talking. "What'd you mean yesterday, though, about no miracles?"

"I meant I'm not a magician," she said. "I can't do anything about *your* problem."

"I know that, Jo. That's not why I suggested you be on the commission."

She stopped at the bottom of the stairs and stood in the lobby, confronting Clay. "Then I'm curious, Clay," she continued. "Why the hell *did* you put my name out there?"

"Just seemed like the thing to do at the time, Jo," Clay said. "I told you that. I just thought maybe there'd be something . . ."

"Okay, let's get one thing straight right now," she said and held her forefinger in the air. "Before there's a vote or a discussion or anything else tonight, okay?"

"What?"

"Even if it happens for the first time in history that there is a woman on the county commissioners, and even if it happens to be Jovita Seals, there's no way in hell I could ever get old Henry's casket moved somewhere else in that cemetery, even if I wanted to. You gotta understand that, Clay." She stopped with this, caught herself just short of saying that this too was not hard to figure out.

Clay stood silent for a long while, then simply nodded, once, but Jovita was not certain he did understand—or wanted to. But if clinging to something this far-fetched might help Clay get through the next week, she would just accept it. She shook her head and turned and walked through the double doors at the front of her Hotel Solitario.

Outside, she crossed the street to the county commissioners' meeting room, Clay matching her, step-for-step. In the meeting hall, townspeople from Solitario and Presidio and area ranchers stood talking in tight clusters against the walls, some already seated in folding chairs. Though it was a mixed group from the county, there was only one female face for every ten males. Jovita and Clay took seats near the back of the room, next to Bea, who had shut down the restaurant for the evening. They all nodded but none spoke. Doc Maddox had come over from Presidio, despite the fact that Friday was not a regular day for his clinic. Even though his property lay inside the county boundaries and he would be a legal voter, Gus rarely attended these meetings and was not at this one. Alvaro had never been seen inside any county commissioners meeting.

At the long table in front of the room, Dobb sat

with his head bent over a sheaf of papers. Yebbie sat next to him, looking out over the unusual gathering crowd, his face like a deer in headlights. Both sat hatless, a rare if not unheard of indication that something somber, if not desperate, was about to happen.

Dalton Simik sat alone in an outside seat on the front row. He too held his head bent over a handful of papers and he too had dispensed with his high-dollar Stetson hat for the evening. Occasionally, Simik lifted his head, angled his body and surveyed the room, stopping his sweep for a long slow-burn when his eyes met Clay's. At seven, Dobb stood in the front of the room, looked out over the crowd and cleared his throat.

"Maybe we could get started," he said and then, "Could everybody just sit down, please?"

"Y'all sit down," Yebbie echoed, his voice feigning authority. The talk subsided and the crowd began to take seats.

"Yebbie agreed I should start this off," Dobb continued when the room fell silent. "But I ain't in no official position, just next in line as the secretary and treasurer of this commission."

"That's official enough, Dobb. Henry'd be pleased to have you take over," someone said from the room.

"Well, speaking of Henry, and you all know he's passed and we put him in the ground already," Dobb continued. "I think it'd be nice to just all stand back up and give Henry a few minutes of silence in recognition for all he's done for this county."

Dobb crossed his hands in front of his belt buckle, bowed his head. Yebbie stood and did the same as did everyone else in the room, even Clay, who did not hesitate at all. When everyone was seated again except Dobb, he picked up a sheet of paper and held it up to the crowd.

"Henry and me and Yeb roughed out an agenda earlier this week," he said. "I'll just go down the items. There's one added thing we'd never have suspected, of course, and that's a replacement for old Henry himself."

"Temporary replacement, Dobb," someone corrected him.

"That's right," Dobb said. "Only until the regular election in November." He paused and let this sink in and said, "Then, there's been a last minute request to be added to the agenda." He turned to Simik on the front row. "If there's no objection, Mister Simik here has asked to speak to the group tonight."

Simik turned back to the crowded room, flashed a fake smile and waved curtly. Dobb turned to Yebbie and went on. "Hearing no objection, write that down at the bottom of the agenda, Yeb. But the first item of business has to be getting Henry's replacement seated up here. And if we have a tie vote between me and Yebbie here . . . ." he smiled and gestured at Yebbie who sat sternly as if determined to have his voice and vote properly recorded, no matter what Dobb Campbell might say, " . . . well at that point then, the law says we have to go to a referendum election for Henry's seat, even though it'd still be temporary. Any questions?"

"You gonna take names from the floor?" a hard looking woman in the front row asked. "I drove over a long and bumpy dirt road for this."

"Gotta take them from the floor," Dobb said.

"We have a suggestion, but we don't have any official nominations yet." He looked at Clay and then at Jovita. "As long as you're a property owner in the county and you want to nominate somebody, that's legal."

"I am and I do," said the woman, who stood and stated her name and gave the location of her small ranch at the edge of the county line. "And I nominate Jovita Seals. Her daddy done a lot for me and my family way back when we was about starved out. I'm by myself out there now. And truth be known, I'm still 'bout starved out." The woman sat down.

Nods of understanding and a sympathetic chuckle worked through the room. It was unlikely that anyone in the room had not heard about Clay's earlier suggestion at the funeral that Jovita's name be on the table anyway. Dobb nodded, turned to Yebbie. "Write Jovita Seals's name down, Yeb. Get it official. And get this woman's name and property verified too." He pointed at the massive record book at the end of the table. "In there. Any more nominations?"

He raised his hand and stood silent for a long while, as if he were an auctioneer giving the going, going, gone warning. "Any more nominations . . ." he said again and frowned this time. "Got another name? Or two?" The crowd remained silent as he surveyed the room. "Anybody? Not one more?"

He stalled again till someone from the back of the room said, "Second the nomination. Get on with it Dobb. I got cows to feed."

Dobb cleared his throat and turned to Yebbie, who sat blinking into the crowd. "Well, okay then," Dobb said. "The nominations are closed." He sat.

Yebbie tore a sheet of paper in half, handed one half to Dobb and kept the other. "Write down your choice," said Yebbie. "I'll write down mine."

"Well, it ain't like there's a lot of selection," Dobb grumbled.

"Sure there is," said Yebbie. "It says we can select anybody we want to, right?"

"Well, yes," Dobb admitted.

"Then it don't have to be somebody who's name come in here tonight, right?"

"Yeah," Dobb said. "Long as they're eighteen and property owners in the county."

"Okay," Yebbie said. "Then write. . . ." He commanded and lifted his pencil and scrawled words on the torn paper. "Here's mine." He folded it and gave the sheet to Dobb and having cast his official vote, sat proudly, tapping the eraser of the pencil against the table top.

Dobb looked at him, shook his head and wrote down his choice. He lifted the two folded ballots in the air and pointed at three people on the front row, one of them the woman who had placed Jovita's in for consideration.

"Wanna tally these?" Dobb sighed.

The three stood in a huddle, quickly looked at each ballot in turn and gave them back to Dobb. He stood and said, "Sorry for all the delay. Looks like it's official. Your new temporary county commissioner is gonna be Jovita Seals."

A small applause rose from the crowd at first, then got louder and finally Jovita rose and smiled at the faces. "Thanks," she said. "I guess . . ." The crowd chuckled and fell silent again.

Dobb stood and motioned her to the front. She took the vacant seat and Dobb picked up the agenda again. "Let's move on," he said, but before he could continue, the woman in the front row held up her hand. "Yeah?" Dobb said to her.

"How come you're doing that?" the woman said.

Dobb frowned again, "Doin' what?"

"Leading the meeting?" she said.

"What do you mean?"

"You said you was getting a replacement for Henry Bennett," she said.

"So?"

"So, Henry Bennett was chairman, right?"

"That's right. . . ." Dobb said.

"Well, she ain't a man, but she sure as hell can be a chair*woman,*" the lady pointed out. "Look that up in your legal book."

"Hold it, hold it," Jovita said. "I know where you're going with all this, but I'm not interested in leading anything, just doing what I can for the county, that's all. And I've got a lot to learn. But if it needs to be formal and legal, I nominate Dobb Campbell here for chairman." She turned to Yebbie. "He's doing a pretty good job as far as I'm concerned. What do you think, Yeb?"

"Well . . . sure," Yebbie said. "Works for me."

"Then the vote's in and it's a majority, right Dobb?" Jovita said. "Doesn't matter how you'd vote. It'd be two to one, so looks like you're it. Officially now."

Jovita looked at him and for the first time this evening, Dobb Campbell smiled. "I believe we can work together just fine," he said. "Just fine." He turned back to the crowd. "Let's take a short break so's we can get organized up here. We'll pick the agenda back up in, say, fifteen minutes, okay?"

The crowd dispersed, some left the hall, others stood in the outer entryway, smoking and talking. Clay and Bea sat silent in the back, Jovita's chair now empty between them. Jovita huddled in secret conversation over the Texas Book of Statutes in front with Dobb and Yebbie. Dobb carefully traced a passage in the book with his forefinger, word for word, nodding and explaining it to Jovita and Yebbie, who both nodded back. All three occasionally glanced over at Simik who sat without emotion, watching them through narrowed eyes. Dobb finally straightened and cleared his throat and said, "Tell 'em to come on back in now, Clay."

Clay nodded, rose and went to the lobby and soon returned to the meeting room followed by the majority of the previous crowd. Dobb stood in front, waiting for everyone to be seated. When the room quieted, he said, "This meeting is called back to order with a full official quorum now."

He looked at Jovita and then back down at the agenda. "As the duly elected chairman of this commission, I'd like to now swear in our temporary replacement for the deceased member, the honorable Henry G. Bennett," he said. "Jovita Seals, would you please stand and raise your right hand and repeat after me?" She stood with her hand already in the air. *"I, Jovita Seals . . ."* Dobb said and then spoke the remainder of the oath of office.

Jovita echoed his words, " . . . *do solemnly swear to uphold the Constitution of the United States of America and that of the Great State of Texas with all laws and regulations pertaining to Solitario County therein, so help me God."*

"Please take your seat with this honorable body of citizens and property owners of Solitario County, State of Texas, now in legal session on this Friday, May the seventh. And without objection from other members of this commission . . ." he paused for a microsecond, looked at Yebbie and then said, "And hearing none, as chairman and as my second official act of business, I hereby appoint you, Jovita Seals, as temporary secretary and treasurer of this body." He shoved over the book of minutes to a surprised Jovita.

"Well," she said. "Thanks again . . . I guess." She opened the book to the blank page with this date at the top. "Looks like I'll have to write down later what's already happened tonight."

"That's your new job," Dobb said. "However you wanna do it. But right now, we'll address the next item on the agenda, the establishment of a Solitario County Water Control Board."

Simik stood and shifted for attention, then waited to be recognized. Dobb had moved to the middle of the table to chair the meeting. "The chair will not recognize any more speakers from the floor at this time," he said to Simik.

"But . . ." Simik began.

"But nothing, sir. We've already done that item on this here agenda, heard from any property owning legal citizen of this county who wanted to talk about Henry's replacement, and now we're moving on to the next item."

"But you said . . ."

"Sit down, Mister Simik. You're not on here till the last item tonight. I put you on the agenda, just like I told you I would earlier . . . you're last."

Simik sulked into his chair but he said nothing else. Jovita looked to the back of the room and saw a grin on Clay's face, Bea held her head cocked, looking back at Jovita with a smile as if to say, *Go for it, Jo . . . go for it.*

"As I said, we'll take up the next item for discussion by this commission," Dobb repeated.

"Mister chairman?" Jovita said.

"Chair recognizes new member of this commission, Miss Jovita Seals."

Jovita looked down at what she had written on a sheet of paper. Idly, she adjusted the scarf in her hair as she read the words evenly, "Mister chairman, I move that you appoint three members of this legally instituted Solitario County Commission to immediately establish a Water Control Board for this county and for that same Water Control Board also to proceed immediately with the posting for one week, not to include legal holidays, which is the legal minimum time required by Texas law, those recommended regulations for same. . . ."

"I second that movement," Yebbie interrupted with glee.

"Discussion?" Dobb said.

"Wait a minute," Jovita interrupted. "I'm not done with this."

"Oh," Dobb said. "Sorry. Go ahead, Jovita."

"And that those recommended regulations be posted in the nearest local newspaper and made available for public comment at a public hearing on the sixth day of that same week and, barring any *legal* objections, shall go into effect at *midnight* on Saturday of that sixth day of that same week." She looked at Dobb and then at Yebbie and finally, at the crowd. "That's it, mister chairman." She sat down.

"Now I'll call for any discussion," Dobb said.

Simik held up his hand, waved it wildly.

"Discussion means from the three *members* of this *legal* Solitario County Commission, Mister Simik," Dobb growled and then said, "Hearing none, I call for the vote. All in favor so indicate by saying *Aye.* And the chair will order a roll call vote on this and also order that this vote be posted in the legal records right there." He pointed at the minutes book in front of Jovita.

"Aye," said Jovita.

"Aye," said Yebbie.

"Motion passes without need for my vote," Dobb said. "Get that down there in that book, Jo."

"Yes sir, mister chairman," Jovita said, paused and cocked an ear toward Dobb Campbell. "And which *three* members of this *three* member commission shall I write down here as newly appointed to the Water Control Board . . . sir?" she said, feigning seriousness.

Dobb beamed back at her, "The three in attendance tonight," he said.

Yebbie crossed his arms and smiled at Dalton Simik, simmering on the front row. Finally, Simik rose and stalked out of the room. As soon as he was gone, Dobb stood and lifted the agenda into the air.

"Next item on the agenda," he said through a tight smile, "Is Mister Dalton Simik, who says he wishes to speak to us." He looked around the room, pretending to search for Simik's face. "Something or other about Texas

Rule of Capture Law and legal but unregulated drilling for water on personal property and . . . well, let's hear from him. Is this Mister Simik here tonight?" Nothing came from the crowd but puzzled looks. "Hmmm . . . Well, hearing no response from the requestor who asked to be on this here agenda, I hereby delete this item and order the newly appointed Water Control Board to meet this weekend, day and night if necessary, for as long as it takes to establish regulations for surface water as well as for drilling water wells in this county and for regulated disposal of any deep well water found during such drilling, and I further hereby order that these regulations be posted in the area newspaper as required by law for five workdays and that on midnight of the sixth day of that same week shall by Texas Statute become legal and binding in Solitario County, State of Texas."

He paused and looked at Jovita and Yebbie, "And I'd just add, that the county is hereby ordered to provide as much coffee and food as it takes to get all this done too. Right now though, I'm tired. I call for adjournment."

"I'll move on that," said Yebbie.

"Second," said Jovita.

"Meetin's over then," Dobb said. ❧

CHAPTER 25

After the meeting, Jovita and Dobb and Yebbie huddled again at the front table, working out plans to meet as the new Water Board over the weekend. Clay and Bea left the room together and walked out into the night. As they crossed the street toward the hotel, Bea said, "Come on in. I'll get some coffee going. Looks like they'll be needing lots of it." Bea paused for a moment and then said, "You've been pretty quiet, Clayton. What do you think about all this?"

"No question in my mind, Bea. I'm happy Jo got on the commission. I wouldn't have suggested her name yesterday after the funeral if I didn't think she'd be good for the county. But I don't think Simik's very happy about anything that happened."

"Yes," Bea said. "He's really something, storming in and out of there like that. What is he up to?"

They had stopped next to the curb in front of the hotel and Bea stood in the wash of light from the ancient chandelier inside the lobby. She looked toward the double doors of the hotel, the broken light through the beveled glass reflecting in her eyes. Then Clay realized that not everyone in the county was aware of Simik and all Clay's problems with moving Serafina, knowledge he had perhaps taken for granted that they knew.

"Well, Bea, it's a long story but I'm sure you've heard at least part of it," he said.

"Some of it," Bea said. "No way I could have missed all that about Perfidia and her baby."

"Right. Well, she's in good hands, Bea. Thanks to you and the others and your help. Don't worry about her. But nobody's found her baby yet, I'm sorry to say. And as far as all this stuff tonight, let's just say that if I don't get Sera out of the ground and into the graveyard somewhere by midnight on Saturday next week, that Simik will move his equipment in and start drilling and probably destroy everything right where she is because they believe near the windmill is the best spot to get down into the aquifer and . . ." Clay paused and studied Bea's face in the dim light. He thought about how all these people had become embroiled in the complex facets of a situation that rivaled the fractured light coming through the glass in the doors of the hotel. "Well, like I said, it's a long story, Bea. And somehow it's snaked into a lot of lives now but maybe it shouldn't be a problem for anybody but me."

"But that's the main thing keeping you awake at night," Bea said. "Moving your Serafina. It's not just this water thing or Perfidia and her baby."

Clay said nothing.

Bea continued, "But they do need to get right on it. I mean, putting those new rules down."

"Yeah, and I don't envy them trying to do it that quick," Clay said. "And if you think about the calendar, five days next week and then a hearing on next Saturday, looks to me like *both* deadlines might happen now about the same time."

Neither spoke for a long moment. Finally Bea said, "But you're not thinking about going ahead with your other thing before that, are you Clayton?"

"Other thing?" Clay said.

"You know what other thing, Clayton," Bea said. "Stop avoiding it. With Serafina."

"Of course I'm *thinking* about it," Clay said and he became irritated. "Hell, I'm always thinking about it. But it's gotten a helluva lot more complicated than just me and Sera and Adelita now, Bea. I know that."

Bea fell silent.

"I'm sorry, Bea. I'm not mad at you, it's just that . . ."

"I understand, Clayton. And I don't mean to stick my nose in. But you wouldn't want to do it now anyway, would you? I mean, not after tonight. They'd never elect a woman to sit on the commission in there unless they knew she'd be a strong vote against this guy, Simik. And you, a *man,* suggesting her name in the first place, just cinched it for them, so you're not *seriously* thinking about moving Serafina any time before they can get something in place, are you?" She waited for Clay to respond. "Well, *are* you?"

Clay said nothing. He had turned and now stared down the dark street where Simik's sedan sat parked at the curb. In the dim light from the hotel windows, he could just make out a silhouette behind the wheel, a cigarette glowing and then fading.

"Why don't you go on inside, Bea," he finally said. "I think I'm gonna take a little walk, clear my head a bit. Maybe go talk to Adelita about all this." He turned toward the sedan and started to leave Bea.

"It's not that way, Clayton," Bea said.

"What?"

"The cemetery," Bea said and she too noticed the figure in the sedan. "If you're wanting to visit with *Adelita*. She's up the other way."

"I know, Bea." He turned around and faced her and they stood there for a long while until Bea sighed and then walked away.

"You be careful, Clay," she said just before she went through the front doors of the hotel.

Clay moved down the street and stood next to the passenger window on the sedan. It did not surprise him when Simik rolled down the power window on that side and said, "Come on inside, Clay. I've been waiting for you."

"I'm okay out here," Clay said. "I figured you weren't just sitting here enjoying a smoke and the night air. Just get on with it, Simik."

Simik sat silent, sucking on the cigarette. After a while, Clay looked up the street one way and down the other. Most of the people from the meeting had already driven away, so he opened the door and quickly got inside.

"I'll get right to it," Simik said. "Since there wasn't much sense trying to stop what's happening inside the meeting there."

"Yeah, that all went pretty fast, didn't it," Clay said and smiled into the darkness.

"Well, fast or not, they've still got to get their asses in gear to get something down in time to stop Agua Hondo," Simik said. "But then, you know as well as I do that we didn't get where we are by just rolling over, right?" Clay said nothing. He knew what was coming.

"So to hedge our bets a little, I just needed to visit with you a minute, Clayton."

"I'd be a fool not to guess what you're after," Clay said. "And believe it or not, you and me want the same damn thing. But you go ahead."

"You're wrong on that, Clay," Simik said. "We don't want the same thing."

Clay looked across at him but he could not see his face in the darkness. "How's that?"

"I want the deed to your place," Simik went on. "I want to punch a hole in the ground, way down, right where your old windmill is. That's where we'll drill first because that's the best shot for getting into the aquifer. That's what we want." He paused and sucked again on the cigarette and Clay heard the sputtering of tobacco in the silence. "Now, what do *you* want, Clay?"

"You know what I want," Clay said. "I just want my Serafina out of there and with her mama, that's all."

"Yes, and you're between a rock and a hard place, so to speak, right?"

Clay said nothing.

Simik went on, "And now, all this other stuff is rolling along and the gravesite where you wanted her is taken and . . ."

"You don't need to go over all that," Clay said, anger coming into his voice. He wondered how Simik knew all this. "I know it and you know it now, so just get on with whatever you wanted to say to me."

"So, if she's still in the ground out there at midnight on May fifteenth, well, I can't guarantee what will happen to her gravesite. We'll be moving in some pretty big machinery and big machinery makes a helluva mess out of things sometimes . . . especially in the dark, Clay. Now you just think about that for a minute."

Clay thought about it, but it didn't take a minute. "You can't move shit in there, though, if these regulations go into place."

"You willing to take a chance on that, Clay?" Simik leaned toward him, whispering now. "With these dimwits in charge here? What if they can't get their shit together and it *don't* happen in time? You willing to risk that our big dozer and jackknife drilling rig won't be chewing up the earth right where you're daughter's been laying peaceful all these years? Think about that for a minute too. . . ."

Clay closed his eyes and leaned his head back against the seat. And this time, he did spend several minutes considering everything Simik had said. As much as he wanted Serafina out of the ground and out of the way of Simik and his crew, the conclusion Clayton Elliott arrived at was not submission to Simik's threat. Clay had never had much use for threats. He thought about Bea's words she had just spoken—she had said that a *man* had suggested Jovita for the commission—and he wondered if he would have used that term to describe himself. But when he sat forward and opened his eyes to confront Simik, he held a white envelope up to Clay's face. Even in the dim light, Clay could see it was stuffed fat.

"You don't need to count this," Simik said evenly, and the threat was gone from his voice. "I assure you, though, it's enough to make it well worth your while. Take care of all your wife's medical bills for good and then some. And when we get the deed, there's all that final settlement to boot, plenty to take a long trip somewhere till all this blows over. And there's enough in this right now to hire somebody to help you dig up your kid out there and get her moved." Simik let this sink in. "Get your kid moved right away, *tomorrow* if you want to. Okay?"

Clay studied the envelope. He thought about Adelita, up there under the big cottonwood tree, bound there by graves now on either side. And he considered his Serafina, still alone under twenty-five years of hardpan, waiting for her father to do as he promised her he would: release her and put her up there with her mother. And he thought about the citizens of Solitario County who had driven many miles this evening and supported his good friend, Jovita Seals, and how their very livelihood might be at risk because no one, not even Simik himself, knew what pumping billions of gallons out of the aquifer might do to the water on their property.

And then Clay thought about Gus and that young woman, Perfidia, and his commitment to helping her find her missing infant and all this whirled inside Clay's head in a barbed-wire tangle of all his own false starts and sudden shifts. And then he thought about the money in the fat envelope, held seductively in Simik's hand. But most of all, Clay thought about the words Simik had just spoken.

"*Hire* somebody?" he said. "To help *dig up my kid?* Is that what you just said, Mister Simik? Like I'd just pay some goddamned drifter off the highway to help me get my baby out of the ground? Dig up my *kid* is what you said. Like you might just dig up some garbage or something and move it?" Clay reached down and pulled the latch on the door. He exited, shut the door quietly and then leaned back through the window. "I ain't interested in your problem, Mister Simik," he said. "And I'd explain why, but you know what? A guy like you just wouldn't get it." He turned and walked up the street toward the cemetery to tell Adelita that it might take him a little longer to do what he had promised her. But somehow, in his own way and in his own time, he would get it done. ❧

CHAPTER 26

After Alvaro had left the yard with the *corrientes* on Friday morning, Gus stood watching as the dust cloud billowed into the air and finally settled back onto the hard earth from which it had sprung. It would do no good to get angry at Alvaro, he thought. That approach had never worked. And Gus had to admit that Alvaro had brought back information, thin as it was.

Gus turned then and walked toward the house to report to Perfidia what he had learned. As he neared the patio, he saw the curtain over a front window drop suddenly back into place, but when he went inside, Perfidia was not at the window in the entryway as he expected. He went on back into the kitchen and then finally down the hallway to the door to the bedroom where she had been sleeping this past week. When he tapped on the door, there was no answer. For a moment, he considered that she might have fled, but when he tried the door, he found it locked. Perfidia did not show herself outside the bedroom all day on Friday.

Now on Saturday in the early morning light, Gus sat on the east-side patio watching the sun inch into the sky. In the quiet, he sipped his mug of coffee and tried to make some sense of the young woman in the back bedroom. He could only conclude that she had refused to come out on Friday because she feared the news that her baby might have already been sold . . . or worse. And so when Perfidia padded up behind him on the patio and touched him on the shoulder, he turned and feigned a smile as if he had good things to tell her.

"Good morning," she said. "You should have got me up."

"I know how to make bad coffee," he said. "I just don't do so good with the rest of it."

"I can do that," she said. "Later." She took the mug from Gus and went back into the kitchen and refilled his and brought one out for herself. "Alvaro was here. . . ." she said, giving the coffee mug back to Gus. They sat at a thick wooden table on the patio.

"Yes," Gus said. He would pretend she had not been at the curtained window, watching him and Alvaro argue in the yard. "Yesterday."

"I know," Perfidia said. "I watched you two through the front window."

"Why didn't you wait for me to talk to you?"

"I don't know. . . ." she said and traced the rim of her mug with a fingertip. "I don't know."

"Well, don't matter," Gus said. "I figured you must have been pretty shook up just waiting to hear something. . . ."

"Something . . . yes."

"Well, good news, bad news, whatever. I guess I'd be afraid to hear too."

"Hear what?" Perfidia looked up at Gus and then waited. So did he.

"I wish it could be good," Gus began, "but maybe

it ain't bad either. Fact is, Alvaro didn't find out anything about your baby."

When he said this, Gus watched Perfidia's face and he thought she seemed relieved, but he decided he might have been confused in the quickening dawn. He went on, "He did talk to one of the bastards who beat you though, but the guy wouldn't say anything about your baby. He did say there was *another* baby in the group. . . ."

Perfidia nodded and then averted her eyes.

"He said a young couple had brought their baby too," Gus went on. "A baby boy."

"Yes."

"He also said you all came across at the canyon," Gus stopped and waited for a response from Perfidia. "In Santa Elena?" Perfidia looked up at Gus but in the gathering light, he could see her eyes had glazed over, as if she did not hear what he had said so he repeated it. "Santa Elena Canyon? You crossed the river there? All of you, right?"

Perfidia did not answer. Instead, she rose and came around the table and took the empty mug from Gus and then went into the kitchen. There, she began to set the table and take out utensils to cook breakfast. It was if she had not heard this at all. Gus sat watching her through the open doors to the patio. Finally, he rose and went into the kitchen and stood leaning against the countertop next to Perfidia. "If you did, you were nuts."

"I lost my job," she said, bringing anger into her voice. She cracked eggs in a ceramic bowl and began to whip them with a fork. "Along with five hundred others. At the *maquiladora* just south of Ojinaga. The American owners closed down the assembly plant and sent the jobs somewhere else where labor was cheaper. To India, I think." She poured the beaten eggs into a skillet and took out a knife, chopped hard at the onions and peppers and scraped them from the cutting board into the eggs. "Do you know what all that means, Gus?" She shook the knife at Gus.

"It wouldn't be good," Gus said. He looked at the knife.

"No, it was not good." She lowered the blade. "Sorry," she said and went on. "We did nothing all day long but assemble clothes for Americans on sewing machines, ten and twelve hours a day, and the pay was not good either, but it was a living over there." She stirred the mixture in the skillet, her back to Gus now. "It was a job. And working that sewing machine is all I know, except this." She lifted the pan and set it down hard onto the stove burner. She twisted the knob and then touched a lighted match to the propane. "Unless you count having babies as a skill also."

Perfidia turned around and looked hard at Gus, who averted his eyes this time. "And so, you say it's crazy to cross the river? You say it's crazy to come down into Santa Elena Canyon to cross where the water boils between those rock walls? Risk my life and that of my infant baby?"

"Well, I meant . . ."

"No, that's okay," she interrupted. "You are correct. Maybe it *is* crazy. Maybe it's crazy to pay *coyotes* as much as I did to help me, everything I had been able to save. Maybe it's crazy to leave the drunken and worthless father of my baby—and no, he was *not* a husband—and set out on this journey by myself with nothing but the clothes on my back? Do you think I didn't know about the Border Patrol, Gus, and about people dying trapped inside boxcars over here and dying of thirst out there in the desert? But you get a little crazy when you have no future and your baby has no future and the only thing left to do over there is whore to survive."

"I . . ." Gus began but once more Perfidia interrupted him.

"And so I came, Gus . . . any way and any place I could. Like thousands of others."

"Okay," Gus said. "I believe all that." He came toward her and lifted a hand to place on her shoulder but he stopped and lowered his hand to his side, embarrassed. "Hey, you don't owe me an explanation. Or anything else."

"And you don't owe me anything either," she said. She looked up into his face. "But why are you doing all this, Gus?"

"Well, for my friend, Clayton," he said. "For one thing."

"And that's all?" she said. "You could get into big trouble for this, Gus. So could your friend, Clayton."

"And I'd do it for anyone who's been treated like you've been."

"Anyone?"

"Especially you," he whispered and cleared his throat and added quickly, "And we're going to find out what happened to your baby. I mean, we're going to *find* your baby and she'll be okay."

She had no reply to this. She turned around to

the stove and touched the handle of the cast iron skillet, jerked it back, put her fingers into her mouth. *"Caray!"* she said. "I've burned your breakfast."

"Hey, that's okay too," Gus said. "I'm used to that." He took a dishtowel and wrapped it around the handle and scooped the eggs into the trash can with a spatula. "Put your hand under this." He turned on the cold water faucet.

"I'm sorry," she said, cooling her fingers under the water.

"You make another round when that feels better. I'll put some tortillas into the oven. We make a damn good team, right?" he teased. "But hey, I thought you said you knew all about this cooking thing?"

She looked up at him and for the first time this past week, he saw a small smile come to her lips. "Usually I do. Unless I burn my fingers. But I don't plan on ever, ever doing that again," she said and continued to stare at Gus for a long silent moment. Finally she looked down at the fingers she held under the cool water. ☙

CHAPTER 27

"I'm done with it, Locket," Sheriff Gil said. He sat behind his desk early on Monday morning, Locket in the chair on the opposite side. "We've done all we can."

"You're going to just drop it, Gil?" Locket said.

"It's all the time and money we can spend on this one, Locket," the sheriff said. "Hell, we've spent more on this than most of them anyway."

"It's a kidnapping," Locket reminded him. "A baby. And that's a little different, isn't it?"

"Yes, it would be," Sheriff Gil said. "If, in fact, we knew that, which we don't. And now apparently, the mother's disappeared too. Where's our case, Locket? No mother, no baby, and so far, no real evidence that either existed, right?"

"I saw her," Locket said. "And so did several others including Doc Maddox and I'm convinced something happened to her baby. What we had was a young woman who looked beat up and had been nursing a baby and she didn't have it with her."

"I don't doubt you, Locket," Sheriff Gil stood and snapped on the cantankerous air conditioner behind his desk, whacked it with the fat of his palm and it rattled awake. He turned back to Locket. "Don't misunderstand.

It ain't me. I just can't build a case on that alone. It's got to be strong enough to convince the FBI and all them others and they couldn't go on just that. And neither can the immigration folks who had at least a couple dozen more illegals come across just this past weekend alone."

"So this one just gets buried, huh?"

"Bad choice of words, Locket, but I'm afraid so," Sheriff Gil said. "Becomes paperwork now, just like thousands of others. That's about it. The BP's got its hands full. It's a shooting war out there and when they ain't being fired at, those agents right on the river get rocks throwed at them. Hell, they've even started putting armored plates on their four-by-fours and I ain't shitting you one bit, Lock. You know about that?"

Locket knew. But he also knew what he had seen in this young mother's eyes and in his heart he simply could not let this one go. Not yet. "Okay, so what now?"

"Well, the Texas Highway Patrol already pulled back on Friday because nothing showed up on the highways out of here. Nothing unusual anyway. Immigration is still on the roads, of course, regular checkpoints and they'll watch as usual. Here again though, Lock—and you know this too—they probably stop fifty to seventy-five vehicles a day and go through them and gather up lots of illegals, put them on a bus, send them back over to Ojinaga and then they'll have to gather some of same ones back up again in a couple more days. It's a revolving door.

"Yeah . . ."

"Hell, they ain't even having legal hearings anymore on them," Sheriff Gil went on. "Too many of them. You know what they're saying to the BP agents who load them on the busses now, Lock?"

Locket knew this too.

"They're smiling and saying *hasta mañana,"* Sheriff Gil said. *"See you tomorrow,* like they was best of friends. And I shit you not. Chances are, several of those will have babies with them too, maybe kidnapped or for sale or God knows what. We got no last name, no photo of the mother you're talking about, Locket, or the baby or the scum who apparently brought her over here. And it ain't likely those *coyotes* would be heading north anyway now, not with all this law heat that's been on them. They're back across gathering up another load on the Mexican side. So if she's still around, which I doubt, she may even be together again with her child in El Paso or Denver or Dallas or even in Ojinaga, who knows where?"

"Yeah," Locket said, but his mind had wandered. "We done here, Gil?"

Sheriff Gil sighed, sat back down. "Yeah," he said and looked at Locket for a long time. "But I know you ain't. Just don't tell *me* about it, okay? Now get the hell outta here."

Locket rose and went to the door and paused, "You know I'm not one of them renegade deputies, don't you Gil? Like on TV?" he said. "But you know what?"

"What?"

"I've been in every alley and abandoned shack here, up and down the back roads lifting lids off stinking garbage cans, and I ain't seen nothing or heard a peep from nobody about this."

"So?"

"So my gut tells me something's not right about

her just disappearing and all, Gil."

"They teach you that gut reaction shit back there in law officer school all them years ago?" Sheriff Gil said.

"I didn't go, remember?" Locket said and then cocked his head. *"You* taught me everything I know about gut reactions and tracking somebody down."

Sheriff Gil cleared his throat and looked down, began shuffling through the paperwork on his desk. "Don't let the doorknob hit you in the ass," he said.

When Locket drove up in front of his office in Solitario, he saw Clay come out of the hotel. They had not spoken since Henry's funeral on Thursday and Locket had been scouring the back alleys in Presidio all weekend for any sign of Perfidia or her baby. But when Clay saw Locket's patrol car, he stopped and ducked his head as if he had not seen Locket and then turned the other way.

Locket pulled to the curb and got out. "Where you going?" he called and Clay could not ignore this. He turned and faced him and smiled and Locket said, "Ain't you curious about what I found out? Come on inside. Let's visit." He went to the door of his office and unlocked it and waited for Clay.

Inside, Locket sat official behind his desk which, like Sheriff Gil's, was stacked with postponed paperwork. Clay took the chair opposite him.

"You look wore out," Clay said.

"You don't look so good yourself," Locket said.

"Yeah, well it's been a long weekend," Clay said. "You missed the big meeting on Friday night."

"Yeah."

"You probably heard about it though?"

"Nope," Locket said. He picked up a pencil and tapped it on top of the sheaf of papers. "I been pretty busy too."

"Figured you were," Clay said. "You find out anything?"

"What happened at the meeting?" Locket said, ignoring Clay's question.

"Well, first of all, they did put Jovita on the county commissioners," Clay said. "And then they made her secretary and treasurer."

"That's a surprise," Locket said. "But in a way, it ain't. She'll make a good one."

"Yeah. Folks seemed to think that. They didn't even put another name in," Clay went on. "Simik from Agua Hondo was there to talk but he didn't stay."

"The outfit that bought your land, right?"

"Yep," Clay said and smiled. "He just got up and left after Jo and Dobb and Yebbie appointed a County Water Board."

"Who'd they put on it?"

Clay chuckled and then said, "Themselves."

"No shit?"

"No shit."

"Is that legal?"

"Guess so," Clay said. "Leastwise that's what they done, legal or not."

"Must be then," Locket said. "Yebbie might not, but Dobb'd know whether it is or not. He woulda researched it or asked Henry about it. . . ." Locket paused, looked down. "Course Henry's in the ground up there now where . . ."

"Yeah." Clay also looked down, massaged one thumb through the opposite palm and then the other, splayed his fingers and then closed them. "Yeah," he repeated.

"By the way, how'd those clothes fit that woman?" Locket said. "I mean, before she just up and suddenly disappeared, you know?"

"Clothes?"

"Yeah," Jovita brought them over, remember?"

"Well . . . I dunno," Clay said and studied his hands. "Fine, I guess. How would I know?"

Locket sat tapping the pencil, the only sound in the office for a long while. Finally he said, "Where is she?"

"You mean Sera?" Clay looked up, feigned a puzzled frown. Locket's words were the same he had heard from Jovita the morning after he took Perfidia out to his old place to meet Gus. "You know I can't bring her up here now," Clay said, continuing the pretense. "Where would I put her?"

"I wasn't asking after her," Locket said. "You wouldn't make a very good criminal, Clayton. I'm sorry about all your problems with getting Serafina where she belongs, but that's not who I mean."

Clay looked first at Locket and then over to his large map of the county tacked to the wall. He stood and went closer to the map, red circles marking the places where Locket had retrieved the corpses of illegal Mexican immigrants. Some of the circles overlapped, indicating multiple deaths from heat exhaustion and thirst or suffocation inside a boxcar or whatever sad fate had brought their dream to an end at that lonely spot. Clay turned back to Locket.

"Come on with me," Clay said.

"Where we going?"

"Just get in my pickup and don't ask questions," Clay said and held the door open.

"Your pickup?" Locket balked. "That damn thing still running?"

"I said don't ask no questions," Clay said. "Yes, it's running, asshole."

"Let's just take the patrol car," Locket said. "Air conditioner works in it."

"So's mine," Clay said. "Patrol cars draw too much attention and we don't want that right now. So just go on out and get in it."

Locket shrugged, adjusted his hat and went out onto the sidewalk and then down to Clay's pickup. He ducked to get inside but had to remove his hat to squeeze his huge frame through the narrow door. Inside, he rubbed the spot on his forehead where he had scraped it getting in. "Damn," he said to Clay who entered easily on the driver's side. "I hope this is important." He rolled the window down.

"Shut that window," Clay said. "And your mouth too." He cranked the engine till it finally caught and sputtered thick blue smoke out behind. Locket rolled the window back up as Clay switched on the air conditioner which, to Clay's amazement, began to churn out air a little cooler than that outside the cab. "See," he said and smirked at Locket who sat, hatless, looking straight ahead.

Clay backed out and pointed the pickup north on the blacktop and then when he reached it, east on the rough dirt backroad toward Casa Piedra. When he got to the spot of his close encounter with Alvaro's eighteen wheeler the past week, he stopped the pickup and got out and stood leaning against the fender on the driver's side, his back to Locket still inside. Clay studied the rangeland to the north until Locket finally got out, put his hat on and came around and leaned next to him.

"They've called off the search," Locket said, serious now. "At least officially."

"You ever think about that big old hunk of rock out there, Locket?" Clay said. "I always stop and study it a bit when I'm crossing through here over to Gus's place. I guess it's not really rock though, but a big old busted bubble of lava." It was not necessary to do so, but Clay pointed out the huge landmark to the north, The Solitario, the only thing breaking an otherwise flat terrain for hundreds of miles. "It's like a volcano that never quite made it to being a real volcano," he turned to Locket who was also squinting at the formation.

"Know what I mean?" Clay went on. "Just popped up out there and then collapsed into itself. That's what the guy from the university said, that one time he come over here and talked about it. Remember?"

Locket nodded but said nothing.

"It just petered out, I guess," Clay said. "Couldn't get done what it was supposed to do. . . ."

"Yeah, guess so. Hadn't thought that much about it," Locket said and then, "You bring me all the way out here in this heat to give me a geology lesson?"

"You ever feel like that, Lock?" Clay went on, ignoring his question. He looked at his friend, but Locket did not look back at him. Locket continued to blink into the bright morning sunlight toward the landmark, as if it might suddenly erupt again.

"Well . . . maybe it ain't done yet," Locket said. "Maybe it's still rumbling under there and someday it'll finish what it set out to do."

"Damn," Clay said and looked back at The Solitario. "It's been like that for thousands of years, Lock. Ain't it about time it made up its goddamned mind and either give up or get with the program?"

"Things take time, Clay," Locket said and looked at him. "Things like becoming a volcano, shit like that, they just take a lot of time, I guess." Locket turned and walked around, removed his hat and got back inside the hot cab. He waited but he said nothing more to Clay who remained leaning against the fender for a long while, regarding The Solitario and considering what Locket had said to him.

When Clay got back inside, he said, "You said *they.*"

"They?"

"You said *they've* called off the search."

"Yeah," Locket said. "Sheriff Gil and the others."

"How about you?" Clay fired up the pickup and slapped the dash to awaken the air conditioner. It rattled and groaned and spat out hot air for a few minutes and then cooled as Clay moved back onto the dirt road toward the east. "Don't sound like you have."

Locket sat silent for a few miles and then said, "I guess I'm like that petered out old Solitario there, Clayton. I just don't give up too easy on something I think's worthwhile."

Clay was silent for several more miles down the

road and then finally said, "Maybe I shouldn't either, Locket," and then he repeated, "Maybe I shouldn't either."

Nothing else was spoken between the two until they pulled into the work yard at Los Arbolitos. Gus was in the big corral moving several crippled and worn out *corrientes* into a smaller area with a loading chute. He stopped and latched the gate when he saw Clay's pickup and then climbed over the rail. Clay and Locket exited the pickup and approached Gus.

"Fast food." Gus said. He jerked a thumb toward the steers. "Your next hamburgers. Or bologna sandwiches. Let's move over there in the shade." He walked to the covered patio around the front of the house and moved three leather bottomed chairs closer together. "Sit."

"Why don't we move inside," Locket said. "Where the cold beer is?"

It was a sudden and impolite suggestion. "Well . . ." Gus began and looked at Clay and searched for words. "Clayton drank up ever beer I had," Gus said. "Last week. Besides, the house is a mess too. Alvaro's been home, you know, and . . ." After a thick and lengthy silence, Gus continued, "I could bring out some cool water though?"

Gus rose to go inside but Clay said, "Sit down, Gus. Locket knows about her . . . I think?" Clay turned to Locket and waited. So did Gus but he did not sit.

"You guys are gonna get me in some deep shit," Locket finally said. He sighed and took off his hat and wiped the inside hatband with a palm. "Seems like I been having to say that a lot lately, though. Yeah, it wasn't hard to put all this together once I stopped long enough to sit over a couple of cold beers at Julio's this past weekend and think about it. Think about how I'd pounded every goddamn back alley and shack and every foot path down by the river there in Presidio and never saw hide nor hair of Alvaro or that baby or nothing else." Locket paused and let this sink in. "Or that woman you two got hid inside, so just sit back down, Gus. Don't make her any more nervous than she already is, probably in there peeking out at us right now." Locket said. "Peeking out at *me*, anyway. Alvaro in there too?"

Gus glanced at the front window curtain and then sat again. "He's back on the road," he said. "Up to the Pecos rodeo."

"Alvaro was in Presidio last week, though," Clay said. "Wasn't he Gus? Did he do what we talked about?"

"Yeah," Gus said. "Cinco de Mayo and the next day. You wouldn't have seen him though, Locket. Not where you were looking."

"Yeah, Julio told me he'd been in the bar. Maybe I ought'a deputize your brother," Locket said. He knew all about Alvaro Muñoz and his friends and his problems and he felt a little pity for Gus. "Maybe I'd solve more of my cases that way."

"Alvaro's got problems," Gus flared. "But he's no criminal."

Locket let this slide. "Well, what'd he have to say?"

"I can tell you that he didn't find out a damn thing about Perfidia's baby daughter," Gus said. "But he did find out about another baby."

"Another baby?" Locket said.

"Yeah," Gus said. "I guess Perfidia came across with a couple also carrying a baby."

"Maybe that's hers?" Clay said. He sat forward, speaking to Locket. "Maybe they've got hers somehow?"

"That's what I thought," Gus said. "And that's what I said to Alvaro. But it ain't hers. Alvaro said this other baby was a boy."

Locket nodded. Clay sat back in his chair but said nothing.

"And that ain't all," Gus continued. "Alvaro said his . . . well, his *information* . . . told him they'd crossed inside the canyon, not on the flatlands above or below it."

"Santa Elena?" Locket sat forward now. "Across that deeper water?"

"That's right," Gus said. "He said they've figured it's the most likely place *not* to be seen by the Border Patrol anymore."

"He's got that right," Locket said. "Not to be seen by the BP . . . or anybody else if you slip on them smooth rocks and get crossed up in that swift water. Damn lucky any of them made it. Damn lucky." No one spoke for a long while as they considered this, and finally Locket said, "I think I need to find this couple and their baby though. That is if the BP ain't caught them yet."

"Why them?" Clay said.

"I think I might be able to get some information out of them that we ain't getting anywhere else." Locket spoke this as he looked at the two and then attempting as much tact as possible he said, "I mean, it seems we might be getting some confusing information about certain things . . . or rather, *she's* maybe a little confused." He looked at the window. "Couldn't blame her, I guess."

"Alvaro said that couple is probably still over here on this side of the river," Gus went on. "But I don't think it's where you been searching, Locket."

"Okay, where the hell *should* I be looking?" Locket shot back. "California?"

"Redford," Gus said. "Probably somewhere down here in this area. Or nearby." He looked to the south where the dais of his high desert rangeland gave way to dry washes and rock fractures and an occasional spring, secreted between ridges like splayed fingers, tipped and pointing toward the Rio Grande.

"Hell, there ain't enough places to hide anybody down there. Not for long anyway. Redford ain't got but maybe fifty people living there. Not a place tp hide a couple with a baby who needs lots of stuff for . . ." Locket began.

"You'd be surprised how many little adobe houses are out there," Gus interrupted and he swept his hand across the horizon to the south, his voice dropping now into a quiet reverie. "Not in Redford itself, but away from it, in those hills coming up this way from the river. Probably a dozen or so. It's like they're just part of the land itself, almost invisible because that's exactly what they're built of. Adobe mud from the dirt, just like this one here. All of them with goat and sheep people living there, making it on nearly nothing. A lot of them work in the onion fields around Redford too. That is, the farms that still have irrigation rights and haven't gone busted in this drought and had to sell their water rights downriver just to get out of debt. You find those *ojitos de agua*, those little eyes of water in Arbolito Creek, or maybe a small spring, and you'll usually find somebody living there."

Clay shifted in his chair. He thought about Simik and his company and what sucking billions of water out of the aquifer might do to those little sources of water. Like Gus and Locket both, he said nothing as he studied the rangeland to the south.

Finally, Gus droned on, "And lots of them still have family south of the river. Lots of family. And they all want a piece of what they think is the American dream over here." Gus sighed and once more gestured at the hardpan, already sending up dust devils in heat thermals rising from nothing but beige rangeland with a complete absence of anything green.

Locket considered what Gus had said. He thought about all the discarded infant items he had discovered in the abandoned house in Presidio. And he thought about the clerk at the store over in Presidio and what she had told Jovita about a man buying great quantities of throwaway diapers and baby formula and cigarettes. Enough to last several days. Or even weeks. Enough to last until all this extra law pressure was off the highways, long enough so that his family could later get packed into a van or some eighteen wheeler with a dozen more and get transported completely out of the area. Or die at some truck stop, abandoned and locked inside without water and disappearing oxygen, like had happened just this past week near Sweetwater. And two weeks before that in Dallas.

"Maybe enough for *two* babies," Locket muttered to himself. "I'll need a horse, Gus," he said suddenly. He stood and lifted his hat and swiped his forehead with the back of his hand. Then he narrowed his eyes at the rangeland to the south of Los Arbolitos. "Water him good, too."

"A horse?" Gus said.

"Yeah," Locket said. "Just for today, if you don't mind. And you'll probably need to let out the stirrups on your saddle for me."

"Right now?" Clay said.

"Right now," Locket said. "And a canteen of that cool water you offered and never brought out, Gus. I think I'll ride across there and poke around a little bit today."

"Just like the Old West," Clay said and smiled at Locket.

"Well, not exactly," Locket grumbled. "My Winchester's still in my patrol car back in Solitario, thanks to you, asshole. And I ain't been on a horse in months." He arched and stretched and pressed the heel of his hands into the small of his back, anticipating what was to come.

"I've got a rifle," Gus offered. "You sure you ought'a go snooping around out there by yourself?"

"Yeah," Locket said. "But I don't need a rifle. County issued sidearm here is plenty."

"How do you know what you're looking for?" Gus said. "Don't you want to talk to Perfidia first?"

"Nope," Locket said. "I got enough clues from that clerk I talked to in Presidio."

"Clues like what?" Clay said.

"Cigarette brand, diaper brand, formula brand and a little physical stuff about the guy who bought all of it." Locket said. "It's enough. And besides, each one of those little adobes out there will have a burn barrel or somewhere they'd put dirty diapers and wrappers and stuff."

"Yeah," Gus said. "If they haven't burned it all."

"Maybe," Locket said.

"I don't understand why you won't just come inside and talk to Perfidia?" Gus pressed. "Wouldn't she give you a better description and stuff?"

"I doubt that she'd . . ." Locket said and then caught himself.

"Why not?" Clay said.

"Yeah?" Gus said.

"Well, what I meant was the minute she sees this badge and all, she might just clam up, you know? I don't want her disappearing again."

This did not make good sense to Gus and Clay and Locket noted the silence from the other two, both standing now. "Well, whatever," Gus said and then repeated, "I ain't a lawman but are you sure you don't want some help out there with this, Locket?"

Locket turned back to them. "Hey, it ain't like I'm trying to be brave or nothing, okay? Or stupid. It's my job, though, and this might get a little tricky and I don't wanna have to worry about anybody else."

"Alright then," Gus said. "And by the way, I think you'll like the horse I'm gonna saddle for you."

"How's that?" Locket said.

"Well, she's sort'a like you, Locket. Big and tough," Gus said and he grinned at Locket. "And she ain't been rode in months either." ❧

CHAPTER 28

It was late on Friday night when Jovita came back across to the hotel from the special commissioners meeting and told Bea all that had to be accomplished by Monday morning. Bea had stood with her hands on her hips and said, "If you want *cold* food and *cold* coffee over there, that's fine with me. I can do that. You're the boss. But if you want me up night and day all weekend fixing hot food and hot coffee and waiting on you three hand and foot, then you'll have to park yourselves right here." She moved to the corner and shoved two tables together and then went straight back to her kitchen without waiting for Jovita to respond.

"And I thought I was the boss," Jovita said to the empty room. She smiled and then returned to the meeting room across the street to help Dobb and Yebbie bring over the materials they would need.

Now at five o'clock on Monday morning, the three sat drained and red-eyed over many pages of handwritten notes Jovita had scrawled for the past two days. They had huddled at the tables inside the hotel restaurant behind a fortress of boxes filled with state water regulations and worn statute books from the commissioner's office across the street. Each had taken turns sleeping for a couple of hours in the first guest room just down the hall. Bea emerged from the kitchen, she, too, strained and sluggish. She came to the work area with a coffeepot.

"More?" she said.

"Not for me." Jovita held up her hand. "What I need's a bath and some fresh clothes and a couple days' sleep. You go on to bed, Bea. And thanks. . . ."

"Yeah, thanks Bea," Dobb said and Yebbie echoed this.

Bea turned and left the room. Dobb stretched and yawned and said, "I think we got it down, even if it is pretty rough. It's good enough we can go ahead and post it in the Alpine newspaper this week, both today's and Wednesday's issues."

Yebbie also stretched and yawned and then pulled out his pocket watch, wound it. "What time was it they said, Jovita?"

"Well, the man I talked to on Saturday at the newspaper said they had to have it in their hands by eight o'clock this morning if we wanted it in today's issue."

"A reporter or what?" Dobb said.

"He didn't say," Jovita said. "But it was six in the morning on a Saturday when I called over. My guess is he was probably the night janitor."

"I hope you can make it in time, Jo," Dobb said. "It has to be in today's paper and also in Wednesday's to make it legal by midnight this coming Saturday."

"Yes," Jovita said and sighed. "That's what it says in here." She put her hand on top of the massive binder of Texas statutes and read from a note she had made. "'*Legal notices shall be published at least twice in a local or area newspaper.*'" But that's just the *notice* that these regulations will be effective Saturday, May fifteenth at midnight. We don't have to print the actual regulations in there too. These only have to be here at the commissioner's office." She held up her scrawled notes. "Typed up and available for anyone to read."

"What about that hearing?" Yebbie said, getting his second wind.

"That's all day Saturday, May fifteenth also," Dobb reminded him. "Deadline day. Agua Hondo can begin drilling at one second past midnight if these aren't in place. That is, unless Clayton does something foolish like . . ."

"You mean drill whether he's got her moved or not?" Yebbie said. "If we don't get all this done in time?"

"None of what you're saying is going to happen," Jovita scolded. She remembered the anger in Clay's voice when he told her about Simik's attempt to bribe him but she declined to disclose this. "Dammit, just trust me on this, you two."

"Well, anyway," Dobb continued. "After midnight, they'll have to go through us and these new regs. One way or the other."

He looked at the other two, who said nothing. All three knew this and none of it bore repetition, not even Clay's dilemma. Dobb went on. "It'll have to be another special meeting on Saturday, and, by the way, someone will need to post a notice about that meeting here in town and what's to be on *that* agenda too." He looked at Yebbie, changed his mind and then went on. "I'll post it local, Jo. You ought'a make sure that's also in the newspaper over there though. And I'll drag your ass in for that hearing too, Yebbie, don't worry. It'll be a long one so catch up on your sleep and your chores."

"The legal notice in the paper has to mention the time of the hearing," Jovita corrected Dobb. "That's what it's all about. But before then, we have to run these notes by the county attorney today, then read through them on Saturday and then take any oral or written comments and consider them," Jovita said. "With an open mind." She looked at her two partners this time. "That doesn't mean we have to make major changes as long as there's no legal problem."

"Something legal like maybe from that skunk Simik?" Dobb said.

Jovita smiled and nodded and then said, "Or anyone else. It has to be public and like I said, we have to keep open minds on it."

"Well, far as I'm concerned, it's done right now," Yebbie said. "But my mind's open, just like always."

Jovita raised her eyebrows but said nothing.

"How long's that Saturday meeting have to be?" Yebbie went on.

"Doesn't say," Dobb said. "But long enough to give anyone a chance to comment, all day and after work hours too, I'd guess. What do you think, Jo?"

"I think unless we want a long legal hassle over this later on, we ought to just sit right there across the street and listen, right up till the last second on Saturday night," she said and then glanced at each man. "With *open* minds, right?"

"Right," Dobb said.

"Right," Yebbie said.

"Well, why don't you do whatever you need to do

upstairs, Jo, and then drive on over there to Alpine with the notices," Dobb said.

"The only thing I'd need to do upstairs would be to get rid of some of this coffee," Jovita said. "And I can do that right down here in the restroom." She stood and picked up the notices she had written. "Or somewhere behind a bush between here and there. It's sixty-seven miles over there, you know," she continued. "Winding two-lane blacktop. That usually takes me an hour and a half, in broad daylight. And it's only half-light out there right now. I can push the speed limit a little after sunup though." She turned to Yebbie. "What time's your trusty railroad watch saying, Yeb?"

Yebbie made a great show of retrieving his pocket watch, wound it and squinted at it. "Well . . . in twenty-two seconds, it'll be exactly five forty-five A.M."

"That gives me about fifteenth minutes to swing by the restroom and then get this stuff loaded in my car and be on the road," Jovita said. "And no, I don't powder my nose any longer, if that's what you two are wondering. I just pee."

Dobb cleared his throat at this and Yebbie looked down as if to make certain he returned his watch to its correct pocket, an act he had done without having to observe it thousands of times. "Yeah, well, that'll give you two hours to get over there," Dobb said. "More or less. I hereby adjourn this Solitario County Water Control Board work session at . . . what time is now, Yeb?"

"Two hours, more or less . . ." Jovita interrupted. "If I don't run into a deer or fall asleep at the wheel or. . . ." She stopped and shook her head. "Just thought of something. There's no way I can push the limit today."

"Why's that?" Dobb said.

"Roads will still be crawling with state troopers and BP agents and maybe even FBI by now."

Dobb grew somber with her comment. Yeb lifted his watch to report the official time the meeting had adjourned. But Jovita did not wait for an official winding of Yebbie's watch or the reporting of the exact time, nor did she stop at the restroom. She left the two sitting at the table, bent over Yebbie's watch.

Jovita had driven the speed limit a full thirty miles north on Highway 67 toward Marfa before it became apparent that she could push it a little. She had seen one truck moving south but not another vehicle, much less any parade of law officers searching for a kidnapped baby and its now missing mother.

Locket had been nowhere around Solitario the past weekend and even if he had been, Jovita was buried in the meeting and would have missed him. So the disposition of Perfidia and her baby were as unknown to Jovita at this moment as was the outcome of all this county commissioner business.

Even Clayton had avoided her earlier this morning. He had risked poking his nose into the restaurant for a moment and then pulled it back like a touched turtlehead the moment he saw the scowl on Bea's weary face. Jovita had no idea where he had gone and if Bea had known anything new, she would have called Jovita aside and told her.

So when Jovita arrived at the edge of Marfa around six forty-five, she decided to stop at the only gas station in town. It was twenty-six more miles to Alpine and she was making good time without any pressure on the roads. But it was not as if she was feeling no pressure at all; she simply could not postpone a restroom break. Nor could she hold her curiosity about Perfidia and her baby any longer.

The attendant scowled when she asked for the restroom key. "You gonna need gas?" he said.

"No," Jovita said. "But I do need to make a phone call."

"We don't make shit off phone calls, lady," he grumbled but she had already scurried away with the key and ducked into the facility.

When she came back with the key, she opened her purse and handed the man a ten-dollar bill. "I'll need change for the phone," she said. "A couple dollars of quarters . . . please."

He stared at her for a long moment as if he would suffer no further indignity, especially this early on a Monday morning. He stood looking at the bill but he did not move.

"Could you hurry?" she growled but when he made no movement toward the cash register, she added softly, "Please?" But he did not punch open the machine until Jovita said, "Okay, you can keep the rest of the ten."

No one answered the phone at Locket's office in Solitario and the person on the line down at Sheriff Gil's office began to quiz her immediately about any emergency. Jovita shifted her feet inside the phone booth and said, "No, it's not an emergency. I just need some information."

"About what?"

"Just let me speak with the sheriff, okay?"

"About what?"

"Okay, it's about a missing person," Jovita said. "Or I should say *persons.* Is that emergency enough for you?"

Sheriff Gil's voice sounded weary when he came right on the line. "This is the sheriff."

"Jovita Seals here," she said. "Sorry to bother you but I can't raise Locket."

"Is he the missing person?" Gil said evenly. "If so, what else is new, Jo?"

"Listen, I don't have time for your bullshit, Gil," she said. "I just drove up from Solitario to Marfa and I didn't see a single patrol car. I'm wondering if maybe you found that woman's missing baby?"

"Well . . ." Sheriff Gil began and there was a long silence on the line. "Well, we *have* called off the search."

"Then you did find it?"

"You know, this ain't even hit the newspaper yet, Jovita," he said. "Now goddammit, why should I tell you?"

"I think you know why," she said. "It's not exactly like I'm a stranger to all this, Gil. And I'm not the *New York Times* but I *am* late for something already and it's Solitario County business, so just say what's happening, okay?" Jovita's voice rose as if she urgently needed the key again from the attendant.

"Oh yeah," Sheriff Gil said. "I heard. Congratulations." When there was nothing but thick silence again on the line, he quickly said, "Everybody decided to just put this one down a notch in priority, Jovita, that's all."

"Down a notch?" Jovita said, incredulous.

"Everybody?"

"Yep," he said. "And you can just hold on a minute. It's not like we ain't got nothing else we're working on. And I didn't say we'd just dropped it or . . ."

"Everybody?" Jovita interrupted.

Sheriff Gil paused for a long moment and then said, "Everybody except maybe some renegade deputy."

Jovita held the receiver away from her face, looked into the mouthpiece as if to decipher what the sheriff had just said. "Bye, sheriff," she said. "Have a great day." She hung up the phone and exited the booth and walked briskly to her car.

As if it were some dire warning, the digital clock on her dash flashed seven-thirty. Jovita drove straight through the little town and turned east at the intersection toward Alpine, still twenty-six winding miles away. She pushed the accelerator to the floorboard until she was up to the speed limit, focused her waning attention solely on the road, ignoring some of the most beautiful scenery in West Texas: Paisano Peak and the Cathedral Mountains to the south.

In Alpine, she parked in front of the office of the *Alpine Dispatch* and went inside with the notices she had written. The desk attendant was pleasant but firm. "See that clock?" she said. Jovita glanced at the wall clock, now reading ten minutes past eight. "Well, I don't know if you're aware of this, but today's paper went to bed at eight o'clock this morning. Sharp. So does Wednesday's. So if you want that notice published in Wednesday's paper, I can sure do that."

Jovita said nothing.

"But like I say, if you wanted it to come out in today's paper, we needed it before eight this morning and preferably by last Friday.

"Look, I'm a new member of the Solitario County Commissioners," Jovita began, her voice rasping now, but she could see from the woman's face that this was not the first time she had heard something like this. "And see, we had no idea we'd even be scheduling something like this so soon because our chairman Henry Bennett . . ."

"I'm real sorry," the woman said.

Neither said anything for long and wasted minutes. Jovita refused to show desperation. She stood there, thinking about the enormous events that had transpired in her tiny spot on the map these past ten days and it seemed that a mere ten minutes in whatever was left of eternity bore little relevance in comparison.

Then Jovita thought about her phone conversation with Sheriff Gil, not an hour ago. "May I speak with your editor," she said evenly and fidgeted with the red scarf in her hair.

"Well . . ." The woman looked back toward an open office door.

"Right now."

The woman turned around and when she saw Jovita's eyes, she appeared as if perhaps she did need reinforcements. She spun around and disappeared into an office behind the counter and soon, another woman came out to the front. The clerk moved to her desk and began working on file folders.

"What seems to be the problem," the editor said.

"No problem," Jovita said and smiled. "I just

wonder if you've heard the latest on that woman who's baby was abducted this past week?"

"The latest?"

"Well, yes," Jovita continued. "You may know the woman's also disappeared."

"We did hear that," she said. "But no official statement yet on it."

"Well, as of . . ." Jovita squinted at the wall clock. "About thirty minutes ago, I guess they've called off the search. County Sheriff's Office, State Highway Patrol, all of them. Maybe even the FBI for all I know."

The woman lifted her eyes at this. "Oh, really?"

"Yes."

"And what's your source of information on this Miss . . ."

"Jovita Seals. I'm a new member of the Solitario County Commissioners and I don't think we've met, but that's okay," Jovita said. "I'm a little green at this, but I think we'll be seeing a lot of each other in the future and by the way, my source is Sheriff Gilberto Romero over in Presidio."

The woman nodded, looked over her shoulder at two reporters working feverishly at computers. "Hold up a minute on that," she said to them. Both frowned and glanced back but stopped what they were doing.

"Go on," the editor said.

"Well, you should give him a quick call," Jovita said. "And when you do, just tell him I told you this, okay?"

"Sure," the woman said and she wrote down Jovita's name. "And I understand you had something else you think should be in today's issue?"

Jovita handed her the notices. "Could you get these in?"

The editor looked at them, smiled at her and said, "I think we can do this . . . Miss Seals."

"My friends call me Jo." Jovita said.

"Thanks, Jo," the editor said and held up Jovita's notes. "Don't worry about these."

Jovita nodded, turned and sauntered out of the office. Outside as she stepped down from the curb, she wobbled, then leaned on the front fender of her car and took in a long breath of morning air before she got inside. ❧

CHAPTER 29

"How long you think it'll take him?" Clay said to Gus as they stood in the work yard at Los Arbolitos. Locket had mounted the big mare and put her forward to the south and now had disappeared into the dry wash that led down to Arbolito Creek.

"Depends on how long he stays at each place," Gus said and turned back toward the patio with Clay behind him. "And whether or not they'll even let him inside and what they'll volunteer to say."

"Yeah," Clay said. He paused and looked back in the direction Locket had ridden. "He's got no warrant or anything, though."

"Most of them are friendly enough," Gus said. "They wouldn't want any more trouble than you or I would. They'll talk to him unless they're hiding illegals." He walked across the patio and held the front door of the house for Clay. "Like I'm doing."

"Yeah, right," Clay said and lowered his eyes. He turned slowly around and faced Gus at the door. "You know, maybe I shouldn't have turned her over to you, Gus. Maybe I should have just let Locket take her to the BP or something."

"Hey, you got enough on your mind anyway," Gus said. "And if Locket didn't handcuff her and load her into your pickup by now, I don't think she needs to worry about that. Neither do you. Come on inside. I'd guess it would take him all day and maybe then some just to stop and knock on doors. We got time for another long visit."

Clay nodded and went through the door into the entryway and Gus followed him back to the kitchen. If Perfidia had spied through the front window at Locket and Clay's arrival, she had quickly disappeared into the back bedroom.

"Where is she?" Clay said. "She'll want to know what's happening."

"Sit down," Gus said. "I'll check on her in a minute. I imagine she's getting pretty tired of hiding out back there. You want something hot or cold to drink?"

"Both," Clay said. He sat at the little kitchen table. "If that's okay. It was a damn madhouse at the hotel all weekend and right up till early this morning. Wasn't any way Bea was up to fixing any food for a live-in bum like me."

"Yeah, you don't want to cross Bea, especially if she's cross herself," Gus observed. "You said *madhouse?*"

"Yeah," Clay said. He told Gus about the meeting on Friday night and Jovita's appointment and about the work sessions all weekend. "Anyway, it was a real crunch to get the water regulations spelled out and the hearing for Saturday posted. I mostly just stayed outta sight."

"Sounds like a good idea," Gus said. He refilled the coffeepot and put it on the stove. "Sure you wouldn't rather have a cold beer?"

"Oh no, you ain't getting me into that again." Clay said.

"That's good," Gus said and brought over a pitcher of cool tap water. "I'm out of longnecks anyway. You owe me big time." He sat across from Clay at the table. "Sounds like you been up to your ears in all that. What about your property and the transfer? What's happening with all that?" He paused and looked at Clay. "And with Serafina?"

"Simik was there, of course," Clay said. "No way he'd been in the dark about what was happening. But I didn't talk to him till after the meeting on Friday night."

"What'd he say about all this?" Gus said. "Bet he cussed and groaned."

"Nope," Clay said. He sipped his glass of cool water. "He was pretty calm . . . well, maybe *determined* is a better word."

"How so?"

"Tried to bribe me, Gus," Clay said. "I sat with him in his fancy car in the dark right there on the main street of Solitario and he poked a big fat envelope under my nose."

"Cash money?"

"Probably," Clay went on. "I never looked inside it. It pissed me off so bad I just told him since he'd stuffed it so full he knew where he could stuff it now."

"You told him *that?*"

"Well . . . not in so many words, but yes," Clay said. "I just refused to look inside it or to even touch it. I got out and he knew I was mad as hell."

"Don't blame you."

"Yeah, thinking I could be bribed was bad enough," Clay said. "But it was the other that really got to me."

"What?"

"He said if I didn't get her moved by the deadline on midnight this Saturday, he'd start bulldozing that area flat, knock over the old windmill and set up his drilling rig. Said it wouldn't be a pretty sight."

"Oh yeah?" Gus said. He rose and brought over the coffee. "Sounds like you won't have to worry about that now though. I mean, with these regulations in place there's no way he can do that. Not legally."

Clay looked down. "Seems like that's all we've been talking about lately, Gus."

"What's that?"

"Things legal and things illegal," he said. "And people." He picked up a spoon and stirred nothing into the coffee, staring at the swirls.

"Yeah, does seem like that," Gus agreed.

"Well . . ." Clay said. "Somehow I just don't know if that'll stop a guy like Simik." He looked up at Gus. "What if he just goes right on in there at say, one second after midnight, and starts tearing up stuff and ignores those regulations? Or claims they didn't have them posted in time or some bullshit legal deal like that? What if he just flattens the old house and bulldozes Serafina's gravesite at the same time? Even if Locket goes out there and hands him some kind of legal paper and stops him from drilling right then, Simik could still do all that destruction in less time than it took you to make this coffee, Gus. How do I know that won't happen if I leave her there right up to the last second?"

"I see what you mean," Gus said.

"Sure, I could sue him, or the commissioners could sue him, and maybe we'd get all kinds of money,"

Clay went on. "But hell, I sure don't want, or need, my old place back. That's his, one way or the other. And he's still gonna owe me the rest of what's in the contract, one way or the other."

"Yeah."

"I just want my baby out of there."

"I know," Gus said. He stood and walked to the door leading to the back patio. Clay watched his friend study the horizon to the east for a long while. "Then let's just move her, Clay." Gus said quietly and he turned back.

Clay stared at him but said nothing at first and then, "What do you mean?"

"I mean *now,* today or tomorrow or whenever," Gus continued. "Anytime between now and midnight Saturday."

"But that'll give Simik exactly what he's wanting," Clay said. "We can't do that, Gus. Not now. Not with all Jovita and the others have got in place. They also need time to—"

"Sure we can," Gus interrupted. "If Simik doesn't *know* we've done it, right?"

Clay thought about this for several minutes and then said, "But that'd break my contract and if he found out about it, he could go right in there. And if I didn't tell Simik, wouldn't I be doing something . . ."

"Illegal?" said an angry voice from the hallway. Perfidia came on into the kitchen from the hall where she had lingered, listening to all this. "How can moving a baby from a bad place to a better place be called *illegal?*"

Clay rose and stood facing Perfidia. Both men

looked at her and saw the painful indignation in her face. Neither dared venture a comment, not even to agree with what she had said.

"And I want to help you, Clayton," Perfidia said and her anger gave way to determination. Her eyes welled up. "I want to give you a little of what I can never pay back."

"You don't owe me anything," Clay whispered. "And I don't know exactly what Gus has in mind, but you got more important things to do right here. Locket'll be back this evening. Maybe with some good news and—"

"And maybe with some bad news?" Perfidia interrupted. "What can I do here but wait? And worry? Maybe I don't want to hear what he'll have to say. . . ." She took in a deep breath and turned her head and the detachment came back to her face.

"We can't do it in broad daylight," Gus said and he moved toward the two. "We'll have to drive over in the dark, do it in the dark, come back in the dark. If Simik—or anybody else finds out what we're doing—it would just be too risky. Word might get out, questions asked. It would bring everything else to a brickwall stop. It's gotta happen at night. And it may take several sessions to get it done with just the two of us."

"The *three* of us," Perfidia insisted. "I want to help, Gus . . . please. I *need* to help."

"Well . . ." Clay sat back down and stared blankly into space but could only repeat, "Well . . ."

"Whatta you think?" Gus pressed and he sat again across from Clay. "It's your call."

Perfidia moved and stood behind Gus with a hand on his shoulder, waiting for Clay to speak. When Clay looked at them again, he nodded as if these words made all the sense in the world. And so did her hand resting on Gus' shoulder. In a few short words, she and Gus's had managed to say more than all the words Clay had spoken since Adelita's death, all his well-considered and legitimate words about *not* moving Serafina. Gus and Perfidia were talking now about how he *could* move her.

"But what if they stop us on the road with you?" Clay said to Perfidia. "I still think that's too risky for you."

"Locket said the pressure was off now," Perfidia said. She looked awkwardly at the two. "I was listening through the window at all that," she admitted.

"Then you also know what he's looking for," Gus said. "I should say, *who* he's looking for?"

"Yes," she said and for a moment, she was not there again. "My baby . . ."

"What if he comes back and we're gone?" Gus said.

Perfidia looked first at Gus and then at Clayton. "What if he comes back and we *are* here? Maybe I'm more worried about that?"

Gus stood silent for a long while. Finally he said, "Clay?"

"Guess it's not my call after all, right?" Clay said.

"Okay then," Gus said. "I think if we stay to the back road and then just straight through Solitario and then it's only the two miles south on the blacktop and then right onto the dirt road out your way, Clay, we'll be okay. It's bringing her back into Solitario that might get tricky." Gus looked at Perfidia and then to Clay. "For Perfidia . . . *and* your Serafina."

"But what about Henry Bennett's grave?" Clay said, still hesitant. "Henry's right where I wanted to put . . ." Clay stopped himself. Gus knew all about this. And what Clay was about to say were the same kinds of words he had heard coming from his mouth his entire adult life. Words that had always stalled him in his tracks, isolated him from the world. Words that had prevented him from going forward with too many plans and too many deeds he knew now he should have done. And maybe even the kind of words that had caused his Serafina to be right where she was at this moment, locked inside the caked earth for all these years.

"You don't worry about where we're gonna put her when we get her into Solitario," Gus said. "I've got an idea that just might work. Let's just get out there tonight and every night this week if we have to and focus on bringing your Serafina up, okay?" He looked over his shoulder at Perfidia. "You and me *and* Perfidia."

Clay thought about this and about what Perfidia had just said about her own child and moving her baby across the river against far worse odds. He knew all along his mission would not be easy either, but when he looked into the face of this young mother, he saw courage he had never thought possible. And then he remembered it was the same kind of courage he had seen many years ago in the face of his new bride, Adelita.

"We'll need to fix that old wagon wheel too," Clay declared and he stood. "It won't take long with a couple of bolts and some axle grease."

"Wagon wheel?" Gus said, baffled.

"Yes," Clay said. "If we're gonna get her moved without anyone seeing us, we need to bring her into

Solitario the back way."

"Back way?"

"Yes, up the dirt county road till we're close enough and then across the rangeland the last few miles inside that dry wash and into town that way," Clay said and he seemed a man transformed now. "We can't risk being seen driving on the blacktop even that last two miles and especially through the main street of Solitario with a tarp covering something in a pickup bed. Not even at night. The BP would be all over us if they saw us. And no pickup can drive across that rough stuff like these old giant wheeled prairie wagons could. Weren't no blacktops back then, right?"

"Right . . ." Gus said. He was not convinced this would be a problem for his four-wheeled drive rig but he did not protest Clay's plan. He knew he was witnessing a Clayton Elliott he had not known in decades, perhaps ever.

"But that ain't the reason why," Clay went on evenly. "Not the main reason anyway. It's just something else I gotta do, Gus, don't you see? Fix it up and bring her in here in that old wore out wagon. It's what I shoulda done twenty-five years ago. I shoulda had it repaired and useful even then, even though I thought of it as some worthless thing from the past."

Gus said nothing and Perfidia now seemed mystified by all this, but she too remained silent. Finally Gus said, "I know you still got that old harness, Clay, but I don't have a single critter that's broke to pull a wagon anymore." He shrugged. "Just a thought."

"I don't either," Clay admitted but he did not seem to be stalled by this.

"Then how are you gonna pull it?" Gus said.

"Palo," Clay said and he smiled. "He's gonna pull it. And like you said about that other problem, Gus, you don't need to worry about how this one's gonna get done either. This problem's mine." ❧

CHAPTER 30

When Locket turned the mare down the steep slope into Arbolito Creek she balked, sidestepped into the loose shale but then finally acknowledged that someone firm was astride her and moved on down. The midday sun had borne down on them for several hours as they inquired without any results at first one lone house and then another, all at the end of rutted two-track dirt roads, and now, when the mare heard the stream, she stiff-legged more rapidly down to the *ojito de agua,* the little eye of water, trapped behind rocks at the bottom.

"Easy," Locket said. "I won't put you where either one of us would get hurt."

He dismounted and loosed the bridle and took out the bit. "You'll enjoy it more this way."

He slipped the reins over her neck and held them in one hand and then loosened the cinch and let her drink unencumbered. He crouched and with his other hand, brought up several cupped palms of water for himself. "Sure better'n that warm canteen stuff."

He stood and reached for the canteen, emptied the remainder onto the rocks and bent over to refill it. As it filled, he glanced down the cut to the little settlement of Redford some four miles south, the furrows of the green onion fields serrated with glistening irrigation water from the Rio Grande.

"No need to go down there," he muttered and took in a deep breath. "Sheriff and every other lawman in the area's already been there. Probably twice or three times." The mare brought her head up, mouthed the cool water dripping from her muzzle and turned her head to him as if she agreed. "Why the hell am I telling you this?" Locket said but he admitted it felt good being horseback again. And he was no stranger at all to conversing with a horse. "Maybe it's because you don't argue, right?" The mare looked at him and then returned to her business of filling her gut.

When she had her fill, Locket stood and allowed her to nibble at the few blades of grass that were teasing her along the edge of creek. "I don't think we could have missed many," he mused, remembering the houses where he had inquired today, all within easy reach of Arbolito Creek and no indication of an infant in any of them. At least, not one they would admit to having, not at their front door which was where he had usually been stopped. But he had seen no evidence around the burn barrels of clues to a baby either.

"Gus said maybe a dozen or so. Said find those little sources of water and there'll be a house there." And then Locket reconsidered Gus' words. He had not said just Arbolito Creek. He had said *sources of water.* Small springs. "Maybe we need to spread our circle a little," Locket said.

He stood and tightened the cinch a little, let the mare exhale the breath she had taken in to prevent a final tightening, and then he tugged it further. "Good trick but it won't work on me," he said. "Sorry. We ain't done yet." He replaced the bit and buckled the headstall. "You'll get oats tonight," he said and rubbed his hand along her neck and mounted. "Promise."

Locket knew well how high the heat could rise and dehydrate a person in this area, even in May. But he had not been out on horseback in a long while and so by four in the afternoon it had become almost unbearable, not only for himself, but also for the mare. He had moved several miles east of Arbolito Creek and as Gus had said, there were a few houses scattered in this area, some with children, but like the others today, none bore any positive clues to an infant. By six o'clock, he had decided to turn the mare back northwest toward Los Arbolitos.

"Maybe we'll try again tomorrow," he said and then let the reins go slack, giving the mare her head. He knew she could find her stall better in the fading light than he could. "Or on the other hand, maybe we won't. . . ."

Once she had her head, the mare quickened her pace a little and seemed to know exactly where she was going. In the tempering evening, Locket slumped forward with the rocking motion, almost dozing. After another hour or so, the mare stopped suddenly and lowered her head. Locket straightened, looked to the west where a slice of coralline sky on the horizon said the sun was just down. He knew they could not have crossed the miles back to Los Arbolitos yet. When the mare began to drink from a small flow of spring water he said, "Well, close but no cigar. But water's water, I guess, and I don't blame you a bit." He dismounted to join her and when he did, Locket saw the thin shaft of light from a window some hundred yards on east. "Well, maybe close enough," he said and stood silent while the mare drank. "Maybe close enough," he repeated and stared at the silhouette of the little adobe house.

He waited until the mare had her fill and then remounted and put her forward toward the house. As he neared, he smelled the smoldering of a burn barrel and nudged the mare in that direction and stopped her at the source of the smoke. Locket leaned over and looked into the glow of various items inside the fifty-five gallon drum. He sniffed and instantly knew the distinct stench to be from plastic throwaway diapers, not something he enjoyed smelling, but something he knew from the burning trash piles county crews had collected from alongside the highways.

He jerked back and reined the mare toward the front door of the house. When he dismounted, he made certain there was enough noise to announce his presence. "Easy," he said, though the mare stood dead tired, like a rock when he dropped the reins to the ground. *"Hola,"* he called, *"Hello?"*

He did not have to knock on the door. It was suddenly ajar and a squat and balding Hispanic man filled it. *"Que pasa?"* the man said and when he saw the wash of light fall across Locket's white shirt and badge and then the sidearm on his hip, he smiled and repeated his words in English, "What's happening?"

"Good evening," Locket said. "Sorry to bother you at this hour, but I wonder if I could talk to you a minute?"

"Sure," the man said and widened the door a little. "Some problem?"

"Not really," Locket said. "I'm Deputy Locket Wagner, from over at Solitario."

"Sure," the man said. "I know you. Come on in."

"Sorry, I don't remember you," Locket said. He removed his hat, came on into the room and held out his hand.

"You probably wouldn't," the man said and shook Locket's hand. "I'm Paco Sanchez. We've talked over a beer or two at Julio's. This is my wife, Consuela.

The woman standing across the room came closer and took Locket's hand and nodded but she said nothing. He noticed they both seemed uneasy.

"Well, I'll get right to the point and then get out of your way here, folks," Locket said. "I'm looking for a missing baby."

"A baby?" the man said.

"Missing?" his wife said.

"Yes, maybe kidnapped or something worse. We don't know."

The couple looked at each other and then back to Locket. They said nothing.

"Is there a baby here?" The woman shook her head but the man did not. Locket continued, "I looked into your burn barrel and saw . . ."

"Yes," the man interrupted. "My brother's baby is here."

"Your brother?"

"Yes," he said. "He's here. With his wife and their baby." Locket nodded but waited for the man to continue. "They've come across the bridge. At Presidio. To visit for a few days. . . ." He turned to his wife and both nodded vigorously.

"Look folks," Locket said and he smoothed the brim of his hat with his hand. "I'm a deputy sheriff . . . not Border Patrol . . . *no la migra.* I've got no authority over illegal immigrants. That's not what I'm here for, so just relax, okay? *Esta bien.*"

This seemed to calm the two but they did not speak. The woman pulled a chair from the kitchen table and offered it to Locket.

"Can't stay," Locket said. "But thanks anyway." He turned to the man. "Could I talk to your brother? And his wife?"

The two looked at each other again and then back at Locket and the man became very somber and he nodded. When he did this, the woman disappeared into the back of the house and soon came out, a young couple behind her. The young woman carried a baby, asleep inside a blanket.

"This is Emiliano," the older man said. "And Josefa, his wife."

Locket nodded but he did not approach. The couple hovered silent against the wall near the door to the back of the house. "I'll just ask them a few questions and then I'll go," Locket said to the older man. "Okay?"

"Okay," the older man said and he motioned the young couple to a sofa where they sat.

Locket moved the proffered chair over now and sat close to them. *"Como esta su niña?"* he said and this seemed to ease them.

"Niño," the woman said, correcting the gender in Spanish, and then in English, "Not *niña.* It's a boy."

Locket nodded. The young woman had said this with the proud and obvious conviction of a new mother who knew exactly what sex her child was. When the young man also smiled and kept nodding, Locket had no doubt that this infant was indeed a boy and not Perfidia's baby daughter. He did not have to verify this fact. What facts he did need to verify were something else.

"You came across the border," Locket said evenly. "With a woman named Perfidia, right?" He began the list of facts, without accusation or emotion, the way he might write it up in his report tomorrow. "Through Santa Elena Canyon. . . . with this other woman and her baby." The young man became somber again, nodded, but then looked at the floor. Locket went on, "Hers was a baby girl, right?" The father nodded again.

Locket went on, "But she could not pay enough to the *coyotes* so they beat her and took her baby, right? Left her to die in the desert, without her shoes?" Locket waited a long while and then repeated, "Took her baby, right?"

Locket had said all this with much sympathy. But when the young man looked up at him, his face was drawn. "No," he said quietly. "It was not that way. That's not what happened to her baby." ❧

CHAPTER 31

"Stop here, Gus," Clay said. They sat in Gus's pickup at the top of the small hill that dropped down to Clay's old place. Clay got out and stood in the darkness for a moment looking at the wash of headlights from his truck. Gus had insisted they bring his rig instead of Clay's because it was faster and could carry all the tools they would need tonight. The beams opened up a slice of night down the rise and on into the yard where shards of broken glass sent back tiny spikes of light.

Clay leaned inside the door and said, "I'm gonna walk on down from here."

Gus looked at him around Perfidia, seated in the center. "Nobody's down there, Clay," Gus said. "We don't need to worry about anybody being here tonight."

"I ain't worried about that," Clay said. He looked again toward the gravesite where a huge tumbleweed had been blown in and now lay trapped inside the little picket fence, almost covering the grave. "I just wanna talk to Serafina a minute, let her know what's going on." He leaned again into the open door. "Okay?"

"Sure, Clay," Gus said. "You just wave when you want us to come on down."

Clay walked away in one rut of the two-track

road and on past the old adobe to Serafina's grave. He reached over and took hold of the thick stalk of the tumbleweed and pulled it free. He tossed it next to the corral where a puzzled Palo stood, his eyes also reflecting Gus's headlights.

"Sorry, baby," he began. "I should have come out more often last week but . . ." Clay caught himself apologizing again for something he had not done. He had come out just two days ago on Saturday and tossed a bale of hay in to Palo and the tumbleweed was not there, nor were any of the little purple flowers he had been seeking.

"Don't need to do that anymore, do I Sera," he said. "Just need to get this done. Ain't nothing me or you either one can do about wind blowing weeds around." He put his hands on his thighs and leaned forward. "Fact is, that's what I'm doing out here in the dark. Me and Gus and a friend," he continued. "Get this thing done. And they're gonna help me. It's what I been promising you I'd do and I gotta do it in the dark so don't you to worry none, hear?"

He straightened and looked around into the darkness and he remembered how those many years ago Serafina had sometimes come into their bedroom in the night, frightened by some animal sound from the darkness outside. Adelita always lifted the child and placed her snug between herself and Clay and soon she was asleep again and after a while Clay would lift her very gently and take her back to her own bed and put the rag doll next to her cheek and tuck the covers around her. And often during the full moon, he would then stand for a long while and watch Serafina sleep.

But there was no moon at all tonight. The task he and Gus and Perfidia had to do would have to be done in the bright glare from Gus's pickup beams and there could be no lingering or reminiscing or fond talk from any of them.

"Time to get busy," he said and then repeated, "But don't you worry none, Sera."

He turned into the headlights and waved to Gus, who brought the truck forward and parked it just so the light would flood Serafina's gravesite. Then Gus leaned out his window and said, "That gonna be okay?"

"It's fine," Clay said. He went to the bed of the truck and brought back wire cutters and cut the wire at the corner of the picket fence where he had twisted it shut just ten days ago. Gus shut off the engine and came out one side of the truck and Perfidia out the other but neither offered to assist with this.

"You need to be the boss on this," Gus said. He held out workgloves first to Perfidia and then to Clay. "You gotta let us know what you want us to do, Clay. But also what you *don't* want us to do, okay?"

Clay nodded but he said nothing. He put on the gloves and folded back the sides of the picket fence into an accordion, dragged it and propped this against the legs of the old windmill. Then he came back and stood at the little mound, covered completely by the flagstones he had patterned there twenty-five years ago.

"We'll stack these rocks out of the way," Clay said. Though he always knew what his limitations would be in doing this thing, he had never actually pictured the task they were about to perform. Inside his head, he was working out step-by-step what needed to be done and how. He bent and picked up one of the flagstones and took it over and dropped it on the ground next to the picket fence. Gus bent and brought over another as did Perfidia and one-by-one each stone was carried away until the little mound of earth lay exposed.

Clay moved and stood next to the headstone he had carved from a white rock slab. He paused as if he might not touch this one, but then said, "This needs to come out too. Don't matter where she winds up, this goes with her." He bent over and pushed on the stone but it did not move. He looked up into the headlights, put his hand up to shade his eyes and said, "Gus?"

Gus came over and stood next to Clay and when they both pushed on the buried stone, it moved a little. The two rocked it back and forward until the hard earth gave way enough that they could lift it free. "Good," Clay said. "Let's put it over there with the others. But it'll have to go back here when we're done tonight."

"I'll do this," Gus said. He did not ask about Clay's comment, just carried it over and placed it gently beside the other stones, returned and stood next to Perfidia.

Clay went on, "If we don't get her up tonight, I mean." Clay stood looking at the mound of earth. He seemed suddenly immobilized by all of this and spoke now to himself or to Serafina and not to the other two. "And see, even if we do, the headstone and fieldstones and the fence still have to be right back where they were in case Simik or somebody comes by and takes a look."

Gus understood. But he did not understand how they would disguise their work unless they finished bringing Serafina up tonight. How could they dig partially down and then cover it right back up, build the mound, put the flagstones and headstones and picket fence back in place so it would look as if no one had touched it?

Gus could stay quiet no longer. He moved over and stood next to Clay with his hand on Clay's shoulder. "Without bringing her up, Clay?" he said. "I don't think we can just dig part way down and then make it look the same tomorrow unless . . ."

Clay stood silent, continued looking down at the mound of earth. "How deep is she, Clay?" Gus said but Clay did not answer. "How deep?"

Clay shook his head, hesitated and finally said, "About three feet. I'm trying to remember, Gus." He turned to Gus and frowned. "I was pretty dazed about it all, you know?"

"Sure," Gus said.

"I remember it being about waist deep though, when I dug it. So it's maybe three feet to the top of the little casket Yebbie built from that galvanized horse trough."

"Listen, Clay," Gus said. "It's not going to be that hard. I'll go over there and get the picks and shovels and we're all three going to get with it, hear? We'll get her up and we'll do it *tonight.*"

"I'll get the tools," Perfidia said. She turned and went to the truck and brought back a pickax and two spades and stood holding them.

Clay looked at her and then at Gus. "Okay," he said. "Like you say Gus, it ain't gonna be that hard. That makes sense to me."

But it was that hard. The packed earth gave no sign of yielding. Gus started with a couple of gentle thumps, but then raised the pick higher and slammed it into the mound as hard as he could. "Three feet, you say?" Gus said.

Clay nodded. "About that, I'd say."

"Stand back," Gus said. He removed his hat and spun it onto the hood of his truck. Then he hammered again at the earth. Thirty minutes later, there was enough soil broken loose that Gus stood aside and let Clay and Perfidia move in to shovel it. Then Gus went right back to work with the pickax.

By midnight, Gus had loosed enough soil for Clay and Perfidia that they stood thigh deep in the gravesite as they shoveled it out. "It's a little more loose now," Gus said. He leaned against the hood of the truck between the headlights, swiped his forehead with his shirtsleeve.

"Get yourself a drink of water, Gus," Clay said. "Over at the windmill. You too, Perfidia. Not enough room in here now for both of us to work anyway." He scraped the shovel in the bottom of the hole, brought up half a spade full and tossed it out. "We ought'a be getting close now anyway."

Clay cleaned out what remained of the loosened soil and struggled out of the hole. Gus returned and brought the pickax over once more but paused at the edge. "Whose waist was it you were talking about, Clay?"

"What?"

"You said about waist deep? Whose waist, yours or Yebbie's?"

"Mine," Clay said and then, "But I don't really remember now . . . could have been Yebbie's, I guess. Why?"

"Well, if it was Yebbie's," Gus said. "Then we're right on it. If it was yours, we're maybe a foot away yet."

"Yeah," Clay said and thought some more. "I just don't know for sure, Gus."

"Then I ain't slamming this pick into the bottom any more," Gus said. "It'll have to just be shoveled out now, you understand. I mean, I wouldn't want to break through and . . ."

Clay nodded. "Yeah, I see. . . ." He looked for a long time into the shadow of the hole they had scratched out. Then he got back down inside and began tapping the point of the shovel into the soil, slowly scraping away what he could loosen this way and tossing it out.

"This'll take a little longer," Clay said. "You two might as well sit in the truck now." It was obvious neither Gus nor Perfidia intended to move. Clay stopped and looked up at them standing at the edge of the gravesite, watching him, but he could not see their faces with their backs to the glare from the headlights. He nodded and turned back to doing what he had been promising Serafina he would do.

It was well past four in the morning when Clay finished carving the soil from around the sides of the little casket with just enough room for his feet to fit at one end. Gus had turned off the headlights and brought over a flashlight and he and Perfidia knelt now as Clay struggled with the corner of the casket, trying to lift it loosc, but it refused to move.

"Open up a little bigger hole under there," Gus said. "I'll work my hand under it too."

"Not enough room for you to stand down in here

too," Clay said.

"Just do it," Gus said. He handed the flashlight to Perfidia and dropped to his stomach and leaned his body over as far as he could into the hole, reaching down until he felt the bottom edge of the little casket. "Right under here," he said and sat back up. "Dig me out a place to grip."

"Oh," Clay said. "I see. Okay, hand me something smaller to dig with, Perfidia. Can't get the shovel in there."

She went to the truck and brought back a screwdriver. "Will this do?"

"I think so," Clay said. He took the screwdriver and stabbed at the dirt just under the edge where Gus had indicated. "Try it now, Gus."

Gus leaned back into the hole and worked his hand under the edge. "Got it."

Clay reached under the other side where he had been lifting. "Okay, on three . . ." he said and counted, but when they pulled up, nothing moved.

"Do it again, Clay," Gus said.

Clay stopped and stood, breathing hard. He looked at Gus. "Maybe it's rusted out under there, Gus. Maybe the whole damn bottom will just come loose and stick right where it's been. And if that happens, then she'll . . ."

"Yeah, and maybe it *ain't,* Clay," Gus scolded. "Hell, everything ain't always gonna be against you, Clayton. Now bend over and help me tug, dammit."

Clay nodded and bent over. He said nothing else and so Gus counted this time and when they pulled, the little casket came loose, intact with the bottom still attached. Clay lifted one side and Gus the other and in his mind, each man thought it to be far lighter than they had expected, as if only some diaphanous soul occupied it. They placed it beside the empty grave and Gus held out his hand and Perfidia held out one of hers and they helped Clay come up from the hole.

"Now you're both free," Perfidia whispered. She gave the flashlight back to Gus to hold while she began to brush the dirt from the top and the sides of the casket. In the darkness, Clay was smiling and breathing hard and soon his breath was coming out in little gusts and neither of the other two could tell if they were laughter or sobs or both.

CHAPTER 32

When Locket rode back into the work yard at Los Arbolitos he knew it was well past midnight. The mare had stood outside the little adobe house for more than an hour as Locket quizzed the young couple inside. Now after at least two more hours riding, she was pulling at the reins and had broken into a trot as they neared the barn in the darkness.

Locket saw that the house was dark. "Looks like everybody's gone to bed," he said and then noted the single truck silhouetted in the starlight. "Or just gone, period. Front door's probably locked either way."

Locket reined the mare toward the truck but she would not turn until he pulled the rein harder and tapped her sides with his boot heels and clucked. "Don't blame you a bit. You've had a long tough haul and so did I," he said. "But we can't see a damn thing inside there without a flashlight. And I got no idea where a light switch might be . . . if there's one at all in the barn."

He dismounted and in the dim light saw it was Clay's truck and immediately wished it had been Gus's. "Damn," he said. "Probably won't even work, even if Clay's got one at all inside here somewhere."

He held the reins as he felt his way and opened the door on the passenger side and groped in the glove box where he did find a flashlight. "Well . . ." he said and pushed the button. Nothing. "Just as I figured." He slapped the light against the reins in the palm of his hand and tried again. Still nothing.

Locket sighed and reached across to check for the ignition key thinking he might move the truck and direct the headlights into the barn, but again, nothing. He tossed the useless flashlight onto the seat, shut the door and led the mare toward the angular outline of the barn. "We'll just have to go by feel, I guess," he said.

He found the latch and opened one side of the double doors and held out his hand as he walked the mare on into the barn. When his hand touched a huge rough-sawn column, Locket slapped the reins around it and tied them off.

"Steady," he said. He moved his palm down her neck as he walked alongside her, loosened the cinch and girth strap. Then he lifted the saddle free with one hand and pulled off the wet saddle blanket with the other. "There," he said. "At least you'll breathe better now."

He leaned the saddle upright against the wall of a stall and draped the wet blanket over its edge. When he bumped the wall with the saddle, he heard the rattle of a wire bale from a gasoline pump lantern on a nail driven into the side of the stall.

"Why didn't you tell me about this, old girl?" He lifted the lantern from its nail and shook it and heard the liquid slosh inside. "Guess I'll have to take up smoking," he said. "Not one damn match in these pockets, my friend, and my chance of finding one in here somewhere are slim to none."

He went back over to the mare. She shifted but then

she stood easy. "You just hang on a minute more," he said and walked back through the barn door and crossed the yard to the house. Just to be certain, he tapped first on the front door and listened for a long while. When he heard nothing inside, he pounded louder and again he heard nothing so he opened the door and called out, "Anybody home?" When this brought no response, Locket reached inside and snapped on the lightbulb in the entryway. Then he worked his way back to the kitchen and found the match holder above the propane stove. He fingered several matches out and went back through the front and over to the barn.

Inside, he heard the mare shifting again. "I know," he said. "Oats. I promised and I'll deliver." He found the lantern, pumped it and primed it and then scratched a match across the wall of the stall. The mare turned her head toward the burst of match flame which spread orange light into the corners of the barn, brighter than seemed possible. Locket twisted the knob on the primed lantern. It spewed and sputtered until he stuck the match inside the glass cover and touched it to the woven nylon bulb and it erupted into a fierce white glow, far brighter than the match. He whipped the match out and held it until the end was cold to his touch and then stuck it into his shirt pocket. "Don't need no fire out here tonight, do you, old gal?"

He hung the lantern on a higher spike and then crossed and led her into the stall and took off the bridle. Then he went into the grain bin and brought back a bucket of oats.

"Here you go," he said. He went to the end of the barn and carried over half a bale of hay. Finally, he took a five gallon bucket out to the water trough in the corral behind the barn and brought it back, poured it into the empty water tub in the stall and did this twice more before he stopped. "Happy now?" He smiled and then he saw a currycomb hanging on the wall. "Okay, maybe just a little more."

He took the comb and worked it over her damp back as she munched the oats and the memory of doing this many years ago in his youth made him feel good. When he finished this, he killed the lantern and went back over to the house.

Inside the kitchen, he found some cold beans and tortillas in the refrigerator and he wolfed these down and filled up with cool water from the tap. Then he set a pot of coffee on the stove, lit the burner and waited. When the coffee was done, he poured himself a mug and took it out to the entryway and put his hat on the steerhorn rack and then flipped off the light and went into the great room at the front of the house. He sat in the dark on an aged leather sofa in front of the massive rock fireplace, blew across the lip of the mug, tested and then sipped on the steaming coffee. He could feel the sweat on his back, now cooling against the leather of the sofa and he considered lighting the fireplace but he did not want to break the darkness because it gave him the solace he needed to think.

In his head, Locket worked over the words he had tried to put together for the past few hours, but nothing seemed right. When he tried the words as a lawman, they seemed awkward and empty and cold as the rock hearth in front of him. When he tried them simply as one human being to another, they ran together as feigned emotion, even though he would never intend them so. When he tried to arrange them in some fiery and impassioned diatribe, they burned his tongue just like the coffee in his mug. Locket dozed off with no resolution to the words he might say, the mug now cold and balanced between his palms.

The opening of the front door jolted him awake. He blinked and cleared his throat and heard the soft voices of Gus and Clay in the entry. In the muted dawn, he could now see the big face of the ancient railroad clock above the hearth: six thirty.

"You just get up?" Gus said as he entered the room. "Or just back?"

Locket put the coffee mug on the hearth and stood. "Dozed off right here," he said. "I been back a couple hours, I guess." Clay and Perfidia moved into the room and stood but neither said anything. "Y'all look pretty weary," Locket ventured but he stopped short of asking where they had been. "I made coffee but it's cold by now."

Gus went on back toward the kitchen. "I'll put on some more," he said. "Sit down, sit down. Won't take long."

Locket sat again on the leather sofa, Clay in an adjacent armchair and Perfidia on the rock hearth. Clay inhaled deeply but to Locket he seemed somehow peaceful. Perfidia shifted on the uneven rocks and Locket wanted to ask her to move to a soft chair, but again, these words seemed patronizing. That would be something Gus could say and so Locket also sat silent until Gus entered with the handles of three more mugs laced inside the fingers of one hand, the handle of the coffeepot wrapped with a potholder inside his other fist. "How'd she do?" Gus said. He poured the fresh coffee all around.

"Your mare?" Locket said. "Oh, she did fine. Lots better than me. I watered and put her up with some oats and hay." He sipped. "Even curried her bit."

Gus smiled. "Wish you hadn't done that," he said and sat on the opposite sofa, next to Perfidia who remained on the hearth. She held the mug between her hands but Locket did not see her taste it yet. She had her head cocked to the side as if she had fallen asleep, but he saw her eyelids open and close and open and close in a slow and unnatural rhythm.

"Why?" Locket said.

"She'll expect it every time," Gus said and then a quiet, weary chuckle went around the room, then thick silence except for the sipping. It seemed everyone was tiptoeing around the words suspended unspoken in the morning air.

Finally Locket said, "I won't even ask where y'all have been. But from the looks of your clothes, I probably could guess."

"I don't mind you knowing," Clay offered. "But it's probably good you don't know everything, Lock. At least not yet. I mean, in case someone should ask you about it."

"Speaking of asking about stuff . . ." Gus began. He looked down and then up at Perfidia who raised her head now. "Why don't you sit somewhere softer," he said to her. "Let's hear what Locket has to say." Perfidia looked at Gus, her eyes wide now, and she shook her head. "Over here, okay?" He placed his hand on the seat cushion next to his. "Might as well be comfortable."

Perfidia looked at Gus and then across at Locket. Finally she rose and moved toward Gus who shifted for her. But she did not sit on the sofa. Instead, she knelt and curled her legs back and sat on the woven rug under Gus's feet. Then she placed a palm on Gus's knee and leaned her cheek against the back of her hand there and locked her half-closed eyes onto the gray dawn coming through the window. Gus seemed puzzled by this at first, then cleared his throat but said nothing. He looked over at Locket and then at Clay. Finally, he placed his hand on top of Perfidia's hair.

"Well . . ." Locket began. "I did find that couple." He waited for these words to clear. "And their baby."

Suddenly, Locket wanted the security and authority of his hat or perhaps his battered desk between him and the three others inside the room. Or even to be back astride the mare and inside the comfort of the darkness, which he could see through the window had now disappeared with the sunrise crossing the work yard outside, pulling back the shadow of the great adobe house.

"Their baby boy," Locket said. "And that was all they had." He thought about the Spartan little house and the broken furnishings and he said, "And I mean that's *all* they had, trust me."

Locket stopped. It was as if an epiphany had struck him and he knew then that it would not be his own words but only the answers to the questions in the words from Gus and Clay. And Perfidia, if she chose. It was obvious to everyone that if Locket had brought back good words, he would have already spoken them.

Clay asked first. “What’d they say?”

“They said they crossed in the canyon,” Locket said. “Just like Alvaro told you Gus.”

“In the dark?” Gus said.

“Yes,” Locket said. “Well, I guess there was just a closing moon and that was all the light they had.”

“And Perfidia was with them?” Gus leaned forward but he could not see Perfidia’s eyes. “You were with them, right?” Perfidia did not respond.

“Yes,” Locket answered for her.

Gus looked up at Locket. “And her baby?”

“Yes.”

“Her daughter?” Gus said.

Locket nodded.

“And she didn’t have enough money,” Gus said quickly. He bent forward trying to see Perfidia’s face but he was speaking for her more than to her now. “Right? And so they took the baby and beat her and . . .”

“No.” Locket could not simply answer questions now so he said, “They said it wasn’t that way at all. . . .”

Gus opened his mouth to speak but nothing came this time. Clay frowned and looked first at Locket and then at Gus and then brought his eyes to Perfidia who raised her head now. She looked back at Clay as if to say something to him. Instead, she leaned her head aside, looked steadily at Locket and waited for him to continue.

Locket returned her stare and went on with the most official and compassionate and even voice he could muster. “They said she held her baby tight in her arms, the laces of her shoes tied together around her neck, just like the rest of group. Just like the father of that baby boy, following the *coyotes*. But when Perfidia got into the waist deep water, she slipped on the rocks, lost her balance and fell forward into the swift water. They said they lost sight of her then in the fading moonlight. But they heard her screams. The others got out on the north side of the river and waited. But I guess the *coyotes* yelled at them to get their shoes back on and threatened them and so they scrambled up the rock bank. The young man said he waited until the last minute and then he too went up with his family. At the top, he said he looked back once more and saw only the weak moon flashing on the ripples and then he could just see Perfidia coming up out of the river and collapsing facedown on the rocks without her shoes. . . ."

Locket stopped and inhaled deeply. He thought someone would now ask the question that he had struggled to find words to answer. But no one did. The only sounds in the room were soft sobs from Perfidia who once again laid her head on Gus's knee.

"Without her shoes . . . and without her child," Locket whispered and there were other words he held in his mind, words like sharpness of rocks and stings of cacti and coldness of the night water. And the cruelty of the *coyotes* who lifted not a finger to go back into the river. But Locket could only repeat, "Without the baby."

No one spoke or moved, the only sound now coming from the big clock ticking on the mantle. Locket watched Perfidia for some sign of denial to all he had said, something to indicate he was wrong and the young man was wrong and all this was some kind of conspiracy to do her harm. But she remained silent, still as death itself.

When the clock had ticked for several long minutes, Locket rose and walked over to Clay and nodded and Clay also rose and the two went without words into the entryway. They put on their hats and walked out onto the patio and paused long enough to breathe in the cool, clean air of the morning. But when they moved toward Clay's pickup in the yard, the stillness was breached by the agony of Perfidia's cries piercing the thick adobe walls. ❧

CHAPTER 33

After she dressed on Wednesday morning, Jovita stood at her window and as usual checked the street below. When she had looked out early yesterday morning, Locket and Clay were just emerging from Clay's truck. Both looked ragged and worn and she wondered where they had been all night. Locket went straight to his patrol car and drove off toward Presidio. Clay then came up the stairs and she heard him close the door on his apartment across the hall, but that was it. She assumed he was sleeping all day Tuesday because she had not seen him.

"What're you guys up to?" she muttered at the window and noted that Clay's truck sat parked where it had been all day on Tuesday and Locket's patrol car was still gone. She walked to her door to go downstairs but stopped when she heard Clay quietly close his door and move down the hallway. "What're you two guys up to?" she repeated. When she heard Clay descend the stairs, she peeked out her door and then came out and also went down.

Clay was standing in the kitchen when Jovita walked in. Bea made no move to offer Jovita her usual morning strip of bacon. She stood tense next to Clay who had his hat in his hands and seemed as worn and frazzled as Jovita had seen him the morning before.

"You look like hell," Jovita said. She poured a cup of coffee and handed it to Clay and then one for herself and turned to Bea. "You had coffee yet, Bea?"

"Yes," Bea said and then, "He wants to talk."

"Lost track of you, Clay," Jovita said. "Lots going on this week I guess. First notice came out in Monday's paper. Got that done at least and the other one's due out today. That'll make it . . ."

"I went over to Gus's on Monday," Clay interrupted. "Locket and me. They called off the search and I thought Gus needed to know."

"I heard," Jovita said. "That was probably a good idea, letting Locket know where she was. Hey, why don't we just go into the restaurant and get comfortable?"

"Well, all this is kinda private," Clay said. "I wouldn't want someone . . ."

Jovita turned to look out of the kitchen door into the restaurant. "Not a soul out there yet," she said. "Is that private enough?"

Clay nodded. "Bea needs to hear this too."

"You two want breakfast?" Bea said.

"Not yet," Jovita said. "Sounds like this might take some time."

Bea and Clay followed Jovita out into the restaurant. Jovita then crossed to the restaurant entry, closed the doors and flipped over the sign to CLOSED and then came back to her table where the other two had already sat.

"Go on, Clay," Jovita said.

"Well first, Perfidia seems fine," Clay said and he saw neither one of the women believed a word of this.

"Okay, maybe she's not doing so well now."

Clay told them about Locket finding the other couple and how their story had not matched what Perfidia had been saying. "Anyway, they told Lock she had slipped in the dark on the rocks while she was crossing the river in the canyon and when she come out on this side . . ." Clay stopped and looked out the restaurant window.

"Well?" Bea pressed.

"Well, I guess she'd lost hold of her baby there in the dark and the guy said when she come up outta the river, she'd lost her shoes and . . ."

"And the baby too?" Jovita whispered.

Clay nodded but he said nothing.

"The baby?" Bea said. She shook her head and repeated, "Her baby?"

"Yeah," Clay said quietly. "That's what he said."

There was a long silence. Tears welled in Bea's eyes and Jovita turned away. Clay lowered his head.

When she turned back, Jovita said, "She denied all this, didn't she?"

"At first," Clay said. "Well, she didn't exactly *say* anything, but she just seemed . . . not with us, you know what I mean? She never said a word the whole time Locket told about all this, didn't even shake her head. She was sitting on the floor next to Gus there and I didn't know if she was even hearing Locket."

"Then what happened?" Jovita said.

"Well, when Locket had talked it all out, said all he'd found out, him and me just got up and went and put our hats on and walked out onto Gus's patio there. And then that's when we heard her."

"Heard her?" Bea said.

"Yeah," Clay went on. "She was wailing and screaming something fierce."

"*Not* cussing at Locket?" Jovita said.

"Nope. It wasn't that. I don't know what she was saying but it sounded more like . . . just grief to me," Clay said and then he turned his head away from the other two. "Reminded me of someone else doing that. . . ."

"Sounds to me like the story's true, Clay," Jovita said. "There's no doubt in my mind that she had been nursing a baby, that's for sure. I'm just real sorry to hear this." She reached over and placed a hand on Clay's and he looked at it and then up at Jovita and he let her hand stay there. "But maybe it all makes sense, if you think about it."

"But she used that little pump Doc Maddox gave her," Bea said and now there was both hope and anger in her voice. "I *know* she did. Why would she do *that* if she knew her baby was gone and she'd never see it again?"

"Maybe to fool us," Clay offered. "Hell, I don't know about all that kind of stuff. . . ."

"But she did not know that I knew she had used it," Bea said and turned to Clay. "But I *did* know."

Jovita sighed and there was a long silence as they thought about this and then she said, "Okay, Bea, but I don't think she was trying to fool us," Jovita said. "I think she had fooled herself and that's all. That's why she used it."

"Fooled *herself?*" Bea said.

"Yes," Jovita went on. "I think she probably

believed her own story right up till Locket laid out the truth. I think she just didn't want to accept that her baby was dead. And I think she was so filled with guilt that she just refused to believe it because she knew that somehow she had been the cause of it and . . ."

"I gotta go," Clay interrupted. He pulled his hand away from Jovita's and shoved back the chair and stood and then repeated, "I gotta go."

"Why?" Jovita said, startled by the sudden action.

"Well, I was wrong just a minute ago when I said I didn't know about that kind of stuff, about fooling yourself, feeling guilty. It's something I know a lot about," he said and turned and left the room. ☙

CHAPTER 34

When Clay reached the little hill above his old place, he saw Gus's pickup parked beside the windmill. He drove on down and parked next to his and got out but he could not see Gus.

"Where you hiding?" he called.

"Over here," Gus said. He stepped from behind the tool shed.

When Clay walked over, he saw that Gus had jacked up the axle on the old one-horse ranch wagon and blocked it in place. He had also pulled the damaged wheel out of the weeds. "You been busy," Clay said.

"Well, didn't get to make it over yesterday," Gus said and smiled. "So I figured I owed you some time."

"Yeah . . ." Clay said. "I didn't get outta bed either yesterday. Except to take aspirin about every three hours." He held up his hands, spread the fingers and worked them into fists, back and forth. "Already took a couple today too so I'm ready to go."

"Yeah," Gus said.

"How is she?"

"Doing as well as could be expected, I think," Gus said. "She also slept all day yesterday or at least I guess she did. I didn't see her again till late in the evening when she came out of the back."

"She say anything about it?"

"Not much. She didn't have to, Clay," Gus said. "What's there to say? It's all true, she knows that and I think she admits it to herself now and that's about it."

"Maybe they'll find it," Clay said. "Somewhere downriver . . . maybe they'll . . ."

"It's happened before in that canyon," Gus said, shaking his head. "Not a lot, but you know, people get desperate to get across and they'll try it. And usually it's with kids, dammit."

"Yeah," Clay said.

"They don't ever find their bodies," Gus said. "Or at least, nobody ever admits to finding them. No telling where it might have got swept down to."

Both fell silent, considered this for a long moment, then Gus said, "But hey, we gonna do this thing or not?" He slapped the dust from the wooden seat at the front of the wagon. "She's still pretty solid, this old warrior. After I pulled all the weeds from around it, I saw she was in better shape than I thought."

"Oak," Clay said. He leaned against the sideboard and inspected the undercarriage. "Solid oak. That's what my old man said anyway and she does look to be that, don't she?"

"I'd say so," Gus said and then he looked toward the gravesite where they had worked all night on Monday. "How's that look over there, though?"

Clay turned to the gravesite, the fieldstones back in place, covering their fresh dirtwork and the white picket fence wired together and in place, and they had also buried the bottom of the headstone and stood it erect again. "Looks the same as always," Clay said and glanced at the tool shed. "Except . . ."

"Maybe you'd want to check on her?" Gus offered. "I'll knock the rust off the inside of this wheel hub." He pulled a round file from his back pocket and began to work on the hub. "I hope you brought grease."

Clay nodded. "Some inside here," he said as he walked around to the front of the shed. At the door, he reached in his pocket for the key to the padlock and opened the lock and then swung the door open. Inside, he could see Serafina's coffin where they had propped it across two sawhorses in the shadows. "Hi, baby," he whispered and went inside.

He found the can of axle grease and a wooden spatula and took in back out to Gus. "This'll work," he said. "I brought out the new axle washer and nut. They're in my pickup."

Gus raised his head and shook it, "Won't need them for a spell. This thing's in pretty bad shape. And then there's this. . . ." He tapped the end of the oak axle, its blacksmithed metal sheath over the end pitted with years of rust. "This has to be filed smoothed too. What's left of the metal at least. Inside of this wheel hub has to mesh with that end pretty close or she'll just wobble loose again."

"Yeah," Clay admitted. "I can work on that axle."

"Then there's the harness inside that needs to be limbered up a little," Gus went on. "And old Palo over there ain't even tried that on yet either, right?" Gus looked at Clay and paused for a while and finally said, "You sure you wanna do it this way, Clayton? My four-by-four over there'd cross that back rangeland into

Solitario in the dark as good as this, trust me."

"Might," Clay said. "Won't argue that with you. It's just that I got my mind made up on this, Gus. Maybe it's a little crazy, but it's just something I gotta do. You understand?"

Gus nodded, gave it up. "Tell you what," he said. "You got any steel wool inside there?"

"Probably. Why?"

"Well, that little old horse trough held up fine," Gus said. "I noticed it last night in the headlights. It must be half an inch thick and old Yebbie brazed it up fine, brazed that little crucifix right on top and those four little brass handles on the sides. And hardly a speck of rust at the seams where I worried it would be."

"Yeah," Clay said and he thought about Yebbie back then and he thought about Yebbie now and he remembered he had thanked a younger Yebbie years ago. He promised himself he would thank the older one the first chance he got.

"But it looked a little dull, don't you think?" Gus went on and now Clay understood.

"You just want me outta your way, don't you?" Clay said.

"Well, no," Gus said. "Not exactly. I'll need you in a bit. I just think it deserves to be shined up a little, don't you? With that steel wool? If you got some inside there?"

"I could do that," Clay said and then again, "I could sure do that." He smiled at Gus and went into the tool shed where Serafina waited.

Inside, he dug through boxes of junk parts and small nail kegs of miscellaneous and worthless items and finally found a large wad of steel wool, itself rusted but still stiff. He turned and tried the steel wool on a corner of the top, rubbing softly, but there was little to show. He put on his leather gloves and pushed the steel wool harder against the metal and soon had a spot cleared of the oxidation and after another minute or two, this area shone bright in the sunlight coming through the door.

By noon, Clay had the top and sides shining silvery and had brought the brass crucifix on top back to life. "I'll do you four next," he said and tapped on one of the little brass handles. "Better get my hired hand a drink of water and something to eat first though."

He walked out into the sun and went behind the shed where Gus toiled now with the file on the axle sheath. Gus looked up and lifted his hat and ran the back of a gloved had across his brow. He glanced up at the sun, averted his eyes and replaced his hat and said, "You coulda ordered up a rainstorm or something."

"Let's take a break," Clay said. "I got some beans in the truck."

"Beans?"

"Pork 'n beans," Clay said. "I keep them handy for emergencies just like this. You know, them little canned kind with a lift off lid? And part of a box of crackers." He saw Gus glance back at the sky and mutter something but Clay did not understand what he said. "And all the cool water you can drink," he went on. "Right over there. . . ." He pointed to the windmill.

Gus nodded and walked toward Clay's truck. "Right over by that shade tree?" he joked.

"We can get inside the truck and turn on the air conditioner," Clay offered.

"Let's just take it over to mine," Gus said. "No sense in getting yours all dirtied up, right?"

The only problem with eating in Gus's truck was that it was so cool that Clay began to feel drowsy after they had opened the cans of beans and scraped them onto their tongues with pocketknives. They finished the stale crackers and then got out and went over to the windmill and drank deep from the cool water after which they returned and sat again in the cool of the idling truck, watching the heat fingers quivering up from the yard.

"How much longer, you think?" Clay said. He leaned back and stared out the windshield.

"Maybe by dark," Gus offered. "What I'm doing anyway. Maybe."

"You think we can work Palo some tomorrow and maybe take Sera in tomorrow night?" Clay said.

"If he's a genius horse," Gus said. "You said he'd never been in a harness, right?"

"He ain't a genius," Clay said. "But he's smart and he's gentle and he'll take the harness okay."

"Don't matter if the damn thing's stiff as wood," Gus said. "You need to saddle soap it up and work it back and forth some, soften it up, especially the bridle and reins."

"I ain't planning to use that old headstall," Clay said.

"You're not?" Gus looked over at him. "What are you gonna do? Just explain to him that he needs to pull this strange thing right behind his butt in the dark of night and when he gets close enough to town, cut across in that dry wash while you and I ride along in there with

Serafina and Perfidia?" Gus said. "He must be a damn genius."

Clay sat forward and looked at Gus. "I'm planning to put my regular bridle on him and just walk him right in. Walk right alongside him, Gus." He paused and blinked at Gus. "Lead him in."

"With your knees?" Gus said. "Walk sixteen miles in them boots?"

"I'll be okay," Clay said. "Take enough aspirin and I'll be okay."

He paused again and studied Gus who had turned and now he looked out the front windshield. "But you said with *Perfidia?* You said with Serafina *and* Perfidia?" Clay said.

Gus nodded. "I asked her yesterday evening when she came out of her room what she wanted to do now," Gus said. "I don't think she had any idea what to do. Said she might as well go on back across the border."

"Back across?" Clay said. "To what? She's got nothing over there now. Nothing."

"That's what I said," Gus went on. "She just felt Locket probably had no choice but to send her back now. Said she was tired of hiding."

"He's not interested in that," Clay said. "He would have already done that if he was. And like he told her himself, it ain't his jurisdiction. Hell, he runs into hundreds just like her every year. He'd get nothing else done if he took all of them in to Immigration. It's the scumbag *coyotes* he looks for."

"Yeah," Gus said. "I told her that too. I said she could stay as long as she wanted. I don't think she believed me, not now, not after what Locket knows."

"But she still wants to do this with us?"

"Yep," Gus said. "Said she owed you this, Clay. Said she promised you she'd help move Serafina. She said she'd never forget how you helped her."

"She owes me nothing," Clay said. "She doesn't need to do a thing."

"I think she does, Clay," Gus said and he looked again at him. "I think she does."

Clay said nothing. He leaned his head back and reached to the side air vent and directed the cool air into his face. Then he pulled his hat down and shut his eyes under it. He had just dozed off when he heard Simik's sedan pull up beside Gus's truck, a billow of dust settling around the car. Gus had left Clay sleeping in the cab, the engine idling and the air conditioner still on.

Clay sat forward and then reached over and killed the engine. He got out at the same time Simik exited his car and they stood face-to-face inside the remaining fog of dust.

"Nice truck," Simik said and tapped the front tire with the toe of his boot. "What're you hauling?"

"You know it ain't mine," Clay grumbled. "Can't afford something like this. Belongs to my friend." He turned his head toward the tool shed. Gus had come from behind, holding the file in his hand. He stood frowning, his head cocked to one side as he looked over.

"Just getting that old wagon out from back there," Clay said and he tried to move into Simik's line of sight when he noticed just the end of Serafina's coffin, glinting in an angular stream of sun falling through the open door of the shed. "And some other stuff in the shed."

"Hmmm . . ." Simik said and he craned to look

toward the open door. "Junk, huh?"

"Some of it is," Clay said and then tried for indignation, just as he had done the past Friday night sitting inside Simik's sedan. "And some ain't. What the hell you doing out here in the heat of the day anyway?"

"Just inspecting my property," Simik said.

"Ain't yours yet," Clay said.

"Will be soon," Simik said. "Just wanted to see where the best place might be to park our drilling rig." He walked around Clay and went toward Serafina's gravesite. "Just looking it over."

When his back was turned, Clay waved frantically at Gus who understood and came around and closed the door on the shed. He stood there, guarding it.

"You won't need your rig," Clay said. "Not out here, anyway."

"That's what I hear," Simik said. "Saw that one notice in Monday's paper." He stopped at Serafina's gravesite, studied it carefully, walked around it and came back and stood with his face close to Clay's. "That's one. If they got their shit together and put another one in today's paper, it appears you might be right. Might be. Unless somebody screwed up some other way." He squinted his eyes over toward the tool shed but Clay could not tell if Simik was looking at Gus or if he had noticed the door to the shed was now closed.

"I am right," Clay said. He tried to sound convincing, keep his voice even.

"Well, what the hell am I gonna do then with this wore out hardscrabble you call a ranch?" Simik said. "Raise Christmas trees?"

"Don't know," Clay said. "I just want the rest of

my money you owe me. I told you that when we signed the contract. It'll be your problem come midnight on Saturday."

"Maybe," Simik said. "Maybe it'll be yours." He spat on the ground and bumped Clay's shoulder as he strode back to his sedan. "I'm leaving right now for a quick run back to El Paso to talk with some others who just might think it's your problem too. Nice meeting you. . . ." He waved at Gus. "What was your name again?"

"I didn't say," Gus said. He did not return Simik's wave.

Simik smiled and nodded. He got into his sedan and spun around in the yard and soon disappeared back down the two-track road toward Solitario.

When he was out of sight, Gus came toward Clay and said, "That him?"

"That's him," Clay said.

"A real asshole, ain't he."

"You think he saw it?" Clay said. He looked at Gus and then toward the shed.

"I don't think so," Gus said. "Hell, dust was everywhere. And I shut the door right away."

"Yeah, but I seen it," Clay said. "I seen the end of it, shining real plain. If I seen it, he could have seen it too."

"Well, what if he did?" Gus said. "So what?"

"He'll know we brought her up."

"Hellfire, Clay," Gus said. "He saw the grave, studied it, walked around it and everything. Nothing looks disturbed there, right?"

"Not to us."

"And not to him either," Gus said. "Otherwise

he'd have said something about it."

"Maybe," Clay said. "Maybe not."

"Let's get this finished," Gus said. He turned back toward the wagon. "We should be done by dark and then maybe we can move her tomorrow night."

"Gus . . ." Clay said.

Gus stopped. He turned back and looked at Clay who stood riveted to the spot. He waited for Clay to continue.

"Let's get finished as quick as possible," Clay said.

"That's what I just said."

"Quick as we're done with the wagon, you need to go on back and get Perfidia if she's gonna be in on this." Clay looked over to the corral where Palo stood dozing in the hot sun. "I'll work with him a little."

"What?"

"Tonight, Gus," Clay said. "We gotta move her tonight." ❧

CHAPTER 35

By the time Gus and Clay had finished with the wagon, it was six in the afternoon. Unlike most wagons, the one-horse ranch wagon had no single tongue. Instead, two oak rails ran from the axle and up each side of the horse and then attached to the chest strap around its neck. Gus and Clay each grappled one of the side bars out of the weeds as they spun the wagon around and managed to pull it into the yard. Clay went into the tool shed and brought out the stiff leather harness but only his regular bridle which he planned to put on Palo. He was leading Palo out of the corral when Gus drove off in his pickup.

"Just you and me again," Clay said. "And damned if I can remember exactly how this fits." He lifted the harness and put the straw-stuffed leather collar around Palo's neck. The old horse stood but when Clay tried to back him between the oak rails, he balked and sidestepped away. "Okay, it's all new, I know," Clay said and he stroked Palo's neck as he led him around and around the wagon. "Let's give it another go, okay?" he said and this time walked beside him, his hand on his neck as Palo finally backed between the rails. Quickly, Clay lifted one rail, attached it to the collar, then went around Palo and did the same with the other. He returned in front of the old horse and walked ahead, leading him with the familiar reins and in short order, Palo seemed to accept his new role.

Gus did not return with Perfidia until almost nine that evening. Clay was still leading Palo around with the bridle when the headlights from Gus's truck swept the yard. Gus stopped his truck and stepped out into the cool of the night, leaving his headlights on.

"Genius," Gus said when he saw Palo pulling the wagon.

"Told you," Clay said and smiled. He stopped the rig in front of Gus.

Perfidia walked over and moved her hand along Palo's mane and over his back. "You don't remember me," she said. "But I know you. We shared water."

"He knows you," Clay said and then, "Thanks for coming. This is all a little nuts. You don't have to do it. It's risky for you."

"Yes I do," she said and touched Clay's arm. "Yes I do."

Gus moved over and the three stood in the glare of the headlights. "Let's get moving," he said. "It's a long walk from here."

Clay led Palo just past the toolshed so that the rear of the wagon was near the door. He dropped the reins to the ground and the old horse stood as if he had done this many times.

"I'll put my saddle forward in the wagon," Clay said. "Then a couple boxes of junk in case we run into someone on the road."

"It's probably ten miles before we can cut across. If we run into anyone between here and there, nobody in their right mind is going to believe we're just cleaning out your junk," Gus observed. "Not in the middle of the night and especially with a horse-drawn wagon."

"Good point," Clay said but he said nothing else. He went into the shed and came back with his ancient high-backed saddle and put it in the wagon. Then he went back inside and brought out a box filled with odds and ends and Gus brought out another and they put these in too.

"Okay," Clay said. "Now Sera." He looked at Gus standing with his back to the headlights, his face shadowed. "Let's put her over the axle and leave some room for someone to sit in there with her."

"Someone?" Perfidia said.

"Yeah," Clay said and he looked at her. "I'm gonna be up front walking with Palo. I'll be leading him."

"You won't make it all the way, Clayton," Gus said.

Clay turned back to Gus and said, "Maybe not, Gus." He stepped over to Perfidia and said, "Would you ride back here with her?"

"Of course," Perfidia said. "If you want me to. I hoped you would ask."

"Okay, enough of all this," Gus said and he moved quickly back inside the toolshed. "Grab that side, Clay."

Clay nodded at Perfidia and moved inside, took the two brass handles shining now in the headlights and he and Gus lifted Serafina out the door and put her inside the wagon. Perfidia said nothing as she sat on the open tail of the wagon and swung her legs inside. Clay went forward and took up the reins and led Palo back out to the two-track as Gus went back inside the shed briefly and then came out. He closed and padlocked the door on the shed.

As soon as Clay had the wagon situated in the road, Gus got back into his truck and moved it behind the shed where the wagon had been and where Clay had parked his pickup earlier in the afternoon. He came toward the wagon with his flashlight in one hand and the two shovels they had used in the other, but he did not carry the pickax.

"I'll ride up here," Gus said. He tossed the shovels into the wagon and then climbed up into the seat. "Won't have any reins to work with but I can put a little light on the road for you." He moved the flashlight across the road. "If that'll help, I mean."

Clay dropped the reins and Palo stood as Clay walked back and looked up at Gus, now sitting. "Not much moon yet but that might be good," he said. "What's in your other hand there?"

"Coffee," Gus said and shook the thermos he had brought. "Passengers only, though."

"Right," Clay said. "Now if you see headlights coming at us, you should kill the flashlight."

"So's they can slam into us in the dark?"

"Yeah, another good point," Clay said and then, "Why just the shovels, Gus?"

"Tell you what," Gus said. "You let us worry about stuff back here, you just get into Solitario the back way and to the cemetery. In the dark if possible, hear?"

Clay nodded. "Then what?"

"I told you I'd worry about that too, remember?"

Clay nodded but he wondered how far he could go with some part of a plan he knew nothing about, even if was from his best friend. But he thought about his own insane plan now in motion and he said nothing more, but turned and went back forward and picked up the reins and led Palo up the rise of the two-track with the wagon and his two friends inside. And with Serafina inside.

By midnight, the procession had reached the culvert Clay had been looking for. He saw it in Gus's flashlight, each end extending on either side of the road into the dry wash. He had seen the culvert many times as he drove this rough road and rarely did it carry sudden rainwater from one side to the other as intended, but when it did, he never once stopped to celebrate the moisture. But he remembered this spot well. Each time he saw it, he thought about the night his mare had foaled Palo right next to the road here. Foaled and died here. And he remembered walking down the dry wash that night on into Solitario but the memory stopped there except for the sorrow and agony of the next few days that he had tried, without success, all these years to erase from his mind.

Clay stopped and dropped the reins and walked back to the wagon again.

"This wash leads right down behind the cemetery," he said. "I'll lead Palo down into it. It's sandy but firm and probably even smoother than what we've been on."

"Want me to spell you?" Gus said. He flicked on the light and moved it to Clay's face. Clay shifted his feet and twisted his face into a wince.

"Get that outta my eyes," Clay said. He held his palm in front of his face. "Hell, this is the easy part now."

"No it ain't," Gus said. He jumped down. "Get up

there, open that thermos and take some aspirin. We ain't done yet." Gus reached to help him up in the seat but Clay refused his hand.

"Step aside," Clay said. He went back to Palo and led him off the road and into the sandy bottom of the wash and dropped the reins again. Gus followed him down and stood holding the flashlight.

"If I'm gonna ride, it won't be up there," he walked to the back of the wagon and Gus held the light.

"Turn that damn thing off," Clay said. "Or just shine it up there if you don't think you can follow a dry wash with just starlight."

"I can," Gus said and he flicked off the light.

"Just stay in the wash," Clay said. "It ain't far now. We should start seeing some lights in an hour or so . . . if anybody in Solitario is crazy enough to be up this time of night."

"Yeah," Gus said. "Crazy." He walked to the front and picked up the reins and led Palo down the wash, his eyes adjusting to the starlight on the sandy soil.

Two hours later, Gus saw a few lights in the distance. "Thought you said *one* hour or so," he called back but no one answered. He dropped the reins and walked back to the rear of the wagon.

But he did not flick on the flashlight when Perfidia whispered, "He's asleep. Took three aspirin with a sip of coffee and dropped right off."

Gus looked at Clay, his head resting on one arm draped over the top of the little coffin. Perfidia held his hat. "It ain't far now," Gus said. "Just let him sleep."

"Okay," Perfidia whispered. "Are you alright up there?"

"I'd take a shot of that coffee," Gus whispered.

Perfidia opened the thermos and poured out the hot liquid into the lid. It steamed into the coolness of the early morning. Gus hunkered on the soft sand and wrapped his fingers around the hot lid, blew across and sipped.

"Can you help me with something?" Gus said. He stood and placed his warmed palm on her cheek and she placed a hand on top of his. Clay stirred, groaned but he did not awaken.

"Sure," she said.

"I don't want him to wake up until I get us where I plan to be inside the cemetery, okay?"

"I won't bother him," she said.

"I'll wake him up then," Gus said. "And he'll either cuss me out or go along with what I got in mind."

Perfidia raised her head and Gus saw her face in the starlight and her full smile which he had never seen. "He'll be fine with it, Gus," she said. "I would be. . . ."

CHAPTER 36

Clay came downstairs late on Saturday evening just as Bea was taking plates back to the kitchen. "I'm closing," she grumbled.

"Just wondered if Jo had been over for supper?"

"No," Bea said. "I took food over there, though. That hearing's been going on all day."

"Till midnight," Clay said. "That's what they put in the notices."

"Yes," Bea said and when Clay turned to leave, she softened. "Clay?" He stopped and turned around. "I made tacos tonight. My special."

"Sounds good, Bea," Clay said. "But I really gotta get going."

"You sure?"

"Yeah," he said. "One thing though, Bea . . ."

"What?"

"Would you come up to the cemetery in the morning? I'm trying to get some others too."

Bea looked at him and understood. She nodded. "Sure," she said. "What time?"

"Early," Clay said. "About dawn, maybe five thirty or six? Is that gonna be too early? I know you got your Sunday brunch an' all, Bea, but I'd appreciate it."

"It's no problem, Clay," Bea said.

Clay nodded and left the hotel. He walked across the street in the darkness and went into the county commissioners' meeting hall. Jovita and Dobb and Yebbie were sitting at the front facing a small group of residents. One of the ranchers from the area was talking and Jovita was writing down what he was saying about the new water regulations.

When Jovita saw Clay standing at the back of the room, she gave the notepad to Dobb, rose and walked back to Clay.

"Can you come out in the entry a minute?" Clay whispered.

Jovita looked back to the front then turned again to Clay, "Sure, just a minute, though."

"This won't take long," Clay said and when they had left the room he went on, "I haven't had a chance to talk to you, but I wanted to thank you again for taking us out there to get our trucks Thursday morning."

"Sure," Jovita said.

"And for not asking what the hell is going on. . . ."

"Sure."

"How's it going in there?"

"Except for Simik," Jovita said. "It's going fine. Most of those who've come in just thank us and ask for clarification on what's going to be happening after tonight."

"Simik?"

"Yes. He's back in town. He came in this afternoon bellowing and flinging a stack of papers at us and making threats."

"Y'all read them?"

"Dobb told him we'd look at them later when we

got a chance."

"Well, did you?"

Jovita smiled. "Looked at them, yes. Read them . . . no. Didn't waste time on that."

"What'd Simik say?"

"He said he was moving his jackknife drilling rig out the county road toward your place."

"When?"

"This afternoon, I guess," Jovita said. "And a heavy dozer too. He's probably out there as we speak."

Clay thought about this and then said, "Well, I'm going over and see if Locket will go out there with me tonight. I'm meeting Gus out there around eleven."

"Don't need to do that," Jovita said.

"What?"

"Ask Locket to go out."

"Why?"

"I already asked him," Jovita said. "He's out there also as we speak and he's got the complete regulations with him."

"I see," Clay said.

"Just in case anyone who might be standing by out there wants to see exactly what goes into effect at . . ."

"Midnight," Clay said and he smiled.

"That's right. Now I gotta get on back in there. It'll take till then to hear all these folks," Jovita said and then, "Oh yes, Simik also said he might just have a surprise for you if you come out."

"A surprise? He say what?"

"No," Jovita said. "But you need to be cautious about how you plan to do it if you and Gus are thinking about . . ."

"Moving Serafina?" Clay interrupted again and then said, "That's something else I wanted to ask you."

"Go on."

"I was wondering if you'd come up to the cemetery around five thirty in the morning? Maybe you could ask Dobb and Yebbie too?" Clay paused and then said, "That is if they want to. I may not be their friend anymore, but they're still mine, Jo. And you can ask anybody else you want."

Jovita looked at him and nodded. "I'll be there, you know I'll be there. For whatever you've got in mind. And I think they'll be there too."

"Thanks."

Jovita put her hand on Clay's arm for a moment and said, "You be careful out there, Clay." She walked back into the meeting hall.

It was eleven thirty when Clay reached his old place. He stopped in the road, his engine idling. In his single headlight, he could see Simik's equipment parked in the ditch alongside the county road. He could hear the idling diesel engines on the equipment and saw several men leaning against the fenders. "Smart," he said. "No trespassing yet. . . ."

He drove on down past the equipment and when he turned into the yard, he saw Locket's patrol car parked nose-to-nose with Simik's sedan in his headlights. Locket was leaning against the front fender of his car but Simik was not in sight. He did not see Gus's truck until he turned into the yard. Gus had parked beyond the windmill near the toolshed, the tailgate down as if to remove the final items from the shed.

Clay stopped and turned off his engine and killed

his light. He got out and walked back toward Gus, who came out of his truck. He did not see Perfidia and decided if she had come, she remained out of sight in the darkness of Gus's pickup cab. "I need your key," Gus said. "That is, if you want to take all those treasures left inside here."

Simik stepped suddenly from the darkness and said, "He won't need a key to get what he's come for."

Clay turned to him. "You might be trespassing, Simik."

"Nope," Simik said. "Just a friendly visit."

"None of my visitors ever shows up with dozers and drilling rigs," Clay said.

Locket had now walked over, his flashlight in his hand. "Nobody's trespassing anywhere," he said and he shone the light in Simik's face. "Not yet anyway."

"You ready?" Gus said. He walked past Simik in the darkness, bumping his shoulder as he passed him.

"That might be assault, sheriff," Simik growled.

"Assault?" Locket said and he flicked off his flashlight. "Pretty dark out here tonight, Mister Simik. Hard to see things like that. And by the way, it's *deputy*, not sheriff."

"What time you got, deputy," Clay said.

Locket flicked the flashlight back on, shone it on his wristwatch. "Eleven forty-five," he said.

"Let's do it, Gus," Clay said. Gus got into his truck but instead of the toolshed, he moved slowly back so that the tailgate neared the edge of the picket fence around the gravesite. "That'll do," Clay called out and waved his hand.

Simik stalked over and stood opposite Gus's pickup

on the other side of the white fence. He had his hands on his hips and the shadows from Gus's red taillights made his face appear even more sinister.

"Where's your shovels? And your pickaxes? You got some very hard digging to do," Simik began over the sounds of the idling pickup. "And quick too. And you might think about this. If you take your kid outta here right now, before that deputy's watch there says midnight, the place transfers immediately to me. I can have that rig over here in two minutes and have a hole started way before then."

Clay said nothing. He put on his work gloves, removed the wire from the corner and then folded the picket fence very carefully as he had done on Monday night. He placed this in the bed of the pickup. Gus came out of his truck and stood next to the gravesite and pulled on his pair of gloves. Clay turned to Locket and said, "What time is it now?"

Locket flashed his light on his watch. "Eleven fifty."

"You ain't gonna make it," Simik yelled and he was frantic now. "Goddammit, you ain't gonna do it in time if you don't get with it." He moved over and stood with his face just inches from Clay's. "And one final thing, asshole," he said through his teeth. "If your kid ain't outta there in time, I'll flatten that pile of shit you called your house and that junk shed back there and that rotting corral and that windmill." He paused because he had run out of breath, sucked in a final gasp and went on. "And gouge the hell out of this spot we're standing on right here because it'll be ours. In *ten* goddamn minutes. This will make a great place for a mud and tailing pit. It won't make a shit to me if your kid's down there. Don't be a fool, Clayton. Let some of my boys come in here and get the remains of your kid outta there for you." Simik's voice came more as a plea than a threat now.

"My *kid?*" Clay said quietly. "You mean *Serafina* don't you?" He turned to Locket. "What time now, Locket?"

"You got about a minute and half, Clay," Locket said. He shook his head as if it was hopeless, but Clay knew Locket was feigning the worry in his voice. Clay knew that even if Locket Wagner was only the deputy of Solitario County, he was not a stupid deputy.

"Okay, Gus," Clay said and the two walked to each side of the little white headstone, worked it back and forth in the soft earth a few times and it came free. They carried it to the bed of the truck, placed it gently inside and closed the tailgate. When they made no further effort at the gravesite, Simik said, "What about these fieldstones? And what the hell are you going to do about what's *underneath* them?" He gestured to the gravesite. "The *remains* . . . you gotta take all that too, you idiot!"

Clay stood for a moment and then said softly, "Those are rocks on top, Mister Simik. Just fieldstones. And what's underneath them is just dust by now. That's all. . . ."

Without another word to Simik, Clay went past Gus's truck toward his own pickup, but when Gus opened the door to his truck, Clay saw Perfidia inside. She had her forehead on the passenger side window and Clay thought he saw tears on her face but he could not be certain. Gus put his truck in gear and drove down the road into the darkness.

When Clay got into his truck he rolled down his window, started the engine and pulled up next to Locket, who held his light on his watch. "Just a minute, Clay," Locket said and he counted, "Five, four, three, two . . . one." He turned the light into Simik's face, now drawn and white. "Here you are, Mister Simik," Locket said. He handed Simik the printed sheaf of papers. "Brand new regulations for water drilling in the county of Solitario." He flicked off the flashlight. "Regulations for drilling on this place that I understand is yours now. Or any other place as well. And they're official as of right now. I'd read through these carefully if I was you before I did anything with that rig over there. That is, if you happen to have a flashlight on you." He turned to Clay and said, "Let's go, Clayton. I'm tired." He went to his patrol car and got inside and drove out onto the road, but he sat idling as he waited for Clay to drive in front of him.

Clay turned his truck slowly toward the road. In the momentary flash of his single headlight, he saw Simik holding the papers by his side, a few sheets now slipped and lying white on the ground. Simik wore a look of total shock on his face. Clay rolled up his window and swung onto the road in front of Locket. "Go ahead, Mister Simik," he whispered. "Flatten away. . . ."

CHAPTER 37

Clay walked up from the hotel to the cemetery at five o'clock on Sunday morning. He had slept hardly any, worrying about Gus and Perfidia. Gus had said he would park as far out of sight as possible on the backside of the cemetery, behind the old ranch wagon where they could get a few hours of sleep. When Clay arrived at the cemetery, he saw just the top of Gus's truck. He walked back and tapped on the window. Gus lifted his head from the seatback, blinked and rolled down the window.

"All set?" Clay said.

Gus nodded and yawned and Perfidia rose from the seat where she had slept bent sideways, her head resting on Gus's thigh.

"Sorry about this," Clay said. "Y'all shoulda just come on inside and got a room."

"We're fine," Gus said. "Didn't want to raise any suspicions late at night. Or any eyebrows, either. People know me but they don't know her. And we didn't need immigration knocking on a hotel door this morning."

He turned to Perfidia, who pulled the silver combs from the sides of her hair, used them to push back her long black locks and then reset the combs. "We still got lots of things to do," Gus said.

"Yeah," Clay agreed. He straightened and took

in a long breath of morning air. "Well, I see some showing up." Several people had walked through the wrought iron gate and were wandering around looking for what they all expected to be a freshly opened grave for Serafina. "They'll all be pretty confused."

Gus nodded. "Yeah, guess they will. You still okay with all this, Clay?"

"See you over there," Clay said.

"Okay," Gus said and smiled. "Can't promise I'll shave but I'll take care of my hair." He picked up his hat from the dash and covered his disheveled hair with it.

"I ain't worried about that," Clay said. "And neither will Sera." He walked toward Dobb and Yebbie, who meandered side-by-side along the narrow gravel road that wound through the cemetery, inspecting each gravesite.

"Morning," Dobb said and Yebbie echoed this but then he added, "What's up?"

"Just a few memorial words," Clay said.

"Where?" Dobb said. "I don't see no . . ."

"Over here," Clay interrupted and walked away. "Over here," he repeated, louder to Locket and Jovita, who had just entered through the gate with Bea in front of them. Several more people came in, some dressed for church, some still in chore clothes.

Clay went over and stood at the foot of Henry Bennett's grave and waved back to Gus, who started his pickup and moved into the narrow road. Slowly, he brought the truck in front of Henry's grave but stopped with the tailgate in front of Adelita's, the crushed white rock atop the mounded earth glowing in the orange rays of the rising sun. Gus got out on one side and Perfidia on the other. They walked back to the tailgate and Gus lowered it.

Clay moved away from Henry's grave, came behind Gus and Perfidia, and stood with his hands folded in front of him. The entire crowd had now gathered around the pickup watching Clay, but neither Gus nor Perfidia turned to Clay. Clay took off his hat and then moved forward and gave it to Jovita. Then he took one of the shovels from the bed of the truck and dug a small trench at the foot of Adelita's grave. He went back and stood next to Gus and Perfidia and said, "Okay. Let's do it."

Every face there seemed puzzled by what was happening, all casting furtive glances at Perfidia, whom most of them had never seen. The men followed Clay's movements and took off their hats too and the women moved closer to look inside the bed of the pickup. As Perfidia watched, Gus and Clay lifted Serafina's white headstone from the bed of the pickup and struggled with it to the foot of Adelita's grave, where they bent forward and allowed it to slip from their hands slowly into the trench Clay had made. Then Clay righted it, and Gus scraped the fresh earth back around it and packed it secure with the heel of his palm. Finally, Clay rubbed the dust from the name on the front of the stone with the sleeve of his shirt.

Clay stood silent for a long while, looking first at Serafina's gravestone and then at Adelita's and then he turned to the crowd. Gus returned to his truck and moved it out of the way down the little road. He walked back and stood at Perfidia's side. The crowd moved around the foot of the grave and as they stared in confusion at what they had just witnessed, their baffled faces turned mellow and Clay looked up at them and each one in turn nodded at him and he knew at that moment no words were necessary. Nothing but a simple, "Thank you for coming," which he whispered to each person as they walked past him in silence, took his hand or wrapped their arms around him.

Last in line were Dobb and Yebbie, holding their hats in their hands. "Guess I didn't get that paperwork in again," Clay apologized. "Sorry. . . ."

Dobb opened his mouth to speak, but Yebbie elbowed him aside, took Clay's hand and spoke first, "Thanks for what you did, Clay. You don't need no more paperwork."

Clay smiled at him. Dobb looked at Yebbie, then at Clay as if for the first time in memory, words had been taken right out of his mouth. Dobb shook Clay's hand and said, "See you inside the restaurant, okay?" Clay nodded and Dobb and Yebbie walked away and Clay noted another first, the two walking hatless under a Solitario sun.

"My turn," Bea said. She walked up and held her arms out. "Lean down here," she said and Clay had to bend a little so she could hug his neck and kiss him on the cheek. She turned quickly. "I gotta get brunch on the table," she said as she hurried off but Clay knew that it was only a gruff excuse for the tears forming in her eyes.

Locket moved forward now and he took Clay's hand and shook it and then put on his hat. "See you inside," he said and walked away.

"Lock," Clay said and Locket looked back.

"Thanks for everything."

"It's my job," Locket said.

"Just like on TV?" Clay said and smiled.

"Yeah," Locket said. "Just like on TV." He turned and walked toward the hotel.

"What now?" Clay said when Gus and Perfidia came to him. "For you two, I mean?"

"Back across," Perfidia said and lowered her eyes. "Tomorrow."

"Back over?" Clay said. "Tomorrow? I mean, I understand but isn't there some way . . ."

"We're meeting Locket in Presidio in the morning," Gus explained. "I just talked to him. He said he'd work it out with Immigration, tell them the whole story."

"What'll happen?"

"They'll take her back over," Gus said but Clay could see he did not seem worried about this. "Just like everybody else, inside the deportation bus."

Clay nodded, waited.

"But I'll be following right behind you crossing the bridge." He looked at Perfidia, who smiled at him. "You know Clay, you ain't right very often," Gus said. "But like you once said to me, a man ought not live his life in solitary. We'll take as much time as we need to get better acquainted and then get all the paperwork done on both sides of the river. And then, if she's feeling right about all this of course, sometime down the road we'll get married over there."

"Well . . ." Jovita had moved up and overheard this. She hugged them both and when she did this, Clay noticed a small wicker basket, looped over one wrist.

"She's a citizen over there, of course," Gus went

on, explaining all this more for himself than to anyone listening. "But see, if she marries a citizen from this side, she can become a citizen here too. She can cross back over with no problem. Over the bridge this time."

"Well, your problems might just be starting, Gus," Perfidia said and smiled at him.

Gus shook his head and looked at her. "No chance," he said and then to Clay, "We'd better get moving."

"You're not coming in for Bea's famous brunch?" Jovita said.

"Not this time, Jovita," Gus said. "Maybe next week. Or the next, who knows? I got Palo back there at Los Arbolitos to feed and water anyway." He turned to Clay and took his hand. "I'll bring over my flatbed and haul your old wagon if you want it over there too."

"That'd be good," Clay said. "That'd be real good."

Perfidia moved to Clay and put her hands on his cheeks. "How do I thank you?" she whispered and tears filled her eyes. "How?"

Clay looked at Serafina's headstone catching the bright sun now, her mother's headstone on the other end just coming into the sunlight crowding out the shade of the big cottonwood tree. "You already did," he said.

She reached up and kissed him first on one cheek and then on the other. Gus nodded at Clay and then put on his hat and took Perfidia's hand. The two got into his pickup and left Jovita and Clay standing alone at the foot of the gravesite.

"Makes sense to me," Jovita muttered when they had left but Clay was not sure she said this to him.

She handed the little basket to Clay, who had

himself fought a valiant battle against tears the entire morning. But this time as he looked at the little purple flowers inside the basket, he lost the war.

"Where'd you find these, Jo?" he said, his voice trembling.

"Not that hard," she said. "Sometimes it just takes a woman to know where to look for things like this." She turned her eyes toward Serafina's headstone. "Or a little girl. Want me to wait for you?"

"That's okay," Clay said. "You go on. I'll just be a minute here."

"Sure," she said. She turned and went out the cemetery gate and onto the sidewalk.

Clay watched her walk away and then turned to the gravesite. He bent over and propped his free hand on his thigh and lowered himself on his knees onto the softest mound of stray earth he could find next to Serafina's headstone. He placed the basket of purple flowers adjacent her stone and thought back across those years when the stone was freshly carved by his younger hands and the purple was vivid on top of another fresh grave that held Serafina.

"It's your kind, baby," he said. "Purple. Just like always. But a nice friend brought them this time and I think you'll come to like her a lot." Clay looked at the words on Adelita's gravestone and then back at Serafina's and it seemed finally right to see them now both facing the morning sunrise. "And I'll bring more when I can find them," he said. "Or she can bring them but I'll practice the bird wings too, Sera. If I try them every day when I come out here, maybe it'll get easier and I'll hear you laugh again and ask me to do them over and over like you always did and you know I will." He paused and took his time as he stood and repeated, not just for Serafina, but also for Adelita. "And maybe it'll all get easier. . . ." Then he turned and walked toward the iron gateway.

"Them getting married?" Clay said when he saw Jovita waiting just inside the lobby of the hotel. "Is that what you meant back there about something making sense to you, Jo? Gus and Perfidia getting hooked up?"

"Well yes, but something else," Jovita admitted.

"What?"

"Well," Jovita said. "You know business has picked up in here a little. . . ."

Clay heard the voices from the restaurant, packed with paying customers. He looked at Jovita. "Yeah, seems like it. At least today anyway."

"I'm thinking it just might make sense to get Bea a new stove," she said. "But I doubt if she'd even listen to me about that."

"Probably not."

Jovita went on, "Well, I've also been thinking about how tight it's getting with so few tables inside."

"Yeah," Clay said. "A little bit, I guess."

"Doesn't make much sense to try putting any more tables in such a small area though, does it?"

"Guess not."

Jovita paused for a moment and then came close to Clay and put her arms around his waist and put her face directly in front of his face, right there in the lobby, and he did not know what to do with his hands, so he held them awkwardly at his side.

"Well, Clayton Elliott, don't forget there's that

other chair at my table inside. No sense in it being empty any damn longer," she said and then stood back and adjusted the red scarf in her hair. "That'd free your table up, right? And anyway, it's like you told Gus yourself, no sense in anyone spending their lives in solitary." She turned and walked toward the entry to the restaurant.

Clay stood blinking for a long while after she disappeared. Finally, he scolded himself for those times he had stood here like this in the past and he thought about all the other wasted minutes in his life. "No damn sense in that," he muttered and followed Jovita into the restaurant as he repeated, "No sense at all." ❧